The Aunt Hill

A NOVEL BY

Marie Elena Martin

Beaver's Pond Press, Inc.
Edina   Minnesota

ISBN 1-59298-069-4

Library of Congress Catalog Number: 2004108334

Printed in the United States of America

First Printing: July 2004

08 07 06 05 04   6 5 4 3 2 1

Cover design by Alberto Gonzalez
Cover photograph courtesy of Washington County (MN)
    Historical Society
Interior design by Rachel Holscher
Typesetting by Stanton Publication Services, Inc.

Beaver's Pond Press, Inc.

7104 Ohms Lane, Suite 216
Edina, MN 55439-2129
(952) 829-8818
www.BeaversPondPress.com

to order, visit www.BookHouseFulfillment.com or call
1-800-901-3480. Reseller discounts available.

The Aunt Hill

For Sharon,

Warm wishes,

Marie Elena Martin

FOR MY DEAR GRANDMOTHER,

Julia Elizabeth Oviatt Martin

Acknowledgments

I would like to thank Milt Adams for guiding me through the publishing process; Cindy Rogers for her wonderful editing; Matthew Fort for his encouragement, criticism, and synopsis; Alberto Gonzalez for his fabulous cover design; Rachel Holscher for her perfect interior design; my high school English teachers, Margie MacNeill and Robert Shandorf, for planting the seed and teaching me to write; and my husband and son for being so patient.

Chapter One

A lone maple leaf, vibrant with autumn color, fluttered in the crisp breeze, clinging to the security of the only home it had known during its lifetime. Suddenly, a gust of wind wrenched the leaf from its branch and took it for a wild ride, sending it soaring like a bi-plane to the sky in a series of loop-di-loops, finally leaving it to fall back to earth on its own. Gently, it drifted down through the barren branches of the tree and alighted on the tip of a scuffed brown shoe.

Lightly tapping her shoe on the dying grass, Harriett Hayden O'Connor stood on the boulevard in front of her house with her arms crossed over her ample chest. A sudden gust of cool autumn air forced her to pull her ragged cardigan closed as she skeptically watched her sister, Mildred, drape artificial cobwebs in between the columns on the front porch of their family home. The porch columns were already entwined with strings of pumpkin lights, and there were skeletons, goblins and witches dangling from the eaves, as well as from a rope that ran from the porch to the sugar maple on the boulevard. A pile of Styrofoam tombstones and bedsheet ghosts sat in a heap near the porch steps, waiting to be strategically placed on the front lawn, along with the hay bales and cornstalks propped against the arbor at the garden gate.

Harriett surveyed the scene and shook her head in disgust, and when she saw her sister gently placing rubber spiders in the cobwebs, she could hold her tongue no longer. "For crying out loud, Millie," Harriett shouted, "that looks absolutely cheesy! Every year you go one step further and this year you have gone too far."

"Oh, don't be such a spoil sport, Hattie," Mildred said, hanging another spider in the cobwebs. "This is for the children. They love this stuff!"

"Yes, simple children . . ." Harriett mumbled to herself.

"Oh, where is your imagination and sense of adventure?" Mildred said lightly.

Unable to come up with a witty retort, Harriett did not respond. Instead, she paused to consider her sister's question and was saddened to realize that she had no idea where such things had gone to in her life. Dropping her head in self-pity, Harriett noticed a brilliantly colored maple leaf resting on the tip of her shoe and she slowly bent over to pick it up. She was not one for pressing leaves and flowers into books but something about the leaf made her want to hold on to it. As she was examining the delicate veins in the leaf, Harriett heard the unmistakable squeak of the garden gate's hinges and she looked up to see her other sister, Gertrude, passing underneath the rose arbor.

Dressed in a floral print dress, muddied pinafore and ratty cardigan, Gertrude clomped toward Harriett in green rubber boots dusted with dirt. She pulled off her worn garden gloves and said, "What is going on out here?" Wiping the back of her hand across her smudged cheek, she added, "I could hear you yelling from down in the rose garden, Hattie."

"Oh, Hattie is just being a spoil sport, as usual," Mildred said, carefully stepping down off the porch and lumbering toward her sisters. "Take a good look, Gertie, and tell me what you think."

The three women came together near the maple tree on the boulevard and silently gazed back at the house, standing together as they had posed for many photographs throughout their very long lives—Harriett, the eldest, in the middle, Gertrude, the second eldest, on her right, and Mildred, the youngest, on her left. Never any rhyme or reason to the line-up, they had just always come together in this manner like the pieces of a jigsaw puzzle that had to be in their proper place in order for the image to materialize. It was a habit that had formed when they were all young girls.

As the three sisters stood together, silently assessing Mildred's holiday decorations, Harriett, as usual, found more disparaging words to utter. "Doesn't it look stupid, Gertie? Millie always overdoes it," she snapped, her arms still crossed over her sagging bosom.

"I think it looks marvelous," Gertrude said joyfully. "The neighborhood children are going to love it! I bet some will even be quite spooked by the ghouls and goblins."

"Or," Mildred said evenly, "we could pop a black pointy hat on Hattie's head and set her out on the porch. That would certainly give the children a fright."

"You're hilarious," Harriett said, scowling.

"Now stop it, you two," Gertrude scolded. "You did a fine job of decorating, Millie." She gave her younger sister's arm a gentle squeeze and walked back toward the side of the house. "I'll bring the pumpkins in from the garden and we can carve them while we have our tea," she called over her shoulder.

Excited about the annual ritual of carving scary faces and anxious to taste the cinnamon apple spice cake that Gertrude had made that morning, Mildred hurried toward the house. "I'll put the kettle on!"

"Oh!" Gertrude shouted, stopping short and turning back toward her sisters. "While I was cutting back the roses, a robin landed not a foot from me, cocked his head at me and then flew off. That means we are going to have company, girls!" she said excitedly.

"Oh, goody," Mildred said as she climbed the porch steps. "We could use some excitement around here."

"You and your damn superstitions," Harriett growled, moving toward the porch. "What the hell is a robin doing here at this time of year anyway? The stupid little creature should have flown south by now."

"Language, Hattie, language," Gertrude scolded, before turning away and stepping through the side gate.

Harriett opened her mouth to reply but decided not to waste her breath as she watched Gertrude's angular form disappear from view.

Eager to get out of Harriett's line of fire, having been the aim of it since lunch time, Mildred hurried into the house and closed the front door behind her. Still scowling, Harriett trudged up the porch stairs, mumbling, "I'm eighty years old and I should be able to say what I damn well please." Glancing around the porch, she added, "And, I should not have to put up with these tacky decorations on my house!" Harriett raised a hand toward the nearest artificial cobweb and considered ripping it down and scattering the little rubber spiders everywhere. The thought of how such an action would upset Mildred forced her to abandon the idea. Despite Mildred's whimsy and silliness, she was still her baby sister and she truly loved her.

Looking up at the hand she held aloft, Harriett noticed that she was still holding onto the maple leaf that she had plucked from the boulevard. Twisting its stem between her thumb and forefinger, she gazed at the brilliant colors that were reflecting the afternoon sun's light. The nagging wonder came to her then, as it had at least once each day for the past year, and she slowly lowered the leaf to her side, her eyes fixed upon the barren maple tree. What was she still doing here? Why hadn't her life come to an end yet? The leaf was making its exit and going out in a blaze of glory, no less, yet Harriett was still trapped on earth. What was God thinking, keeping her here so long? Hadn't she been punished enough during the past eighty years? Gertrude and Mildred certainly did not need her; they did not even seem to want her around, and her children and grandchildren had disappeared from her life as if they had never really existed. Was she that awful to be around?

As Harriett contemplated this, her gray eyes pooled with tears. Frantically blinking her eyelids, she managed to stop the flow. She walked over to the porch railing with the intention of letting the leaf drop to the ground but she stopped short, pulling it to her breast. The small symbol had come to mean something to her, and she decided to keep it—yes, maybe even pressed in the pages of a book just like Gertrude would think to do. Turning to go inside for tea, Harriett took one last look around at all of Mildred's decorations and thought that perhaps the neighborhood children would truly appreciate them.

Inside the tea kettle was whistling, but Harriett made her way down the hallway to the library. As she passed the dining room, she glimpsed Gertrude carefully spreading newspapers over the

Chippendale dining table that had been in their family for generations. She hurried past before her sister could draft her into duty. In the library, she pulled the enormous *Random House Dictionary* from a shelf and cracked it open to find a place for her leaf. The book opened to page 839, with the headings "liver spots" and "load" at the top. Harriett laughed aloud.

"At least I won't forget where I put it," she murmured, placing the leaf on the page and pressing it flat with her finger tips. "With all the rich food I've eaten in my life, I've become quite a load over the years, and one can play "connect the dots" with the liver spots on my arms. So all I have to do is take a look in the mirror and I will remember where I put it." Gently, Harriett closed the dictionary and placed it back on the shelf.

Fires crackled in both the dining room and parlor hearths, and MPR was tuned in on the radio, filling the rooms with the melodic strains of Debussy. Her sisters always kept the house overly warm and cozy which truly irritated Harriett. Wandering into the kitchen with a scowl on her face, Harriett acknowledged Mildred with a nod and made a beeline for the cupboard near the refrigerator. She extracted a bottle of whiskey and hid it under her sweater.

Mildred stopped slicing Gertrude's spice cake, pulled herself to her fullest height and said, "Where do you think you're going with that?" Harriett turned away from her sister and nonchalantly strolled out of the kitchen and into the dining room.

"She's drinking again," Gertrude said quietly as she walked through the kitchen and disappeared into the mud room.

"I heard that," Harriett called over her shoulder.

"There's nothing we can do," Mildred said loudly. "She is eighty years old and probably not going to last much longer, anyway. Besides, the booze mellows her out a bit."

"Ha, ha. You're hilarious," Harriett said sarcastically.

Gertrude entered the dining room with two plump, round pumpkins in her arms and set them on the table. She gave Harriett a look of warning and then went to retrieve the third pumpkin.

"I'm waiting for my tea!" Harriett roared at Mildred as she took a seat at the table.

"Hold your horses!" Mildred called back. "Why don't you take a swig of that stuff already so that Gertie and I don't have to listen to you piss and moan while we're carving our pumpkins!"

"Will you two stop this!" Gertrude cried as she came back into the dining room with the last pumpkin. "You're going to spoil the entire evening."

Mildred walked up behind her and set the tea tray down hard on the table. She noted that Gertrude was looking red in the face and as if she were about to cry. Patting her sister's hand, she said, "Don't worry, Gertie. We'll stop."

"This is holiday time," Gertrude said anxiously, her pale blue eyes welling up behind the small oval spectacles perched upon her pointy nose. "It's supposed to be fun and we're supposed to act like a family."

"I know. I know. I'm sorry and so is Hattie," Mildred said, glaring at her eldest sister. Harriett made a face at her in response. Hugging Gertrude's shoulders, Mildred said, "I promise it will be fun, Gertie. You always make it fun."

"Oh, will you two stop your bellyaching," Harriett said impatiently. "We haven't got all night! We have to carve these damn things and get over to the church."

Gertrude and Mildred looked at one another and rolled their eyes. Harriett grabbed the teapot off the tray and filled her cup in an attempt to ignore them both. Then, most defiantly, she broke the seal on the whiskey bottle and poured some into her tea. Angrily stirring her hot "toddy," Harriett turned away to look out the bay window toward the river in the distance.

The views of the St. Croix River and the Wisconsin shoreline were best from the porch and gardens of the house. But from her spot in the dining room, Harriett could see several motor boats bobbing near the lift bridge and a few trees still blazing with color on the opposite bank of the river. She had always thought that their house had the best views of the town and the river, which spilled into the Mississippi downstream. The Hayden family home had been standing on the same spot for over one hundred years, and thanks to the marvelous builders and craftsmen who had constructed it, the beautiful structure showed no signs of giving into its age. When the three sisters were suddenly back together under its roof, Harriett's children and grandchildren had dubbed the old house "The Aunt Hill," which was a fitting name for the grand, Victorian edifice perched majestically on a hill overlooking the town of Stillwater, Minnesota.

The house was truly a "painted lady." Five different colors had been employed to cover its many surfaces, including a soaring turret on the southeast corner of the house. And there was a wonderful wraparound porch with a sandstone foundation where Harriett spent the summer months sitting on the porch swing, spying on the town with her binoculars. Sitting grandly at the end of the upper part of Chestnut Street, the views of the town and the river were for the most part unobstructed, so Harriett could keep a sharp eye on the community and the comings and goings of the tourists who flocked to the sleepy river town.

As Harriett sat stewing over her sister's poor treatment of her, she noticed a long string of traffic coming over the bridge from Wisconsin. "Damn tourists," she murmured, adjusting her bifocals. "What do they all want to come here for? They just jam up the streets, crowd the restaurants and litter the sidewalks with their Tremblay's candy wrappers."

"Oh, stop your complaining," Mildred snapped, pouring herself a cup of tea. "Those tourists keep this town going. They come for the antiques, the boutiques, the quaint restaurants and, yes, Tremblay's candy store, and they leave lots of money in their wake. That's what keeps this town alive." Mildred took her tea and cake and sat down in front of a pumpkin.

"Your husband brought all the antique shops to town and really put us on the map," Gertrude said as she took a seat across from Mildred.

"Oh, shut up, Gertie," Harriett snarled. "My husband never did anything but destroy everything and everyone around him."

"That's enough," Mildred warned. "Let's forget about the tourists and Hattie's husband and get on with carving these pumpkins. We don't have much time before we have to leave for church."

"You two forget it," Harriett said, clutching her tea cup and the whiskey bottle and walking out of the room. "I'm going to take a nap. Call me when it's time to get ready."

Silence hung heavily in the room after Harriett's departure, and Mildred and Gertrude stared at one another across the table, their lips pursed, their bodies slumped. Finally, Mildred picked up a carving knife and stabbed her pumpkin. She instantly felt better. "Come on, Gertie," she said, "we have to carve all three of these by ourselves so let's get cracking."

Gertrude picked up a knife and carefully examined the pumpkin in front of her, trying to decide the best place to carve a face. "I just don't understand—"

"Let's talk about Halloween," Mildred said, cutting her off. "I don't even want to think about Hattie until I have to see her again."

After packing their contributions to the potluck supper into a basket, the three sisters piled into their fire engine red 1962 Mercury Comet, with Mildred at the wheel. They drove the few blocks to St. Michael's Catholic Church on South Third Street, where their brother John had once been the pastor. On Saturday evenings, the Hayden sisters always attended five-thirty mass which was followed by a potluck supper and bingo. Feeling rather lucky, Harriett had brought extra money to purchase more bingo cards that night, knowing there would be special holiday prizes. For their part, Mildred and Gertrude were more interested in the socializing that occurred during those evening gatherings and they never paid much attention to their bingo cards. Mildred and Gertrude had many friends in Stillwater, young and old, but Harriett did not, that is, except for Mr. Harmon, who was ninety-years-old, bald, toothless and "only interested in her sexually," as she frequently reminded her sisters.

That evening the bingo prizes were provided by Mulberry's Nursery and Garden Center. An array of bright yellow, burgundy and white potted mums and small pumpkins planted with ivy and philodendra brought life to the drab church basement. When Gertrude, the gardener, saw the prizes, she could hardly contain her excitement and her hopes of winning one of the beautiful plants. Harriett told everyone within earshot that she thought the prizes were cheap, and then she proceeded to win two mum plants and one of the pumpkin planters. Mildred knew that it was not Harriett's competitive nature that had pushed her to purchase extra bingo cards, but rather her desire to please her younger sister. And Gertrude could not have been more appreciative when Harriett approached her at the end of the evening.

"Here, Gertie," Harriett said, handing Gertrude a nursery flat filled with the plants. "You're the flower fanatic. I can't stand the ugly weeds."

"Are you sure, Hattie?" Gertrude asked hesitantly. "They're such beautiful prizes. The little pumpkin would brighten your room."

"Just take the damn things, Gertie," Harriett snapped as she pulled her coat over her shoulders and headed for the staircase leading out of the church basement. "Let's go home. I'm tired and we have to be back here at the crack of dawn tomorrow."

Mildred and Gertrude watched Harriett slowly make her way toward the door. She did look very tired. Placing a hand on Gertrude's arm, Mildred said, "Why can't you just accept things from her without your usual phony protestations? She knew you wanted them so she won them for you. Why do we always have to go through this, Gertie?" Mildred added in exasperation. "You always make her mad."

"I don't know," Gertrude said honestly. "I'm just trying to be polite."

"Why, for goodness sake? It's just Hattie!" Mildred saw the tears beginning to pool in Gertrude's eyes and she snatched up the box of plants and headed for the stairs. Over her shoulder she called, "Let's go, Gertie. Hattie is waiting!"

Outside, the night was clear and chilly. Mildred and Gertrude waved goodbye to their friends as they followed Harriett to the car. An enormous harvest moon beamed down at them, illuminating the still October night with an orange glow that cast eerie shadows along the tree-lined streets. They drove in silence back to The Aunt Hill.

Before crawling into her bed that night, Harriett snuck down the back stairs and tiptoed into the library where she pulled the enormous dictionary from its place on the shelf and quickly located the pages between which she had pressed her leaf. It was there, just as she had left it, soft and radiant with color. She held it up to the light for a moment and marveled at its beauty. Then she put the leaf back in its place, closed the dictionary, and placed the book on the shelf before heading back upstairs to her bed.

Chapter Two

The following morning, All Hallows Eve, the three sisters were up at the crack of dawn and off to church for eight o'clock mass which was always followed by a social hour that included coffee and donuts. The sisters skipped the donuts that morning and rushed home to start work on their enormous holiday baking project which involved making two hundred pumpkin-shaped sugar cookies that they would be handing out to the children as treats for Halloween. This tradition had begun several years back when Gertrude concluded that baked goods would be a lot more nutritious and less damaging to tooth enamel than candy. Of course, Gertrude never stopped to consider the cups of refined sugar that were poured into the cookie dough and Harriett and Mildred played along to humor her. Mildred did it because she loved the baking and decorating, and Harriett did it because it gave her ample opportunity to complain. On an average day, Harriett could find several things to gripe about, but with events likes this, she could stockpile complaints to use for days to come.

During the annual Halloween baking ritual, each sister had her specific duty and Mildred, for the most part, was in charge. Mildred made the batches of cookie dough (her secret recipe), and Harriett rolled out the dough and cut it with the pumpkin-shaped cookie cutter, a task that was accompanied by criticizing Mildred for not achieving the proper dough consistency. After the cookies were baked and the house smelled sweet, it was Gertrude's job to decorate them with orange icing and black jack-o-lantern faces. Children came from all over Stillwater to get the special cookies that the Hayden sisters handed out on Halloween, so in Gertrude's mind each cookie had to be unique and, of course, have a happy countenance.

Finally, when the kitchen had been cleared of the baking mess and the dishes from their lunch and every surface scrubbed clean, Mildred carried a pot of coffee into the dining room where they sat down to begin the arduous task of individually wrapping each cookie in clear cellophane and tying them with black and orange ribbons. They happily munched on the pile of cookies that had not made it as trick-or-treat material and sipped their coffee. Even Harriett kept silent as she performed the mundane task.

Around three o'clock in the afternoon the doorbell rang and Gertrude was sent to answer it. "Who could that be?" Mildred wondered aloud.

"Probably some little urchins starting early, hoping to get the best pickings," Harriett growled.

"Honestly, Hattie, the things you come up with," Mildred said, tying a perfect bow on a wrapped cookie.

They heard Gertrude open the front door and then heard her cry, "Goodness gracious! Molly! What a surprise!"

"Molly? My Molly?" Harriett said, shoving herself out of her chair and hurrying from the room with Mildred two steps behind her.

Still standing in the doorway, Gertrude embraced the girl warmly and then stood back, beaming at her sisters. "Look," she said excitedly. "It's Molly!" Smiling sheepishly at all of them was a young woman with rich auburn hair and creamy skin sprinkled with freckles. Her bright green eyes were fringed with worry.

"We can see that, you idiot," Harriett snapped. Trying to conceal her excitement, she stood where she was and nodded at her granddaughter in greeting. "How are you Molly?" she asked in a clipped tone. "Did we invite you for Sunday dinner and forget about it?"

The young woman stepped forward and cautiously hugged Harriett. "Hi, Granny," she said quietly. "It's good to see you."

Harriett did not embrace the girl but simply asked, "What are you doing here? Aren't you busy with exams? Isn't it the end of a quarter or something?"

"The university has switched to semesters, Granny," Molly replied evenly.

"Of course, we knew that," Mildred said, stepping forward to pull the girl into her arms and wrap her in a big bear hug. "Oh, Molly darling, how good it is to see you." She rocked back and forth with the girl tightly wrapped in her arms and cried, "Gertie said we were going to have a visitor, and here you are!"

"For God's sake, give her some room to breathe," Harriett said, pulling Mildred away from her granddaughter. "Now, who drove you down from the cities? Did you drive by yourself or did you ride with someone? We don't have to feed some boyfriend of yours, do we? You've only been in school a few weeks so you had better not have picked up a boyfriend already."

Mildred noticed that her grandniece was nervously glancing around and that her skin was quite pale. Molly had always been able to absorb all of her grandmother's verbal blows and continue as if things had never been said, so whatever was bothering the girl went well beyond Harriett's nasty cracks. Stepping between Harriett and her granddaughter, Mildred placed her hand gently upon Molly's shoulder. Looking into her grandniece's eyes, she said, "What is it Molly? What has brought you to us?"

Molly dropped her head on Mildred's shoulder and quietly said, "I need your help, Aunt Millie." Taking a deep breath, she looked up into her great-aunt's eyes. "I am in a bit of a pickle, as you always say."

"And what pickle is that?" Harriett asked, her voice hard and her expression severe.

Mildred and Gertrude waited anxiously for the girl to respond while Harriett eyed her suspiciously. Molly swallowed down the bile that was creeping its way up her throat and said, "Mother and Father threw me out, took away my car and told me never to come home again." There was a collective gasp. "I had to drop out of the University because I'm pregnant and they stopped paying my tuition."

"What?" Harriett screeched. "Pregnant!" Molly immediately dissolved into tears and Gertrude joined her. "Your parents let you go away to school so that you could exercise your independence and this is what you did with it!" Mildred held onto Molly as Harriett wailed, "Your parents paid good money to send you to the University and you blow it before the first quarter is over! Apparently those university boys had a lot more to offer you than the curriculum!"

"That's enough, Hattie," Mildred yelled. "Gertrude, close the door," she instructed. Then she turned to Harriett and furiously said, "Keep your mouth shut."

Sobbing uncontrollably and clinging to Mildred, Molly cried, "I think I'm going to be sick."

"Shh, everything is going to be all right," Mildred cooed. "Come with me upstairs and we will take care of everything." Gently, Mildred guided the girl toward the stairs while Molly fought not to be sick until she reached the bathroom.

Before closing the front door, Gertrude stepped out onto the porch to collect Molly's duffle bag and suitcase. The bag's weight was too much for her so she grabbed it by the strap and dragged it inside, leaving both pieces at the bottom of the stairs. She looked up to see Harriett standing in front of the bay window in the parlor and hesitantly walked toward her. Pulling a handkerchief from her skirt pocket, Gertrude dabbed away her tears and quietly said, "Millie will sort things out and find out the true story. Then we will be able to figure out how best to help Molly." She turned and left the room.

Harriett did not turn away from the window. She stood like a statue, staring out at the town below her and at the beautiful autumn day. She cursed the fates for allowing human beings to make the same mistakes that their ancestors had made. She had such hopes for Molly. Molly was the bright one, the beautiful one, with so much potential and with such a promising future. Now what kind of future could she have? Would she now suffer the same miseries that had defined Harriett's life?

Upstairs, Mildred sat on the guest bed with Molly's head cradled in her lap. As she stroked the girl's thick, dark red hair, Mildred watched with relief as the color slowly returned to Molly's freckled cheeks. The poor girl had been violently ill the minute they had reached the bathroom and had collapsed on the tile floor, bumping her head against the toilet and giving Mildred quite a fright. After helping Molly to a guest bedroom and onto the bed, Mildred pulled an afghan out of the antique armoire and covered the trembling girl. Then she tidied up the bathroom and returned with a glass of water. As she looked down on Molly, a memory instantly transported her to a dreadfully hot August afternoon in 1946 when she and Angelo had come home from a day at Lake Phalen and she had run straight through the house to the bathroom and was terribly sick. That night, Doctor Dooley told Mildred that she was pregnant. The memory flooded Mildred's warm brown eyes until tears spilled over her sparse lashes and rolled down her weathered cheeks.

Molly looked up to see her great-aunt crying and her heart suddenly swelled with remorse. "I'm so sorry, Aunt Millie," she said. "I should not have come and dumped all my troubles on your doorstep like this. I just didn't know where else to go."

Mildred blinked away her tears and looked into her grandniece's bright green eyes. "You have nothing to be sorry about, Molly. I promise you that we will do our best to help you in any way that we can." Mildred wrapped her arms tightly around Molly and pulled her close. As she hugged the girl she fantasized about Molly being her own child, someone to whom she could give all the love that she had been holding in reserve for too long.

Reluctantly releasing the girl, Mildred brushed the long strands of hair from Molly's pretty face. "Would you like to talk about it, Molly, or would you rather rest for a bit?"

"I want to tell you, Aunt Millie," Molly said with conviction. "Especially you, because I know you will listen to the whole story."

Touched by Molly's faith in her, Mildred's heart nearly wept; oh, to be trusted and needed by a child, albeit a grown one. "Yes, I promise you that I will listen to your entire story without interruption if you promise to tell me everything. You needn't be sensitive or embarrassed about what happened. And please, above all else, be absolutely truthful."

Looking directly into Mildred's eyes, Molly said, "I promise Aunt Millie that I will tell you the absolute truth."

"Very well." Mildred slid back on the bed and settled herself against the ornately carved Victorian headboard. "Get comfortable and tell me what happened."

Molly took a sip of water, grabbed a pillow for her throbbing head and lay down across the foot of the bed. "I'm such a fool, Aunt Millie. I went to college a naïve fool and now I have to pay for it the rest of my life."

"Now stop that, Molly," Mildred hushed. "I will not have my grandniece making derogatory comments about herself. Just tell me what happened."

"All right." Lowering her gaze, Molly began to draw circles on the quilt with her finger. "You know that when I got to the University I was a little overwhelmed and desperate to make friends. Well, I met some girls in the dorm that first week that loved to go to all the parties on campus, especially the ones at the fraternities. I liked going with them because I met more and more people every week and I knew that I would soon be able to pick some real friends out of the bunches that I had met."

"That's right," Mildred interrupted. "That's good."

"Well," Molly continued, "that first week of school, after orientation, we went to fraternity row to hit all the parties that were going on during their rush week. That's when they are deciding on who to accept into the fraternities. Anyway, we started at a fraternity that one of the girls insisted we go to because she was hot after this fraternity brother who she had met at a football game. So, we got to the house and it was jam-packed with people. Right away someone shoved a glass of this punch concoction into my hand."

Mildred's expression held skepticism. "Punch concoction?"

"No, I knew, Aunt Millie, that it had alcohol in it. Lots of alcohol in fact. I told myself that I'd just have one."

"But you didn't."

"That's just it, Aunt Millie. I don't remember." Molly rolled onto her back and covered her face with her hands. Rubbing her eyes with her finger tips, she sighed and continued, "I remember talking to some boys that I had met at a football game and then they introduced me to some of the players. And while we were all talking, I was drinking the punch. Aunt Millie, the next thing I remember is waking up in a strange bed, naked, with blood stains on my thighs and on the sheets of the bed."

Mildred stared at her grandniece in horror, and Molly's face crumpled as tears once again flooded her eyes. "My mind was so foggy and I felt so awful, as if I were stuck in a nightmare, and I just wanted to run away. My body was so sore and I could barely move, but I climbed out of the bed and found my clothes scattered on the floor." Molly paused for a moment and wiped the tears from her cheeks. "My panties were torn so I couldn't put them back on and when I saw them I threw up all over the bed. After I was done being sick, I got dressed fast and got out of there, even though one of my legs did not seem to work. It was about five o'clock in the morning and there were people passed out all over the place. I was so scared and so afraid of waking anybody. And as soon as I was safely out the door, I dragged myself across campus to my dorm." Molly rolled over and buried her face in the pillow. "Oh, I feel sick just thinking about all this again," she moaned.

Mildred slid down the bed and settled herself right next to Molly. Gently rubbing the girl's back, she said, "Molly, did you report it to the police?"

"No. No I didn't," Molly cried. "I was so ashamed. I felt like such an idiot for getting so drunk and allowing it to happen to me." Molly turned to look at Mildred and with great distress in her voice said, "I told one of the girls what had happened to me, and she said that there is this rape drug going around college campuses called GHB, or something like that. She thinks that whoever gave me that first drink put it in there and waited for me to pass out so he could do what he did to me. But I don't remember who gave me the drink," Molly wailed in frustration. "It was so crowded and there was so much confusion, and I can't remember Aunt Millie. I can't remember!"

"Shh. It's okay," Mildred said, pulling Molly into her arms. "You are not to blame for anything, my dear girl. A violent crime was committed against you, and no matter how naïve you think you were being, you did not deserve to be assaulted like that." Mildred's insides were boiling with rage. When she was inclined, she could produce one of the nastiest tempers the world had ever seen, and at that moment she truly wished that she was standing face to face with the monster who had harmed her grandniece.

With grim determination, Mildred beat back the violent thoughts and calmly said, "Did you go to the hospital or see a doctor?"

"No," Molly replied sheepishly. "When I got back to the dorm, I took a hot shower and scrubbed myself until my thighs started to bleed," Molly explained. "I was still very woozy and I collapsed in the shower and got sick again. After that, I crawled into bed and fell asleep, and I didn't wake up until dinner time when the girls came knocking at my door."

Molly sensed reproach in Mildred's watery eyes and all the distasteful remorse flooded back into her body, making her feel ill once again. Burying her face in Mildred's ample bosom, she murmured, "I know I did the wrong thing, Aunt Millie, but I was so ashamed. I just wanted to forget that it had ever happened. If my mother and father found out, I knew they would freak and blame it all on me, so I thought I could just bury it and try to move on with my life."

"And then, you discovered that you were pregnant," Mildred said evenly.

"Yes, and I had to tell them. I had to tell someone. I didn't know what to do," Molly said in despair. "I have been so terribly sick and unable to make it to class or to stay awake to study. I just don't know if I have the strength to make it through all this."

"Have you considered an abortion?"

Molly's head snapped up. "Aunt Millie, we're Catholic."

"Never mind that," Mildred said sharply. "I never thought that I would ever suggest such a thing to anyone in my entire life, but this is a situation in which I believe it should be considered."

"My parents would damn me to hell if I did such a thing!"

"Well, your parents were wrong for throwing you out in the first place, so don't let their self-righteous indignation interfere with your decision." Mildred clasped Molly by the shoulders and gave her a little shake. "This is your body, Molly—your life. I don't believe for a second that God wanted anyone to harm you in this way. It's evil. And He certainly did not have a hand in making you pregnant. That was simple biology. There was no love involved." Mildred shook her head. "No. The sooner you can get over this, the better."

Sighing, Molly confessed, "I did think about it, Aunt Millie. I thought about doing it right away. But then I realized that with my upbringing and my family, I would suffer more from having the abortion than from having the baby and giving it up for adoption. This is my mistake and I guess I have to suffer the consequences."

"No, you don't," Mildred nearly shouted. "This is not your fault, Molly! Your parents are wrong. Your mother preaches Catholicism as if she were the Lord herself, and truth be told, she is the most unchristian, unloving, unforgiving human being that I have ever encountered in my life. And your father, who should know better, does not have the guts to stand up to her, and he should be utterly ashamed of himself. So, let's forget about your mother and father for the time being. The very first thing you need to learn to do is to take control of your life, and coming to us was a good first step, even though I understand that you only came to us because they threw you out and you did not know where else to go." Mildred smiled at Molly and brushed her hair away from her face. "But, we're going to make it through this Molly, dear, and you shall come out on top. I promise you that."

Molly hugged Mildred tightly and whispered, "Thank you, Aunt Millie."

All at once Mildred was overflowing with love for the girl. A peaceful silence descended upon the room and wrapped the two women in a cloak of calm. She planted a kiss on the girl's forehead; then she rose and made her way toward the door. "I had better go and relay your story to Gertrude and your grandmother as I am sure they are most anxious for the tiniest bit of information."

"Please don't let Granny kick me out," Molly begged.

"Don't you worry about your grandmother, Molly," Mildred said confidently as she turned the knob and opened the door. "Your Aunt Gertrude and I will handle her." Molly's face was transformed by an expression of relief. "Now, you get some rest, and I'll have Gertie bring up some broth along with some tea and toast for your supper."

"Thank you, Aunt Millie," Molly said softly. "Thank you for being so open-minded and understanding."

"You're most welcome. When you live to be my age, you learn that things are not always black and white. Every situation is special and comes with its own set of unique circumstances. One needs to consider what these are before coming to any conclusions." Then Mildred winked at Molly before walking out of the room and shutting the door behind her.

A second later, just as Molly was flopping back on the bed, Mildred's head popped into the room. "If it makes you feel any better, Molly," Mildred said softly, "your parents had to get married because your mother was pregnant. And, fortunately for her, she had a miscarriage early on and no one was ever the wiser." And in the blink of an eye, Mildred disappeared.

For a long time, Molly sat staring at the closed door, her eyes wide with astonishment and her heart burning with anger for her parents, who would neither forgive her nor help her in her hour of need.

Chapter Three

Downstairs in the parlor, as Mildred related Molly's tragic tale, Gertrude listened patiently while Harriett erupted every other minute, spewing hot lava in the form of disparaging remarks. Mildred did her best to ignore her comments, but when Harriett snarled, "Her father is absolutely right about her—she is a ridiculous girl who cannot be trusted to be on her own! She deserves what she got," Mildred jumped out of her seat.

Looming above Harriett with one hand raised above her head, she warned, "Don't you ever say that again Harriett Louise Hayden or I will slap your ugly, sour face. Molly most certainly does not deserve what happened to her and the consequences should not be hers to bear." The pathetic sound of Gertrude sobbing into her handkerchief caused the violence in Mildred to dissipate. She lowered her hand to her side and stepped away from Harriett. "Let's get one thing straight from the beginning; this is not Molly's fault. Every freshman college student in America takes a drink at their first big party and in my mind that is not a crime; it is a declaration of independence, a bit of experimentation, a part of growing up. That's all Molly can be accused of doing," Mildred said forcefully. "Some evil boy obviously had his eye on her from the moment she walked into that party. He's the criminal. He's at fault and he should pay the consequences! Not Molly!"

"Well, how is that going to happen when the foolish girl did not have the brains to report the crime to the police?!" Harriett yelled.

Clenching her fists so tightly that the arthritic pain in her wrists shot all the way up to her shoulders, Mildred glared at her older sister. "Watch your tongue, Hattie, or Gertie and I will send you over to the nursing home before nightfall." Satisfied that her threat had garnered Harriett's attention, she continued, "Molly is going to stay here with us and we are going to help her get through this mess and get on with her life. You're either going to join us and be supportive or you can leave this house. It's your choice, Hattie, and I'm dead serious." Mildred gave her one last look of warning and then glanced over at Gertrude.

The doorbell rang, breaking the tension in the dimly lit parlor. Mildred headed toward the front foyer, and as she went she softly said, "Molly is a good girl, Hattie. She was a virgin." Then she stopped and looked back at her older sister and added, "And who are you to cast stones? You made the choices that shaped your life."

Out in the foyer, Mildred straightened herself, smoothed down the front of her skirt, and opened the door. There was Simon Mulberry, standing with his arms akimbo, looking around at her decorations on the porch.

"Simon! How glad I am to see you!" she cried, pushing open the screen door.

"Hello, Miss Hayden," he replied, flashing a dazzling white smile at her. "Sorry I'm so late. Things were crazy at the nursery—lots of last minute pumpkin shoppers—and it took me longer than I expected to get out of there."

"No need to apologize, Simon. You're just such a dear to come and help me."

Simon stepped in front of Mildred, pushed back against the screen door with his rear end, and glanced out toward his pickup truck. "I brought you some more hay bales and corn stalks and some of the pumpkins we had left over from today's sale."

"You're so thoughtful," Mildred gushed. "Come inside and I'll get my coat on."

"If you don't mind, I'll unload the truck while you're getting ready. I'm in a bit of hurry to get home so that I can hand out candy to the little munchkins. I love seeing all the costumes."

"Oh, certainly," Mildred said in perfect understanding. "You run along and I'll be right out to help."

"Who's there?" Harriett yelled from the parlor.

"It's just me, Mrs. O'Connor," Simon called to her.

"And who are you?" Harriett growled, knowing perfectly well who it was.

"I'm here to help your sister put up all the tacky decorations that you despise so much," Simon called, winking at Mildred and charming her with an enormous grin. Giggling, she playfully pushed him out the door and hurried to the closet for her coat.

Harriett gave no response for which Mildred was grateful. She did not relish more confrontation of any kind that day as Molly's troubles were weighing heavily enough upon her, and she needed to put on a cheerful face for the trick-or-treaters who would soon be adding their own brand of excitement to their lives.

When Mildred stepped out onto the porch, she paused a moment to watch Simon heft two hay bales out of the back of his well-used pick-up truck. She sighed softly and whispered, "Oh, if I were only fifty years younger . . ." And then a thought hit her hard, like a slap across the face, and she instantly pulled herself out of her reverie and hurried off the porch, calling, "Oh, Simon!"

"Yes, Miss Hayden," Simon replied, turning to smile at her. "Just tell me where you would like the hay bales to go and I'll get started."

"Oh, forget about the hay bales for a minute," Mildred said dismissively. "I have something that I want to ask you."

"What's that?" Simon pulled off his suede work gloves and slapped them against his rock hard thigh.

"Do you need any help at the nursery right now? Are you hiring anyone?"

Simon eyed her cautiously. "As a matter of fact, we're in desperate need of help. We lost all of our high school and college workers when school began in September, and we don't have enough employees to meet our winter needs. Why do you ask?"

"Because I have the perfect candidate for you!" Mildred said excitedly, thoroughly pleased by her own brilliance. "Hattie's granddaughter, Molly, who is in a bit of a pickle at the moment, has come to live with us and she needs to get out of the house and interact with young people, as well as earn some money."

"Hold on, Miss Hayden," Simon said, raising a hand. "You know that I adore you and Miss Gertrude and would do anything for you, but I really don't need the aggravation of having to deal with Mrs. O'Connor on a regular basis which would surely happen if her granddaughter were under my charge."

"Don't you worry about Hattie," Mildred instructed. "I can handle her, and I promise you that she will not harass you in any manner." She looked hopefully at him. "So, what do you say?"

Simon could see that it meant a lot to Mildred; besides, it would not hurt anyone if he just talked to the girl and got a feel for whether or not there was a place for her at the nursery. God knew they needed the help as the Christmas season was fast approaching. "Oh, all right, Miss Hayden," Simon said, laughing. "You have twisted my arm with your charm." Mildred blushed slightly. "Send her over to the nursery tomorrow and I'll interview her."

"Hooray!" Mildred squealed, clapping her hands together in delight.

"I can't promise you anything," Simon warned, "but I'll give her a fair shot."

"God love you," Mildred said adoringly. Then she clasped his shoulders between her hands, stood up on her tiptoes, and gave him a quick peck on the cheek. "Thank you. Thank you. Thank you," she chanted. "Now, let's get this yard all set up before the little ones start showing up for their treats!"

It took Simon and Mildred all of fifteen minutes to stage the ghoulishly terrifying front yard display. After receiving oodles of gratitude and a plateful of the Hayden sisters' famous pumpkin cookies, Simon sped off in his truck, beeping his horn. Mildred waved goodbye as she stooped to light their scary jack-o-lanterns with a match stick, and singed her finger with the flame.

The sisters hurriedly put together a meager supper, and Gertrude took a tray up to Molly as Mildred had promised. When the first chubby little finger pressed the doorbell and summoned them into action, the evening became a blur of costumed children and thankful parents, and lots of praise and idle chatter. Harriett continued in her foul mood, and Mildred made a point of keeping her behind the scenes so that she would not scare the children with her crabby face. By ten o'clock, they were so exhausted that they went to bed without watching the evening news.

Molly watched the holiday unfold from her bedroom window that evening, catching brief glimpses of costumes as the children passed underneath the street lamps. She wished she were downstairs handing out treats with her great-aunts, but she had neither the stomach nor the desire to face her grandmother's reproachful glare. She'd heard it all from her parents already, and she did not need to be reminded again that she had fallen from grace.

All of her life she had tried to stay within the boundaries her parents had set for her simply because she had wanted them to love her. Now, she realized that her behavior had not made the slightest bit of difference. They did not love her. How could they love her and say the things they said to her? When they had declared that she was no longer their daughter, Molly wondered if they were actually relieved to get rid of her—especially her mother. She had never worn the right clothes, had the right hair style, said the right things or behaved in a manner that pleased her mother. No, George and Gillian O'Connor must be feeling quite relieved to be rid of their disappointing daughter. And Molly crawled into her bed that night feeling tremendously sorry for herself, until she remembered something her Aunt Mildred had said about her parents and the self-pity turned to fury in her heart.

The following morning, while Mildred was busily preparing oatmeal, toast and tea for Molly and telling her about the Mulberry Nursery, Gertrude and Harriett shuffled into the kitchen. When Mildred explained her plan to them, Gertrude cried, "Millie, what a fabulous idea! The nursery would be a perfect place for Molly, among all the new life, everything growing and fragrant and—"

"Oh, will you shut up!" Harriett snapped. "You and your damn flowers. She doesn't know the first thing about working in a nursery. What makes you think that Simon will actually hire her?"

"Careful, Hattie," Mildred warned, glaring menacingly at her elder sister. "Stay out of this if you are not going to be supportive."

Molly jumped in. "Granny, I know I don't have any experience, but I'm willing to learn and I'm willing to work hard." Despite the fact that her grandmother was glowering at her in an attempt to frighten her into silence, Molly swallowed down the bile creeping up her throat and continued, "I need to earn money to pay for school when I go back and this could be a great opportunity for me."

Looking over at Mildred, Molly smiled sweetly and said, "I'm so grateful to you for setting this up, Aunt Millie, and I promise I won't let you down." Then, glaring over at her grandmother, Molly deliberately added, "I'll pay my fair share and I'll do my fair share of work while I am living under your roof. You have my word."

The sound of a pitiful sigh came from the opposite side of the table. "Oh, Molly," Gertrude said. "In your condition you mustn't exert yourself or have too many worries. Why don't you just let us take care of you?"

"What nonsense," Harriett moaned. "You don't know the first thing about having a baby, Gertie, so just stay out of this."

"That's enough, Hattie," Mildred cut her off. "Molly is young, strong, and extremely capable, and if she wants to work to earn money and do her fair share around here so that she manages to keep a modicum of self-esteem, then so be it. This is Molly's predicament and these are her choices to make, and we will provide advice and support as long as it is asked for and accepted." Mildred paused a moment and glanced at both of her sisters. "Do I make myself clear?"

Gertrude nodded her head vigorously without making a sound. Harriett, on the other hand, made a "Harrumph" sound, snatched her plate of toast and cup of coffee off the table, and stormed out of the kitchen.

A ray of pure morning sunlight crept its way through one of the east-facing windows and spilled across the room and the round oak table where the three remaining women sat. The sunbeam, alive with dust motes, found Molly's face, illuminating the anger and disappointment that had crept in around her eyes.

"Don't mind your grandmother," Mildred said, gently taking Molly's hand. "She's just having a hard time with the situation, but she'll come around. You'll see. I know for a fact that her heart is not made of stone," Mildred teased, smiling sympathetically.

"Millie's right," Gertrude chimed in. "She loves you, Molly. And she just wants what's best for you." Reaching her hand across the table to add it to the pile begun by Mildred, Gertrude added, "Deep inside she is just sick about what happened to you, dear."

"That reminds me," Mildred said. "Gertrude and I have a friend at church that we think you should talk with about your situation. She's a younger woman, who is a counselor for victims of crimes, particularly sexual crimes." Molly swallowed hard and Mildred patted her hand in reassurance. "She, herself, was a victim of rape, many years ago," she continued, "and she turned the experience into something positive by becoming a counselor for others who have suffered in the same way."

"She's a tremendous person, Molly," Gertrude added, desperately trying to be helpful. "You'll really like her and I know that she'll be able to help you."

"Gertie's right," Mildred said confidently. "You need someone who will completely understand all that you have gone through. And at some point, we need to address the criminal aspect of your situation and find out who did this to you. I know that she can help us with this, as well."

Molly's stomach began to turn at the thought of having to relay her sordid tale once again. But maybe they were right. Perhaps she did need to talk to someone who had had a similar experience and who might be able to help her leave it all behind. Molly caught sight of the dust motes swirling about in the warm light of the sunbeam, and as she watched them dance about joyfully, a jolt of energy pushed her to sit up straight. "All right, I'll go and talk with your friend if you think she will help me. And I would like to go and talk to Mr. Mulberry today about a job at the nursery if one of you can drive me there."

"Good girl!" Mildred said happily, clutching Molly's cheeks between her hands and planting a loud kiss on her forehead. "You see . . . you have been here less than twenty-four hours, and we're already making progress. What a fine team we make!" Both Mildred and Molly rose from the table.

Gertrude could not have agreed more. She wanted Molly to stay with them forever so that they could help her. The girl would bring purpose to their lives. All Gertrude had ever known was a lifetime of taking care of people. As a young girl, she had been the most popular baby-sitter in the neighborhood, and as a young woman, she had been the most popular first grade teacher at the elementary school, where she happily taught until she was forced into early retirement by their father's untimely stroke. Gertrude was persuaded by their hopeless mother to give up her own life to move home and take care of him. And when Avery Hayden had finally died of a third and final stroke in 1968, their mother, Alice, began to suffer from angina, and Gertrude stayed on to become nursemaid to her. In all her years on earth, Gertrude had never met the man who had the potential of fulfilling all of her romantic fantasies born of the romance novels she had been reading since her teens. She realized that she had been born to serve, and in the romantic recesses of her heart, she imagined herself to be a kindred spirit of the Queen of England, sacrificing all for her country, or in Gertrude's case, her family.

With her parents gone and her sisters in good health, Gertrude saw Molly as a new golden opportunity. She began making mental lists. First, she would drive Molly to the nursery for her interview and then make sure she was home for a meal and an afternoon nap. Then she would need to find a good doctor for Molly and set up appointments and get her to the doctor's office—however often pregnant women had to go to the doctor—then monitor her grandniece to make sure she was getting the proper nutrition, drinking plenty of fluids, exercising, taking her vitamins, etc. Then there would be the sewing of maternity clothes, and if Molly kept the baby, there would be baby clothes to knit and sew as well. If nothing distracted her, she could dream about such possibilities all day.

"Are you going to keep the baby, Molly?" Gertrude blurted out, surprised by her own bluntness.

Stopped in her tracks by the question, Molly turned from the kitchen doorway to look back at her great-aunt. "No, Aunt Gertie," Molly said softly. "I really don't think that I am in any position to take care of a child. This baby would be better off with two parents who will love it and take care of it for a lifetime."

Gertrude slumped in her chair. "That's a very mature way of thinking, Molly, and probably the right decision." Giving herself a good shake, Gertrude rose and walked across the room to embrace her grandniece. "I am so proud of you," she whispered.

"Are you going to come with us to the nursery, Gertie?" Mildred asked impatiently. "I thought I would take Molly now so that we can catch Simon before he gets too busy." She walked into the front foyer and Molly and Gertrude hurried after her.

"I thought you and I could pick up some more mum plants for indoors so that we have plenty for Thanksgiving," Mildred called over her shoulder. "Then I thought we could have a look around to see what else we need while Molly is having her interview."

Gertrude passed her sister up in the hallway and reached for her coat. "I was planning to take Molly to the nursery myself," she said, hurrying into her coat and reaching for her handbag and the keys to the Comet. "But you can come along if you'd like."

"Yes, I would really like to come along if you two don't mind," Mildred said smiling.

"Please come," Molly begged.

"Yes, do come," Gertrude encouraged, feeling safely in control with the keys to the car clasped tightly in her gloved hand.

The three women walked out the front door and past all the Halloween decorations that suddenly seemed out of place with the holiday officially over. Dark, cold clouds were fast approaching from the western sky, bringing with them a vicious, biting wind which propelled them quickly toward the car.

As the Comet pulled out of the garage and backed down the asphalt driveway toward the street, Harriett stood on the upstairs landing, spying down on them from behind a lace curtain. No one had invited her along or included her in the decision to take Molly to Mulberry's Nursery for an interview. Harriett was Molly's grandmother, her true blood relative, and she should be deciding what her granddaughter should and should not do. Mildred and Gertrude had no business interfering, especially when they insisted upon shutting the door on her every time she opened her mouth to express her opinion on a matter. This was exactly what her sons had been doing to her for most of their lives and Harriett resented it bitterly. She perfectly understood that she would never win a mother-of-the-year award, but she had never been physically abusive to her children or a drunken ogre like her husband. So why did they turn against her and shut her out of their lives as soon as they had left home?

Harriett's resentful thoughts dragged her down into a depression that she did not welcome. She slowly sank onto the window seat. "You miserable, old fool!" Harriett shouted at the empty house. "You had your chance and you blew it."

Harriett snatched the spectacles from her face and rubbed furiously at her eye sockets. Then placing them back on the bridge of her prominent nose, she hoisted her large frame onto her feet. For a moment, she stood like a statue on the staircase landing and stared at the dusty chandelier hanging in the foyer. She had no idea what to do or where to go. Millie and Gertie always had a plan for the day and her job was to gripe about it and purposely get in their way and annoy them until they gave her a project or shooed her away. The wheels in her brain turned slowly like the pulley of a drawbridge until Harriett resigned to descend the staircase and search for her binoculars in the parlor. There, she stood formidably in the big picture window, binoculars pressed against her glasses and her feet spread for stability, slowly scanning the town in the hopes of witnessing something interesting.

While Harriett was spying on the town of Stillwater, Mildred, Gertrude, and Molly were zooming west of town in the red Comet. The two giddy aunts were overloading Molly with information about the Mulberry family, interrupting each other mercilessly and giving the poor girl a blistering headache. From what Molly could gather, her great-aunts thought that Simon Benjamin Mulberry was the most handsome, most generous and well-mannered man alive, and he was beginning to sound too good to be true.

After what she had been through and the way her father had treated her, Molly did not exactly have a lot of trust for the opposite sex, and she doubted that Simon Mulberry was as wonderful as they claimed.

"Simon has the most beautiful milk-chocolate brown skin," Mildred was saying, "and deep, dark eyes. And his hair is black, thick and curly—soft curls, not tight ones."

"He's bi-racial," Gertrude interjected. "His biological parents were two different colors." Molly nodded in response, as if she had just learned something fascinating.

"Henry and Lillian Mulberry adopted him when he was just a baby," Mildred explained. "They tried for years to have children of their own, but it just wasn't meant to be. And when they laid eyes on Simon, they fell instantly in love with him. He was such a cute baby, with a gentle disposition, bright eyes, and the best belly laugh I've ever heard."

"Henry and Lillian were hoping for a boy to take over the family business. You know, the nursery has been in their family for three generations," Gertrude said quite seriously. "And Simon surprised them by taking a genuine interest in the business and educating himself so that he could one day take over. In fact, his father handed over the day-to-day operations to him awhile ago, and he has proved to be quite the good businessman and manager," Gertrude added proudly.

"Yes, Simon is their pride and joy," Mildred concurred. "And he seems to love them unconditionally. He is extremely devoted and loyal to Henry and Lillian, which is more than most parents can say about their own biological children."

"Like me and my parents," Molly said sarcastically.

"That's different," Mildred said sharply, turning to look at Molly in the back seat. "Your parents, especially your mother, never expressed their love and devotion to you or showed you any respect. Everything begins with the parents. They set the stage for their relationships with their children."

Molly opened her mouth to respond just as Gertrude cried, "Here we are!"

Gertrude turned into the parking lot at the Mulberry Nursery and Garden Center and parked the Comet close to the front door of the store. At the entrance, a woman with salt and pepper hair, dressed in denim overalls, a tattered old barn jacket and green rubber boots, was taking down a Halloween display and neatly stacking the decorations in an old wagon. What Molly noticed most about the woman was the long, thick plait of hair hanging down her back and the fringe of bangs that hung like an awning off the right side of her forehead.

"Hello there, Lillie," Mildred called out as she stepped around the wagon.

Lillian Mulberry turned from her task, and then beamed with delight, clapping her hands together in excitement. "Well, what a treat to have you two here this morning!" She approached Mildred and Gertrude with outstretched arms and gave each of them a quick hug. "How was your Halloween? Were you just swamped with little ghouls last night?"

"It was business as usual," Mildred replied. "I think we passed out one hundred and fifty cookies."

"That many!" Lillian gasped. "Well, they are the best cookies in the five-state area! Simon can't live without them."

"Speaking of Simon," Gertrude interrupted, "do you know where we might find him?"

"He's back in greenhouse number fifteen, I think," Lillian said, suddenly noticing Molly. "Do you need Simon's help in the garden today, Gertrude?"

"No," Mildred answered for her sister, "we've brought our grandniece to see him about a job here at the nursery." Gently taking Molly by the arm, she pulled her forward and said, "Lillian, this is Harriett's granddaughter, Molly O'Connor."

Lillian held out her hand to the girl and smiled warmly. "Hello, Molly. It's a pleasure to meet you."

Molly shook her hand timidly and attempted to return her warm gaze. "Hello, Mrs. Mulberry."

Gertrude quickly said, "Molly is staying with us for awhile and she needs to find a job to make some money for school. Simon said that he needed some help in the greenhouses and told us to bring Molly over for an interview this morning."

"Well, we are desperate for help right now," Lillian concurred, "so I'm sure he is anxious to talk with you, Molly." Molly smiled at Mrs. Mulberry's encouraging words. And seeing the hope in Molly's bright eyes, Lillian steered her through the entrance to the garden center. "Come with me, dear. We'll hunt down my son in the back forty."

Glancing over her shoulder at her great-aunts, Molly was a bit alarmed when they just waved at her and then turned their attentions toward a shopping cart. "We'll be shopping and visiting, Molly," Mildred reassured her. "Come and find us when you're done."

"Okay," Molly stammered.

"Don't worry. You'll do just fine," Lillian said. Wrapping an arm around Molly's bony shoulders, she teased, "Simon won't bite. But, he does growl a bit . . ." Lillian laughed out loud and then winked at Molly. "I'm just teasing, sweetie. Although I'm his mother and am therefore biased in my opinion of him, I can assure you that you will never meet a better human being than my son." Lillian's chest puffed with pride as she thought about Simon.

Across a greenhouse filled with potted, white mum plants, Lillian caught sight of one of the employees. Pulling her arm from around Molly's shoulders, she called out, "Jacob, do you know where Simon is right now?"

Watering the plants around him, the young man called back, "Last time I saw him, he was on his way to the office to check on some seed shipments."

"Thanks, hon." Lillian waved a hand in his direction. To Molly, she said, "It gets to be a bit of a maze back here so just follow me and keep your eyes to the ground so you don't trip on any hoses."

Lillian took off at a good clip down a narrow path between benches of potted mums. Molly sped after her and immediately stumbled over a hose that was snaking its way underneath the flower tables. For a brief second, she envisioned flying mum plants pelting Mrs. Mulberry and knocking the poor woman to the ground. Refocusing, she fell into step behind Lillian as they wound their way through greenhouse after greenhouse. Molly was amazed and delighted by the rows and rows of colorful flowers and plants. One greenhouse held flats of seedlings, the green sprouts dancing about as enormous fans circulated warm air through the building, and another stored larger plants with big green leaves and red stems, and yet another greenhouse contained ornamental evergreen trees that stood at attention, as if they were a military assembly waiting to be addressed.

Such wonders, Molly thought. She had never really considered where flowers came from, how they were started, and who grew them. She had grown up in her parents' house in Evanston, Illinois, where a full-time gardener brought flats of seedlings in both the Spring and Fall. She had never had any interest in what he was doing but she had always enjoyed the results, especially the fifty-foot impatiens border that wrapped around the front of their brick mansion situated on the shore of Lake Michigan. Molly abruptly shook the thoughts of her family from her head and focused her attention on Mrs. Mulberry's thick braid. The surprisingly speedy woman was increasing the distance between them. How could she move that fast, Molly wondered, stumbling over another hose. Mrs. Mulberry had to be in her late fifties/early sixties. Maybe the woman ran marathons in her spare time.

Finally, they entered a greenhouse with miles of yellow and burgundy mums blanketing the flower benches that ran the length and width of the area. At the far end of this sea of color sat a white clapboard building with a bright green door, above which hung a hand-painted sign that read, "Office." Molly sighed in relief. The trek through the maze of greenhouses had taken a bit out of her, and all she wanted to do was sit down for a minute and catch her breath.

As the two women approached the office door, another employee sauntered in from an adjacent greenhouse, slapping a pair of gloves against her denim jeans. The girl had a smirk on her overly made-up face and she was swaying her ample derriere from side to side as if it were on display in a fashion show. Molly noticed that she was not wearing a gardening apron like the rest of the employees at Mulberry's, and her enormous breasts were bulging out of the scooped neck of her long-sleeved tee-shirt.

Molly heard something akin to a dog growl rumble about in

Lillian's throat and she cautiously took a step back from her. "Tracy! Aren't you supposed to be transferring the flats from greenhouse six to number seven?" Lillian said angrily.

"I'm working on it," the bleached blonde replied, rolling her eyes in annoyance. "I was just helping Simon with today's delivery. The truck arrived." The girl kept moving the entire time she was talking and managed to escape into another greenhouse before Lillian could say another word.

"That girl needs a swift kick in that fat ass of hers," Lillian snarled, moving into the passageway between the buildings.

Molly started giggling and quickly raised her hands to cover her mouth. Lillian turned around to look at her and then laughed too. "Sorry about that, honey." Lillian shook her head at herself. "That wasn't very nice of me, but that girl's just so hot after my son that it burns me." Molly's freckled cheeks, rosy from both exertion and embarrassment, and her eyes, sparkling with laughter, caught Lillian off guard. She suddenly saw how beautiful Molly was and she marveled that the girl was Harriett O'Connor's granddaughter. Remembering her purpose, she spun on her heels and hurried away, calling over her shoulder, "You just wait here, honey. I'll go fetch Simon for you."

Chapter Four

Molly stood alone near the office door, waiting for Lillian to return. The greenhouse was deathly still, and a little shiver tickled the base of Molly's spine. Shrugging off the chill, she scanned the greenhouse and then moved through the sea of mums like a ship sailing on a soft breeze. Standing in the middle of the greenhouse, surrounded by brilliant autumn colors and the earthy aromas of the rich soil and spicy mum plants, Molly suddenly understood why someone would develop a passion for gardening. What a reward to plant a tiny seed in the soil and nurture it until it grew into a strong, brightly colored flower that filled a room or garden with its alluring fragrance. If she stood there long enough, she thought she might actually be able to see the flowers growing and hear them stretching up toward the sun, begging for its prized energy. Just then, the sun came out from behind a cloud and poured its brilliance into the greenhouse, making the mums more vibrant in color. Closing her eyes against the blinding light, Molly raised her face toward the glass ceiling and sighed contentedly. The sun's heat seeped into her pores and filled her with soothing warmth.

As she stood in the midst of the autumn hues with her face raised in worship and her dark red hair cascading down her back, Simon Mulberry paused near the office and silently observed her. His first thought was that there was absolutely no way that Molly could be crabby old Harriett O'Connor's granddaughter. His second thought was that he had just fallen in love at first sight. Suddenly, his knees began to wobble and he moved his legs to steady himself. Simon thought he had better clear his throat to alert Molly to his presence, but before he could make a sound, she turned and caught sight of him standing near the office door, gazing at her across the tables of mums. "Hi," he called, waving a hand.

Molly stood rooted to the spot where she had been standing. Her very first thought was, "Holy moly! Aunt Millie and Aunt Gertie were right! " and her second was, "Get a hold of yourself!" She had never seen a man as handsome as Simon Mulberry. Mildred and Gertrude had described him in detail but she could not have imagined, by any stretch of the imagination, the amazing color of his skin, which, at the moment, contrasted beautifully with the ivory turtle neck that hugged the well defined muscles of his upper torso. Struck dumb, she stood there staring at him in awe, her mouth actually hanging open.

Taking a few steps in her direction and with his eyes glued to her pretty face, Simon said, "You must be Molly O'Connor. I'm Si–" At the corner of the office building was a wooden support pillar from which someone had hung a basketful of multicolored mums which collided with Simon's head at the very moment he was uttering his name. "Shit!" Molly heard him exclaim as he reached for his forehead. Thrown off balance by the blow to his head, Simon spun round and fell back against the wooden support beam, smacking the back of his head on its corner. This last jolt sent him crashing to the ground with a loud groan.

Molly watched in both horror and amusement as the scene played out before her. When he fell to the floor and out of sight, she bolted forward. She dropped to her knees beside him and unconsciously placed a hand upon his chest. Half laughing, she said, "Are you all right?"

Cradling the back of his head with his left hand and rubbing his forehead with his right, Simon groaned, "That's gonna leave a mark!"

Suddenly, Molly broke into laughter. Realizing that he had just unintentionally performed a physical comedy sketch for her, he began to laugh as well. Their laughter grew, like a crescendo, until they were both crying and holding their stomachs. Then Molly collapsed on top of Simon's chest and the laughter stopped abruptly.

Pulling herself back together, Molly sat up straight and said,

"Sorry about that. I shouldn't have laughed and gotten so carried away."

Hoisting himself up onto his elbows, Simon responded, "Don't worry about it. That had to be pretty hilarious to witness." Utterly embarrassed by his performance, he added, "I really am normally not such a klutz."

Unable to help herself, Molly giggled again. Cupping her hand over her mouth, she looked down at Simon in horror and said, "I'm so sorry. I don't know what's wrong with me today. I'm not purposely being rude. I think that I'm just a bit nervous."

Utterly and completely charmed by her, Simon looked into her twinkling green eyes and said, "I know you're not being rude." He sat up, held out a hand to Molly, and said, "Now, help me up and we can get on with your interview in the safety and comfort of the office."

"Are you sure you're all right?" She held up two fingers in front of his face. "How many fingers do you see?"

Simon looked at the fingers and then looked back at Molly's serious face and burst into laughter again. Completely helpless in the situation, Molly joined him, their next bout of laughter lasting longer than the first. Finally, Simon hoisted himself off the ground and pulled Molly up to her feet beside him. Simon was so tall that she had to tip her head back to look up into his face and when she did, she fell in love with his dark brown eyes, his long thick lashes, his elegant, pointed nose, and his gorgeous, broad smile. With the nearness of him and a sudden surge of hormones, Molly's knees buckled, her vision tunneled, and she headed for the ground once again. Catching her just in time, Simon hefted her into his arms and, laughing, he carried her toward the office door.

"Oh, no you don't," Simon said, grinning from ear to ear. "I'm not going to let you bang your head and sue us right out of business."

Extremely offended and terribly uncomfortable in Simon's arms, Molly tried to wriggle free and said with indignation, "I'm not the kind of person who would do a thing like that."

Reaching for the knob on the office door with Molly still safely cradled in his arms, Simon looked at her with incredulous eyes and said, "I was just kidding, Molly." At the realization that she had not picked up on his joke, Molly's cheeks burned in embarrassment.

Inside the dark office, Simon carefully placed her in a chair near an enormous metal desk, and then walked over to a refrigerator in the corner of the room. Still woozy, Molly leaned over in the chair and dropped her head between her knees to try and draw some blood to her brain.

Simon turned from the refrigerator with a bottle of spring water and saw Molly doubled over in the chair. Unscrewing the cap on the bottle, he crouched down beside her. Simon nestled the water bottle in her palm, closed her fingers around it, and said, "Take a sip. It'll help."

Molly carefully raised herself to sit back in the chair, praying with all her might that she would stop feeling faint and not get sick in front of him.

Watching her closely, Simon reached over to brush back some of the strands of hair that had fallen into her face. "What happened out there? Do you have an issue with low blood sugar or something?" Simon liked the idea that she actually may have been swooning over him.

"Something along those lines," Molly replied, telling herself that she could not and would not lie to Simon if he was really serious about hiring her. The fact remained that she was pregnant and she would not be able to hide this from anyone for much longer and then explanations would be required. Molly was making herself sick just thinking about such things.

Eyeing her curiously, he said, "Would you like something to eat? You still look really pale."

"No thank you."

"Are you sure?" Simon pressed. "I've got my lunch in the fridge . . . fruit, sandwich, veggies?"

Molly shook her head and did not open her mouth to reply for fear that something might come out of it at the mere mention of food. Swallowing hard, she closed her eyes in an effort to collect herself. Now, more than ever, she wanted this job. To work with Simon Mulberry every day would be anything but a hardship, and in the short time she had been in the greenhouses, something had awakened in her and she was curious to discover more.

Molly opened her eyes to find Simon's gorgeous brown eyes staring back at her. She was sure he would turn away, so she remained transfixed and he surprised her with his unwavering gaze. Feeling the heat begin to rise again, Molly cleared her throat politely and said, "May I please have an interview, Simon."

"Of course. That's what you came here for in the first place, not to watch me make a complete fool of myself with a hanging pot and a post, or to nearly faint in my arms, right?"

Molly giggled. "Right."

"Okay," he stood and made his way around the desk. Taking a seat across from Molly, he leaned back in his chair and propped his feet up on the edge of the desk. "Let's get this interview underway."

Molly smiled and he was happy to see the color coming back into her cheeks. "So, Molly, why do you want to work here?"

Sitting up straight in her chair, she leaned forward. "In all honesty, I desperately need a job so that I can pay for school in the future, and Aunt Millie and Aunt Gertie thought this would be a wonderful place for me to work. They certainly think the world of you and your family, and of course, Aunt Gertie thinks the only place to really experience life is in a garden."

Simon smiled. "Do you have any experience with flowers, plants, trees . . . ?" he asked.

Molly looked directly into his eyes so that she could read his reaction and said, "No, absolutely none whatsoever." Much to her chagrin, Simon's eyes gave away nothing. She quickly added, "But I'm willing to learn, and I promise you that I'll work hard. I promise . . ." Molly said, her voice trailing off as she considered Simon's unchanging gaze.

"I believe you." Tearing his gaze away from Molly in order to formulate a relevant question, Simon picked up a pencil from the blotter on the desk and grabbed a sheet of paper.

Molly thought this was a good sign, indeed. Simon was actually going to take notes which meant he was considering her employment, or maybe he was just going to hand her an application to fill out and send her on her way. Her hopes were dashed with this last thought.

"How many days a week do you have classes?" Simon asked, writing something down on the piece of paper.

"Oh, I'm not in school at the moment," Molly stammered.

"When do you plan on going?" Simon asked, erasing what he had just written down.

"I want to go back as soon as I can, but it won't be for at least eight more months," Molly replied, thinking that she was helping her situation by saying that she would be available to work for that long a period of time.

The pencil in Simon's hand suddenly stopped on the paper. He put together all the clues: Molly nearly fainting, Mildred saying that she was in "a bit of a pickle," and Molly talking about going back to school in eight months time. There was only one logical conclusion. Suddenly, he felt ill. And looking up from the paper into Molly's eyes, his suspicions were confirmed.

Molly sat back in the chair and braced herself for Simon's next question, the answer to which would certainly end the interview right then and there.

"Molly, are you pregnant?"

There was a long pause as they held a staring contest across the desk while Molly decided on her answer. Finally, she whispered, "Yes."

An awkward silence descended upon them. Molly shifted uncomfortably in her chair and averted her eyes. She wondered if she should just leave without saying a word. Perhaps it would be best that way and it would save him from having to tell her that there was no job for her at the nursery. For some reason she wanted to spare him from having to let her down, even though she was miserable at the thought of never seeing him again and at the thought of him thinking so ill of her.

Simon was trying to sort through his conflicted feelings. So, some creep got Molly pregnant and bailed out on her when she told him about her condition. It happened to girls all the time. In fact it had happened to one of his good friends at university and he certainly had not condemned her for it but had helped her through the whole ordeal. The difference with Molly was that he was attracted to her and he wanted the situation to be much different. But facts were facts, and the truth was that he could no more alter Molly's situation than he could change the earth's orbit. There was no sense wishing things were different. If he could not have Molly O'Connor the way he wanted her, then he could at least have her as a friend. A movement distracted him. Molly was rising from her chair.

Jumping up out of his seat, Simon held a hand toward her as if by magic he could detain her. "Molly, wait." The words were louder than he had intended. Startled by the tone of his voice, Molly froze.

In a softer tone, Simon said, "I'm sorry. Your personal life is none of my business. It was wrong of me to ask that question."

Shrugging, Molly replied, "It's all right. You needed to know what my limitations might be in the future. I didn't want to lie to you because you would have eventually figured it out and then you would think less of me." Pausing a moment to take one last look at Simon's beautiful face, Molly turned to leave. "Thank you for the interview. I completely understand why you wouldn't want to hire me."

Simon was around the desk in the blink of an eye and had his hands on Molly's shoulders before she had taken two steps. Slowly turning her to face him, he smiled. "Can you start tomorrow? We really need the help."

"What about my problem? What happens when . . ."

"When what? When you start getting leg cramps and pinched nerves and you're too tired to stand up?"

Molly nodded.

"Then I put you on a stool at the cashier up front or at the information desk," Simon said easily. "We can make this work, Molly. It won't be a problem."

"Really?"

The hope in Molly's eyes and voice touched Simon's heart, and at once, he knew that he could take the high road. He would become a friend to her, something akin to a big brother (after all, he figured that he was at least eight years older than she), and if he had her close by, he could look after her. Smiling down on her, Simon nodded his head and said, "Really."

"Oh, thank you. Thank you. Thank you!" Molly cried, launching herself at him and wrapping her arms around his neck, completely caught up in her own excitement. When Simon stiffened against her, she immediately pulled back. Without meeting his eyes, she softly said, "Sorry. I got a little carried away. This is my first real job and I'm just so excited."

"Don't worry about it. I understand." Simon crossed the room and opened the office door. Looking at the watch on his wrist in an attempt to regain his composure, he cleared his throat and said, "I don't mean to be rude, but I really have to get back to work."

"Oh," Molly exclaimed. "I should've realized that you were so busy. I'll just go find my aunts and get out of your way."

"The Hayden sisters are here?"

"Yes, they drove me over this morning."

"Well," Simon said, smiling, "I'll walk you back to the store and say hello. I can certainly spare a couple of minutes to see my favorite gals."

Relieved that he was going to lead her back through the maze she had blindly navigated on her way to meet him, Molly quickly scooted through the door and then waited for Simon to lead the way. Following along behind him, she was able to admire his beautiful form and it struck her that she had never in all her life been so attracted to a man, especially one she had known for all of fifteen minutes. Given her circumstances, she was surprised that she felt anything at all for him. The terrible part was that she knew he had already closed the door to her. She was certain that he had been initially attracted to her, but once he found out about her pregnancy he was entirely different toward her. There would never be anything between them aside from a working relationship—that is, if she did not blow it and get fired in the first week.

Simon suddenly stopped, and lost in her thoughts, Molly plowed into the back of him. "Oops! Sorry," Molly grimaced, stumbling back to restore the distance between them.

Turning around quickly, Simon reached out a hand to grab her. "That was my fault." Convinced that she was steady on her feet, Simon released Molly's arm and said, "Is your grandmother here?"

Shaking her head from side to side, Molly looked wounded and said, "No."

"Oh, I see," Simon said, his heart flooding with sympathy for her. "I don't suppose she's taking your news very well."

"Not at all," Molly assured him. "Not at all."

Nodding his head in understanding, Simon turned and silently led Molly back to the garden center, where her aunts were happily engaged in conversation with his mother. When Simon and Molly entered the shop, the three anxious women all turned their enquiring eyes upon them. Being the gentleman that he was, Simon did not make them wait; he quickly confirmed that Molly had been offered a job. There was much excitement and gratitude, and before Simon slipped away from the celebration, he told Molly to come back the next day at nine o'clock. After she had filled out all her paperwork, including a formal application, she could start her first day of work.

When Molly climbed into the back of the Comet for the drive back to The Aunt Hill, she was grinning from ear to ear. Aunt Mildred was right. Coming to them had been the right choice. She was already making progress. And she had already made a friend, or at least she hoped that she had. In the short time she had spent with Simon Mulberry, she realized two important things: that she felt very safe in his presence and that she needed him. Somehow she knew that she needed him in her life.

Chapter Five

The morning of Molly's first day at the Mulberry Nursery and Garden Center, she awoke to an abdomen full of nerves and hormones and was immediately sick. She was glad to get it out of the way because she instantly felt better. She was counting the days until the first trimester was over so that she would experience some relief from the nausea. The nurse practitioner she had seen at the University of Minnesota Hospital had given her some hope that this would be the case, and she prayed that the woman had not been feeding her a line and giving her false hope.

Mildred looked in on her just after she had been sick and when she understood what had happened, she marched Molly downstairs to fill her up with oatmeal and toast, her sure-fire remedy for pregnancy nausea. Despite not wanting to eat anything, Molly had to admit that it had worked the previous day. She obediently shoveled the food into her mouth while she watched the morning weather report.

While Molly concentrated on the television, Mildred took the opportunity to look her over. She smiled when she saw that Molly had taken pains to look nice for her first day of work; she had lightly applied some makeup which enhanced her beautiful features. Sipping her morning coffee, Mildred decided that she was happy: happy for Molly and happy that Molly had come to them. Yes, it would all work out. God had a plan for Molly and they were simply following where He led. And the best part was that Mildred got to be a part of the plan and to take an active role in helping mold her grandniece into an adult. What a gift and a privilege. She promised herself, and God, that she would not take her responsibilities lightly.

While Mildred was lost in thought and Molly was captivated by a news story on the television about a professional football player who had dropped dead on the playing field, Gertrude emerged from the mud room carrying a pair of green Wellington rubber boots, which she set on the floor near Molly's chair.

"Good morning, Aunt Gertie," Molly said sweetly.

"Good morning, sweet girl," Gertrude replied, planting a kiss on the top of Molly's head.

"Morning, Gertie," Mildred said cheerfully. "Doesn't our Molly look wonderful for her first day of work?"

Gertrude looked Molly over thoroughly before shaking her head in disagreement. "I think there's something missing."

"What?" Molly said, panicked.

Gertrude pointed down toward the floor next to Molly's chair and said, "Those."

Molly glanced down at the green rubber boots and said, "Really? Are you sure they won't laugh at me, wearing those on my first day?"

"Molly," said Gertrude in exasperation, "did you notice what Simon was wearing on his feet yesterday?"

Molly shook her head. "I don't think I ever looked at his feet."

"Well, what woman would?" Gertrude said wisely. "But never mind that. He wears Wellingtons because the greenhouses are muddy and dotted with puddles and you can rinse them off at the end of the day with a hose." Gertrude liked knowing about things and drawing out her explanations. "I could not live without my Wellies in the garden. You'll see. Once you've tried them, you won't be able to work without them either."

Molly transformed her skepticism into excitement and jumped out of her chair to give her great-aunt a hug. "Thank you, Aunt Gertie. How thoughtful of you."

Gertrude held onto Molly for a bit and simply enjoyed the moment. Then she let her go. "Go ahead. Try them on and see if they fit."

Molly did as she was told and was surprised to find that they fit her quite well. "I thought we had a similar shoe size," Gertrude said, perceptively.

Mildred rose from her seat and walked around the table to examine the boots. "Good thinking, Gertie," she praised. "Well done."

Gertrude beamed, feeling quite pleased with herself. "Well, we should think about going, Molly," she said, snatching a piece of toast from the toast rack in the center of the kitchen table. "You don't want to be late for your first day of work."

"It is not even eight o'clock yet, Gertie," Mildred said, frowning. "Calm down and have some breakfast, and for heaven's sake, let Molly finish eating. It only takes fifteen minutes to get to the nursery."

Just then Harriett lumbered into the kitchen with the morning newspaper and made a beeline for the coffee pot. "You're not leaving already?" she scoffed.

"No, no. Gertie is just a little anxious this morning," Mildred explained, pulling out Tupperware containers and jars from the refrigerator.

"Molly, I'm going to make you a lunch to take along, as well as some snacks," Mildred said. "If you keep your stomach full, you are less likely to get sick. We can stop at the convenience store on the way and get you some of those individual milk bottles for the day," Mildred continued. "And this morning I will go shopping and stock up on the foods you like to eat. So take a moment to write a list for me."

"Please don't go to any trouble, Aunt Millie," Molly protested. "If you'll let me borrow your car later, I can do the shopping for you. I do have some money and I would like to pitch in."

"And you damn well should," Harriett mumbled as she slopped oatmeal from the pot on the stove into a bowl.

Mildred smacked Harriett in the arm as she walked past her toward the counter and said, "Nonsense, honey. You are going to be so tired by the end of the day that it will take all your energy just to get through dinner."

Gertrude placed a hand on Molly's shoulder and said, "Millie's right, Molly. You'll be exhausted. So, you just take care of yourself and the baby, and we will take care of you."

At the mention of the word "baby," the skin on the back of

Harriett's neck prickled and anger welled inside of her. Turning from the stove with her bowl of hot oatmeal, she growled, "You two need to stop coddling her, and she needs to start helping out around here."

"Hattie!" Gertie gasped.

Molly rose from the table and walked over to Mildred at the counter. "Here, Aunt Millie," she said, taking the bread knife from her great-aunt's hand. "Let me do that. You sit down and have your breakfast."

Knowing that Molly needed to prove herself to her grandmother, Mildred stepped away from the counter and left the girl to make her own lunch. Glaring at Harriett, she took a seat at the kitchen table, grabbed a piece of toast and the front section of the newspaper and began to read, purposely blocking out her elder sister, who, at that moment, she wanted to slap hard across the face.

At precisely eight-thirty, Molly gathered up her things, stepped into her Aunt Gertrude's green Wellington boots and made one last stop at the bathroom. Mildred and Gertrude collected their purses and jackets and went to stand near the front door. As they waited patiently for Molly, Gertrude jingled the keys nervously in her hand until Mildred snatched them away from her in annoyance. Then Harriett sauntered by in her coat and kerchief without acknowledging their presence and strolled right out the front door. Puzzled, Mildred and Gertrude watched Harriett step off the porch and walk in the direction of the garage. Both women hurried out the front door and onto the porch. Much to their surprise, Harriett was climbing into the passenger seat of the Comet.

"Sorry," Molly said, breezing by them. "Now I'm ready to go."

Speechless, both women turned to stare at Molly. "What?" Molly said. "Do I have food on my face or something?"

"It seems your grandmother is coming with us this morning," said Mildred.

Angling her neck to peek into the garage, Molly's stomach did a summersault at the sight of her grandmother's babushka-covered head sitting motionless in the front seat of the car. "Oh dear," Molly groaned. "Do you think she's going to make a scene at the nursery?"

Gently patting Molly's hand, Mildred smiled. "I think she just wants to be a part of this big moment in your life. It's her way of showing her support."

"Now, let's not spoil it," Mildred warned. "Nobody make a fuss over her. Just act natural." Turning back toward Gertrude, she ordered, "Gertie, hurry and lock that door. We don't want Molly to be late for work or Simon will be disappointed in all of us."

Molly suddenly got a little woozy and nearly fell backward down the stairs, and Gertrude got a little excited, fumbled with the house key and dropped it. Mildred grabbed onto her swaying grand-niece and then stooped to pick the key up off the porch floor. Handing it back to Gertrude, she said with great exasperation, "Now, do you think you can handle locking up while I pull the car out of the garage?" Gertrude nodded her head and began to fumble with the key again.

With a strong hand on Molly's arm, Mildred led her down the steps, over to the garage, and then opened the car door for her to get in. When Mildred climbed into the driver's seat, Harriett snapped, "What have you been doing? Now she's going to be late!"

"Thank you for your concern, Hattie," Mildred replied in an even tone. She turned the key in the ignition. "We still have plenty of time." She backed the Comet down the driveway to where Gertrude stood waiting. Finally, everyone was buckled in and they were on their way.

As they headed west on Pine Street, Gertrude pointed out Simon's house to Molly. She was surprised to see a well-maintained, romantic little bungalow, surrounded by rose bushes that still had blooms on them. When the house had disappeared from view, Molly tried to decide what it said about Simon. Perhaps he was romantic, meticulous, sensitive—and then her mind really got carried away and continued: beautiful, tall, strong, sexy, kind, funny, and obviously not interested in you. And that was the end of Molly's mental appraisal of Simon Mulberry. Silently, she scolded herself and promised to stop thinking about him.

But when they were approaching the nursery, she prayed that Simon would not be around to see her being dropped off by her elderly relative posse. She did not want him thinking that she was a baby and needed constant adult supervision. She wanted to be strong and independent, the type of woman that she was sure he would be interested in and would most certainly respect more. But, as they approached the employee entrance of the nursery, Simon was standing there, looking more gorgeous than he had the day before, dressed in baggy jeans and a blue denim shirt, talking to what Molly supposed was another employee. Mortified, she slumped down in the seat and wished that her Aunt Mildred would drive right past him and away from the nursery. Unfortunately, her wish did not come true.

As Mildred pulled the Comet up alongside Simon, Harriett frantically rolled down her window and called out to him, "Young man!"

Simon smiled and waved, then excused himself from the conversation he was engaged in. "Yes, Mrs. O'Connor?" he said with laughter dancing in his eyes. "I thought I might be hearing from you." Simon glanced into the back seat and winked at Molly.

"Wipe that smug look off your face, Simon Mulberry, and listen to me," Harriett instructed. Simon bit the sides of his cheeks. "Molly is here to work. You see that she does a fair day's work for a fair day's wages." Looking directly into his eyes with the intention of frightening him, she added, "Do I make myself clear?"

"Perfectly," Simon said, trying to sound respectful and sincere at the same time, for both Molly and her grandmother's sake.

Molly quickly kissed Gertrude and placed a hand on Mildred's shoulder before exiting the car. Out of the corner of his eye, Simon watched her progress and carefully timed his parting remark.

"And don't you worry, Mrs. O'Connor. I'll take good care of your granddaughter." Before stepping back, Simon winked at Harriett and then pounded the roof of the car with his fist as he called out, "Have a nice day, ladies!" Then he turned to escort Molly through the employee's door into the magical and fragrant world of the Mulberry Nursery and Garden Center.

Harriett opened her mouth to say something more, but Mildred stepped on the accelerator, throwing Harriett back in her seat, and sped out of the employee parking lot.

"It had to be a little awkward for Molly to have three old ladies driving her to work," Gertrude said softly from the back seat. "Perhaps just one of us should drive her from now on. One of us can drive her in the morning and the other can pick her up at night."

"I think that's a very good idea," Mildred said, nodding her head. "Good thinking, Gertie. It was very sensitive of you to consider Molly's feelings like that."

"Oh, what rubbish!" Harriett barked. "If Molly is going to live under our roof then she should have to live by the rules we lay out for her. Someone has got to look out for her, seeing as she obviously can't look out for herself."

"I am trying to look out for her," Gertrude snapped.

Mildred pulled to a stop at an intersection and turned to look at both of her sisters. Even though she was the baby of the family, she constantly felt like the mother. "Now, that will be the end of this discussion. Do you want to come with me to the grocery store or should I drop you two at home?"

"Oh, please let me come," Gertrude said pathetically. "I want to help you choose good foods for Molly."

"And you?" Mildred said, looking over at Harriett.

Simmering inside like a pot of soup on the stove, Harriett kept her eyes glued to the windshield and muttered, "Just go."

Oh, good. Just what I need! thought Mildred. Two hours in the grocery store with Hattie and Gertie arguing over what foods Molly should and shouldn't eat. I'd rather have someone shoot paper clips at my face with a rubber band!

Mildred clicked on the blinker to indicate her turn onto Highway 36, and when the traffic light changed to green, she took her turn and focused on her route to Cub Foods, hoping for several minutes of peace before she entered the grocery store with the harpies that had disguised themselves as her sisters that morning.

At the nursery, things were going well for Molly. She had filled out her application and all the subsequent paperwork that coincided with employment, and she had been given a brand new green garden apron with the words "Mulberry Nursery" embroidered across the top. Simon had commented on the Wellington boots, informing her that she had made an excellent decision in wearing them. He had been terribly sweet and helpful since she arrived, but when it was time to give her a task, he called on his mother to show Molly around and get her started. Molly felt extremely uncomfortable and self-conscious and wished that Simon could have been the one to show her what to do. Even though she had known him for merely a day, she felt at ease with him.

Lillian was terribly nice to Molly and took time to explain everything as she moved Molly from one task to another. Together, they watered the mum plants in greenhouses number seven and eight and then they spent the rest of the morning loading up carts with mums that were going to be distributed to small flower shops around the Twin Cities. After a short coffee break, during which Molly ate some soda crackers and a container of yogurt all the while keeping a sharp eye out for Simon, Lillian and Molly got to work loading one of the delivery trucks with the plants they had gathered.

Molly's stomach and heart did a flip-flop when Simon showed up with Jacob, the boy she had seen the day before, at the loading area. "Molly, get down out of that truck," Simon ordered abruptly. Then he reached up and carefully lowered Molly out of the truck and placed her gently on her feet. Without looking at her, he turned away and called for Jacob to take her place. "Mom," Simon said with authority, "you and Molly hand the plants up to Jacob. The job will go a lot faster this way."

Simon was gone from sight before Molly had completely understood what had happened. She did not understand why he seemed so angry with her. She and Lillian seemed to be doing the job fast enough, and it hurt her feelings to be singled out in front of her co-workers. The hurt feelings soon turned to humiliation, and her faced flushed with the heat of resentment.

With great curiosity, Lillian looked over at Molly and she began to wonder. Simon had been acting strangely since he had met Molly the day before. She could not quite put her finger on what was troubling him, but Lillian knew her son better than she knew herself, and she was certain that something was upsetting him with regard to the girl.

When Lillian, Molly, and Jacob had finished loading the truck
with the mum plants, it was time for a lunch break for everyone.
After escorting Molly back to greenhouse number five, where
there was a platform surrounding an enclosed lavatory that served
as the break area, and after introducing her to some more of the
Mulberry employees, Lillian excused herself and went in search
of her son.

Feeling out of place around the other employees who were so
familiar with one another, Molly pulled her lunch bag and bottle
of milk out of the small refrigerator that sat next to an old kitchen
cabinet. On top of the nearby counter sat a grimy coffee maker
that was brewing fresh coffee. As the aroma swirled up from the
machine with a cloud of steam, Molly's face turned a putrid pea
green and she nearly vomited into the sink. Steadying herself,
praying desperately that no one had noticed, she walked away
from the counter and sat down at the end of one of the picnic
tables that completed the employee break area. Closing her eyes
and swallowing hard, she gripped the table with her hands and
willed the nausea away. Thankfully, there was a sudden commotion as another person approached the break area.

"Hey, Mr. Mulberry!" Jacob said, "How's it goin?"

"Hi, Mr. Mulberry," another girl said.

"Hello, gang!" said a very tall man dressed in denim overalls
and a plaid shirt. "Breaking for a little lunch, are we?"

Molly watched the man she now knew as Mr. Mulberry with great
interest. He was tall, barrel-chested, and had the thickest gray hair
she had ever seen. His shoulders were broad and looked as solid as
a rock, as did the rest of him. Years of working in the nursery had
kept him extremely fit and permanently tanned. His face and fore-
arms were well weathered, and charming laugh lines sprang from
the corners of his twinkling blue eyes. Molly liked him instantly.

"Well, who have we here?" he said, turning his attention to
Molly and smiling broadly. "You must be Molly O'Connor, our
newest employee."

Molly could not help smiling back. "Yes, I am," she said quietly,
waiting for him to direct the conversation.

Henry Mulberry sauntered over and took a seat across from her at the picnic table. "Well, I'll be damned if Simon wasn't right," he said, shaking his head. "You are a pretty one." Molly blushed from the tips of her toes to the top of her head. Lowering her gaze, she fidgeted with her lunch bag and relished the thought of Simon actually saying such a thing about her.

"Don't be embarrassed," Henry said, chucking her under the chin like a toddler. "My son just calls them as he sees them. He's very smart, my Simon."

Molly peeked up at him from underneath her eyebrows and smiled. Henry winked playfully at her and then rose to leave. "I'm out in the back forty digging up saplings for a new home development today so I am a dirty, smelly mess." He chuckled. "I won't stick around and spoil your lunch." With great disappointment, Molly watched him begin to walk away.

"Welcome to the family, Molly. That's what we all are here at Mulberry's," he called over his shoulder. Then Henry stopped and turned to face her again. "I hope you'll be happy here, and let us know if for any reason you're not." Again, Henry winked at Molly and gave her a wave. Then he looked at the rest of the group and said, "Bye, kids."

"See ya," the group chimed in unison.

Molly stared at the back of his head as he navigated his way out of the greenhouse and wished with all her might that she could have a father like Henry Mulberry.

After a brief search, Lillian found Simon stewing in the office, slamming file drawers and kicking the desk. She demanded an immediate explanation of his behavior. Seeing no viable exit route as his mother stood with her arms crossed barring the office door, Simon slumped down into his desk chair, sighed heavily, and covered his eyes with one hand.

"What's troubling you this morning?" she asked in a no-nonsense tone of voice.

Knowing his mother would not let him leave the office until he had answered her, Simon took a deep breath and exhaled the words, "I just don't want Molly climbing up on things."

"Why not?" Lillian asked completely baffled.

Simon took a moment to chew on his bottom lip which his mother recognized as his way of stalling. "Why not?" she demanded.

When Lillian Mulberry demanded information, she got it. Always had and always would. To resist her would be an exercise in futility and Simon just did not have the strength to fight her that afternoon. "Because she's pregnant, Mom," he blurted.

Lillian stared at him in shock and then quietly said, "Oh, dear." She inched her way across the room and plopped down into the metal chair that Molly had been sitting in the previous day.

"Now do you understand?"

"A bit," Lillian said cautiously, "but I still don't understand why you are so frustrated and angry."

"Because," Simon said pitifully. He stood up, shoved his chair hard against a file cabinet and turned away from his mother.

Patiently, Lillian waited for her son to explain himself as he leaned his elbows on top of a file cabinet, buried his face in his hands and moaned. Then he lifted his head and turned to look at his mother. "Because I thought she was 'the one,' Mom," Simon said miserably. "Yesterday, when I saw her for the first time, something inside me came alive. I've never been attracted to any woman like that. And then I find out she's pregnant, only nineteen years old, and had to drop out of the University. Who knows what her relationship is with the baby's father . . . I can't get in the middle of all of that."

"Why not?" Lillian said evenly. "That's what your father and I did for you."

Simon stared dumbly at his mother, and she just smiled at him and rose from her chair. "God brought Molly to us for a reason, my dear boy. Why don't we just take a little time to figure out why."

"Because I don't want to take the time," Simon snapped. "I want things to be different. I want her to be free so that I can ask her out and get to know her better."

"Patience, Simon. Have a little patience," Lillian said softly.

Simon sighed in frustration and pushed away from the file cabinet.

Turning to leave the office, Lillian said. "I promise that I'll keep an eye on Molly and keep her off ladders and out of trucks if you promise never to act like that again." Having learned what was bothering her son and having said her piece, Lillian left Simon alone in the office.

After a very long and arduous first day on the job, Molly was ready to collapse in a heap at five o'clock. Her feet ached, her back ached, her neck ached, and her breasts ached, the latter, of course, being related to her pregnancy. Lillian had been her teacher and mentor all day long, and she had been most kind to her, especially in the afternoon. Together, they had watered hundreds of plants, helped some of the other employees transplant poinsettia seedlings into larger pots, loaded several trucks for deliveries (with Jacob's help) and moved one greenhouse full of plants to another. The day had gone by so quickly that she never had had time to think about feeling sick or tired, but now that Lillian was releasing her from duty, she began to feel every ache in her muscles and an unpleasant sourness in her stomach. What she needed desperately was a warm bath, some ginger ale and a box of soda crackers.

At the end of the day, Simon could always be found in the office doing book work, placing orders for seeds, supplies, or merchandise for the store, or filling out payroll. After a day full of physical activity, he enjoyed propping his feet up and having a Coke while he listened to the radio and completed his office tasks. He was up to his elbows in time cards and payroll forms, singing along to an old R.E.M. tune, when there was a loud knock at the office door.

"Come in," he called out, reaching over to turn down the volume on the radio. Simon looked up to see Molly's pale face peeking cautiously into the room, and without intending to, he scowled at her. After her unpleasant encounter with Simon that morning, Molly was extremely leery of him and she held back in the doorway.

"Ah, Simon," Molly stammered, "your mother said I was done for the day and I was wondering if I could borrow the phone to call one of my aunts to come and pick me up?"

"Sure," Simon said, waving her into the room. He lifted the desk phone and placed it on the other side of the desk, closer to Molly, who set her tote bag on the floor before reaching for it. As she was dialing the number for The Aunt Hill, Simon glanced at her face and was shocked to see how pale and tired she looked. He reached over and hung up the phone before Molly finished dialing. Alarmed, Molly looked up at him.

"I've got a better idea," Simon said, leaning closer to her across the desk, in part to get a better look at her face. "You're looking pretty beat, like you could use a few moments of peace before going back to The Aunt Hill and your curious aunts and grandmother." Molly smiled. "So," Simon continued, "why don't you prop your feet up, have a soda and a snack and give me thirty minutes to finish up what I'm doing. Then I'll drive you home."

"I can't ask you to do that," Molly protested.

"You didn't ask," Simon corrected. "I offered. And it's on my way home and absolutely no trouble at all." Taking his finger off the disconnect button on the phone, Simon instructed, "So, call your aunts and tell them that I'll be giving you a ride home. And tell them not to tell your grandmother or we'll both never hear the end of it."

Molly dialed the number, and Mildred immediately answered the phone. "Hi, Aunt Millie, it's me. I'm just calling to let you know that Simon is going to give me a ride home when he is done with his work so you don't have to come and get me."

"Oh, that's so nice of him," Mildred cooed on the other end of the line. "You tell him that I said thank you."

"I will," Molly assured her. "Oh, and just tell Granny that one of my co-workers is giving me a ride. Otherwise she will make a big deal out of it and give Simon the third degree, if you know what I mean."

"I couldn't agree more, honey," Mildred said, fully appreciating her grandniece's concern. "So, how was your first day?"

"It was good," Molly said, trying to sound upbeat despite her devastating exhaustion. "I'll tell you all about it when I get home," she promised. "I should be there in about an hour."

"All right, dear. We'll have dinner ready when you get here."

"Thanks, Aunt Millie."

"Bye, dear."

While Molly had been talking, Simon collected a can of Sprite from the refrigerator and a box of crackers from a file cabinet drawer. After setting the snack items down in front of Molly, he replaced the receiver on the telephone and shoved it back across the desk. Then he silently walked back to his chair, turned up the volume on the radio and went back to work. Trying to focus on his task, he observed Molly in his peripheral vision, taking note when she popped the top on the soda can and started to munch on some crackers. He looked up at her and smiled warmly, and then quickly refocused on his work.

Molly looked absolutely drained and rather sickly, and Simon felt directly responsible for her poor condition. He decided then and there to give her the next day off so that she might recoup some of her energy, and when she came back to work the following day, he would make sure to outline a less physically demanding day for her and personally oversee her workload. He would just need to remember to act professionally around her and not treat her like a child, as he had done earlier that day. After working everything out in his head, he glanced up at Molly only to find her looking directly at him. He quickly lowered his eyes and pretended to focus on the work in front of him, again cursing the fates for making her situation so difficult. Despite what his mother had said earlier, he still believed Molly was totally off-limits; getting involved with a pregnant woman could only lead to disaster.

Chapter Six

Molly was more than grateful for Simon allowing her to take the following day off. At first, she had thought that he was firing her, but when he explained that he had noticed how tired she seemed, she was truly grateful for his understanding and concern. And even though he appeared to not want anything to do with her, Simon seemed to care about her well being, which completely confused Molly. On the ride to The Aunt Hill, he had been cordial, making small talk and focusing on his driving instead of his passenger. She had sensed his aloofness and understood it to mean that he did not want to get involved in the mess she had made of her life, and for this she could not blame him. Her life was a big train wreck and despite the casualties—her innocence, her education, her chance for a future with someone as wonderful as Simon Mulberry—it was her responsibility to get herself back on track and get the wheels moving forward again. If she could do this, she knew she could have some sort of happy future and perhaps one day be able to put all of this miserable business behind her.

The following day, after falling asleep at the dinner table the previous evening and with no workday ahead of her, Molly was able to get a full ten hours of much needed sleep, and she woke up feeling refreshed and ready to take on the world. Well, a corner of it anyway. Once again, she managed to keep down one of Aunt Millie's hearty breakfasts, after which she bundled up and went out into the garden to help her Aunt Gertrude cut back the rose bushes in preparation for winter. The day was bitter cold and the dark clouds hovering in the sky held the promise of snow. A biting wind sliced through Molly's quilted jacket as she snipped away at the hearty stalks of the rose bushes. As she worked, she could swear that she smelled snow in the air.

"Molly, dear," Aunt Gertie cried when a gust of wind tore her kerchief off of her head, "you must be freezing! Go inside and warm up a bit. I can handle this."

"I'm fine, Aunt Gertie," Molly called over the wind. "The sooner we can get this done, the sooner we can both go indoors." Smiling and waving to her great-aunt, Molly turned back to her task and swore under her breath as a sharp slap of wind hit the exposed flesh between her garden gloves and her jacket. Pulling her arms back to stuff her hands into her pockets for a moment, she glanced up at the house and caught sight of her grandmother watching her from inside the library window. Caught like a "Peeping Tom," Harriett jumped back out of view. Molly watched for a moment to see if she would reappear, but her grandmother did not look out the window again.

A few minutes later, Mildred came busting out the back door of the house and scurried across the garden toward Molly. She was dressed only in a pair of slacks and a turtleneck sweater and she immediately wrapped her arms around herself. "Molly, dear!" she called, unwrapping one arm to wave a piece of paper at her grandniece.

Molly stood. "Aunt Millie, get back inside!" she cried. "You'll freeze to death without a coat on out here."

"I'm fine, honey," Mildred said, dismissing her with a little flick of her hand, "but you shouldn't be out here. What if you catch cold?"

"We're almost done," Molly assured her.

"What's all this?" Gertrude asked, suddenly materializing at Molly's side.

Again, Mildred brandished the piece of paper she had been flapping at Molly. "I got an appointment for Molly with Helen Faraday this afternoon," Mildred said excitedly. "Molly, remember, she's the one we told you about who counsels women who have been victims of sexual crimes."

"That's wonderful," Gertrude cried, watching Molly for her reaction. "You're going to like her, Molly. She's very easy to talk with and I know she can help you come to terms with what has happened."

Molly was queasy at the thought of having to talk about her sordid tale again, especially to a complete stranger, but she knew that her aunts only had her best interests at heart and she could not bear to disappoint them by refusing to take the appointment. "What time is the appointment?" Molly asked. "When do I need to get ready?"

Mildred could see the reservation in Molly's eyes despite her attempt to conceal it from them. Wrapping Molly in a big warm bear hug, Mildred whispered near her ear, "The appointment is at one-thirty, and I'll come along with you if you like." In gratitude, Molly hugged her great-aunt tightly.

When an icy gust of wind sliced through Mildred's sweater and into her back, she quickly pulled away from Molly. "Ooh! I had better get back inside before I catch my death!" she cried, turning and heading for the house. The wind whipped her bobbed, silver hair around her head and in front of her multicolored spectacle frames. She held her hair back with her hands and called over her shoulder, "You gals finish up out here and come inside. I'll have some cocoa ready for you and then we'll have a nice lunch together."

Molly watched Mildred retreat into the house as Gertrude, after patting Molly on the shoulder, stepped away and went back to her task. Shivering violently as another gust of cold wind swirled its way up underneath her jacket, Molly blinked as several errant snow-flakes blew into her face and stung her skin. Winter was creeping into town, preparing to settle in for the next five months.

After a hot and hearty lunch punctuated by a discussion about Molly seeing Helen Faraday that afternoon, Mildred and Molly drove the short distance to Helen's office on Third Street. The office was housed in a century old brick building that abutted the neighboring stone edifice and was surrounded on two sides by a quaint white picket fence. It looked homey and inviting enough, but Molly was still very skeptical about discussing her situation with a stranger. Her body was actually trembling when she walked into the building. Inside the brick structure, they stepped immediately into a foyer with a very steep staircase rising up to a second story. Molly noted that the first floor of the building was occupied by a law firm, so she assumed that Helen's office was upstairs.

Taking Molly by the hand and giving it a gentle pat of reassurance, Mildred guided her up the stairs and down a narrow hallway. At the far end of the passageway stood a heavy oak door with a brass plaque that read, "The answers are within you." Molly stared at the plaque while Mildred rang the bell beside the door, above which there was a small sign that read, "Helen Faraday, Counselor."

A moment later, the door was opened by a woman of average height and build with friendly blue eyes and long, thick brown hair held back by a tortoise-shell barrette. She wore a black wool pant suit over an ivory blouse that was buttoned just one short of the top. The only jewelry adorning her body was a gold watch and a pair of small gold hoop earrings. After sizing her up, Molly concluded that there was absolutely nothing threatening about the woman and she felt some of her anxiety begin to dissipate.

"Hello, Millie," the woman said, wrapping Mildred in a warm embrace. "It's so good to see you."

"You, too, sweet girl," Mildred said before pulling away and taking Molly by the hand. "This is my grandniece, Molly O'Connor, Harriett's beautiful granddaughter."

The woman held out her hand and said, "Hello, Molly. I'm Helen Faraday. It's so nice to meet you."

Molly took the offered hand and shook it quickly. "It's nice to meet you, too."

Helen ushered them into her reception room and immediately offered to get Mildred a cup of coffee or tea. While the two older women discussed the particulars of Mildred's beverage, Molly glanced around the small room taking note of the comfortable surroundings. The walls were papered in a rich maroon and gold stripe and in one corner there were two upholstered wing-back chairs with matching ottomans situated on either side of an inlaid lamp table. Several popular magazines were fanned out on top of the table next to which sat a sturdy crystal candy dish filled with wrapped hard candy.

"Have a seat, Millie," Helen said, setting a steaming mug of tea and a plate of sugar cookies on the lamp table between the two chairs. "Get comfortable and just relax. Molly and I will either be back in five minutes or an hour, depending on how Molly feels." Helen smiled at Molly.

Mildred pulled Molly into her arms. "Just give Helen a chance. I really think she can help," she whispered before releasing her and stepping back.

Helen motioned for Molly to follow her. "Step into my office, Molly, and you and I can get better acquainted."

When she passed through the door, Molly stopped dead in her tracks at the sight she beheld. Helen's office was a cozy collection of furnishings gathered around a marble-fronted fireplace in which a fire blazed. There were two large, tufted red leather sofas piled with upholstered pillows sitting in front of the fireplace with a glass-topped, wooden coffee table between them. Beyond the leather sofas there was a small kitchenette and beyond that was a sliding glass door which opened out to a rooftop garden terrace.

Compared to her parents' home, Helen's office was one of the most inviting places Molly had ever been in. The house she grew up in was so sterile and expensively decorated that she had been afraid to touch anything for fear of disrupting the perfect order. This room invited her to flop on a sofa and put her feet up on the coffee table, or to grab a soda from the refrigerator and set herself down to bask in the sun on the terrace. The atmosphere in the room immediately tore down Molly's defenses and she easily removed her jacket and hung it on the coat stand that stood inside the door.

Helen strolled over to the kitchenette. "Would you like something to drink, Molly? Tea . . . soda . . . water?"

"Water would be fine, thank you," Molly replied, taking a seat on one of the sofas near the fireplace. Holding her hands up to the heat radiating from the hearth, she dared to look around the room at all of the artwork on the walls.

"Sparkling or still?" Helen asked placing two glasses on the counter.

"Oh," Molly said, surprised that she had a choice. "Um, sparkling would be nice."

"Sparkling it is," Helen said, holding up a bottle of Perrier for Molly's inspection before pouring it into the glasses. Helen placed the filled glasses and a bowl of pretzel twists on a tray and carried it over to the coffee table. She stoked the fire with two more logs and finally took a seat opposite Molly on the other sofa.

Handing Molly a glass, she smiled. "Now, let's get one thing straight. This is an initial meeting and you are under no obligations to me. If you feel like getting up and leaving at any time, please feel free to do so." Shifting to get more comfortable, Helen continued, "We both know why you're here. Millie, of course, gave me a brief overview of your situation, and above all else, I want you to feel comfortable talking to me. I'm here to listen and to help if I can, but you are the one who has to navigate through your problems and find the solutions that best suit you. And I assure you that you have the power within yourself to do just that."

Helen paused a moment to let her words sink in, then she kicked off her shoes and pulled her legs up onto the sofa. "Now, relax. Get comfortable and I'll share my story with you first. How does that sound?"

Placing the glass of Perrier on top of the coffee table, Molly silently weighed her options. Then she kicked off her shoes and stretched out on the sofa with a pillow plumped under her head. "That sounds good."

After Helen had finished recounting the nightmare of violence that characterized her personal experience with rape, Molly excused herself to go into the bathroom and be sick. When she reemerged, Helen was waiting with a cold compress and a cup of weak tea and a shoulder to lean on. Getting Molly comfortably situated on the sofa again with her feet up and the compress on her forehead, Helen sat down beside Molly and began their session in earnest.

"So, tell me how you feel about what I just told you," she said, lifting the cup of tea to Molly's lips.

After taking several deep breaths and a few sips of the tea, Molly said, "I feel like I have no business being here. My experience doesn't even come close to what you went through and I feel like I should get a backbone and stop whining about it." Molly rubbed at her eyes and cried, "How did you survive that? My God, how can you walk around and live your life without that haunting you every minute?"

Looking directly at Molly, Helen said, "Because I took the time to think it all through. It was one moment in my lifetime, and I decided that I could either curl up in a ball and hide from the rest of the world until I died or I could get beyond it and live all the other moments of my life. You see, I realized that I was only going to get one life, and I wanted to make something of it, to see and do so much. I certainly did not recover from the trauma overnight," she assured Molly, "but I found my way through it all and now I have the life that I wanted."

Lifting the cup of tea for Molly to drink, Helen paused a moment and then continued, "I have a wonderful husband who is a tender and generous lover and who has reassured me that sex is a wonderful expression of love between two people and not a vile act of hatred. Sure, I still have nightmares and I still get spooked, but he's there to calm me and bring my world back into perspective. I also earned a black belt in karate and I'll be damned if any man will ever hurt me like that again."

Rising and walking back to the other sofa, Helen added, "I'm one of the lucky ones. I lived through it and I found my husband, Richard. But more importantly, I don't blame myself for what happened to me and I don't regret my life."

Helen took a big gulp of water from her glass, then snatched a handful of pretzels and settled back on the sofa. "Now, would you like to tell me your story?"

Molly gazed back at Helen Faraday with admiration, thinking that she was such a strong woman who seemed so at peace. Drawing upon Helen's strength, she found the courage to relate her own story, and Helen listened intently without once interrupting. Several times Helen nodded as if she understood her feelings but otherwise she kept silent and let Molly hold the floor. And when Molly finally came to the end of her tale, she finished with, "so I'm going to have this baby and give it up for adoption because I believe it's the right thing to do."

Leaning forward in her seat, Helen said, "I admire you so much for that. Do you realize how much courage it takes to do what you're doing?"

Molly was shocked to hear such words because she did not

believe herself to be courageous in the least. She was the one everyone called "pampered and foolish," and, therefore, no one should admire her, least of all a woman like Helen Faraday. She was afraid of getting an abortion because of her parents' wrath, when in actuality—if she had been stronger—she probably could have taken care of the whole mess without anyone ever knowing. Molly had always relied upon her parents for everything. She had foolishly believed that they were going to take care of her problem and make things right. Continuing her thoughts out loud, Molly softly said, "I'm not brave at all."

"Well, I disagree," Helen said forcefully. "And I'm going to help you see just how strong you really are. But before we get started on that, I want to ask you a question. Do you think you are at all to blame for that boy drugging and raping you?"

"Yes," Molly said without hesitation. "I'm responsible for myself, and I naively accepted that drink without considering the consequences."

"Well," Helen said, considering her answer, "we have a lot to work on and I believe that I can help you change some of the negative opinions you hold of yourself, that is, if you want to come back and see me again."

"I'd like to, but I'm not sure that I can afford it."

"Don't worry about that," Helen said. "Your Aunt Millie wants to take care of the fees for you." Holding up a hand to silence Molly's expected protest, she added, "Let her do this for you, Molly. It's so important to her. She desperately wants to help you."

"I don't know what I would do without her right now."

"What a gift to be so loved and to know that you are deserving of it," Helen said with great meaning. Molly stared at Helen with a bewildered expression. Helen simply smiled. "Think about it."

Holding out a hand to Molly to help her off the sofa, she said, "Well, that's all our time for today." Molly looked at her watch and was shocked to see that sixty minutes had passed in no time at all. "If you would like, I can set aside an hour each week, more if you'd like, of course. You can let me know what works for you."

Before Molly could say anything, Helen opened the door to the waiting room. "Here she is, Millie—your precious girl."

Mildred jumped out of her seat. "How did it go?" she said, looking at Molly's face for some sort of indication. "Do you think you will come back?"

Molly glanced at Helen, who stood leaning against the door jamb with her arms crossed over her chest and her lips pressed tightly together, waiting for Molly's response. "It went really well, Aunt Millie. And yes, I would like to come back."

"Wonderful!" Mildred exclaimed. "So do we need to set up your next appointment?"

"When Molly gets her work schedule ironed out with Simon, she can give me a call and let me know when she's available," Helen stated. "Then we'll find some time to talk again."

"Thank you so much," Mildred said, reaching out a hand to Helen, who clasped it between both of hers.

"You're welcome." Helen patted Mildred's hand. "And, thank you, Molly, for having the courage to share your story with me."

"No, thank you," Molly said very seriously.

Back on the street, the two women found the Comet blanketed with a thin veil of snow. Molly used a gloved hand to brush off the windows while Mildred started the engine. When they were both belted into their seats, still shivering from the cold air, Mildred said, "What do you say we go over to Starbucks and have one of those fancy mocha coffees with whipped cream? My treat."

"I'd like that a lot," Molly said, smiling brightly, feeling warmed by a sense of belonging.

While Mildred and Molly had been away, Gertrude had been soaking her ice cold body in a hot tub with the hopes of not getting a chill from her outdoor exertions that morning. She didn't want a cold, or even worse, pneumonia. Harriett had been rather preoccupied and extremely quiet during lunch, which had translated into a peaceful afternoon at The Aunt Hill and had tugged on Gertrude's heart strings enough to make her want to bake something special for both Harriett and Molly. She pondered her options as she soaked in the tub and then got out when she had decided what to bake.

After dusting herself with talcum powder, Gertrude put on a

warm wool skirt and sweater set to try and retain the body temperature she had achieved in the hot bath. When she was all put together, she hurried downstairs to make some fresh bread rolls for dinner (Harriett's favorite) and a fresh apple pie to celebrate what she hoped was another good day for Molly. Tiptoeing down the back staircase in the hopes that Harriett was napping and that her treats would be a nice surprise, she alighted in the kitchen only to hear Harriett's angry voice trailing down the hallway from the library.

"Listen to me, you self-righteous little worm," she was yelling. "You and that snooty wife of yours had better stop hiding behind your priest and church and show a little compassion and forgiveness toward your daughter! All this nonsense about her breaking commandments is ludicrous." Harriett paused a moment to listen. "Don't you dare talk to me that way, George. I'm still your mother, despite your attempts to deny the fact, and I am disgusted by your hypocritical behavior. Who are you or Gillian, for that matter, to throw stones at anyone on such a subject, especially when Molly's situation is so different? This was not her choice. A heinous crime was committed against her and it disgusts me that you can't find the compassion for her that a father should have for his daughter."

She listened to his reply and erupted, "How could you ever think such a thing? Why on earth would she make up such a terrible lie? She's your daughter, for crying out loud," Harriett cried, "and she deserves your understanding and respect."

Harriett paused once again to listen to her son on the other end of the line and then shouted, "This is not about me or my relationship with my children, and don't you dare glorify your father. He was a drunk, a mean drunk, and he spoiled you children with money and left me to try and mold decent human beings out of you through discipline. Quite obviously, I failed miserably. Your behavior is more than proof of this fact."

Harriett never talked to her children except on the holidays when they placed their obligatory call, and here she was pounding George to dust over the telephone for disowning his daughter. Suddenly, Gertrude felt a strong urge to pick up the phone and give him a piece of her mind as well, but instead, she tiptoed across the kitchen and leaned up against the wall near the doorway, cocking her ear to listen.

In a quieter tone, Harriett said, "Don't think you're fooling anyone, George. People will eventually learn the truth and your precious social standing will be downgraded a notch or two, and it will not be the end of the world. I know you. And I know that Molly is your favorite, so how can you do this to her?"

There was silence as Harriett received the answer to her question, and then she burst out with, "Oh, please! Spare me the histrionics. Gillian should be popped into a mental institution this minute. Molly is not a material asset! She's an innocent girl with a good heart who is trying to make the best of an awful situation. Sure, she's a bit naïve and foolish, but that's your fault. You cloistered her and did not prepare her for what was awaiting her in the everyday world."

There was another pause on Harriett's end of the line, and then came more. "Well, I can see that aside from slamming your thick head against a wall to try and knock some sense into you, there's nothing more I can say. The facts are this: Molly is living with us, going to counseling, starting a new job, and having some son-of-a-bitch's baby that she will give up for adoption. If you get around to finding some forgiveness in that rock of a heart you possess, you will find her here with us. Otherwise, you and Gillian stay far away from her. I won't have you upsetting her further. And it's your duty to tell her brother where she's staying and that he's welcome to visit her any time. She needs Tim's support if he is willing to give it."

Harriett paused to take a breath. "I don't want to hear from you again, until you're ready to ask her forgiveness for your despicable behavior. This is not about you, George. She did not do this to you and Gillian, you selfish morons. This is about what was done to Molly; it's about her life and her future." In a softer tone, Harriett said, "If you could only see through the anger, you would be so proud of her for the way she is handling all of this."

Harriett switched tones again when she signed off, saying, "You're a fool, just like your father, and your wife is a barking lunatic. And that's all I have to say to you." Harriett slammed the receiver down and sat staring at the wall in front of her. She wanted to punch something or someone—preferably her son and daughter-in-law.

As soon as she heard Harriett hang up the phone, Gertrude

quickly tiptoed back across the kitchen and up the back staircase. There was no reason on earth to let Harriett know that she had been eavesdropping. Her plan was to come back down the main staircase, making lots of noise as she did so to alert Harriett to her presence, and then go about her business as if she had heard nothing. And when she stomped off the last stair in the front hall, she innocently called out, "Harriett, are you around? I was just going to make some tea. Would you like some?"

"No!" Harriett snapped, as she rose from her chair and slammed the library door.

Gertrude flinched as the door banged shut and then shrugged. She was too excited to tell Mildred what she had overheard to let Harriett's anger rattle her that afternoon. She just hoped that her elder sister could find a way to convey her feelings to Molly before it was too late.

Chapter Seven

Molly's next few days at the nursery went much more smoothly than the first, and Simon was pleased with the progress she had made. She quickly learned to navigate her way through the maze of greenhouses and learned which greenhouse housed which plants. After transplanting hundreds of seedlings, she developed a gentle and efficient technique of transferring the delicate little plants into flats, and she gained more knowledge than she ever imagined about mums and poinsettias. She had even taken a turn at the cash register in the store, which proved to be a bit nerve wracking and which Simon immediately recognized and remedied.

Much to Molly's delight, Simon had taken charge of overseeing her work and checking on her at various intervals during the day. And for their part, Lillian and Henry took their turns working with Molly, helping her acclimate to her new job, and they both treated her with respect and care which quickly endeared them to her. Often, at the end of the day, Molly wished she could crawl into Henry's pocket and go home with Simon's parents. She imagined that they were the perfect example of how parents were supposed to act toward their children, and she envied the way they loved Simon.

As for the rest of the employees at the nursery, Molly was slowly getting to know them in her own way. Tracy Benedict proved to be more than Molly could handle, as the girl made it her mission to make Molly feel uncomfortable and unwelcome at Mulberry's, so she avoided her as much as possible. But the elderly women who worked the cash registers in the store easily befriended Molly and did their best to make her feel at ease, as did Jacob, who had taken quite a shine to Molly during her first few days on the job.

Simon and Molly had worked out a schedule that would give her Sundays and Wednesdays free, which gave Molly a weekday on which to schedule her counseling sessions with Helen Faraday and her regular medical checkups with the obstetrician. Sundays were reserved for church and family dinner. Mildred had found Molly a female doctor who was highly recommended by all the young mothers at church. And after her first appointment with Dr. Rachel Johnson, Molly was quite pleased with her great-aunt's choice.

The first week of Molly's employment, either Gertrude or Mildred drove her to work in the morning, and then Molly would wait around for Simon at the end of the day to drive her home. After several days of this arrangement and recognizing that it was ridiculous for the aunts to drive Molly all that way every morning when he lived so close by, Simon offered to pick Molly up for work if she could be ready by seven o'clock. If it meant going to bed at seven o'clock at night so that she would be rested enough to get up in time for Simon to drive her to work, Molly was more than willing to make the adjustment.

With the help of Mildred's food regimen, Molly was beginning to get over her morning sickness which was a blessing. She could not afford to be getting sick and having everyone wonder why, and she was beyond grateful to her Aunt Mildred for forcing her to eat the heaps of carbohydrates that were not only settling her stomach but also giving her the energy she needed to do her job. She was still five pounds under her normal weight, but the doctor assured her that it was perfectly normal and that she would soon start gaining weight as the baby grew which, in turn, would increase her appetite.

At The Aunt Hill, the four women settled into an unconventional shape of a family that seemed to please them all. Even Harriett appeared to be quite comfortable with their arrangement. Her attitude toward her granddaughter had clearly changed and she was a tad bit softer on the girl. When Gertrude had told Mildred about Harriett's conversation with her son, Mildred had not been as excited as Gertrude had hoped because she was not in the least surprised by her elder sister's behavior. If nothing else, Mildred knew that Harriett could always see the wrong and the right in a situation. Whether or not she would admit to it was an entirely different story.

As the days passed, Harriett became more protective of Molly and was having a difficult time disguising this interest as merely her disapproval of the girl's behavior. She made regular wise cracks about Molly seeing a counselor and made it very clear that she had issues with Simon escorting her granddaughter back and forth from work. And even though it was completely unnecessary, she badgered Molly about helping out around the house, doing her share of the cleaning, laundry, cooking, etc. And much to everyone's surprise and delight, under Mildred and Gertrude's tutelage, Molly was becoming an amazing cook and baker. She used the same ingredients as the older women but somehow Molly's food came out tasting so much better. After growing up in a world where she was neither asked nor expected to be able to do anything, Molly was gaining confidence in her own abilities and taking pride in her accomplishments. Her co-workers were benefiting greatly from her newfound talents, as she brought her baking experiments to work on a regular basis. It soon became a forgone conclusion at the nursery that no one made better cookies than Molly O'Connor.

All this newfound confidence was helping Molly make great strides with Helen Faraday who was pleasantly surprised by her rapid progress. Molly enjoyed her sessions with Helen and looked forward to them each week with an anxious excitement. She was always nervous about admitting to feelings that she had believed to be wrong or judgmental about others, including her parents, but Helen helped her to see that such feelings were very normal and often justified. Even when Helen made her drop back into the dark recesses of her life, Molly knew that she would be safe with her aunts, her grandmother, Helen, and Simon in her life. She was not certain how long Simon would be there, but she hoped and prayed that it would be forever. In a very short period of time, Molly had come to trust and love him like no one else in her life. For now, they were friends, but she held out hope for something more. At best, her hope was a long shot. Right now, Simon treated her like a little sister, but one of the many important things she had learned from Helen Faraday was to never give up hope.

One dark and snowy evening a week before Thanksgiving, when Simon was driving Molly home from work, she felt a rush of emotion for him that she did not completely understand. She suddenly found herself saying, "Simon, I want to tell you how I got pregnant."

Cautiously, he said, "I would like to know, Moll, but you don't have to tell me."

"For some reason, I want you to know," Molly said firmly. "It's important to me."

"All right," Simon agreed, "let me pull over." Simon steered the truck over to the curb and slipped it into park. Turning in his seat, he looked nervously at Molly. "I'm listening."

For a moment, Molly stared into his eyes. Then she averted her gaze to the windshield, focusing on the wiper blades as they scraped the falling snow from the glass. She softly said, "I didn't get pregnant because I had sex with a boyfriend. I was drugged and raped at a fraternity party at the University my very first week of school." Molly glanced at Simon to see his reaction and for reasons unknown to herself, she whispered, "I was a virgin, Simon."

Simon's heart felt as if it were being squeezed by an iron fist, as if it might pop right out of his chest. "No, Molly. No," he said softly. If he had thought his dreams were shattered before when he found out she was pregnant, now they were completely obliterated. He had no idea what to say to her. He could say he was sorry, but the word was not enough; it could hardly begin to convey what he felt. Lowering his forehead to the steering wheel, he closed his eyes and wished with all his might that he and Molly shared a much different reality.

Molly had never dreamed that his reaction would be so dramatic. Either he truly cared about her or he was completely sickened by what she had just told him. Whatever his feelings, she knew for certain that there was no way Simon would ever want her now. She had been a fool to tell him. At that moment all she wanted to do was vanish. Then Simon could look up from the steering wheel and be relieved that she was no longer sitting beside him.

"I'm going to take you to my house for dinner, Moll," Simon said suddenly, and he surprised her by reaching for her hand. "I want you to tell me everything." He had told himself that he would never ask her out on a date or dare to bring her into his private world, but at that moment he simply could not help himself.

"I'm not sure I want to tell you any more," she said truthfully.

"Why not? You trusted me enough to tell me this much." Simon gently squeezed her hand. "I won't betray you to the world, I promise."

Molly gazed deeply into his eyes and thought for a moment. "All right."

Simon was surprised by her answer. Then he remembered something and said, "But I have to tell you that my mother knows you're pregnant. She wondered why I pulled you out of that truck your first day."

"That's all right. Pretty soon everyone will be able to see that I'm pregnant. I won't be able to hide it forever," Molly said sadly. "Anyway, I know that you're really close to your parents and you probably share everything with them."

"Not everything." Simon smiled at her, and then his expression became more somber. "If you don't want me to tell my parents anything more, I won't."

Molly shrugged. "You decide. I just don't want the whole town knowing what happened."

"Don't worry about that." Simon looked down at her hand and noticed how fragile it looked in comparison to his. Once again, he felt compelled to protect her. "Do you still want to go to my house?"

"Yes," Molly said without hesitation.

"Then let's go."

With Simon still clutching her hand, they drove the remaining miles to his house. They entered the bungalow through the back door and stepped into the dimly lit kitchen. Immediately, Molly unzipped her jacket to let the warm air get close to her body.

Simon helped her with her coat and then switched on the overhead light.

Molly glanced around the cheerfully bright room, with its yellow
walls and white cabinets, and smiled. She kicked her boots off and
placed them on the mat just inside the door, wondering if Simon actually used the kitchen for anything other than a storage room for
refreshments and snacks; it was as neat as a pin. The vase of fresh
cut flowers in the middle of the small round kitchen table did not
surprise her in the least. She had noticed that he brought a bunch
of cut flowers home from the store at least twice a week. Up to that
moment she had assumed he was bringing them to a girlfriend, and
now she was relieved to know that her assumption was false.

"It's usually not this clean," Simon confessed as he turned on the
chandelier in the dining room. "The cleaning lady came today."

"I see," Molly said as she followed him into the living room.

The living room felt very masculine, a reflection of the man
who had put it together. The walls of the room were beige and
they were framed with a dark-stained oak trim that continued into
the adjoining, small dining room where the woodwork displayed
itself grandly in the form of an ornate, built-in buffet. Antique
mission-style furniture and two Persian rugs blanketed the honey-
colored wood floors.

While Molly looked around and got a feel for Simon's lifestyle,
Simon quickly started a fire in the hearth in the living room and
pulled a chair close for Molly to sit in. "Have a seat, Moll," Simon
said, pulling an ottoman in front of the chair, "and I'll get dinner
started."

"Do you mind if I use the bathroom first," Molly asked awkwardly.

"Not at all," he assured her as he took her by the hand. "Come
with me."

Completely thrown off balance by Simon's touch and with her
heart pounding a deafening drumbeat in her ears, Molly followed
Simon blindly down a corridor toward the back of the house. "Here
you go." He pushed open a door and flipped on a light switch.

"Thanks." She stepped past him into the small room tiled in
white and black porcelain. Safely inside, with the door closed and

locked, Molly took a moment to regain her equilibrium. She whispered to herself, "You've got to get a grip. He just wants to be your friend."

She took note of the gleaming white porcelain toilet and pedestal sink, the shiny chrome fixtures and towel racks, the gray and white plush terry cloth towels, and the gray and white striped shower curtain hanging around the tub. Again she thought about how the room reflected Simon's personality; everything was bright, neat, and coordinated, just like Simon.

While Molly was hiding out in the bathroom, Simon was frantically raiding the cupboards and refrigerator for ingredients for their supper. When he was pleased with his menu plan, he opened a bottle of red Italian wine, poured himself a glass, and got down to business. By the time Molly came out of the bathroom and had made her way back through the hallway, Simon had a pot of water working up to a boil on the stove and Italian sausage browning in a skillet. He pulled a Tupperware container out of the refrigerator, caught sight of Molly in the doorway, and smiled. "My homemade vodka sauce," he said, holding the plastic container up for her inspection. "I hope you like it."

"I'm sure I will," Molly said, impressed with his culinary skills. "What can I do to help?"

"Not a thing." He picked up a glass of wine and walked toward her. "Here," he said, holding it out to her. "I know you're not supposed to, but I don't think one glass will do any harm, and it might make you more relaxed when you tell me your story."

Molly stared at the glass of alcohol and had a quick flashback to the fraternity party.

"Moll, what is it?" Simon asked, worried.

Molly looked into his eyes and realized that there was no reason to be afraid. She trusted Simon. She truly liked him. But she was determined not to make any more stupid mistakes in her life.

"I just don't think it's a good idea," she said, refusing the glass of wine.

"That's all right," Simon said lightly. "What else can I get you? Some sparkling water?"

"That would be nice, thank you."

"Coming right up." He raced to the refrigerator and returned seconds later with a bubbling glass of water. Taking Molly by the arm, Simon escorted her back into the living room and had her take the seat by the hearth. He stirred the fire, handed her a throw rug, and then hurried back to the kitchen.

"Dinner won't be long," he called over his shoulder. "Just relax for a moment."

Molly did just that. She propped her feet up on the ottoman and took a sip of the cold water and relaxed back into the chair. She was completely comfortable sitting in Simon's living room in front of a blazing fire while he raced around the kitchen preparing their meal. Somewhere in the midst of all his clattering around in the kitchen, he found time to put a compact disc into his player and the sounds of light jazz suddenly filled the house.

As she sat staring into the fire, taking small sips of her beverage, Molly began to fantasize about being married to Simon and imagined coming home from the nursery together at the end of a long day and winding down in this manner, with Simon preparing dinner and her relaxing by the fire with her feet up. She did not waste time envisioning their meal. She just knew they would have a long wonderful discussion while they ate and that there would be laughter and hand holding. And then Molly's romantic sensibilities really kicked in and she started dreaming about their after-dinner activities that she was certain would include Simon carrying her off to the bedroom to make love to her. As she fantasized about what this would be like, Simon popped his head around the corner from the kitchen and said, "Dinner's ready!"

Lost in her erotic fantasy, Molly did not hear him and simply stared blindly into the flames. Simon wondered if Molly was having second thoughts about telling him what had happened. He quietly approached her and softly placed a hand upon her shoulder.

Startled, Molly jumped in her seat and stared up at him with alarm. "Oh, Simon," she gasped, her cheeks flushing in embarrassment.

"Sorry. I didn't mean to startle you," Simon said, looking down at her apologetically. "Dinner's almost on the table, and I thought you might want to call The Aunt Hill first and let them know where you are."

"Oh, good idea."

Simon took the glass from her hand and replaced it with a cordless phone. "Come to the table when you're finished."

Molly smiled at him and then quickly dialed the number. Unfortunately, her grandmother answered. "Hello, Granny. It's Molly."

"I know that," Harriett snapped. "Where are you? You should be home for supper by now."

"Um . . . Simon invited me to dinner at his house," she stammered. "He'll bring me home right after we've eaten," Molly added for good measure.

"Well, that had better be all you're doing over there, young la–"

"Molly? It's Aunt Millie, sweetheart," a gentle and loving voice said over the phone. "Whew, just got the phone away from your granny. You relax and have a lovely evening with Simon," Mildred instructed. "I'll wait up for you, dear."

"Thanks, Aunt Millie," Molly said in complete gratitude. "I won't be late."

"Say hello to Simon for us and enjoy yourself," Mildred said happily. "Love you!"

"Bye." Molly smiled when she hung up the phone, and then she thought about what her grandmother might be saying at that very moment and the depressing thought wiped the smile away. She padded in her stocking feet into the dining room where Simon had set the table with placemats and a collection of various-sized candles. How wonderfully romantic, Molly thought, and her face once again broke into a smile.

Back at The Aunt Hill a storm was brewing in the kitchen. Mildred was setting the table for their dinner and Gertrude was serving things up at the stove, while Harriett was pacing and ranting.

"She has already gotten herself into enough trouble and now she's going to add to it by sleeping with a black boy!" Harriett screamed.

"Simon is not black!" Gertrude interjected. "He's mulatto."

"Whatever the hell he is," Harriett yelled, "she's over there right now, doing God knows what with him and she's going to undo all that she has accomplished!"

Mildred said, "Molly is a very smart girl, Hattie, and she is not going to do anything stupid. Neither, for that matter, is Simon. They are simply friends, and maybe Molly just needs to talk with someone closer to her own age. For God's sake, she lives with three old women. Who can blame her for wanting to be around younger people?"

"Simon is eight years older than Molly!" Harriett cried.

"What difference does that make?" Mildred screamed. "He's certainly closer to Molly's age than we are."

"Harriett," Gertrude said calmly, "Molly needs friends, friends who will be there for her when her troubles can no longer be hidden. Maybe she just wants to talk to Simon about what happened to her in order to get his perspective."

"Oh, what do you know? Maybe he thinks that she's an easy conquest because she's already pregnant and willing to go to bed with a man," Harriett growled.

"Hattie!" Mildred yelled. "How dare you talk about your granddaughter that way! Molly is not a loose girl and Simon would never think about her in that fashion. They're just friends, Hattie, and even though I pray that it develops into something more, I know that Simon has no physical interest in Molly at this point. She says that he has made that abundantly clear to her."

"Well then, why does he drive her to and from work everyday?" Harriett snapped. "Why is he always sniffing around her at the nursery when I go to check on her?"

"Because he likes her, Hattie!" Mildred cried. "It's not a crime to have warm feelings toward another human being of the opposite sex, and it does not mean that the feelings are merely sexual. Men and women do have platonic relationships and they are perfectly acceptable."

"I'm telling you that he has more than friendship on his mind," Harriett warned.

"So what if he does, Hattie?" Gertrude said quietly. "Why would Simon falling in love with Molly be such a bad thing?"

"Because she needs to get rid of that baby and get on with

her life," Harriett said in exasperation. "She needs to go back to school. It is essential that she goes back to school so that she has options for her future."

"She is going back to school," Gertrude said, becoming quite agitated.

"Do you think for one minute that Simon would ever stand in her way?" Mildred said, shaking her head in disbelief. "You have no idea about these two people, Hattie; you don't know them at all."

"I know Molly," Harriett said defensively.

"No, you don't, Hattie," Mildred said sadly. "Not if you really believe any of the things you've just said about her."

"Oh, shut up," Harriett snarled as she brushed by Mildred and stormed out of the kitchen. Slamming the library door behind her, she hurried to the big oak desk and opened the top drawer. Frantically rummaging through a pile of papers in the right-hand corner, she found the scrap that she had hidden there that morning. She took a seat in the desk chair, reached for the telephone, and dialed the number written on the paper. A message recorder at the Albrecht Detective Agency of Minneapolis answered her call. Harriett cursed under her breath and hung up the receiver without leaving any information.

Chapter Eight

Molly and Simon sat down in the candlelit dining room of his bungalow and immediately dug into the food. Molly devoured the penne pasta, Italian sausage and homemade vodka sauce, lightly sprinkled with freshly grated parmesan cheese. The dish was so tasty that she could not stop herself from eating every morsel. Simon had also prepared warm garlic bread and spinach in a butter sauce. A plate of frosted brownies sat in the middle of the table, tempting them into saving room for dessert. Molly told Simon how fabulous everything was and how impressed she was with his cooking.

Secretly delighted that she enjoyed the meal he had prepared, Simon merely brushed her compliments aside by crediting his mother for teaching him a thing or two in the kitchen when he was a teenager. Then he turned the discussion around to Molly's baking talents and her accomplishments at work.

When the meal was finished, Molly cleared the dishes from the table and helped Simon load them into the dishwasher. Then Simon heated the tea kettle on the stove and started the coffee maker. He amazed Molly at every turn because it seemed that he could do just about anything without becoming in the least flustered, and with each passing minute she became more infatuated with him.

With the kitchen spic and span, and a cup of herbal tea and a mug of coffee resting on a small tray, Simon led Molly back to the living room and the fireplace. Then he dashed back to the dining room and returned with the plate of brownies and one of the lit candles which he placed upon the mantel. After tossing another log on the fire, Simon handed Molly the cup of tea and then sat down opposite her. "All right, Moll, tell me what happened to you."

Saying a silent prayer that Simon would never turn away from her, Molly stared at him for some time. Simon returned her unwavering gaze in silence, and then softly said, "Go ahead. I can handle it."

Remembering some of the things that Helen had told her, Molly took a deep breath and then quietly began her tale. Simon listened with rapt attention, his eyes never leaving Molly's face. Several times she noted his hands gripping his mug as if he might crush it and she wondered what he was thinking. She also noticed that he clenched his jaw at one point. And several times Simon closed his eyes for a brief moment as if he were in pain.

It made Simon's stomach turn to imagine what had been done to her. Violence bubbled up inside of him, requiring all his will power to keep it restrained. He wanted to kill the bastard who had raped Molly, and the wheels were turning in his mind, devising ways to find the little frat boy and get him carted off to jail. Then his anger turned to sympathy and he wanted to touch Molly. He wanted to hold her in his arms, rock her back and forth, and make the nightmare vanish, as if none of it had ever happened.

"I don't know why I wanted to tell you all of this," Molly said softly, drawing Simon out of his tortured thoughts. "I can see that you are absolutely disgusted with me."

Simon leaned forward and rested his hands upon Molly's knees. "I'm not disgusted with you," he assured her, "I just want to bash that creep's brains in for what he did to you." Simon looked down at the floor for a moment and then back at her. "I'm sorry this happened to you, Moll."

Gently placing her hand on top of his, Molly whispered, "Thank you for not thinking less of me."

"Why would I think less of you? It's not your fault."

"I was stupid enough to take the drink without questioning where it came from," Molly explained.

"No, Molly, nothing about this was your fault," Simon said firmly.

"You were just being a college freshman which is what you were expected to be. How were you to know what that son-of-a-bitch had premeditated?"

Molly was unable to control her feelings in the face of Simon's sympathy and kindness, and tears filled her eyes and poured down her cheeks. Simon pulled her into his arms. And knowing that it was as intimate as he was ever going to be with her, he held her close, prolonging the moment when he would have to let go. As he pulled her even closer to his body, Simon suddenly realized why she had refused the wine he offered her and it made him feel sick.

"I'm going to get you a tissue," he said, abruptly letting her go.

Simon returned a moment later and handed Molly a box of Kleenex. She blew her nose and wiped her eyes, and he grabbed the used tissues and tossed them into the fire one by one. As he watched them be consumed by the flames, he asked, "Why don't you get an abortion, Moll?"

"Because I'm Catholic and I'm afraid I will burn in Hell if I do such a thing. Plus, my family would hate me even more than they already do."

"Bullshit!" Simon said forcefully. "I'm not a Catholic and I'm certainly not God, but I don't think anyone could condemn you for it. You have to do what's best for you so you can get over this."

"You sound like my counselor," Molly said, pulling another tissue from the box and blowing her nose. "Anyway, I think it's too late, and I've already made my choice."

"It's not fair that you have to put your life on hold for nine months to carry some criminal's child while he walks around free as a bird, possibly doing the same thing to some other girl," he said furiously. "I want to find this creep, Molly, and I want him to suffer for what he's done to you."

"No!" Molly said, grabbing Simon's arm. "I don't ever want to know who he is."

"Why not?" Simon asked in disbelief.

"Because this way I can almost believe that it never really happened. There's no face and I have no connection to him. Do you understand?" Molly released her hold on Simon's arm. "Besides, my life's not on hold. I've got a job, new friends, and I'm developing a wonderful relationship with my aunts. This is all positive for me. I'm finding out who I am and just how strong I am. Although it all began with something evil, I think it will end with something good."

Simon stared at her for a long time. Then he reached up to cup her cheek with his hand and whispered, "You amaze me."

Closing her eyes to savor Simon's words, Molly dared to rest her cheek in his hand. For a brief moment, the world was bliss. Simon pulled his hand away and her eyes shot open in response. Then she said, "I can give this baby to two loving parents that want it and pray the baby will be as fortunate as you."

Simon ran a hand through his curly hair. "How true, Moll," he said, smiling. "How true." He stood and held out a hand to her. "Come on. I'd better get you home before your grandmother sends the police over here to retrieve you."

She laughed as she smoothed down the front of her denim overalls. "You know my grandmother pretty well."

"Yup, I do," Simon replied. "She's a stubborn, cranky old lady."

"You're right," Molly agreed as she bent down to pick the throw rug up off the floor.

"Leave it," Simon said, taking her by the arm.

In the kitchen, Simon helped her with her coat, making Molly feel like a child as he zipped her jacket up and wrapped his scarf around her neck. "You should wear a hat and scarf to work. It's really starting to get cold and you don't want to get sick."

"Yes, Dad," Molly said in a childish voice.

"Watch it," Simon warned playfully as he pulled his leather jacket on.

Molly placed a hand upon his chest. "I know you didn't mean to, but please don't treat me like a child, Simon. That's all my parents have ever done and I'm trying to leave all that behind me."

Thrown off balance by her remark, Simon stared at her in silence.

Molly turned away from him and he gently grabbed her arm. "I'm sorry. I didn't mean . . ."

"I know. I shouldn't have said that." Molly could not look at him. "You were just joking and I was being overly sensitive."

"No, I was serious about the hat and scarf because I'm genuinely concerned for your health," Simon corrected. "But I can see how you took it a different way." He turned Molly around to face him. "I apologize and I won't do it again."

"Thank you." Molly smiled at him. All was forgiven.

He smiled back at her. Then he zipped up his coat and pulled his gloves on. "We'd better go."

While Molly pulled her boots on, Simon grabbed his keys and mobile phone from the counter, turned off the overhead light, and slipped his feet into a pair of Sorel boots without bothering to tie up the laces. Then he held open the door for Molly, who was immediately taken aback by a blast of cold air that slapped her face as she stepped outside.

"Ooh," she cried, covering her face with her hands.

"What'd I tell you?" Simon said, wrapping an arm around her to shield her from the wind as he locked the kitchen door. Taking Molly by the hand, he said, "Let's run for it." And they dashed across his driveway to the garage.

As they were pulling onto Pine Street, Harriett was backing the Comet out onto Chestnut Street. Molly had been gone too long for her liking and she was becoming increasingly suspicious. She had snuck out of the The Aunt Hill after pretending to retire to her bedroom. Mildred and Gertrude were thoroughly engrossed in a television program in the library so she easily slipped out the front door. Feeling quite clever, Harriett did not turn the car lights on until she was several houses away. With a scowl on her face and a big, furry hat on her head, she drove to Simon's bungalow along her own secret back roads route. She was determined to not give herself away before she had a chance to catch her granddaughter doing whatever it was she was doing.

Turning off her lights half a block away, Harriett rolled the Comet up to a stop in front of Simon's neighbor's house and quickly killed the engine. Then she crawled out of the car, being careful not to slam the door, and crept toward the bungalow with her shoulders hunched. She saw a light burning in the living room and hurried up the porch steps to peek through the windows. She was fortunate that Simon had forgotten to turn on the overhead porch light that evening.

There were red coals in the fireplace and a candle burning on the mantle but Molly and Simon were nowhere to be seen. Cupping her hands around her eyeglasses, Harriett pressed her face up against the window pane and tried to see beyond the living room deeper into the house. A moment later, she heard a growl and turned to find a little white poodle standing on the porch, baring its teeth at her.

"Oh go away," she snarled at the dog. "Get out of here! Shoo!"

The poodle started yapping maniacally and then lunged for Harriett's ankles. She was glad that she had worn her boots. Frantically looking around for something to hit the dog with, Harriett cursed Simon for not leaving her some sort of weapon. The porch was empty, except for the porch swing and the mat in front of the door, and she did not think the piece of rubber-backed carpet would do much of anything to the feisty animal.

"Fifi!" a voice called from the side of the house. "Fifi, come!"

Harriett had no place to hide so she quickly thought up an explanation for her presence on Simon's porch. She kicked at the dog and called out, "Who's there?"

"Who's that?" A form materialized below the end of the porch.

Harriett squinted to make out the face looking back at her through the rungs of the porch railing, but could not see a thing in the dark.

"Harriett? Is that you?"

"Yes," Harriett said in exasperation, trying to shake the dog loose from her ankle. "Who's that?"

"It's me, Betty Sullivan, from church. Fifi, stop that. Let go of Harriett." The elderly woman hurried around to the front of the house and climbed the stairs. "Fifi, no!" she yelled, yanking the dog away from Harriett's boot and collecting it in her arms. The dog immediately quieted. "I'm so sorry, Harriett. Fifi must have thought you were a prowler."

"Well, I was just trying to find Simon," Harriett stammered. "We've got a clogged drain in the kitchen and were hoping he could help." Quickly changing the subject, she added, "I didn't know you lived next door to him."

"Yes, we have been good neighbors for years," Betty said proudly. "Simon is such a nice young man. He takes care of the yard and the sidewalk for me and I bake him bread in return."

"How nice," Harriett said snidely. "Well, if you'll excuse me . . ."

"Oh, Simon's not home," Betty informed her. "I saw him drive away about ten minutes ago with a young woman. I didn't get a good look at her because she was all bundled up in a scarf, but they were holding hands and they looked very cozy together."

Betty's casual observation did not help Harriett's mood and she stomped right by the woman and off the porch. "I'd better get home. It's late."

"Good luck with your drain! See you at church," Betty called, waving the poodle's paw at Harriett's back.

When Harriett arrived home, the house was dark and quiet. No one had noticed that she had been missing which made her feel both smug and sad at the same time. Climbing the stairs to go to bed, she noticed light spilling out into the hallway from beneath Molly's door. She stood quietly and listened to voices murmuring. Molly was telling Mildred about her evening with Simon, and although she was dying to know what had happened, Harriett would not knock and ask to join them. She moved down the hall to her bedroom and shut the door behind her.

Chapter Nine

After dropping Molly at The Aunt Hill and seeing her safely to the door, Simon hurried back to his truck and dialed his parents' number on his mobile phone. He needed to talk to them and hoped that they were still up and willing to listen. They were. It took Simon twenty minutes to drive the distance from The Aunt Hill to his parents' house in Marine on St. Croix, nestled on the banks of the river north of Stillwater, which gave him more time to think about what Molly had told him. He realized that he did not want to think about it and that he wished none of it were true. The images flashing through his brain tormented him, and he tried to distract himself by scanning the radio stations on the car stereo. When he finally pulled into his parent's driveway, the light above their door went on and his father stepped out into the cold to greet him.

"Hey, kid," his father called. "Welcome home." His father wrapped him in a bear hug and pulled him indoors. Henry Mulberry performed this little ritual every time Simon came back to their house, and despite the predictability of it all, Simon found great comfort in it.

Inside, Lillian was waiting with open arms and three mugs of cocoa with marshmallows. After planting a kiss on her cheek, Simon pulled off his gloves and shrugged himself out of his jacket. "Gosh, it's cold out there tonight!" he exclaimed.

"Yes it is," his mother agreed. "Now, no more small talk. What's got you so worked up that you are driving all the way out here in this weather to talk with us?" Lillian took a seat at the pine farmhouse table and indicated that her husband and son should join her.

"Well," Simon said, sitting down opposite her while his father took the seat at the head of the table, "I learned something incredibly disturbing tonight and I just needed to talk it out. Otherwise, it's going to eat away at me, and, Mom, you always said that it's better to address worries right away or they will gnaw at you and drive you crazy."

Nodding her head, Lillian said, "Yes, I do believe that. So, what's worrying you?" Lillian was actually worried herself about what might be tormenting her son. She folded her hands together tightly.

"Molly," was all Simon said.

"What about Molly?" Henry asked nervously. "Has something happened to her?"

"No. She's fine, Dad," Simon assured him, "except for the fact that she's pregnant."

"Pregnant?" Henry was completely taken aback.

"Yes, pregnant," Simon said miserably. "I found out tonight how she got pregnant and it's tearing me up inside."

Lillian's sharp instincts told her that they were not going to like what they heard but obviously their son needed to tell them. Reaching for Simon's hand across the table, Lillian gripped it tightly and said, "What happened to Molly, Simon?"

Looking back and forth between his parents, pausing a moment to consider whether or not he was doing the right thing by telling them, Simon said, "You have to promise you won't tell a soul."

Without skipping a beat, Henry and Lillian said in unison, "We promise."

"And don't let on to Molly unless she brings it up to you."

"You have our word, son," Henry assured him.

Formalities out of the way, Simon took a deep breath and began to relay Molly's story. Lillian slowly lost her composure and Henry pulled a handkerchief from his pocket and handed it to his wife. They both listened quietly as Simon continued, and Lillian cried while Henry patted her hand in sympathy, his jaw clenched in anger.

When Simon finished the story, Lillian let herself go, and removing her glasses to soak up the tears on her face with Henry's handkerchief, she wailed, "How could anyone do such a thing to that dear girl? How could any man do such a thing?"

"Calm down, Lil," Henry urged, as he rubbed her shoulder with his hand. "We're not talking about a man, here, but some little bastard who actually thought it would be fun to rape a woman. What the hell is wrong with kids, today?"

"Poor, Molly," Lillian whispered. "That sweet, innocent girl . . . and to make the choice to go through with the pregnancy, what an admirable decision on her part."

"Exactly!" Simon nearly shouted. "She's sweet, she's admirable, she's beautiful, and she has all this baggage that I am afraid to deal with."

Henry looked curiously at his son. "Are you in love with her?" Now he was getting the picture and a better understanding of why Simon was so upset.

"I don't know," Simon said angrily. "All I know is that from the first moment I laid eyes on her, I had this feeling we were supposed to be together, and I've been on a roller coaster of confusion and doubt. And tonight, I got sent screaming down an enormous hill and I just want to get off the ride."

Lillian sat up tall in her chair and looked her son squarely in the eye. "Why?" she demanded. "What are you afraid of? If you really like Molly and think she may be 'the one' as you said, then why should what happened to her have anything to do with the two of you cultivating a relationship? Please don't tell me that you are afraid of what people might say."

"No, Mom," Simon said angrily. "I could care less what other people think. But what if Molly can't get over this and it completely destroys her chance at a healthy relationship? What if she's afraid of a man's touch for the rest of her life?" Simon demanded, looking to his mother for answers.

"My dear Simon," Lillian cried reaching across the table to take his face between her hands, "You know better than to let 'what ifs' dictate your life. Tell us what you feel. Tell us what you want!"

"I just want things to be different," he whispered. "I want Molly's life to be different."

"That's a lovely idea." Lillian released his face. "But you can't change the past. So start thinking about what you can do. How do you think you can make a difference in her life?"

"I would venture a guess that you already have," Henry said wisely. "She seems to trust you."

"Yeah, but tonight I nearly blew it by treating her like a child." Simon dropped his face into his hands and rubbed at his eye sockets. "I feel this incredible need to protect her. I have from the beginning."

"Then maybe you're more in tune with her than you think," Lillian suggested. "Perhaps you've had a sense from the beginning that she'd been hurt and that is the basis of your feelings for her."

"I don't know," Simon said in exasperation. "All I know is that I love the way she laughs and the way she sings and talks to the plants when she's watering them. I love the way she tilts her head when she's talking to me and the way her eyes look directly into mine . . ."

Lillian leaned back in her chair. The confession had been more than she had bargained for and she was reeling from his words. She always prayed that he would one day find the woman of his dreams but now that he perhaps had, she felt a pain deep inside.

Staring down at the untouched mug of cocoa in front of him, Simon softly said, "I want her, Mom, more than I've ever wanted any woman in my life, and I'm afraid she won't want me because of what happened to her. And it really pisses me off that some ass-hole did this to her and ruined the experience for her."

"I see," Henry said. Pausing for a moment to consider Simon's admissions as well as his own thoughts, Henry suddenly asked, "Has she ever recoiled from your touch?"

Simon thought for a moment about his father's question. The memory of touching Molly that evening as she rested her cheek in his hand gave him his answer. "No," Simon said frankly. "As a matter of fact, she responds warmly to my touch, but that's just because she trusts me, I think. Besides, touching her on the cheek is a far cry from being intimate."

"Oh, I beg to differ," Henry said. "I don't claim to understand women very well, but I think that if she had issues with being touched, she would shy away from you no matter where you touched her."

"I agree with your father, Simon," Lillian chimed in. "You said yourself that she's receiving good counseling and working through the whole experience, and maybe she's making great progress. Or, the simple fact that she never experienced the pain of being brutalized because she was unconscious could mean that she is less traumatized than she would be if the situation had been different."

"Your mother is one smart cookie, son," Henry said, reaching for Lillian's hand, "and I think she just hit the nail on the head with that last assumption. But, the truth is that you'll never know what Molly's feelings are unless you discuss them with her."

"How do you even start such a conversation?" Simon asked hopelessly. "I can't just ask her if she is afraid of sex, but that's exactly what I need to know."

"I think you're getting a little ahead of yourself," Lillian said cautiously. "What do you think, Dad?" She gazed at her husband, tapping her fingers on the table top.

Henry said, "I think that if you're serious about having a life-long relationship with Molly, you had better find out if she has issues before you make such a commitment."

"Wait a minute. Wait a minute," Lillian said, holding up a hand. "Molly is still at the beginning of this terrible experience and I think it's much too soon for you to be thinking about testing her intimacy boundaries." Looking very seriously at her son, she continued, "You need to take this slowly and you need to give her some time to sort through her fears. She's very young, Simon, and she needs to get rid of that baby. If she feels the same way you do, and if her counselor helps her work through some of the issues she may have with regard to what happened to her, then you may have something wonderful one day."

"You're right. I guess I'm just being impatient," Simon admitted. "It's not like she's going anywhere in the next eight months."

Chuckling, Henry looked over at his wife and said, "Well, Dr. Freud, I think we've helped him with his paralyzing dilemma."

"I sure hope so, Dad," Lillian wished aloud as she rose from her chair and walked around the table. Wrapping her arms around

Simon's shoulders, she rested her cheek against his and softly said, "We just want you to have a happy life. That's all."

Reaching behind him to wrap his mother in a hug, Simon pulled her close and said, "Do you realize how happy you've made my life, so far?"

Lillian dissolved into tears. Reaching for his handkerchief and then dabbing at her eyes, Henry said with great sarcasm, "You'd better get going, kid, before she pulls out your baby book, the photo albums, and the home movies."

Simon rose from his chair, pulled his mother into his arms, and tenderly kissed the top of her head. "Thank you for listening."

And then Simon reached for his father as he was rising from his chair. As they gave one another a hug, Simon said, "Thanks for everything, Dad."

"Our pleasure, son." Henry slapped him on the back. "That's what we're here for."

"Well, I really should go." Simon headed for the mud room to get his coat. "I need to be by myself for awhile and think about all this. Again, thank you for talking this through with me. You really are the greatest parents in the world." Simon shook his head in playful disbelief. "Twenty-seven years running and you have yet to be dethroned."

"Quit bothering us and go home and figure out your own problems," Henry teased.

"Okay, okay," Simon laughed. "I'm going!"

As Lillian watched her son leave, she realized that she had never seen him so unraveled by a woman. Over the years, he had dated so many women; a varied and interesting lot, to be sure, but none of them had ever stolen his heart the way Molly seemed to have done, and in such a short period of time. This situation was definitely different—something special.

Chapter Ten

The morning after Molly had divulged her secret to Simon and then had spent half the night talking over her feelings with her Aunt Mildred, she awoke with a start from a nightmare that had her gripping the bedcovers, holding on for dear life. In the dream, she was falling from a tremendous height, falling to her most untimely and certain death. The one thought flooding her mind was that she would die without knowing what it was like to be with Simon. And just as she was about to hit the ground and splatter to pieces, Simon materialized and caught her in his arms, utterly taking her breath away. She woke up gasping for air. What had it all meant? Was she dreaming about Simon because she was truly in love with him, or was it because she spent so much time with him every day? She knew that she trusted him and felt safe with him and that she was incredibly attracted to him physically. But did her feelings go deeper? Could his feelings for her ever go beyond friendship?

She did not have the answers at that moment, and she did not relish the confusion in her heart and head. Fortunately, it was the day before Thanksgiving and Molly's day off from work. With all the preparations for the feast the following day, there was more than enough to occupy her mind and keep her from thinking about Simon. When she finally made it downstairs, it was after nine-thirty, and her grandmother and aunts were just returning from daily mass.

"Well, well," Harriett sneered when she entered the kitchen

and saw Molly sitting at the table eating her breakfast. "Look who finally dragged herself out of bed. You and Simon must have had quite a night."

"Hattie!" Mildred snapped as she brushed by her elder sister. "Just stop it!"

Mildred wrapped her arms around Molly's shoulders and gave her a peck on both cheeks. "Good morning, dear," she said cheerfully. "Did you have a good sleep? I'm glad you slept in and got some rest."

"Thanks, Aunt Millie," Molly said, resting her cheek upon Mildred's soft arm. "I did have a good rest, and sorry I kept you up so late."

"That's perfectly all right, dear."

"But now I'm ready to get to work," Molly said, glaring at her grandmother. Releasing Molly and smiling to herself, Mildred stepped away from her grandniece and reached for an apron.

Gertrude came blowing into the room like a brisk autumn wind that pulls the leaves from the trees. "Oh, Molly! Did you hear?" Gertrude rushed over to take a seat beside her grandniece. "This morning, Mildred called and invited Simon and his family to Thanksgiving dinner and they accepted!"

The spoon with which she had just taken a bite of her oatmeal fell from Molly's grip and clattered against the porcelain cereal bowl. Harriett noted Molly's reaction to Gertrude's news and watched with curiosity as her granddaughter fidgeted nervously with the breakfast dishes in front of her and kept her eyes hidden from all of them.

"Aren't you happy?" Gertrude asked, her face falling in disappointment.

Mildred slid into the chair across the table from Molly and reached for her grandniece's hand. "Sweetheart, what's the matter?" Mildred asked with great worry. "I just thought that they might enjoy being with a bigger crowd during the holiday since it is just the three of them and Simon's aunt and uncle, and I thought you would enjoy having a friend here since none of your family could make it."

Molly was uncertain how Simon would behave toward her now

that he knew what had happened and after the way she had reacted to his concern for her. "Nothing's the matter," she said putting on a brave face. "I think it's a wonderful idea. After all, that's what Thanksgiving is all about, being with family and friends." Squeezing her aunt's cold hand, she added warmly, "Thank you for thinking of me. It will be really nice to have Simon here to talk with."

Molly could not help noticing her Aunt Gertrude breathing a sigh of relief beside her and her grandmother eyeing her from across the room. "Well, we'd better get to work!" she said cheerfully. "We've got a lot of preparing to do!"

Mildred said a silent prayer of thanks to God, and then rising from her chair, ordered her sisters to start setting the dining room table. "And no nonsense or dilly dallying, Hattie," she warned. "You never help with any of the food preparation so you had better contribute without any complaining."

Harriett did not respond but walked silently and blindly out of the kitchen in the direction of the dining room. Gertrude and Mildred looked at one another and simultaneously threw up their hands in exasperation. Then Gertrude made herself a cup of tea before making her way to the dining room to endure the hardship of trying to work with Harriett.

With Gertrude and Harriett gainfully employed, Mildred and Molly set about making their list of what needed to be done in preparation for the following day, prioritizing their duties and dividing the responsibilities. They dedicated the remainder of the morning to cleaning the house, taking care to make sure that the bathrooms sparkled, the woodwork gleamed, and that everything was neatly settled in its proper place. Several hours later, famished and exhausted, Molly and Mildred made a light lunch for the crew at The Aunt Hill and then sent the sullen Harriett and the slowly unraveling Gertrude over to the church to help decorate for the Thanksgiving Day mass, after which they were to pick up the fresh turkey from Mr. Larkin's farm just across the bridge in Wisconsin.

With Gertrude and Harriett out from under foot, Mildred and Molly got down to the business of baking pies and bread rolls and making the stuffing and cranberry sauce. Molly worked on the pie crusts and fillings while Mildred concentrated on the cranberry sauce, each regularly consulting with the other in regard to ingredients and technique.

Molly was rolling out a pie crust for her pumpkin pie when out of the blue, she said, "Aunt Millie, why is Granny so angry all the time? What happened in her life to make her so miserable?"

"Why do you suddenly want to know, dear?"

Firmly focused on her pie crust, Molly answered, "Because I want to understand her better and try to make her love me."

"Oh, Molly," Mildred cried. "She does love you. She just does not know how to show you."

"But why, Aunt Millie? I want to know why."

"Take a seat, dear," Mildred said, pointing toward the table with a wooden spoon, "and I'll tell you what happened to your grandmother to make her so bitter and unhappy."

Excited that Mildred was actually going to enlighten her, and most anxious to hear what she had to say, Molly wiped her flour-caked hands on her apron and pulled out a chair at the table and took a seat. Mildred sat in the chair beside her and paused a moment to decide where to begin her tale.

"Your grandmother was nineteen years old when she fell in love with a man named Raymond Archer," Mildred began. "He had come down from the Cities to help Papa with the accounting for the business. I think he was probably twenty-three years old at the time." Mildred paused a moment to think. "Anyway, he was gorgeous and sophisticated and always wearing a dashing suit and beautiful shoes. At least that's what I remember most about him. He also had thick, straw-colored hair and was always suntanned. Come to think of it, he looked a lot like a young Robert Redford," Mildred said, glad to have found a visual reference that Molly could use for her imaginings.

"Well, it was summer time and we were all out of school. Hattie liked to help Papa at the office when she had the free time. She liked keeping track of all the properties that he owned. You know, your grandfather owned most of the buildings on Main Street, and your great-grandfather practically built this town with his lumber mill," Mildred said proudly. "Anyway, Hattie liked the money side of the business and liked taking in all the rent checks and adding them up. Papa was rather unnerved by Hattie's interest in the business and tried to discourage her. It was a man's world, and our brothers were to inherit the business. But as you know, your uncle John became a priest, Tim died of tuberculosis when he was twenty-four, and Joe died in the war."

Molly glanced at her aunt sideways. "I know, I know, dear," Mildred said, patting Molly's hand. "It was a much different world back in the nineteen-thirties and forties; we women did not have Oprah to inspire and empower us."

"Anyway, back to Raymond Archer," Mildred said, determined to keep the story on track. "He came down from the Cities and got a room at Thompson's boarding house. He was to stay for as long as it took to help Papa get the business accounts in order and then he was to go back to his firm in St. Paul. Well, Hattie got one look at him and fell head over heels in love. She was quite a looker in her day and she turned his head so quickly I was surprised it did not snap off."

Molly laughed out loud at the image. "Sorry, Aunt Millie," she said, covering her mouth.

"That's all right, dear. It actually was quite funny," Mildred assured her. "From his first day on the job, he was courting Hattie. Or it might be more accurate to say he was sniffing after her like she was a dog in heat. Within three weeks, the little con-artist had Hattie believing that he was in love with her and that he wanted to marry her. And shortly thereafter, he had her uncrossing her legs for him. After she had been with him for about a month, she started making all kinds of future plans that included a big society wedding in St. Paul and a house on Summit Avenue because he had convinced her that his family was rich and well respected in the community. Then one day, he told her that he was married and had a new baby back in the city."

"It gets better," Mildred said in response to the look of disbelief on Molly's face. "After he told her this delightful news, he actually suggested that they continue as they had been because he could see to it that his wife would never find out. Well, you know your grandmother and her temper. She went quite literally insane, I think. She was so hurt and angry because she had let herself be so completely taken in by Raymond that her immediate response was to hurt him back."

"Oh God," Molly gasped. "What did she do?"

"She slept with your grandfather and got pregnant," Mildred said flatly. In further explanation, she added, "Gerald O'Connor was also working for Papa that summer. He was nineteen years old, very cocky and extremely interested in Hattie. Until the night she took him to bed to get back at Raymond, she had done nothing but express her loathing for him, and sure enough, he got her pregnant."

"Oh, dear Granny," Molly said sadly.

As Gertrude drove the Comet over the lift bridge toward Wisconsin, Harriett stared out the passenger window at the dark, cold water of the St. Croix River and was suddenly reminded of Raymond Archer. She was not sure what made her think of him after so many years. Perhaps it was the feeling she got from the water just then, but it occurred to her that the drive would provide her with a perfect chunk of time to revisit the past and make some comparisons and assessments. Her granddaughter's predicament and behavior weighed heavily upon her mind, and she was very curious to know about Simon Mulberry's intentions. Like Raymond Archer, Simon was very handsome and charming, and she wondered if he would also turn out to be a cad and a cruel deceiver.

Harriett had believed in Raymond Archer so deeply and had given herself over to him body and soul. In return, he had destroyed her heart, leaving an empty hole inside of her for the rest of her life. Harriett did not like to be made a fool of and she was sure as hell not going to let anyone make a fool of Molly. Mildred and Gertrude thought the world of Simon, but, then again, her father had thought the world of Raymond Archer. There truly was no knowing a person until you had spent a reasonable amount of time with them.

What had she been thinking when she went off with Gerald O'Connor to exact revenge on Raymond Archer? Even now, the thought of Gerald made her sick. The memory of some of his drunken tirades still made Harriett's bones ache. He had fractured three of them during their marriage and had bruised Harriett's face so many times that her cheeks were permanently splattered with broken blood vessels. She had saved her sons from Gerald's heavy hand and had successfully concealed her situation from her family and the world around her, but she had lost her spirit, youth and beauty before her twenty-fifth birthday. Harriett had become pregnant when she was nineteen years old, just like Molly, and it had ruined her life. How could the Fates be so unkind to come full circle like this? And how was Harriett going to prevent history from repeating itself?

If only her father had not threatened Gerald's life and forced him to marry her; how different Harriett's life would have been. At least her father had received a dose of his own medicine when he discovered that Gerald had been embezzling from him, forcing him to sell off many of his properties. It had frustrated Harriett that no one ever saw the real Gerald O'Connor, but she was, in part, to blame. Her pride had caused her to conceal the truth from her family, and they never realized how much he drank, gambled, and cheated on her. When he stole her idea to save some of the buildings they owned by leasing them out to antique dealers, Gerald was welcomed back into the family fold, and Harriett was made a fool of once again.

Molly's situation was already quite different from hers, but the few similarities were enough to put the fear of God into Harriett. Fortunately, there were so many more options for her grand-daughter, including a safe abortion, and she was surprised to find herself actually considering it a choice. It was interesting that as a Catholic she believed abortion to be a sin for anyone, but with her granddaughter being drugged, raped and possibly robbed of a happy life, she thought it just might be acceptable in the eyes of God. Harriett thought it funny how right and wrong became blurred when a struggle involved oneself or a loved one.

What she wanted more than anything was to turn back time for both Molly and herself, but that was impossible. Thanks to her circumstances, she had become a realist and a pessimist. Fairy tales did not come true and there were no knights in shining armor.

Simon Mulberry was just another man with selfish motives, and she would be damned if he would harm her granddaughter. She could see that Molly was in danger of falling in love with him and this raised Harriett's defenses. He would have to prove himself worthy of Molly long before she would consent to him taking her granddaughter out on a date. And as Molly's parents took no interest in her, Harriett felt that it was her responsibility to look out for the safety and well-being of her granddaughter.

"Hattie, we're here," Gertrude said, shutting off the engine. Startled, Harriett glared over at her sister. "We're at the Larkin Farm," Gertrude explained. "To get the turkey, remember?"

Harriett turned and looked out the windscreen to see a big red barn with its door gaping open. "Yes, I remember," she snapped. "Let's get this over with and go back home." Harriett opened her door and placed a foot on the ground. Turning back to Gertrude, she said, "Don't start talking or we'll be here all afternoon."

Molly finished the crusts and ingredients for her three pies and moved on to the dough for the crescent rolls. Mildred chopped celery for the stuffing while she kept an eye on the cranberry sauce simmering on the stove. They had been back to work for an hour since discussing Harriett's past, and Molly had been silently considering all that her great-aunt had relayed to her. She felt sorry for her grandmother and wished that there was something she could do to make up for the bad choices Harriett had made so long ago.

"Now, I see why Granny is so angry with me," Molly blurted out. "She's probably afraid that I will make the same mistakes that she did, or that I already had when I arrived here that night. No wonder she's so hostile."

Mildred stared at her grandniece in amazement. "I'm very impressed. That's exactly why Hattie acts the way she does."

"Whatever became of Raymond Archer?" Molly asked, abruptly changing the subject.

"Oh, his was a sad ending," Mildred said dramatically. "He got involved in another sex scandal in the Twin Cities which was made very public and then he lost his wife's fortune in some very bad investments. Shortly after that, he killed himself." Molly gasped. "I can't exactly remember how, but I think he hanged himself," Mildred said absently. "Anyway, I can remember thinking that he got what was coming to him after ruining my sister's life the way he did without an ounce of concern for her well-being."

"Did Granny know that he killed himself?" Molly asked, fascinated.

"I think I sent her the newspaper article," Mildred said, trying to remember the facts of her distant past. "She was living here in Stillwater at the time, and your grandfather was still working with Papa at the business. She had just told me about her affair with Raymond Archer several years earlier, when my marriage ended, so the article jumped right off the page at me."

"You were married?" Molly asked, shocked by the revelation.

"That is a story for another day," Mildred said woefully. "Some day I will tell you, but not today." They both went back to their chores and worked in silence.

As Molly was kneading the daylights out of her bread dough, Mildred stopped chopping the celery. "Are you sure you're all right with Simon being here tomorrow?"

"Yes, it's all right, Aunt Millie. I'm just a little afraid of how he is going to act toward me now that he knows the whole truth," Molly confessed.

"I thought we talked about this last night, dear," Mildred said, pausing to look over at her grandniece. "I'm sure he will not treat you any differently. From all that you told me, I'm certain that he cares very deeply for you, and I don't believe the revelation of your misfortunes is going to change his feelings."

"Oh, I hope not, Aunt Millie. I truly hope not."

"You really like him, don't you?"

"Yes, I do."

Harriett and Gertrude returned at around four-thirty that afternoon with the biggest turkey Molly had ever seen. She guessed that she would be packing turkey sandwiches for lunch for the next month and a half, but Gertrude assured her that it was just the right size for their holiday crowd. With the majority of their crowd being elderly women, Molly was certain that her Aunt Gertrude had grossly overestimated the appetites of their group. But regardless of her thoughts, she did not want to ignite an argument with either her grandmother or her Aunt Gertrude because they returned from their afternoon errand in the foulest of moods.

Quickly, Molly prepared a light supper in anticipation of the following day's feast. She was so physically exhausted that she could hardly lift her fork to eat. And after a combined clean-up effort and some final preparations, Molly stole away to soak in a hot bath before she collapsed into bed. When she emerged from the steamy bathroom wrapped in a plush, terry cloth robe, looking as pink as a newborn piglet, she nearly slammed into her grandmother in the hallway.

"Oh, Granny!" Molly gasped, raising a hand to her chest. "You startled me."

Harriett stopped and silently eyed her granddaughter. "You look tired. Did you overdo it today? You shouldn't overdo it."

"No, Granny. I'm fine," Molly assured her. "I'm going right to bed."

"Well, goodnight then," Harriett murmured, looking down at the floor.

"Goodnight, Granny," Molly replied sweetly. Then she stepped toward her grandmother and lightly hugged her. "I love you, Granny," she said softly.

At Molly's touch, Harriett's body went as rigid as an elm. Sensing her grandmother's discomfort and feeling awkward herself, Molly released Harriett and backed away toward her own room, softly closing the door. For a moment, Harriett stood motionless in the hallway. When she regained her mobility, she propelled herself into the safety of her private chamber and closed the door securely behind her.

Chapter Eleven

Gertrude awoke at five o'clock in the morning on Thanksgiving to stuff her prize turkey and pop it in the oven so it would be ready in time for their scheduled dinner. With all the other women of The Aunt Hill still fast asleep, she took advantage of the quiet time, made herself a pot of coffee and an English muffin with jam and then went out to retrieve the paper from the front porch. She was pleasantly surprised by how mild the air felt and was thoroughly enchanted by the lacy white flakes drifting down from the sky. There was not even the slightest breath of wind and the town was cloaked with a thin, fresh blanket of snow.

Gertrude noticed several other houses with lights on in their windows, and she smiled. The golden glow from the houses spilled out across the snow-covered yards and into the streets causing the ice crystals to glisten in the darkness. She straightened and released a sigh of contentment, her warm breath steaming as it met the cold air. The morning was magical, and she felt a part of some secret early morning society which gave her a bit of a thrill.

Unfortunately, her cherished peace seemed short-lived when Harriett came shuffling into the kitchen around six a.m. in search of coffee and the newspaper. She looked awful, as if she had been up ill during the night. Gertrude's early morning contentment was instantly replaced with worry.

"Hattie?" Gertrude nearly whispered. "Are you all right? Are you ill?"

Standing at the stove to pour herself a cup of coffee, Harriett grumbled, "I'm perfectly fine. Where's the crossword?"

Quickly rifling through the newspaper, Gertrude found the section with the day's crossword puzzle and held it out to her sister. Harriett grabbed the paper and walked over to the telephone table to retrieve a pen.

"Would you like me to make you some breakfast?" Gertrude asked cautiously.

"That would be nice, thank you." Harriett plopped down in a chair at the table. "But just something light," Harriett snapped, true to form. "We're having a big meal today."

In silence, Gertrude went about making Harriett a poached egg on toast. After she had served her sister, she checked on the turkey and then went to inspect the dining room to make certain they had not forgotten anything.

By eight o'clock that morning, The Aunt Hill had completely come to life and the sounds of doors opening and closing, taps running, and voices calling back and forth comprised something of a morning symphony that had a special rhythm and harmony. By eight forty-five, Mildred had them all marching out the door and crawling into the Comet to make the short journey to church for the Thanksgiving Day mass.

Harriett made a point of steering clear of her granddaughter, maneuvering toward a seat at the opposite end of the pew from her. But she looked upon Molly with pride that morning as she noted all the appreciative glances that were directed at her. As she watched Molly gracefully greet acquaintances before sliding into the pew beside Mildred, Harriett decided that her granddaughter was surely not the foolish child who had landed on their doorstep three weeks earlier, but that she had quickly grown into a woman of poise, beauty, and grace. Harriett felt a lump growing in her throat and she grabbed a hymnal and started rifling through it distractedly.

After the lovely mass of thanksgiving, the Hayden sisters and their young charge stopped for a quick donut and coffee with their fellow parishioners in the church basement and then zoomed home to get ready for their holiday company. When the doorbell rang, announcing the arrival of their dinner guests, the hunger pains in Molly's stomach were replaced with a host of fluttering butterflies. She chose to stay back in the kitchen while her aunts ran for the door.

Gertrude was first to the door and she flung it open in excitement. "Simon!" she cried. "Come in. Come in." Gertrude motioned for him to step inside. "Welcome. Welcome," she said with pure delight, and Simon leaned in to give her a peck on the cheek.

"Happy Thanksgiving, Miss Gertrude." Simon handed her a plastic floral bag tightly stuffed with deep red roses. "Your favorite," Simon said, winking at her.

"Oh, Simon," Gertrude cooed, "how thoughtful of you. They're so beautiful!"

"Oh, quit your gushing," Harriett sneered, "and give the man some room to breathe."

"Hattie," Mildred said in warning.

"Ah, Mrs. O'Connor," Simon said, walking toward Harriett and reaching into the handle bag that he was carrying. He pulled a bottle of single malt Scotch whiskey from the bag. Holding up the bottle for Harriett to inspect the label, he said, "A little something for you. And don't even pretend you don't like to drink it."

The boy surely had charm; she'd give him that, but it would take a lot more than charm to give Molly the happy life that she deserved. Harriett eyed Simon and he leaned in and gave her a peck on the cheek.

"Here, Simon," Mildred said, stepping around Harriett who was momentarily stunned. "Let me take your coat."

"Miss Hayden," Simon said, pulling a box of Godiva chocolates from his carrier bag. "These are for you, and you don't have to share them with anyone if you don't want to. Molly said they were your favorites."

"Oh, Simon," Mildred cried, genuinely pleased. "Thank you very much. Yes, they most certainly are my favorites."

As Simon shrugged out of his coat with Mildred's help, Molly crept out of the kitchen and into the foyer. When Simon caught sight of her, all movement ceased within his body, and without realizing it, he whispered, "Molly." Having seen her in nothing but overalls since she started working at the nursery, he was captivated by the way she looked. The short, gray skirt and ivory turtleneck sweater, with her shiny auburn hair swept off her face and curling down her back, made her a vision. He realized that he had never seen her legs before, and he was delighted to discover they were long and shapely.

Suddenly aware that the collective crowd in the foyer was staring at him, wondering of course why he was standing there paralyzed, Simon tried to act as if he had not been gawking at her like a drooling, infatuated teenager. "Hi, Moll!" he said with a bright smile. "Happy Thanksgiving!" He stepped toward her and planted a soft kiss upon Molly's cheek, just as he had done with her grandmother and great-aunt.

"Happy Thanksgiving," Molly replied, beaming back at him. Simon looked absolutely gorgeous in a black, cashmere turtleneck and dark brown corduroys. Molly had to tell herself not to stare. Lowering her eyes to draw them away from Simon's beautiful face, Molly was suddenly mortified to realize that she was staring directly at his crotch. Her head flew back as she frantically looked around for a neutral object to focus on.

"Don't worry, Moll. I've got a hostess gift for you, too. I brought you a bag of cheese popcorn from the candy store because you said you've had a craving for it."

"That's really sweet. Thank you," Molly said, tilting her head and daring to look back into his eyes.

Just then, there was a light tap on the storm door. As it was pulled open, they all heard Lillian Mulberry sing, "Happy Thanksgiving!" She stomped the snow off her boots on the mat outside and then her rosy-cheeked face popped inside with a genuine smile of happiness lighting up her countenance.

"Gertie!" she cried, catching sight of the middle Hayden sister standing just inside the door. "Happy Thanksgiving!" She handed Gertrude the baking dish she was carrying. "You're so lovely to invite us. This is going to be so much fun. I've brought the yams and a Jell-O salad, and Henry is bringing some bottles of wine that Simon recommended, so they are sure to be good."

Stepping up to assist Lillian with her coat, Mildred said, "Here, Lillian, let me help you."

"Oh, dear, sweet Millie," Lillian replied, escaping from her coat before wrapping her arms around Mildred. "Happy Thanksgiving." Stepping away from Mildred, Lillian caught sight of Harriett, who was backing away. She caught her up in a hug before she could utter a word in protest or escape to another room.

"Oh, there's my son," Lillian said, with complete adoration. "My goodness, you look handsome today!" Simon wrapped his arms around her and lifted her off the ground, making her laugh happily.

"Does he ever," Molly whispered, as she watched the two of them with great envy.

"Happy Thanksgiving, Mom," Simon said, placing Lillian gently back on her feet. Clamping his face between her hands, Lillian pulled Simon down to her and kissed his cheek with a loud smack.

"Hellooo," a voice sang like a little calling bird, and everyone turned to see a new face enter the house.

"Girls!" Lillian cried in excitement. "You remember my sister, Louise."

"Hello, Louise," the three Hayden sisters said in unison.

"Hello, girls," Louise replied. "It's so good to see you again and so nice of you to have us for dinner." Handing Mildred a plastic bag containing a velvety purple African violet plant, she said, "This is just a little Thanksgiving present. Lillian said you had a collection of violets in your kitchen window."

"Yes, we do!" Gertrude said, excited by the prospect of a new addition to their plant family. "How kind of you."

"Thank you," Mildred said, smiling appreciatively at Louise.

Leaving Simon, Lillian crossed back over to the front door and took the plate containing her Jell-O mold away from her sister. "Where are those two gentlemen?" Lillian asked, glancing out the storm door to see if they were on the porch.

"Oh, Arnie and Henry are quickly sweeping the snow off the walk," Louise said, as Mildred helped her out of her coat. "They should be along any minute."

"How sweet of them," Gertrude said dreamily.

Molly walked toward Lillian with outstretched arms and said, "Here, Mrs. Mulberry. Let me take that from you."

"Molly!" Lillian shouted as she looked the girl over. "Look at you! You're lovely!"

"Thank you, Mrs. Mulberry." Molly wondered if Simon thought the same thing.

Quickly handing over the dish, Lillian wrapped her arms around Molly's shoulders and hugged her over the plate of Jell-O. "Happy Thanksgiving, dear." She hugged Molly a bit longer than might be considered appropriate but she did not care. Her heart had been aching to comfort the girl since Simon told them her story.

Lillian finally released her and Molly backed into the kitchen with the Jell-O mold.

"Here, Miss Gertrude," Simon said, rushing over to take the dish of yams out of Gertrude's arms. "Let me take those from you."

"Oh, thank you, Simon," Gertrude gushed. "You are such a gentleman."

"Oh, Simon," Louise said, pushing open the storm door. "Your father left the box of wine just outside the door here. Do you want to bring it inside for us?"

"Certainly," Simon said, stepping out the door and placing the dish of yams on top of the wine box. Then he hefted the load into his arms and carried it inside, hurrying toward the kitchen in the hopes of having a moment alone with Molly.

Harriett motioned for their guests to follow her and said, "Let's move away from the door and into the warmth of the parlor, shall we?"

"Good idea, Hattie!" Lillian said, following Harriett's lead. "Come along, ladies. The men can take care of themselves." And the group of gray-haired women dressed in wools and tweeds moved into the parlor to entrench themselves by the crackling fire.

In the kitchen, Molly had her head stuffed into the refrigerator where she was trying to find a spot for Lillian's Jell-O mold on one of the packed-to-capacity shelves. She was just balancing the plate on some pickle jars and a carton of cream when Simon entered the room. To his great delight, he was treated to the most pleasant view of Molly's rear end sticking out of the refrigerator, and he paused a moment to admire her form.

"Need any help there, Moll?" he asked, grinning from ear to ear.

Shooting straight up like a catapult, Molly spun on a heel, lost her balance, and fell backward into the refrigerator. Clutching a hand to her heart and trying to brace herself with an arm, she gasped, "Simon, you scared me!"

Simon raced over and extracted her from the refrigerator. "Are you all right?" He pushed some jars and containers back into place on the shelves. "You didn't hurt anything, did you?"

Laughing and running her hands down the back of her skirt to check for globs of food, she replied, "No, I'm perfectly fine. Just don't sneak up on me like that."

Simon smiled down at Molly, and when she looked back at him, he was suddenly caught up in a moment of déjà vu. He felt as if they had both been there before, standing together in the glow of the refrigerator bulb, staring deeply into one another's eyes and getting chillier by the minute. Pulling Molly closer to him and out of the way, Simon reached for the refrigerator door with one hand and shut it tightly. Then he looked back at Molly whose eyes appeared to be posing a question. "What is it?"

She was flustered to be asked what she was thinking and knew that there would be no way of dodging Simon's question. "I was afraid that you might feel differently toward me now that you know what happened."

"I'm sorry about what happened to you, Moll, and more than anything, I just want to beat the shit out of the punk who hurt you, but it doesn't change the way I feel about you. We're friends and I hope we will be forever."

"Me, too."

"Um . . . Excuse me, Simon, Molly," Henry Mulberry said sheepishly as he stood in the kitchen doorway. Molly attempted to pull away from Simon but he kept her close by holding on to one of her arms.

Gently massaging Molly's arm with his fingers in an effort to reassure her and calm her nerves, Simon smiled at his father and said, "Hey, Dad! Happy Thanksgiving!"

Crossing the room with his arms outstretched, Henry Mulberry approached Simon, who happily stepped into his father's embrace.

"Happy Thanksgiving, son." After a quick squeeze and a slap on the back, Henry released Simon and reached for Molly.

Wrapping his arms around her and lifting her off the floor, Henry spun her round and said, "Happy Thanksgiving, little lady." Then, placing her gently on her feet, Henry held Molly at arm's length and whistled. "You're looking downright gorgeous, today!"

"Yes, she is, Dad," Simon agreed. "Who knew she had legs under those baggy overalls!"

"And mighty fine ones, too," Henry teased as he bent to inspect her legs.

"Stop teasing," Molly scolded.

"Sorry, sweetie," Henry apologized, planting an affectionate kiss on top of Molly's head as he wrapped her up in one arm. "Now, I need you two to help me find some alcohol for those crazy women in the parlor before things get ugly out there."

"We've got just the thing!" Simon moved toward the kitchen table. "Moll, can you please scare up some wine glasses and a tray, and I'll uncork a couple of these bottles."

"I'll help you, Simon," Henry said, taking Molly by the hand. "Molly, just point me in the direction of some wine glasses and you can go join the crowd in the parlor. Simon and I will take care of the drinks."

"There are wine glasses and a tray in here," she said, switching on the overhead light in the pantry.

"Wonderful!" Henry said, taking her by the shoulders and steering her out of the kitchen. "You go take a seat, and we'll be out in a minute." Molly strolled out of the kitchen.

"What was going on in here when I walked in?"

"Nothing," Simon said in exasperation. "I swear to God, nothing."

"Uh-huh," Henry mused.

Henry and Simon served the wine to the assembled crowd and then joined in the lively conversation that buzzed around the parlor at The Aunt Hill. Simon had brought Molly a glass of sparkling water and half of a roll to hold her until dinner and to curb the nausea she might be feeling. His kindness and the way he had been looking at her since he arrived made her begin to hope that

Simon might actually be attracted to her and therefore might be able to overlook the mess she had made of her life. When Simon chose a seat clear across the room from her, Molly did not feel slighted because she discovered his eyes on her several times. And when she glanced over at him, he did not instantly look away but held her gaze for a moment before directing his attention elsewhere.

The conversation turned into a lively debate over a proposal for a new bridge that would cross the river at a point south of Stillwater, eliminating the horrific traffic jams in town. With the heated discussion occupying the crowd, Mildred rose from her chair and excused herself to see to the final preparations for their meal. Gertrude excused herself, as well, to check on her turkey, and Molly joined them to offer her assistance. Lillian and Louise would not be denied a part in the proceedings, and soon all that was left in the parlor were the three men and Harriett.

When Simon suggested that he would join the ladies in the kitchen to offer his assistance, Harriett grabbed him by the arm, pulled him back down to the sofa and said, "Sit down, young man. Trust me. You don't want to get caught up in the melee in there."

"Well then," Simon said playfully, "why don't you let me escort you to the dining room and we'll grab the best seats for ourselves."

"You think you're pretty slick, don't you?" Harriett said, taking his hand and allowing him to help her to her feet.

"Not at all," Simon assured her as he wrapped her hand around his elbow and gave it a gentle pat. "I just enjoy spending time with you."

"Hah! Now, I know you're trying to pull the wool over my eyes," Harriett sneered. "No one enjoys spending time with me."

Ouch! Simon thought. He quickly said, "Well, I do. So, get used to it."

"Why?" Harriett asked suspiciously.

"Because you make me laugh," Simon said chuckling. "And I'm not laughing at you. I'm laughing with you," he added. "And don't pretend that you're not trying to be funny."

"Presumptuous boy," Harriett mumbled.

"Overly suspicious woman," Simon mumbled back.

And as they made their way out of the parlor and toward the dining room, Harriett quietly said, "Just what were you up to the other night with my granddaughter?"

"Absolutely nothing, I assure you," Simon said, looking her directly in the eye. "We had dinner and talked. That's all."

"You brought her home pretty late," Harriett noted.

"Is that why you came snooping around my house?" he said, grinning. Harriett stared straight ahead in silence. "Mrs. Sullivan said that she and Fifi caught you prowling on my front porch."

Harriett began to pull away from him but he stopped her. "Listen. I understand your suspicions and respect your love and concern for Molly, but you have nothing to worry about. I promise you I won't do anything to hurt her or betray her trust. I care about her too much."

"How much?" Harriett demanded.

"Probably more than you're comfortable with," Simon answered.

Harriett stared at him for a moment. "Well, at least you're being honest," she said.

Just then, Molly came bursting out of the kitchen with a covered dish in her hands and nearly slammed into them.

When the crowd was finally gathered at the table with place settings and dishes of steaming food covering every square inch of the ivory lace tablecloth, Mildred led everyone in a prayer of thanksgiving. Just as everyone was reaching for the dishes of food, Molly rose from her seat across from Harriett and begged their forgiveness. "I just wanted to say something quickly, if you don't mind," she said nervously. "I just want to say how thankful I am that my Granny and my aunts took me in when I had no place else to go. They gave me a family for which I will be forever grateful." Molly looked at her grandmother and great-aunts in turn, and then looking across the table at Simon, she continued, "And I'm grateful that Simon gave me a chance to prove myself at the nursery. I'm so thankful for our friendship. And I feel very fortunate to be sharing this meal and this holiday with all of you."

"Here, here!" Henry bellowed, raising his wine glass to Molly. "Well put, dear girl."

And all assembled around the Hayden dining room table

raised their glasses in a toast to honor the young woman who had the courage to express her feelings. With such formalities out of the way, Henry began to carve the turkey while Lillian and Louise passed plates and bowls until each person had a pile of food smothered in gravy. They ate until they were full, and then they ate until they could not put another morsel in their mouths. Incapacitated by their gluttony, they sat at the table engaged in subdued conversation, until Molly rose and started to clear the dirty dishes.

"You ladies knocked yourselves out preparing this meal and now it's time for the clean-up crew to take over." Henry placed a hand on Molly's arm.

"That's right," Simon concurred. Rising from his chair and collecting a stack of dishes, he looked over at Molly. "Take a seat, Moll, and just relax."

Nudging Harriett with his elbow, Simon said, "Keep an eye on her. Don't let her move." Then he hurried off to the kitchen with his cumbersome load.

While the women discussed the prospect of venturing out the following day to fight the holiday shopping crowds, Henry and Arnie cleared the dining room table down to the centerpiece and candlesticks while Simon was up to his elbows in soap suds in the kitchen sink. With all the leftovers safely tucked away, the men came limping back into the dining room, gripping their lower backs and rubbing at the muscles in their necks.

As he stood in the arched entrance to the dining room, Simon called out to Harriett, "Are you up for a cribbage match?"

Harriett peered at Simon over the top of her glasses. "Have you got any money?"

"Hattie!" Gertrude cried.

"Oh, calm yourself or you'll have an aneurysm," Harriett said in aggravation. "I'm just suggesting a little friendly wager, and if the boy doesn't want to play, he doesn't have to."

"And the gauntlet has been thrown down," Arnie said, laughing.

"Don't encourage them, dear," Louise scolded without looking up from the cross-stitch canvass she was working on.

"You're on," Simon said, grinning at Harriett. "Let's play."

Hoisting herself out of her chair, Harriett gave a little cry of pain as her arthritic knees nipped at her, sending shock waves down into her ankles. Rushing to her grandmother's aide, Molly wrapped an arm around Harriett's back and grabbed her arm for support. "Are you okay, Granny? I think we all got a little stiff sitting for so long."

"Don't fuss over me," she grumbled. "I'm not an invalid."

"Sorry, Granny." Molly quickly backed away.

Harriett was struck with instant remorse. Reaching for Molly's hand, she squeezed it tightly. "It's okay, dear. I just get a little cranky when my arthritis kicks in."

"Is anyone else interested in playing some cards? Perhaps some Bridge or Hearts?" Mildred asked.

"Count me in," Lillian said cheerfully.

"Me, too!" Gertrude said.

"If you ladies don't mind," Henry said hopefully, "Arnie and I will hide away in the kitchen and check out the football game. Is it all right if we commandeer your television set, Millie?"

"Perfectly all right," Millie assured them. "If you want to be more comfortable, there is another television in the library where there are some chairs you can fall asleep in."

"Now you're talking," Arnie said, making a beeline for the library with Henry close on his heels.

"Molly? What about you, sweetheart?" Gertrude asked, looking expectantly at her grandniece. "Do you want to play some cards with us?"

"Sure. That would be fun."

"Well, then," Mildred said, motioning for everyone to follow her, "let's retire to the parlor for some entertainment. Later we'll have coffee and dessert."

The women followed Mildred into the parlor, where Simon and Harriett were settled at a small table in front of the big picture window, already arguing about whether or not a high or low card draw got to deal first. Harriett, of course, won the deck and started shuffling the cards with the full intention of teaching Simon a lesson.

Simon was handing over a ten-dollar bill to Harriett when Henry and Arnie came moseying into the parlor, wondering if anyone else was hungry. The collective response to the suggestion of some pie and coffee was a resounding yes, and Molly hurried off to the kitchen to cut up her desserts.

"I'll be there in a minute to help," Simon said, stuffing his wallet back into his pocket. "As for you," he said, glaring down at Harriett, "I intend to win that ten dollars back real soon."

"You can certainly try," Harriett said smugly.

"Oh, I will," Simon assured her. "You just name the time and the place, and I'll be there."

"Don't forget your wallet."

"All right, that's enough gambling for today, you two," Mildred said laughing. "Let's all go back to the table to have our dessert."

Simon headed for the kitchen. "I'll go help Molly. Take your time, everyone." He found Molly standing at a counter slicing her prize-worthy pies and her decadent looking pecan tart.

"How can I help?" he asked as he approached her from behind and peered over her shoulder at the desserts. "Those look fabulous! I'm going to have to try them all."

Molly laughed. She secretly savored his compliment and hoped that they tasted as good as they looked. "Can you please get the bowl of whipped cream out of the refrigerator?" Molly dared not turn around because his body was so close to hers.

"Sure thing," Simon said, happy to be of service. He dug through the shelves of the refrigerator in search of the cream. "Molly, I'm sorry that your family wouldn't come and spend the holiday with you." He hoped she could hear the sincerity in his voice. He had been thinking about how she might be feeling all through dinner.

Molly's eyes pooled with tears. Her emotions were simmering just near the surface these days and she did not seem to have any control over them. With her back to Simon, she stood like a statue, silently crying.

Simon watched her carefully for her response. When he realized that she was crying, he tiptoed up behind her, turned her around, and pulled her into his arms. After a moment of reluctance, Molly relaxed and wrapped her arms around his middle, then buried her face in his shoulder. "I just wish they could forgive me and love me. Even though I'm angry at them for what they've done to me."

"Oh, Molly," Simon said, closing his eyes in despair, "right now, they're just being stupid and ridiculous, but they have to love you. How could anyone not love you?" He rested his cheek on the top of her head and pulled her closer. Simon suddenly became acutely aware of the press of her form against his torso and his eyes instantly shot open. And there, standing in the kitchen doorway, was Harriett O'Connor with an utterly unreadable expression upon her face. Simon and Harriett gazed at one another, and then he pulled back from Molly, clutched her face between his hands and kissed her softly on the forehead.

"It's going to be all right, Moll," Simon whispered. "I promise."

"I thought I'd better come and help you since I haven't lifted a finger all day," Harriett said gruffly, stepping into the room without any pretense.

Molly quickly pulled back from Simon, slamming her tailbone into the edge of the counter top and instantly crying out in pain.

"Molly!" Simon cried, reaching out for her but missing her arm and, by some mysterious law of physics, knocking the knife out of the pecan tart, sending it flipping through the air, impaling itself in the wooden floor just an inch from his shoe.

"Shit!" Simon exclaimed, half laughing. "Are you all right?" Simon tried again and managed to grab Molly by the shoulders. "Excuse me, Mrs. O'Connor," he apologized.

Harriett slowly bent over and pulled the knife from the floor boards. Standing there with it in her hand, she shook her head and looked at Simon and Molly. "Calm down," she said with a scowl, "or you are both going to end up in the hospital."

Harriett looked over at Molly and said, "Are you going to be all right?"

"Yes," Molly replied, wincing as she rubbed at her tailbone. "I'll be fine."

"Well, let's have some dessert," Harriett instructed. Then she marched back toward the dining room.

Simon and Molly watched Harriett go. After a moment, Simon said, "I think she likes us." And they burst into laughter.

They heard Harriett coming back toward the kitchen and their laughter instantly ceased. Molly hurried from the room to go fix her face and Simon grabbed the two pies from the counter. "If you can grab the whipped cream, I think we're ready," Simon said to Harriett as she reentered the room.

Holding out a hand to stop him from taking a step, Harriett said, "What exactly is going on between you two?"

"In all honesty," Simon answered, "she's stolen my heart and I don't think I'll ever get it back."

"She's much too young," Harriett said dismissively. "You need to give her more time. There's so much that she needs to do for herself."

"I understand that," Simon replied, "and I'm trying to hold back. I really am. But it's so hard when I fall more in love with her every day."

"Is it truly love or is it just the desire to get her into your bed?" Harriett said skeptically.

"Yes, it's truly love."

"Are you sure, or do you just want to protect her after learning what happened to her?"

"Of course I want to protect her," Simon answered, "because I love her. So do you."

"I'm her grandmother."

"Well I'm the man who loves her, the one who thinks about her all day long and dreams about a life with her," he countered. "She fills my heart and mind and makes them complete. That's what I know for certain."

"If you truly love her, then leave her alone."

"No," Simon said adamantly. "I will stay my current course and hope that she falls in love with me and becomes comfortable enough to be with me."

"But what about her future?"

"It's a wide open book, and I intend to support her in whatever she chooses to do; with her baby, her education, her career, right down to any hairstyle she chooses."

Harriett took the pumpkin pie from his hand, and said, "Well then, just make sure that you make her happy for the rest of her life, or I will make you suffer."

Harriett confused the hell out of him. Simon wasn't sure if she was telling him to stay away from Molly or to go for it. "Are you saying that you approve?"

"I'm saying that she could do a lot worse than you. But, we need to agree that it must be Molly's choice to be with you and that you need to give her time to make that choice. There'll be no pressuring her by declaring your love for her. Do I make myself clear?" Simon nodded. "Now, grab that whipped cream and then you can come back for the coffee."

"You like me," he said smugly.

"I never said that."

"Well, I'm going to prove to you how much I love Molly and hold back until she's ready for a relationship, and then you'll like me."

"Just stick to the plan," Harriett warned. "I'll have my eye on you every minute."

"I don't doubt that," Simon said, smiling. He followed Harriett out of the kitchen.

Chapter Twelve

The day after Thanksgiving, the Christmas season officially began, and the Mulberry Nursery started to buzz with activity. Truckloads of Christmas trees arrived daily, and the employees were busy making strands of garlands and decorative wreaths and swags for the holiday. Orders piled up as they worked frantically to fill them and make deliveries. Simon and Henry were so busy decorating house exteriors that Molly only saw Simon when he picked her up in the morning and drove her home at night. By the end of the day, they were both too exhausted for any meaningful conversation.

Molly missed Simon, and her body began to ache for his touch. Sometimes she would lean back against him when he was opening the pickup truck door for her at the end of the day just to form some sort of physical connection with him. And when she confessed her silly behavior to Helen Faraday at one of her weekly sessions, her counselor was happy to hear that Molly was having perfectly normal feelings for Simon. This led to further discussion of issues with regard to intimacy in reference to what had happened to Molly, and they had their best session yet. Molly completely opened up to Helen, shared some of her fantasies about Simon, and even expressed her fear that he might not harbor the same feelings toward her. In response, Helen suggested that Simon might simply be reluctant to become involved with Molly because of her current situation, but that only time would tell. Molly needed time to heal, and perhaps Simon understood this and was just simply being respectful to show how much he cared about her.

Perhaps Helen was right about Simon. Then again, he did seem to touch Molly quite a lot and he was always standing so close to her. Molly had no experience with any sort of physical relationship, but she knew that she wanted to be with Simon. And her growing feelings for him made her realize that she needed to know something of what it was like to be intimate with a man before her life was completely altered by the experience of giving birth to a baby. But every morning when Molly climbed into Simon's truck for the ride to work, he was preoccupied with other worries and did not have much time for her. She wondered if she had been misguided.

Molly and Lillian were working on a special order wreath one afternoon when Molly began to lose steam, chugging along, drifting in and out of daydreams. Christmas music spilled out of the speakers overhead and lulled her into a hypnotic state. She was staring through the hole in the wreath in front of her when Lillian noticed her posture.

"Are you getting tired, dear? You really have been working much too hard these last couple weeks."

"Oh, no. I was just thinking of all the things I need to get done before Christmas," Molly fibbed.

"You poor girl," Lillian said, rubbing Molly's back. "I'm going to talk to Simon about giving you some days off. I think you could use the rest."

"Please don't. I really need the money. I have some special presents in mind for my grandmother and my aunts for Christmas."

"I think you are probably the best present they have ever received," Lillian said wisely.

"I don't think so, Mrs. Mulberry," Molly said, shaking her head. "I brought some pretty heavy baggage along with me."

"You're referring to your pregnancy, I assume."

"Yes. Simon said that he told you."

"I demanded that he tell me," Lillian assured her. "He was pretty upset about it when you told him what had happened and I wanted to know what was troubling him so that I could help."

"Then you know the whole story?" Molly asked, utterly mortified. Anger bubbled up inside of her at the thought of Simon sharing her secret with his mother. Then she realized that she had left the decision to him.

"Yes, dear," Lillian confessed. "And it won't go any further. I promise you."

Molly recognized the sincerity behind her words.

"I'm so sorry about what happened, and I would like to help in any way I can."

"Thank you. That's very kind of you. But you've already helped," Molly assured her. "You have given me so much self-confidence. You give me responsibilities and you praise everything that I do."

"That's because you are good at everything you do."

"I don't know about that," Molly said humbly. "But I appreciate your support, and I love working here. It's made me happy."

"I'm glad," Lillian said, lightly patting Molly's back. "And Simon is glad that you're here, too."

"Really?"

Lillian nodded. "You like him," she said knowingly.

"Very much," Molly confessed. "I trust him more than anyone else in the world and I feel so safe with him. I hope you're not angry at me for saying that."

"Why would I be angry?"

"I remember how mad you were about Tracy Benedict going after him, and I don't want you to think the same of me."

"Sweetie, Tracy Benedict is a completely different story; she's throwing herself at him despite his disinterest. Simon cares about you a great deal. I know that for a fact," Lillian said forcefully.

Molly smiled brightly. And when Lillian saw the hope in the girl's eyes, she wondered what would come of it.

"Come on," Lillian said, sliding off her stool. "Let's go find Simon so that he can drive you home."

"But I've got two more wreaths to do," Molly protested.

"They can wait until tomorrow, dear. You look exhausted, and right now, you need to pay attention to what your body is telling you."

"All right," Molly acquiesced. "My body does seem to be telling me that it wants to go home, curl up in bed, and take a nap."

"You see!" Lillian said, raising her index finger. "I heard it." Molly laughed and Lillian wrapped an arm around her shoulders. Then they went to look for Simon.

Several days later, on a bright, sunny Sunday morning, Molly had arisen quite late and had missed going to church with her grandmother and aunts. Taking herself to a later mass, she had walked the few blocks to St. Michael's because it was an unseasonably warm day. It was just two weeks before Christmas, and the melting snow made it feel like springtime. After just two months of cold temperatures, she was already feeling the depressing confinement of winter.

After mass, she walked back home, taking deep breaths of the crisp damp air and pausing every now and again to raise her face to the sun to catch some of its warmth. When she approached The Aunt Hill, she was more than delighted to see Simon perched on a ladder, hanging strands of icicle lights from the eaves of the porch. She dashed across the street with a little skip in her step.

"What are you doing working on a Sunday, you heathen?"

When Simon turned to look at her, she was overjoyed to the see the enormous smile on his face. "Well, there she is! I heard you were a bad girl and missed mass this morning. Did you actually go or have you been wandering around town for the last hour? Your cheeks are all rosy."

"I went to church," Molly replied.

"Good girl." Simon climbed down the ladder.

"So, what are you doing here on a Sunday?" Molly asked again.

"Oh, I always decorate The Aunt Hill for the holidays during my free time. Your aunts pay me in baked goods," he explained. "I'm a little late this year because we've been so busy with all the new customers. Of course, your granny gave me an earful this morning so I'll probably just get a lump of coal instead of cookies."

"She just gives you a hard time because she has a crush on you," Molly teased.

"Do you think?" Simon said, laughing.

"I think they all do."

Simon picked up a long evergreen garland. "So, what are you

up to for the rest of the day?" He dragged the garland toward the porch. Molly followed him. "Have you got any special plans or are you just going to relax?" Simon reached up and fastened one end of the garland to a porch column with a wired, red felt bow.

"No special plans," Molly answered, hoping that he might ask her to join him for a coffee, or a walk, or anything.

"That sounds nice," Simon said absently, as he draped the garland down in front of the stone wall and attached the next section with another bow. "You need to catch your breath after the way we've been working you ragged." Simon took a step toward her as he moved to the next section of porch but Molly did not back up. Coming face to face with her, he immediately noticed Molly's red nose and exclaimed, "You're frozen!" He gently tapped the end of her nose with his gloved finger. "Why don't you go inside and warm up. I've got to finish this garland and then do the lighted garland on the garden fence before I get the tree up inside."

Molly turned to walk away from him but he caught a glimpse of her face. Dropping the garland, he reached for her arm. "Whoa, hold on a minute. What's wrong?"

"I just miss you," Molly said honestly. "We never get to talk any more because you're so busy and tired all the time."

"Oh, honey," Simon said, pulling her into his arms, "I'm sorry. This is such a hectic time of year for us. I know I've been a boring old grouch on our car rides to and from work but it won't last much longer, I promise. Dad and I should be done with all the decorating by Tuesday and then I'll be less preoccupied."

Molly laid her head on Simon's shoulder. He wanted to take her face between his hands and kiss her on the lips, but he gently pushed her away. "I'll tell you what," he said, holding her by the shoulders. "We'll leave work early on Thursday. I'll take you out to dinner and we can do some Christmas shopping. We'll go up to the Cities, to the Mall of America; there are some good restaurants there and more than enough stores for us to browse."

"Really?" Molly's eyes twinkled in the sunshine.

"Really."

"Yay!" Molly said, clapping her hands together. "I have some special presents in mind that I'm sure to find there." Now she could look forward to a special night out with Simon. She would be counting down the days until their "date."

"Go inside and get warm and I'll finish up out here." Simon patted her shoulders and then returned to his task. "After I get the tree up in the parlor, maybe you and I can have a quick visit. Then I've got to get back to the nursery and get caught up on paper work," he said wearily.

"Why don't you let me help you with the paper work?"

"Thanks for the offer," Simon said, smiling at her, "but I'll get it done."

Molly waved a hand at him and made her way across the snow-covered lawn.

Simon watched her go, following her every move. When she started up the stairs, he bent over and picked up another length of garland. As he began to hang the next section of garland, he realized that he had not heard the front door open and close. Peering over the porch wall, he saw Molly standing like a statue with her hand on the storm door handle. "What is it, Moll?"

Molly yanked her hand away from the door and spun round to look at Simon. Seeing just his hat and his eyes, she walked across the porch and peered down at him. For a moment, she completely lost every thought in her head.

Simon watched as her eyebrows drew together in dismay. "What are you thinking?"

"I just . . ." Molly mumbled, completely at a loss.

"Just what?"

"I just wanted you to know how much I value our friendship," she said, the words coming out in clusters. "It means a lot to me."

"Me, too," Simon replied, reaching up to her. Molly offered him her right hand, and squeezing it gently, Simon said, "You're very important to me."

The words had come straight out of Simon's mouth, into her ears, and down into her stomach, where her resident butterflies began to flit about in excitement. Molly smiled down at Simon and then backed up across the porch and disappeared into the house.

The following Thursday, the day of their "date," all of Molly's excitement and expectations were dashed to pieces in the first few hours of her day. Simon arrived an hour late to pick her up for work, and he was not in the cheeriest of moods. He had been at the nursery until the wee hours, trying to get caught up as well as get a jump on the next day so that he and Molly could have their evening out. He hated being late, and more than this, he hated oversleeping. It simply threw off his entire day. When they arrived at the nursery, more bad karma greeted them. Henry was in an uproar over a mixed-up commercial poinsettia order and three employees had called in sick.

Molly ran off to the safety of her workbench and quickly got to work on the last two special order wreaths of the season. Around ten o'clock that morning, just as she was putting the last few sprigs of winterberry into the final wreath, she felt someone walk up quietly behind her. She knew that it was Simon.

"That's spectacular," Simon said softly as he peered over her shoulder. "You really are talented."

Tilting her head to examine her work, she decided that it did look spectacular, and she was certain that the customer would be more than pleased. She had used several different boughs to make the wreath itself: blue spruce, Norfolk pine, and Frasier fir, and had then added pine cones and some winterberry branches. Finally, she had entwined the wreath in a sheer red ribbon and a gold rope cord.

Simon moved closer and wrapped his arms around her shoulders. At that same moment, Tracy Benedict was on the prowl, searching the greenhouses for Simon. When she came upon the two of them, she quickly ducked behind a pile of Christmas trees.

"Forgive me for being such a jackass this morning," Simon said softly near Molly's ear. "My behavior was inexcusable."

The feather-light caress of Simon's words upon Molly's ear sent a shiver of pleasure up her spine. Mistaking the shiver as a shrug, Simon pulled his arms from around her shoulders and folded them across his chest. She turned to look at his face. "Don't worry about it. I know you haven't had much sleep lately. You have a lot on your mind."

Simon eyed her with a degree of skepticism, certain that she was simply masking her anger, but he quickly realized that she was being sincere. "God, you're an angel, Moll," Simon whispered, gently brushing the hair back from her face with his hand.

"I understand if you want to cancel tonight," Molly said sadly.

"Don't even say it," Simon said, shaking his head. "I practically worked all night to make sure we could get out of here together this afternoon."

"But if you're too tired . . ."

"I'm not too tired for a fun night out with you."

"Really?"

"Really." Simon absently ran his thumb along her cheek bone.

From her hiding place behind the evergreen trees, Tracy Benedict began to hear the blood pounding in her brain. Molly O'Connor was stealing her man with her innocent little act. Why hadn't she thought of it?

"I brought clothes to change into so we don't have to waste time going back to The Aunt Hill," Molly announced.

"Good. So did I." Simon pulled his hand away from her face as he realized what he was doing. Rubbing that same hand along the back of his neck, he said, "So, let's plan on running out of here at three o'clock."

"I'll be ready." Molly tried hard to contain her excitement.

"I've got some phone calls to return so I have to run. I'll catch up with you later."

"All right." She waved at him as he backed away.

Molly turned back to take one more look at the wreath she finished. Quite pleased with her work, she rose from her chair, picked up the wreath, and headed for the store to hang it in the cut flower cooler. It would be ready and waiting when the customer came to pick it up that afternoon.

Tracy Benedict eyed Molly's back with disdain. When the opportunity to get her revenge presented itself, she was going to damn well make the most of it.

Molly noticed that the huge hanging poinsettia baskets in greenhouse number two were drooping severely when she passed through on her way up front. She saw Lillian in the store and told her about the plants. "Who's on watering duty today?" she inquired of Lillian.

"Tracy has been assigned to that greenhouse for the past week," Lillian informed her. "I'll bet she hasn't watered them once. I'll track her down and send her over to water right away."

"I can do it, but I won't get around to them until after lunch," Molly offered.

"No. It's Tracy's job and she is damn well going to do it." Lillian realized that she was scowling and she altered her expression. "You have enough to do, Molly. Besides, I know you and Simon are trying to get out of here early today."

"It's no problem. I don't want to see them die; they're so beautiful," Molly said.

"Don't worry about it. You go back to your work and I'll see that Tracy gets to the baskets as soon as possible." With a very serious expression on her face, Lillian took off at a fast clip.

Before lunch break, Molly ran up to the store with some simply decorated wreaths for the last minute shopping crowd and noticed that the poinsettia baskets still had not been watered. Lillian had obviously not yet tracked down Tracy Benedict. Molly ate a quick lunch and hurried off to undertake the task of watering the poinsettias herself. If they waited much longer the expensive baskets would be worthless. With a hose and a ladder, she got to work watering, making her way through the sea of red and cream, reviving the thirsty poinsettias.

Simon was breaking for lunch when he took a detour in order to tell Molly that everything was under control and that they were still on for their escape at three o'clock. He was searching for her when he heard her sweet voice drifting out of greenhouse number two as she sang along with the Christmas carols playing over the extensive speaker system that he had installed throughout the nursery. He spied Molly's Wellington-clad feet perched on a ladder and a stab of anger and fear punctured his stomach. Hadn't he made it clear that she was not to climb up on things? And there she was several feet off the ground teetering on a rickety old ladder.

Tracy Benedict had also found Molly watering the poinsettia baskets but she was two steps ahead of Simon. Crawling on her hands and knees under the flower tables, Tracy had snaked a hose underneath the ladder Molly was standing upon and then had made her way back to where the hose was attached to a spigot. Crouching down to remain out of sight, she suddenly yanked on the hose and pulled the ladder out from under Molly.

Molly screamed as she lost her balance and tumbled off the ladder. Simon watched in horror as she fell backward onto a flower table, a host of brilliant red poinsettias breaking her fall. "Molly!" he cried, skirting the flower tables that blocked his path.

Lillian came running into the greenhouse, having seen Molly's fall from an adjoining area where she was carting up some plants. Out of the corner of her eye, she caught a glimpse of Tracy, bent over, trying to slink away. "Stop right there, Tracy!" she yelled, pointing a finger at the girl. "Don't you move a muscle!"

Racing Simon to come to Molly's aid, Lillian knocked several plants off the tables she passed. When they reached Molly, she was lying among a pile of destroyed plants and a mound of dirt, with water spraying from the hose several feet down the table.

"Oh God!" Simon cried. "Are you all right, Moll?" He hovered over her, searching for signs of injury.

"Molly," Lillian said, taking the girl's hand, "before you sit up, I want you to move your legs and arms." Molly did as she was told. "All right, Simon, help her up," Lillian instructed, clutching Molly's hand.

Wrapping his arms around Molly's upper torso, Simon pulled her up into a sitting position and then he ran his arms up and down her body as if he were checking for broken bones. "Tell me if you hurt anywhere. Did you bump your head? How's the baby?"

Molly's eyes darted back and forth between Simon and his mother; she wasn't sure if she was hurt or not. When Simon mentioned the baby, her eyes drifted down to her midsection. For the first time since she had become pregnant, Molly suddenly felt a connection to the life growing inside of her, and she was concerned for its safety.

"I think I'm okay," Molly said hesitantly. "My back feels a little sore but that's about it." Turning to Lillian, she asked, "Do you think the baby's all right?"

"I think the baby is just fine. They are pretty safe floating around in all that fluid. Anyway, you did not fall that far and that wooden table is pretty springy so I think it absorbed most of the impact."

"What the hell were you doing up on a ladder?" Simon demanded angrily. "I told you I didn't want you climbing up on things."

"I was just trying to be helpful," Molly said defensively. "The baskets were dying and needed to be watered. And don't yell at me like I'm a child!"

"I didn't mean to yell. I'm sorry," he said softly, pulling her into his arms. "You just scared the hell out of me."

"Well, everything seems to be fine here," Lillian said, smiling as she reached around Simon to knock the running hose to the ground. She glanced across the greenhouse to where Tracy Benedict stood waiting. "I have some business to take care of so I'll leave you to tend to Molly, Simon."

"I'll take it from here, Mom."

Lillian looked into Molly's eyes and softly said, "Just sit here for a minute to make sure that you're all right." Molly nodded her head as it rested against Simon's chest. "You should take Molly home, Simon, and keep an eye on her," she instructed. Lillian glared at Tracy and pointed in the direction of the office. Then she hurried off after the girl, happy to have a good reason to finally fire her.

Simon held Molly and rubbed her back in a smooth circular motion. "How are you doing, Moll? Do you think you're okay?"

"Mmm-hmm." For a moment, she completely forgot about any aches or pains that she might be feeling. She was utterly content, sitting there among the sea of poinsettias with Simon's arms wrapped around her and Christmas carols drifting softly overhead. There was absolutely no reason to move and spoil the perfect moment.

Simon gently took her chin and lifted her face to his. "The thought of something happening to you . . ." he whispered. And before Molly could respond, he lowered his lips to hers and surprised her with the most perfect kiss, a tender kiss so full of emotion that she did not want it to end.

Suddenly, and to her grave disappointment, Simon pulled back. "I'm sorry, Moll," he said breathlessly. "I shouldn't have done that." Turning away from her, he added, "I should take you home."

"I don't want to go home," she said defiantly.

"I really think it would be a good idea to take you home and get someone to check you out, make sure that you're okay." Simon ran a hand through his hair.

Molly's heart burned with humiliation and fury. "I'm fine," she said through clenched teeth. She slid off the flower bench and started to walk away from Simon. Before she knew it, his hand was gripping her upper arm and he was guiding her toward the employee break area. Molly wanted to stop and tell him what she was feeling but she did not have the courage. The words were there, on the tip of her tongue, but she simply could not propel them out of her mouth. In silence, they got their coats and gear (Lillian had left Simon's things outside the office door) and made their way out of the nursery.

As Simon and Molly climbed into his truck, huge, fluffy white snowflakes were accumulating on the hood and windshield. Inside the cab of the pickup, Simon quickly started the engine and turned the dial for the heater up high. Then, without a word, he fastened his seatbelt and looked to Molly to do the same. Ignoring him, she looked out the window and tried to focus on the falling snow. Simon reached across her, pulled the belt down, fastened it and then shifted the truck into gear. He wondered what Molly was thinking and feeling, but he was afraid to ask. He was afraid of where it might lead, and he was afraid that it might end what they already had.

Several blocks from The Aunt Hill, Molly broke the silence. "Just let me out here and I'll walk the rest of the way."

"Molly, don't be ridiculous," Simon replied.

"Don't call me ridiculous," she snapped. "Now stop the truck and let me out."

"Molly, what's wrong?" Simon asked as he continued to drive. "Tell me."

"No."

"That's great. How the hell am I supposed to understand what's bothering you if you won't tell me?" Simon said in exasperation. "I shouldn't have kissed you. I know that."

"Why not?" Molly demanded.

"Because you're dealing with a lot of emotions and issues right now and you don't need me confusing things." Simon pulled over to the side of the road and put the truck in park.

"How do you know what I need or want?" she yelled, finding the courage to express herself. "I am so sick of everyone telling me what I need or what I should do. Even my aunts still treat me like a child sometimes, and I don't need you doing it as well." Molly put a hand over her eyes and dug her fingers and thumb into her temples.

"I'm trying not to treat you like a child," Simon said calmly. "But you have to tell me what's bothering you so that we can talk about it like mature adults."

Molly lowered her hand and glanced over at him. "You want to know what's wrong? I'll tell you. I'm hurt and frustrated," she said, pounding a fist against her chest. "You're always touching me and acting as if I matter to you and then you pull away and make me feel like a fool for falling in love with you."

"I thought I was doing what was best for you," Simon explained, reaching out a hand to touch her cheek. "I promised your grand-mother I would keep my distance and give you time to get over what happened to you, and I wasn't sure how you would react to my affection."

"I'm the only one who knows what's best for me," Molly said more softly. "Only I know how I feel, what I'm comfortable with, and what I want."

Unbuckling his seatbelt, Simon moved closer. "What do you want?"

"I want you," Molly whispered, looking into his eyes. Then Molly kissed Simon with all the passion that had been building in-side of her.

When Simon's lips drifted from hers and started trailing along her jaw line and down her neck, Molly softly said, "Please, take me home with you."

Pausing to look into her eyes, he asked, "Are you sure?"

"Yes. Absolutely."

Around four o'clock that afternoon, Simon was awakened from what felt like a drug-induced sleep by the ringing of the telephone. Reaching for the phone on the bedside table, he cleared his throat and quietly answered, "Hello?"

"Simon? Where is she? What's going on over there?" It was Harriett. He was expecting this.

Looking over at Molly sleeping soundly beside him, Simon whispered, "Just a minute." He crawled out of bed, grabbed his briefs from the floor, and pulled them on. He could hear Harriett ranting into the telephone, and he covered it with the palm of his hand and crept out of the room. After shutting the door, he put the phone to his ear and said, "Just calm down. Molly's here with me."

"What's going on over there?" Harriett shouted. "Your mother called to check on Molly and told us what happened. She said you two left work over two hours ago. What's going on, young man?"

"I don't think you really want to know."

"Don't get smart with me," Harriett snapped.

"I mean no disrespect. I just don't think you really want to hear what has gone on between me and Molly," Simon explained.

"You agreed to leave her alone and let her get her life in order," Harriett reminded him.

"And I was sticking to that, but Molly had her own ideas. You said that what was most important was what Molly wanted and that I had to wait until she figured it out. Well, she seems to have figured it out. We both wanted this to happen."

"This is ridiculous!" Harriett snarled. "You bring her home this instant or I'm coming over there to get her."

"She's sleeping."

"Well, wake her up!" she ordered.

"Please, Mrs. O'Connor, just listen for a moment," Simon begged. "I love Molly with all my heart and I would never do anything to hurt her. Do you understand? But there's more we need to say to each other, so I'm asking if you'll let her stay with me for awhile."

"What do you mean by 'awhile'?"

Simon walked into the kitchen and noticed that the world had gone completely white. Moving toward the windows, he said, "There's a blizzard raging out there so why don't you let her stay the night. I promise I'll bring her back to The Aunt Hill, safe and sound, first thing in the morning."

Harriett was silent for some time. Simon waited patiently for her answer. "Tell Molly to call me the minute she wakes up." There was a loud click and then a dial tone.

Simon stared out at the driving snow and inhaled deeply. Exhaling slowly, he thought about what he and Molly had started and all the obstacles they were going to face. He was so in love with her now that none of it seemed to really matter, but he did want to help negotiate some sort of resolution to the estrangement between Molly and her parents before things went much further. And then there was the baby Molly was carrying; they truly needed to talk about what she was going to do with it. He had his own thoughts and hopes, but he wasn't sure that she would agree with them. And then he began to question his own motives for being with her, as if Harriett were channeling doubts into his mind, attempting to scare him off.

All the heavy thoughts were too much for Simon. He tossed the phone onto the kitchen counter and went to crawl in bed with the woman he loved. When he pulled Molly into his arms, all the doubts vanished and a sense of peace washed over him.

Chapter Thirteen

Simon awoke the next morning to slivers of bright morning sunlight sneaking through the shutters on his bedroom windows, projecting patterns across floor. Molly slept peacefully in his arms. For one lovely moment, life was bliss, absolute perfection. He had been waiting and wondering when someone special would show up. Now he could stop searching. Molly was more than he had ever dreamed he deserved. Yes, God was definitely smiling upon him, just as He had been the day He brought Henry and Lillian Mulberry into his life. Simon was blessed and he knew it.

He lost the perfect moment when he caught sight of the digital clock on the nightstand. It was already eight o'clock, and they were expected at The Aunt Hill for breakfast that morning. He slid out of bed, snatched a bath towel off the floor to secure around his middle, and walked over to the window. He moved the lever on the shutter and was instantly blinded by a burst of bright light. He quickly closed the slats. After a minute or two, his vision adjusted and he navigated his way out of the bedroom and down the hallway to the kitchen.

Bright sunlight spilled into the house and warmed the rooms. He looked out the kitchen windows and his eyes nearly popped out of their sockets. "Holy shit! It's going to take me an hour to dig us out of here," he whispered.

A deep, thick blanket of snow was mounded into smooth drifts that reminded him of the rolling hills of southern Wisconsin. The sun was so bright and the sky so blue that Simon knew it would be cold outside; the temperature always seemed to dip after a snowstorm blew through Minnesota. He glanced at the neighboring houses and saw steam pouring out of the furnace chimneys, confirming his suspicion. A huge snowplow came barreling down his street, piling the snow several feet high along the curb, completely blocking the driveway. Simon eyed the mountain of snow and glared at the back of the plow as it progressed along its route.

Simon put the kettle on for a fast cup of cocoa and then returned to the bedroom, where he plopped the pile of Molly's clothes that he had collected along the way at the foot of the bed. Before he was tempted to crawl back in with her, he turned away and concentrated on finding something warm to wear. Quickly pulling on some briefs, a pair of long underwear, and jeans, Simon grabbed some wool socks from a drawer and then settled down on the bed beside Molly.

She stirred, and then opened her eyes to the empty space beside her. "Simon!" she cried, sitting bolt upright.

"Whoa," Simon said quietly, taking her by the shoulders. "I'm right here, honey."

"Sorry. I was expecting to wake up in your arms."

"I was hoping for that too." Simon wrapped his arms around her middle and pulled her close. "But it's after eight and I promised your grandmother that I would have you home before breakfast this morning."

"We've got time," Molly said, pulling him back down to the mattress with her.

"Oh, honey, I wish we could, but there's at least a foot and a half of snow out there, with drifts as big as elephants. It's going to take me a while to dig us out." Simon kissed her forehead, then her eyes and nose, and finally her lips. "So, why don't you go back to sleep and get some more rest while I'm clearing the driveway. I'll wake you when I come in to take a shower."

Molly turned her face away from him, "All right, but only if I get to join you in the shower."

"Well, there's a proposal I can't refuse," Simon said, laughing. "We're going to get along famously." Simon sat up and tucked the covers in around her naked body. "Now, try and sleep a bit more. You need it after last night," he teased. "I'll wake you in about an hour. I'll also call The Aunt Hill and tell them when to expect us."

"All right," Molly said, snuggling down into the covers, "although, I'm not sure I can face Granny this morning."

"Why not?" Simon combed his fingers through her thick auburn hair. "I thought you ended your conversation last night on friendly terms."

"It's just that I know she is so disappointed in me."

"Let's not jump to conclusions. Wait until you've had the chance to tell her exactly how you feel."

"You're right," Molly said, smiling. Then she let her eyes roam over his bare chest and abdomen, and softly said, "God, you're beautiful."

"Right back at you," he whispered near her lips.

Simon kissed her tenderly and then sprang off the bed. Pulling first a tee-shirt and then a sweatshirt over his head, he instructed, "Now, go back to sleep, princess, and I'll wake you with a kiss later." He stopped in the doorway to gaze at Molly one last time. "I love you, Moll."

Looking back at him with sleepy eyes, she replied, "I love you, too." Simon left the room and she drifted back to sleep with a smile on her face.

As Simon was cutting a path down the driveway with his snowblower, his father pulled up in his battered old Suburban with the plow on the front. He beeped his horn and motioned for Simon to move out of the way. Simon turned out of the drive and onto his sidewalk, while his father plowed the driveway.

It took Simon thirty minutes to clear his sidewalk and then shovel the stairs and walkway up to the house, after which he quickly cleared off his neighbor's sidewalk and stairs. And as he and his father were finishing up the narrow sidewalk that led to her garage, Betty Sullivan poked her head out of the house. "Thank you, you angels! I'll stop by with a loaf of bread and some cinnamon rolls later this afternoon, Simon!"

Simon and Henry waved at her in response.

After finishing up at Betty Sullivan's, Simon walked his father back to his truck. "Thanks, Dad. I would've been at this for hours!"

"My pleasure, son. I thought you might need a hand this morning," Henry replied, wrapping an arm around Simon's shoulder as they walked along. "I'm actually surprised that you are up and walking around."

"Nice, Dad," Simon said sarcastically, giving his father a playful shove.

"Oh, c'mon," Henry said playfully, sticking a gloved hand into Simon's side. "A little ribbing is good for you." When they reached his truck, Henry grabbed the door handle and turned toward his son. "So, how is Molly this morning? Harriett was so worked up over you two that I thought she was going to have a stroke!"

"Moll is fine. She's great," Simon said, pausing a moment to look at his house.

"What is it?" Henry asked, eyeing Simon.

"I want to marry her, Dad. I want to spend the rest of my life with her."

"I think that's wonderful," Henry said happily. "I know a few gray-haired women that are going to have a tough time with it right away—including your mother—but they'll all come around. I can see that you and Molly were meant to be together."

"There's no doubt in my mind about that," Simon said forcefully. "It's just that . . ."

"What?"

"Oh, nothing. I'm just thinking too much." Simon rubbed at his eye sockets with his gloved hand.

"Simon, you and Molly are lucky to have each other," Henry said, squeezing his son's shoulder. "I think she's especially fortunate to have you in her life after all that she has been through and the way her family has treated her. You can have a bright future together despite the fact that she's carrying someone's child. I'm convinced of it."

"I sure hope so," Simon said, sighing heavily. "I just don't want her to decide in seven years that I'm not exactly what she wanted."

"Why on earth would you say such a thing?"

"Because she's so young . . . What am I saying? I'm starting to sound like her grandmother!" Simon said in dismay. "I just want to be with her for as long as she wants to be with me."

"And you shall be," Henry said decisively. "And I'm pretty certain that it will be for a lifetime. Anyway, you can't worry about things you have no control over or you'll make yourself sick. Just go with what feels right."

"Of course, you're right." Simon smiled and nodded. "Thanks, Dad. Thanks for everything."

"My pleasure." Henry slapped Simon on the back and said, "Well, I'd better get over to the nursery and plow the lots."

"Are we going to open up today?"

"Hell, no one is going to be out driving around today," Henry scoffed. "It'll take most people the better part of the day to dig out." Pulling a tissue from the glove compartment, Henry blew his nose. "No. I think Stillwater can live without the nursery for one day."

"Great!" Simon said, grinning.

"Enjoy the day with Molly," Henry called, waving out the window as he pulled away in his truck. Simon waved until the truck reached the end of the block, where Henry honked the horn and turned in the direction of the nursery. When he had disappeared, Simon gathered his shovel and hurried up his driveway with the snow-blower. Once everything was put away in its proper place in the garage, Simon dashed across the yard and into the warmth of the house.

He found Molly where he had left her, snuggled under the covers, sound asleep. Sitting down beside her, he gazed upon her for a moment. She looked so young and innocent with her seamless face sprinkled with freckles. It was hard to imagine that she was going to be a mother.

Softly, Simon caressed her cheek with the back of his fingers. Molly stirred a bit but remained asleep so Simon started kissing her neck and then her ear lobe, and by the time he worked his way around to her lips, her eyes were open and she was smiling.

"Are you going to wake me up this way every time I spend the night with you?" she asked.

"Probably," Simon said smirking. "Why, have you got a problem with it?"

"Actually," Molly answered as she turned to look up at him, "I would prefer that you were naked and lying next to me when you did it."

"That can be arranged," Simon replied in an even tone. "But

just not today, honey. You need to get out of bed and into the shower or your grandmother is going to come storming through that door and drag you out of here by your feet."

"Okay, okay." Molly sat up and pushed him off the bed and onto the floor.

As they were racing each other to the garage, Molly slid on an icy patch of snow and went down hard on her bottom.

"Molly!"

"Ow, ow, ow, ow, ow!" Molly yelled, rubbing at her rear end. "Why is it that I'm always falling and getting hurt when I'm near you?"

"I'm sorry, honey," Simon said, helping her off the ground. "Are you all right?"

"No."

"Would you like me to kiss it and make it better?" Simon teased.

"Very funny," Molly said sarcastically. Then she looked up at him and smiled coyly. "You could kiss my lips and maybe that would make me feel better." Simon pulled her into his arms and kissed her with great tenderness.

He pulled away from Molly and whispered near her lips, "There, are you all better?"

"Oh, yes," Molly sighed with her eyes closed underneath her sunglasses. "Can you please do that again?"

"Later, honey. Right now, I've got to get you home, so mush! Let's go!" Simon took Molly by the hand and led her toward the truck.

They made their way over to Chestnut Street, fighting patches if ice and unplowed streets along the way, once nearly colliding with a parked car. They were listening to music playing softly on the radio when suddenly Simon said, "Moll, I was thinking about something while you were drying your hair, and I want to talk to you about it."

"All right." She turned in her seat to give Simon her full attention. "What is it?"

"I was thinking that now that we know everything is great between us physically, maybe we should try and abstain for awhile, perhaps until the baby is born."

"I don't understand," Molly said nervously. "Don't you want to make love to me like this? Does it disgust you?"

"God, no," Simon said, reaching for her hand. Pulling up to the curb in front of The Aunt Hill, Simon put the truck in park, unbuckled his seat belt and turned toward Molly. "Honey, it's not that I don't want you. I do. Even as we're sitting here talking, I do. And, I can hardly believe that I'm suggesting this because I'm not sure that I'll even make it a day without giving into the temptation of your body. Hell, I couldn't keep my hands off you last night, remember?"

Molly smiled at the memory.

"But you're special to me, Moll. I'm in love with you. And I don't want this just to be about sex. Besides, it might make our relationship a little easier to swallow for your grandmother."

"Of course you're right," Molly said, turning away from Simon. Blinking away tears, Molly looked out her window at The Aunt Hill. It looked like something out of Currier and Ives, with the snow blanketing the house top and drifts hanging precariously from the porch roof. "Just promise me that you'll be there when this baby is gone," Molly said softly.

Simon turned her face back to look at him. "I promise," he said, staring directly into her eyes. Then he kissed her until the blood left her brain and she forgot about everything except the taste and softness of his lips.

On the porch, Molly fished the key out of her backpack and shoved it into the lock. She pushed open the heavy oak door and stepped into the foyer of The Aunt Hill with Simon close on her heels. The big door slammed behind them. Simon helped Molly out of her coat, removed his own and then hung both of them on the coat stand just inside the door.

"Molly? Is that you?" called a voice from the direction of the kitchen.

"Yes, Aunt Millie," Molly called back. "We're here."

An instant later, Mildred came running out of the kitchen and threw her arms around Molly before the girl knew what was happening. Holding Molly so tightly that she could not breathe, Mildred whispered, "It's good to have you home, sweetheart."

When Mildred finally released her, Molly took in a deep breath and watched in amusement as her great-aunt did the same thing to Simon.

"We've been holding breakfast for you two," Mildred said, releasing Simon and moving them both in the direction of the kitchen. "Your grandmother is as cranky as a starved lion, so watch out."

When the trio entered the kitchen, they found Gertrude busy pouring pancake batter onto the griddle and Harriett just sitting down at the table with a pot of coffee in her hand. Gertrude paused a moment to welcome them and wish them good morning while Harriett simply glared at them from her seat.

Quickly, Molly walked around the table and kissed her grandmother on the cheek. "Good morning, Granny," Molly said cheerfully. "Sorry we are so late but–"

"But here we are, and we're both starving," Simon interrupted, not wanting Molly to make any excuses for their behavior, nor any fabrications. "How can we help, Miss Gertrude?" He wrapped an arm around Molly from behind and pulled her close to his body.

Harriett sneered, "I hope you two are headed to confession after breakfast."

"Hattie, please," Mildred said in exasperation.

"Betty Sullivan called ten minutes ago to say that she saw you two mauling one another in the driveway this morning, and by now the entire town knows what you were up to last night!"

"That's not true, Granny," Molly said defensively.

Simon gave her upper arms a gentle squeeze. "Since when do we care what other people think?" he asked the room in general. "That sounds more like Molly's parents' department to me."

"Don't start getting smart," Harriett warned. "I have a mind to kick you out of this house and never let you back in."

"Granny, stop it!" Molly yelled, startling them all. "I won't let you talk to Simon that way. Neither of us has done anything wrong."

"Now you are changing the laws of our religion to suit yourself," she replied sarcastically. "You have a baby in your belly, girl. This all began with something wrong."

"Exactly," Molly shot back. "The boy who raped me was wrong. Not Simon. Simon loves me and wants me despite all that's happened."

"And what about the baby?" Harriett demanded angrily.

"I want to be a father to it," Simon said softly. The room went silent and all the women stared at him in shock.

Molly turned in his arms and looked at him with wide eyes. "What?" she whispered.

"I know we didn't talk about this but I was up all night thinking about you giving the baby away, and I don't want you to," Simon explained.

"This is absolute nonsense," Harriett scoffed. "No one is going to keep that baby."

"No it's not," Molly replied, still looking at Simon. "You have no say when it comes to this baby, Granny. This is my choice. No one else's."

"Yes, like the choice that got you pregnant in the first place," Harriett said meanly.

"That's enough!" Simon and Mildred said in unison.

"Fine! You all stick together in your little club because *you* know what's best, and I don't!" Harriett yelled. Then she turned and stormed out of the room, slamming the library door behind her.

"Granny!"

"Let her go, honey," Simon said, grabbing Molly's arm. "Give her a minute."

"No. I have more that I want to say to her."

"Simon is right, dear," Mildred said softly. "It's best to leave her alone for awhile."

Molly struggled away from Simon's grip and moved swiftly across the kitchen, bursting through the library door and slamming it soundly behind her.

"Oh, dear," Gertrude said under her breath.

Mildred and Simon looked at one another and held each other's gaze for a long time.

Molly found Harriett sitting at the big oak desk, rummaging through the top drawer. Taking a deep breath, she crossed the room and stood beside her grandmother.

"Granny, stop treating me like a child," Molly said angrily. "You don't need to remind me of the mistakes I've made. I know what they are and I've learned from them. You know that."

Harriett turned away and looked out the window.

"Granny, please," Molly said more softly. "I'm sorry I lost my temper. I'm a little hormonal, as you can imagine, and I'm very defensive of Simon."

Again, Harriett did not respond.

Molly dropped to her knees beside her grandmother and settled her bottom on her heels. "Please understand how much I love him," she begged. "I trust him more than anyone, and I feel as if no man will ever harm me again as long as I'm with him."

"You don't know men," Harriett countered. "I have much more experience than you do, and they can't be so easily trusted."

"He's not Raymond Archer, Granny."

Harriett turned and stared at Molly in surprise. "My situation is so much different," Molly explained. "Simon is not married and I'm the one with a baby on the way. Simon is a good man, the best man. He knows how to love because he has been so truly loved all of his life."

"I told him to leave you alone and wait until you had grown up a bit . . . accomplished some things, and then he goes and pulls a stunt like yesterday," Harriett said, angrily punching her thigh with a fist.

"He didn't force me into anything, Granny. I was the one who pressed the issue. At the moment, I wanted him and needed him, for several different reasons. Can you understand how I needed to know some things?"

"That doesn't make it right."

"Why not? Why can't it be right even though the church says it's wrong?" Molly demanded. "I'm not promiscuous, Granny. And if all goes the way I hope it will, Simon will be the only man that I will ever be with. We truly love each other and we are committed to one another."

"You are nineteen years old, Molly. You can't know what you want or what will make you happy for a lifetime," Harriett informed her.

"That's not true," she replied forcefully. "I've had to grow up very fast since all of this began and have had to learn to make the right choices, which I believe I'm doing. And I've tried so hard to make you proud of me and to try and get you to love me."

Harriett closed her eyes and turned away. Reaching up to cover the hand in Harriett's lap with her own, Molly cried, "Please, Granny, I need you to love me. You and the aunts are the only family I have now. I don't want you to be angry with me all the time or disappointed in me, the way my parents have always been. And I need you to love Simon, for my sake."

Harriett looked back into Molly's watery eyes and clasped her hand. Molly pushed herself up onto her knees and wrapped her arms around her grandmother's middle, resting her head upon her soft bosom. Slowly, Harriett's arms moved to encircle Molly's shoulders and she pulled the girl tightly to her chest.

"Shh. It's not good for you to get upset," Harriett whispered. "We will get this all sorted out." She did not let go of Molly for a long time, and when she finally did, it was with reluctance.

Sitting back on her heels again, Molly wiped the tears from her cheeks and said, "If it makes you feel any better, Simon suggested that we not sleep together again until after the baby is born, and I agreed with him."

"Why? What do you mean?"

"He doesn't want our relationship just to be about sex," Molly said, blushing slightly.

"Well," Harriett said, nodding her head, "I think that's wise."

"See, Granny. He doesn't want to hurt me and he wants so much more from our relationship."

"No, he doesn't want to hurt you," Harriett agreed.

Brushing the hair back from Molly's face, Harriett looked her granddaughter over. "You look tired," she said with concern. "Perhaps you should go upstairs and lie down for awhile."

"I think I might," Molly replied. "I don't feel very well."

"Have you had anything to eat this morning?"

"No."

"Well, get out to the kitchen and eat a good breakfast," Harriett ordered. "You'll feel much better."

"All right." Molly rose from the floor. Looking down at her grandmother, she softly said, "I love you, Granny."

Harriett simply nodded her head in response.

Chapter Fourteen

Molly walked out of the library, and Gertrude served up plates of pancakes and bacon for everyone. They talked in hushed tones at the kitchen table while Harriett remained barricaded behind the library door. Operating on just a few hours of sleep, Molly felt miserable and did not eat very much. She was confused about whether or not things had changed between she and her grandmother. Could she expect different behavior from Harriett in the future? She did not expect her grandmother to throw her arms around her and cry, "I love you!" but she had hoped for some sign of reassurance that they would not be having the same argument over and over again. Most of all, Molly hoped that her grandmother would accept Simon and stop bullying him. Along with the morning sickness, Molly's head began to ache and she slumped in her chair.

"Honey, you look a little green," Simon observed. He swallowed his last bite of pancakes and rose from the table. "Come on. I'll take you upstairs and tuck you in. You'll feel better after a nap." Molly took his hand and let him pull her up out of her chair.

"Here, dear," Gertrude said handing her a glass. "A little ginger ale might help your stomach." She kissed Molly on the cheek and patted her arm.

"Thanks, Aunt Gertie. I'm sure it will help," Molly said optimistically.

"All right, Moll, say goodnight," Simon instructed as he pulled her toward the door.

"Have a good rest and feel better," Mildred said, blowing her a kiss.

"Bye," Molly said, waving.

Simon led her upstairs and sat beside her on the bed for awhile, gently rubbing her back. In a few minutes, she was fast asleep, and he hurried back downstairs. Gertrude was preparing a tray of food for Harriett when he walked back into the kitchen.

"I'll take that in to her," Simon offered, quickly picking the tray up off the table before anyone could object.

"Are you sure you want to go in there?" Mildred asked from her station at the sink where she was scrubbing away the bacon grease from the frying pan.

"Hattie can be pretty nasty when she's mad," Gertrude warned.

"I can take her. I lift weights." Balancing the tray on his right hand, Simon playfully raised it above his head.

"Take care, Simon," Mildred warned. "She really is not as tough as she pretends to be."

"I figured that out a long time ago," he replied. Then Simon left the kitchen and the two women heard him knock on the library door before he opened it and closed it with a gentle click.

"I thought you might be hungry," Simon said as he approached Harriett. She was still sitting in the desk chair, her body as rigid as a tree trunk, and she did not acknowledge him. He noted that she was staring down at a closed file folder sitting on the blotter. He placed the tray on the end of the desk, dragged a chair over, and sat down across from her.

"Did you and Molly have a good talk?" Simon asked softly. Harriett did not respond. "She's overly tired and not feeling very well, so she may have been a bit emotional."

"You're the reason she's so tired," Harriett said flatly.

"Do you really want to go there?"

Harriett turned away to look out the window.

"Listen, I'm sorry," Simon said, hoping that she would turn to look at him so she could see that he was being sincere. "I know that I made an unofficial promise to you and you think that I broke it, but it was Molly's choice. She was ready."

"How do you know?" Harriett sneered, still refusing to look at him.

"Because Molly knew, and you and I agreed that it was all about her. Her decision, her choice."

"I didn't say that," Harriett snapped.

"With all due respect, yes, you did. And you also told me to make her happy for the rest of her life, which led me to believe that you were ready to accept my having a relationship with her." Simon paused for a moment and dropped his eyes to the floor. "Look, I'm just trying to be open and honest with you," he said, gesturing with his hands. "Molly means the world to both of us and it's important to her that we get along. I want to be able to talk candidly with you about anything because that's how I was brought up." Simon looked up at her profile and willed her to look at him. "My parents taught me to respect people's thoughts and opinions, and I'm simply trying to show my respect for you by speaking plainly."

Harriett turned to look at Simon. He did have a point. She stared at him for a moment, and then said, "Why are you here?"

"Because I love your granddaughter and I want to marry her," Simon said evenly. "And I want to ask your permission to do so."

Harriett could not hide her surprise. "Have you asked her?"

"Not yet."

"You've only known each other for six weeks," she said flatly.

"Sometimes that's all it takes to know that you've found the person you're supposed to share your life with," Simon reasoned. "At the risk of sounding overly dramatic, I don't want to live my life without Molly now. She's a part of me, and her happiness and comfort are extremely important to me."

Folding her hands in front of her on the desk, Harriett leaned forward and challenged, "She is only nineteen."

"She'll be twenty in a week," he corrected. "And she's going to have a baby in approximately seven months."

"And you want to be a father to the baby."

"I want to be the father of Molly's child," Simon clarified. "I want it to be our baby. I want to give her that option. That's why I want to marry her soon, so that my name will be on the baby's birth certificate."

Harriett looked away from him and back out the window, pausing to consider all that he had said to her. Simon sat quietly, watching her while he gave her the time she needed to decide how she felt about his explanation.

Harriett turned back to him and quietly asked, "Why do you want that baby?"

Looking her squarely in the eye, Simon replied, "Because I was unwanted and someone rescued me. It's my turn to do the same."

"But that baby will be a constant reminder of what happened."

"Not if Molly can get past the event, which she seems to be doing without much anguish or effort at this point." Simon reached across the desk and covered her hands with his own. "This baby is a part of Molly, and it's sure to look like her and be like her, despite the DNA contributed by the asshole who raped her. I want to be able to love that part of her as well."

Gripping Harriett's hands tightly, he asked, "Don't you want a chance to love your great-grandchild? I thought that's what we all learn to live for when we've gotten beyond the material trappings of life and finally realize what's important."

"My God, you're a wise old soul," she whispered, staring at him. Harriett blinked and shook her head. Then she pulled her hands out from underneath Simon's and asked, "Don't you want children of your own?"

"More than anything," Simon assured her, pulling his arms back and reclining in his chair. "But not until Molly is ready; not until she has finished school and accomplished some of the goals she may set for herself."

"Then why muck things up by keeping this baby?"

"Because I believe it needs us, all of us," Simon replied. "She can still go to school and chase her dreams because she will have all of us, including my parents, to help out with the baby."

Sliding the file folder across to him, Harriett said, "I think you should take a look at this."

"What is it?"

"I hired a private investigator to find Molly's attacker and, with the help of the students at that party, he narrowed the field down to two U of M football players." Simon did not reach for the file. "All we need now is DNA from the baby and we'll have him."

Simon stared at the closed folder for some time. Then he looked up at Harriett and said, "Burn it. Get rid of it before Molly ever finds it."

"What on earth are you talking about? Don't you want to see justice served?"

"For whose sake?" Simon demanded. "Yours or Molly's?" Leaning forward in his chair, he said, "She doesn't want to know. She's made that clear to all of us." Harriett turned away as if she were refusing to listen to him. "Molly has made so much progress with Helen and they've agreed that it's all right that she doesn't want to find this guy or press charges. Don't you see this could set her so far back that it might take years to get her to where she is now?"

"I can't believe that you, of all people, don't want to see this criminal thrown in jail," Harriett said angrily.

"Believe me, I want more done to him than that," Simon said with fury in his eyes. "But more importantly, I want what's best for Molly. I want her to be able to forget about what was done to her so that we can have a happy life together."

"Then why keep the baby?" Harriett cried.

"Because when the moment comes for her to give it away, she might not be able to," Simon explained. "I want her to have the option of keeping it so that she doesn't have to live with guilt and regret for the rest of her life."

Harriett nodded slowly and pulled the file folder back across the desk. "Please, destroy it," Simon begged.

"No," Harriett said firmly. "I am going to keep it in case Molly changes her mind." Simon dropped his head and covered his eyes with his hand. "But, you may ask her to marry you. And if she agrees, you will have my blessing. I can see how much she loves you and trusts you, and I believe you truly love her."

Simon slowly raised his head and looked directly into her eyes. "Promise we'll have your blessing?"

"Yes, yes," Harriett answered, waving a hand dismissively. "Now, go away and let me eat my cold breakfast in peace."

Grinning, Simon rose from his chair and walked toward the door. "I think you and I are going to get along just fine, Granny."

Inspecting the food on the tray with her nose in the air, Harriett replied, "I never said you could call me that."

When Molly awoke from her nap, refreshed and feeling worlds better, the crowd at The Aunt Hill sat down to a late lunch of soup, bread and cheese. Harriett was surprisingly civil which made Molly uneasy. She carefully considered everything her grandmother said, searching for double meanings and sarcasm. After lunch, Simon and Harriett played cribbage while Molly helped her aunts clean up, and she noted that they seemed to be getting along much better. Simon had been sitting beside Molly reading the newspaper when she awoke from her nap, and he had informed her that he and Harriett had had a heart-to-heart talk and he thought things would change for the better between them. Molly was happy to see that his assumption was correct, and she hoped for the same situation between her and her grandmother.

Simon spent the entire day at The Aunt Hill, helping the sisters with household maintenance projects and spending time with Molly, hoping that the day would never end. After knowing the pleasure and joy of having Molly in his bed, he did not relish going home alone to an empty house or cold sheets. Suddenly, his entire world had changed and he knew that he could not go back to the way it was and be truly happy. When Simon said goodnight to her in the foyer that evening, a sense of desperation strayed into his kisses and betrayed him to Molly, who begged him to take her back to Pine Street with him. Resolved to stick to their agreement, he managed to tear himself away from her and walk out of The Aunt Hill. When he stepped out into the frosty night air, Simon realized that he had never felt so alone in all his life and it unnerved him.

The following Sunday, Simon was taking Molly to his parents' home for a family dinner. Thanks to Betty Sullivan, the entire town knew that they were an official item and tongues were wagging about the mismatch. Simon's parents were not at all surprised, but Lillian still had reservations because of Molly's age and situation. Simon hoped that if his mother got to know Molly better and to under-stand how much they meant to each other that she might relax and get over her worries, so a Sunday family dinner seemed like a perfect opportunity to get the ball rolling.

Molly was getting ready for their dinner party that evening when there was a soft knock upon her bedroom door. Snapping the waist band of her tights into place, she frantically smoothed her skirt down around her hips and legs and called, "Come in."

It was Harriett.

"You look nice," she said, eyeing Molly from top to bottom.

"Thank you. I want to look nice for Mr. and Mrs. Mulberry."

"Molly, you don't have to prove anything to the Mulberrys," Harriett said looking directly at her granddaughter. "They already know you and like you just as you are."

"And do you like Simon . . . just as he is?"

Harriett looked over Molly's shoulder and paused for a mo-ment. "Yes, I do. But I still think you are a bit young to know if he is what you want."

"He's what I want," Molly replied firmly. "I just wish you'd have a little faith in my ability to make my own decisions and to know what's best for me."

"I do have faith in you, Molly. You've proven yourself to be ca-pable of making good decisions. I just want you to make the most of your life," Harriett explained.

"I will, Granny. I promise."

"Very well," Harriett replied, turning to leave. "I'll let you fin-ish getting ready."

"All right. I'm just going to curl my hair and put on some makeup. Then I'll be down." Molly watched her grandmother walk out the door and she smiled. The winds were beginning to shift.

Simon arrived to pick up Molly but had to wait with the sisters in the parlor while she finished getting ready. Joining Harriett in a glass of scotch, the four of them had a nice talk about the developer who was trying to buy the land that the nursery was sitting on and that Simon now owned, since his father had gifted it to him several years earlier. Harriett was astounded to hear the sum of money he had been offered and had turned down, and she realized that, with all of his assets, Simon's future was financially secure.

When Molly appeared, she looked quite stunning. Everyone agreed that she was, without a doubt, glowing with health and happiness. The blush in her cheeks from all the compliments added to her beauty which gave them all something else to talk about, until Simon finally came to her rescue and dragged her away. The three elderly women followed them into the foyer and watched as Simon helped Molly into her coat. She bundled up with a scarf, hat and gloves while Simon pulled his coat and gloves on. There were hugs and kisses all around, and Harriett surprised her sisters by taking part in the affectionate display. She even went so far as to smile at Simon when he and Molly walked out the door.

When they were in the truck, Simon immediately pulled Molly into his arms and kissed her hungrily, slowly shifting gears to kiss her with great tenderness. He had been dying to kiss her since he arrived at The Aunt Hill, having not seen her all day. Feeling much better, he turned the key in the ignition and focused on his driving. As they pulled away from the curb, Molly looked out the window at what had truly become home to her and she marveled at all the love and affection contained within its walls. What a world of difference from the house she had grown up in. She was beginning to realize that her family was fading from her life, and she thanked God every night that she had made the choice to come to The Aunt Hill for help when her parents had abandoned her.

"I wish my brother would answer my letters," Molly said to the passenger window.

"What, honey?" Simon said, glancing over at her.

"I was just thinking that I wish my brother would answer my letters and contact me," Molly answered, looking back at him. "He can't think the way my parents do about all of this because he has never seen eye-to-eye with them. He was always there for me when we were growing up, defending me against my mother. His love, affection and friendship were all I had."

"How many letters have you written him?" Simon asked, refocusing the conversation. The mere mention of Molly's parents filled his head with violent thoughts.

"I've written twice since all this happened and he hasn't written back or called at all."

"But, honey, didn't you say that he's studying abroad in Russia? Maybe he hasn't received the letters yet."

"But I sent them through the university address that was given to me by the study abroad program," Molly explained.

Simon sensed that she was starting to get upset and decided to end the discussion. "Don't worry, Moll. I promise you that I'll find him." Simon pulled his leather glove off with his teeth and reached over to caress Molly's cheek. "Tomorrow, I'll call the University of Michigan and get this sorted out. We'll find him."

"I'm sorry. I'm just an emotional basket case today. I'm a little nervous about going to your parents' house," Molly confessed.

"Why?"

"It's just that, now that they know you and I are serious about each other, I can tell your mother is not real thrilled about it."

"Honey, she's just worried about your situation with the baby," Simon explained. "She likes things neat and tidy. But most of all, she's concerned for my happiness. And when she sees that I have truly found it in you, she'll be fine."

Simon smiled at Molly. "We just need to give her time."

"I guess you're right," Molly said, settling back into the seat and looking out of her window into the darkness, searching for house lights in the trees along Highway 95.

Simon marveled at how easily she was able to change her state of mind. Was it a sign of instability on her part or the result of a deep faith in him? Whatever the reason, he certainly wanted to understand it better. It suddenly dawned on him how he could accomplish this.

"I was thinking that I would like to come to one of your counseling sessions with you if it wouldn't make you too uncomfortable," he said cautiously.

"Why?" Molly asked, turning to look at him.

"Because I think it would help us understand each other better and help me more clearly understand what you've gone through," Simon answered honestly.

"I'd like that."

"Really?"

"Really," Molly assured him.

"Well, then, let's set it up," Simon said happily as he turned the truck into his parents' driveway.

The light was already on over the back door. The cottage-style house was outlined in twinkling white Christmas lights that made it look like something out of a fairy story. Peering through the windscreen, Molly took it all in.

"How charming," she said softly as she undid her seatbelt.

"Yes, it is," Simon agreed, doing the same. Simon gave her a quick kiss and added, "Now, get ready for my dad's bear hug. He always greets me with one and I'm sure he'll do the same to you."

"I don't mind," Molly said happily. "I love hugs, and I can hardly remember my parents hugging me. In fact, I don't ever remember my mother hugging me."

Simon stared at Molly for a moment. Then he opened his door, jumped out of the truck, and was racing around to help Molly out of the pickup when Henry burst out of the house and called in his booming voice, "Welcome, welcome, welcome!"

The evening turned out to be one of the happiest and most enjoyable events in Molly's life. She was able to relax and be herself without her grandmother's critical eyes glued to her all evening. And Simon felt comfortable enough to show his affection for her in front of his parents which Molly believed was a strong declaration of his love for her. More importantly, Lillian did not seem in the least bit upset when Simon would place a hand on Molly's knee, drape an arm around her shoulder, or hold onto her hand. In fact, she felt as if she had been accepted as part of their family that evening which made her wonder what Simon had in mind for the future.

Throughout the evening, Henry and Lillian had entertained Molly with stories of Simon's youth which had made her laugh until her jaw hurt and her sides ached. And much to her surprise and amusement, she learned that Simon had not always been so wonderful. In fact, he had been quite a challenge when he was growing up and he had suffered through many severe and lengthy punishments. He, himself, admitted that it was his father's discipline, along with his mother's abundant affection, that had made him into the man he had become. And Molly had been bold enough to thank them for raising Simon the way they had, for she was currently benefiting from all of their hard work.

Molly did not want the evening to end, but both Simon and Henry were being sensible about everyone getting a good night's sleep before the following day's work at the nursery. Even Lillian seemed sorry that their fun had to come to an end. After hugs and kisses, Molly and Simon bid his parents goodnight and crawled into the pickup truck for the journey back to The Aunt Hill. Although she was tired, Molly talked non-stop during the drive home, expressing to Simon, over and over again, how much she had enjoyed herself.

He was glad the evening had been pleasant for her and that his parents had been so kind and welcoming. Simon secretly hoped that his parents could fill the void in Molly's life, left by her mother and father, and that they would soon love her as a daughter. He wanted to marry her before long so that they could be together day and night. Despite his resolve, he was already weakening in his commitment to abstinence. The memories of the night he spent with Molly were too good to let slip away, and they were constantly tempting him.

Chapter Fifteen

The week leading up to Christmas was an absolute mad house at the nursery. Special orders for floral arrangements and gift-wrapped poinsettias kept the staff in a state of perpetual motion. The cash registers rang incessantly as customers unloaded their carts of gift ornaments and holiday decorations. Molly got a chance to arrange some evergreen and floral centerpieces for special orders and she wowed the customers with her perfectly balanced creations. She loved doing it so much that she was disappointed when she was moved back into the greenhouses to help reorganize and get the spring plantings underway. Despite the fact that the world was anticipating the Christmas holidays, Mulberry's was already making preparations for Easter, with the planting of lilies, hydrangeas and mums.

But regardless of the hectic days and the heavy workload, Molly and Simon managed to eat their lunch together every day and to steal kisses when no one was looking. None of Molly's co-workers knew that she was pregnant, and now that she was beginning to show a little bit, she was starting to fret over the eventuality of having to explain just how she got pregnant. Simon tried to ease her anxiety by suggesting they simply say that someone at college had gotten her pregnant, and the coward did not want the responsibility of it. It was not exactly the truth but it certainly was not a lie, and beyond it, there was no need for further explanation.

As promised, Simon telephoned the University of Michigan right away in an effort to locate Molly's brother, Tim. After several tries, he managed to find a helpful woman who informed him that Tim's term abroad had ended the week prior and that no one had any idea if he had returned to the States or if he was off traveling around Russia before his final semester. However, the woman assured Simon that the letters Molly had sent through their offices had definitely been forwarded to her brother at the address they had been given before he left for St. Petersburg. She suggested that perhaps Tim had moved out of the student housing into an apartment over the course of the term and was not checking his mailbox. Simon felt miserable that he did not have better information for Molly, but he promised to track her brother down at school as soon as the new term started in January.

On the Tuesday evening before Christmas, after Molly's last day of work before the holiday, Molly and Simon pulled into the driveway at The Aunt Hill in anticipation of Aunt Millie's famous roast chicken and dumpling dinner. Gertrude flew out onto the porch, motioning for them to hurry inside. Terrified that something had happened to either Mildred or Harriett, they ran to the house, only to learn that Molly's brother was on the telephone talking with Harriett. Molly dashed to the phone in the kitchen. Harriett was still chatting with Tim, and when she saw Molly, she gave her a stern look and pointed toward the library.

"Well, Tim, it was good to talk with you and to get things straight," Harriett said loudly. "Molly just arrived, so I will turn you over to her. Good luck with school and keep up the hard work." Harriett listened for Molly to pick up the receiver in the library and then hung up.

Simon and the sisters puttered about in the kitchen, preparing dinner and setting the table while they waited for Molly to finish her call. They were all curious. Simon was hopeful that at least one member of Molly's immediate family would be understanding and show his love and support for her. Although she had the affection and encouragement of her family in Stillwater, Simon knew that Molly would not be truly happy until she received her family's forgiveness and love.

Forty-five minutes later, Molly emerged from the library grinning from ear to ear. Her joyful mood quickly spread through the kitchen like a ray of sunshine popping out from behind a cloud. "He believes me and he still loves me!" she said excitedly. Dancing across the room and into Simon's open arms, she cried, "What a great Christmas present. *This* is going to be a happy Christmas."

Simon wrapped his arms tightly around her, lifted her off the floor and said, "It certainly is."

"Oh, how wonderful!" Gertrude cried, clasping her hands together under her chin.

"I couldn't agree more," Mildred added, patting both Molly and Simon on their backs.

"I'm starving. Let's eat," Harriett grumbled as she sat down at the table.

Christmas Eve morning, Molly was awakened by Simon bumping through her bedroom door with a glowing breakfast tray and singing "Happy Birthday" in a lovely tenor. Still half asleep, Molly stared at him in bewilderment. For a brief moment, she wondered if she was stuck in a dream. Was it really her birthday? How could she have forgotten?

Sliding onto the bed beside her with the breakfast tray, Simon quickly kissed her cheek and finished the song with backup from her aunts. "Happy birthday," he said, settling the tray on the bed.

Molly sat up and propped herself on a pile of pillows. The breakfast tray was illuminated by two candles burning in a stack of pancakes that dripped with melted butter and syrup. There was also a crystal vase with a red rose and a stack of white envelopes next to the plate of pancakes. Harriett sauntered into the room with a wrapped present in her hands and walked around the bed.

"Wow!" was all Molly could think to say.

"Happy birthday, Molly!" her aunts cried, beaming at her from the foot of the bed. They, too, were holding brightly wrapped parcels.

Slapping the palms of her hands over her eyes and rubbing them in circles, Molly asked no one in particular, "Am I dreaming?"

When she heard Simon's familiar laugh near her ear and the press of his lips on her wrist, she lowered her hands. "You're not dreaming, honey," he assured her. "This is all very real."

Looking up at her grandmother and aunts with bright eyes, Molly exclaimed, "This is the best surprise I've ever had! I completely forgot it was my birthday. I've just had so much on my mind."

"Well, there's more to come," Simon informed her. "So make a wish and blow out those candles and we'll get things underway."

"All right," Molly said agreeably. Closing her eyes and grasping Simon's hand, she took a moment to formulate her wish and then opened her eyes and blew out the candles. Everyone applauded and Simon moved the tray off the bed and onto the floor.

"Now it's time for presents," Simon announced. "Who wants to be first?"

"Oh, me," Gertrude said, handing a large box to Molly. "Please, open mine first."

Molly looked at Gertrude with excitement in her eyes. Settling the big box on top of her outstretched legs, she began to pull away the wrapping paper.

Impatiently, Simon reached over and tore a huge swatch from the box. "Come on. We'll be here all day if you don't get a little more aggressive. Aren't you anxious to see what's inside?"

"Obviously, you are," Molly teased, continuing to slowly pull strips of paper from the box.

"Moll!" Simon cried, reaching for the box again.

"All right, all right," she said, slapping his hands away. "I'll go faster."

Molly wildly ripped the paper and tore open the box. Peeling away layers of tissue paper, she found a neatly folded black wool coat. Pulling it from the box, she held it up to inspect the cut and style and was very pleased with the look of it, especially the fake fur cuffs and high collar. "Oh, Aunt Gertie! It's lovely! Thank you so much!"

"You're welcome, dear." Gertrude beamed in response to Molly's delight. "It should get you through the winter, even when you start to get bigger around the middle," she informed her. "Millie and I talked to the sales girl about your situation and told her your size, and she assured us that this coat would work well and keep you very warm."

Hugging the coat to her chest, Molly looked up at her aunt and said, "Aunt Gertie, I love it."

"I'm so glad, dear."

Simon collected the box and the paper and dropped them on the floor. Then he took the coat from Molly and draped it over the headboard behind him.

"Here, sweetie," Mildred said, handing Molly another brightly wrapped package. "Open mine next."

Molly took the gift and quickly tore away the wrapping paper. "Is that fast enough for you, Simon?"

"Much better," he said, laughing.

Molly opened the large box to find a maternity kit from Bloomingdales that contained several different articles of clothing that could be mixed and matched. She carefully examined the illustrations on the back of the kit to see exactly how it all worked. "Oh, Aunt Millie, this is great! Thank you. I was terrified at the thought of having to go into a maternity store to buy things," she confessed.

Mildred reached over to put a hand on her shoulder and said, "Well, I didn't want you to have to spend any of your hard earned money on things you should never have had to buy in the first place."

"Here, here," Simon said quietly.

"All right, last present," Harriett said, stuffing a box into Molly's face and taking a seat beside her on the bed.

Simon helped Molly stuff the kit back into the box and plopped it on the floor beside him, along with the torn up paper. Taking the package from her grandmother, Molly was surprised by the weight of it. She nearly dropped it.

"Whoa, this is so heavy. What's in here, Granny?"

"Why don't you open it and find out?" her grandmother replied.

Molly unwrapped the heavy package to find three books. One was an encyclopedia of flora and fauna and the other two were gardening books written by the famous British horticulturalist, Christopher Lloyd. "Granny, these are fabulous!" Molly cried, flipping through the pages of the books. "I can't wait to start reading them. Thank you." Molly looked up at her grandmother with a bright smile on her face. "These will really be helpful when I go back to school in the fall."

"What are you talking about?" Simon asked, eyeing her closely.

She looked back at him with confusion and said, "You know . . . when I start the horticultural program at the University."

"No. I don't know," Simon replied.

"What do you mean? I've talked about it . . ."

Simon shook his head at Molly and she looked to her aunts and grandmother, who were doing the same thing. "Oh, my God," Molly said softly. "I thought I had mentioned that it's what I want to do, but I guess I was just thinking about it and discussing it with myself."

"I think it's a wonderful plan," Gertrude said excitedly. "It's the perfect career for you."

"Are you serious, honey?" Simon asked, reaching his hand up into her hair and gently squeezing a fistful of it.

"Yes," she replied, looking directly into his eyes. "I love working at the nursery. I'm good at it and it's what I want to do."

Smiling, Simon pulled her close and kissed her forehead. "Well then, I'll hook you up with my old advisor and we'll get you on your way."

"Really? That would be wonderful."

"I think you've made another good choice," Mildred said, smiling and winking at Molly.

"Me, too," Simon concurred.

Harriett frowned. "Are you sure you're not doing this just because of Simon?"

"No, Granny," Molly said forcefully, feeling her face turn red. She glared at her grandmother. "This is what I'm good at, and I love working with plants."

"All right, then. Here's your other present," Harriett said lightly, pulling a small box from the pocket of her trousers and handing it to her granddaughter.

Molly stared at her for a moment in puzzlement. Cautiously, she took the small parcel and lifted the lid. Inside was a small felt jewelry bag. Daintily, she picked it up, pulled open the drawstring, and tipped the bag onto the palm of her hand. A pair of garnet and diamond drop earrings tumbled out. "Oh, Granny!" Molly whispered. "They're beautiful."

"They were our mother's," Harriett explained. "She gave them to me before she died, and I know she would be happy that I have passed them on to you."

Molly reached out a hand to her grandmother, who had no other choice but to take it. Squeezing Harriett's hand, Molly said, "I'll cherish these, always, Granny, and some day, I'll give them to my daughter."

Harriett could only respond with a nod. Then she pulled her hand away from Molly's and rose from the bed.

"Wow, this is all too much," Molly said sincerely. "This is the best birthday I've ever had."

"Well, I'm going to go down to the kitchen and make you a hot breakfast," Gertrude said, bending to pick the tray up off the floor.

"Oh, don't worry about that, Aunt Gertie. I can eat those pancakes."

"Nonsense," Harriett chimed in. "Those are stone cold. You need a good hot meal on such a cold day." And Harriett tugged Gertrude by the arm and out of the room.

Before the tray got away, Simon grabbed the envelopes from it and said, "These are your birthday cards from us, honey. We'll clean up this mess and get out of your way so that you can read them in peace." Mildred bunched up the wrapping paper and stuffed it into the coat box, and Simon collected the box of clothes and the books and took them over to her dresser.

"You all don't have to leave," Molly protested.

Simon walked back over to the bed and bent over to kiss Molly on the lips. "Just read your cards, birthday girl, and I'll be back with a tray full of hot food. Then you can tell me all about these secret plans of yours."

"Enjoy your morning, birthday girl," Mildred said, waving from the doorway. "Just stay in bed and relax. It's your special day."

"Thanks, Aunt Millie," Molly called to her. To Simon she said, "I honestly was not trying to keep my plans from you."

"I'm just teasing," Simon said, lightly bopping her head with a closed fist. Backing away, he said, "Now, read your cards. I'll be back in a minute." He disappeared and Molly was alone.

Molly looked around at the presents she had received and

fingered the earrings in her hand. She felt completely over-whelmed. A great deal of thought and consideration had gone into each gift, which is something that she had never experienced before. All her life she had been given expensive dolls, clothes and jewelry that her mother believed were appropriate. It was a wonderful feeling knowing that her aunts and grandmother had actually taken the time to consider what she would like or what she might need. Once again, they had made her feel so comfortable, so at home and so much a part of a family. Staring down at the stack of envelopes in her hand, she thought of Simon and suddenly realized that he had not given her a gift.

Shrugging, Molly opened an envelope and began to read. Simon returned awhile later with a tray loaded down with breakfast foods (some of which he intended to eat), and he crawled into bed with her. They both ate heartily and chatted happily about the day and Molly's plans for the future. Then Simon declared that he had to leave and go to work.

"Please don't go," she begged when he rolled off the bed.

"Honey," he said, leaning over to kiss her several times, "there's still one more surprise for you. In case you didn't notice, I didn't give you a gift."

"I didn't want to mention it . . ." Molly teased.

"Well, I'm still working on it so I've gotta go." Simon grabbed the tray off the bed. "You relax and enjoy your day, and be ready for me to pick you up at five o'clock."

"Where are we going?" Molly asked excitedly.

"It's a surprise!" he said in exasperation. "I'm not going to tell you a thing, so don't be calling me at the nursery and pestering me all day. Just be patient and be ready by five o'clock."

"But it's Christmas Eve and your parents are coming for dinner," Molly protested.

Simon set the tray down and stomped back across the room. Molly screamed and ducked under the bed covers. After wrestling with her for a moment, he pulled the covers down and pinned her arms to the mattress. Looking deeply into her eyes, he warned, "No more argument." Then he kissed her sweetly, and pulling back abruptly, he said, "See you at five." In the blink of an eye, he jumped off the bed, snatched the tray up and vanished from the room.

Happily, Molly spent a lazy morning in bed paging through her new garden books. Then she showered, dressed and wandered down to the kitchen. Her aunts were busy preparing for Christmas Eve dinner while Harriett was sitting at the table waiting to be fed her lunch. Molly had to fight to keep from laughing as Mildred and Gertrude rushed about the kitchen, completely ignoring her grandmother who had a napkin on her lap and a knife, fork and glass sitting in front of her.

Molly moved toward the refrigerator and informed the room, "I'm starving. I think I'll make myself a sandwich."

"Oh, Molly," Gertrude practically wailed, "it's your birthday and you should not be doing anything."

"What rubbish," Harriett growled. "You two are too busy to feed us so let the girl make us some sandwiches." Looking to Molly, she added, "I'll have turkey with lettuce and mayonnaise, and some cottage cheese with peaches."

"I'll get right on that, Granny." Molly smiled as she stuffed her head into the refrigerator to search for the requested lunch items.

Mildred came up behind her and quietly said, "You go sit down, dear, and I'll make you some sandwiches."

"Thank you, Aunt Millie, but you're busy with dinner preparations. I can make the sandwiches and the peaches and cottage cheese," she said, unable to contain her laughter any longer.

Mildred started to giggle along with her, and the two of them stood huddled in the refrigerator door, their bodies shaking from laughter.

"What's going on over there?" Harriett demanded. "What are you laughing at? Are you laughing at me?"

"Oh, I want to laugh, too," Gertrude cried.

Mildred immediately sobered and stepped away from Molly. "We were just trying to find the Swiss cheese," she fibbed. Then she returned to her task and continued to ignore her grouchy sister.

"Well, I don't want Swiss cheese on my sandwich," Harriett snapped.

"Don't worry, Granny," Molly called as she rummaged through the drawers in the refrigerator. "The cheese is for my sandwich. Would you like a pickle, too?"

"Why the hell would I want a pickle? The damn things give me indigestion!"

Aware that her grandmother was moments away from a starvation-induced rant, Molly quickly set about preparing their lunch. She kept her head lowered and succeeded in stopping the giggles bubbling about in her throat.

After lunch, Molly wandered into the parlor. She stood for a moment in the big picture window, looking down toward the river. The ice was creeping out across the water from the banks; soon the river would freeze through, and deep, dismal winter would settle upon the town until the warm and gentle breezes of spring arrived to melt away the ice and bring the river back to life. As she thought of this, Molly was reminded that Spring would also bring a baby into her life, a baby that Simon wanted. What exactly had he meant the day he announced his wishes in front of her grandmother and aunts? Why would he want the baby? It certainly would not look like him. This simple thought gave Molly her answer. Simon wanted to give an unwanted child a home just as he had been given. She did not think it was possible to love him even more, but at that moment she did. And the sad truth was that she would have to disappoint him. She had no intention of keeping the baby, and she did not look forward to telling him.

Staring forlornly out at the river, Molly blindly watched the cars going back and forth across the lift bridge. A light snow was just beginning to fall and the flakes captured her attention, drawing her out of her trance.

"See anything interesting?" Harriett asked, materializing beside her with a pair of binoculars in her hand.

"No," Molly replied blandly. "Just more snow."

"The damn stuff just keeps on falling. I think it's going to be a long winter."

Molly smiled. "Can I have a look?" She held out a hand for the binoculars.

Harriett handed them over and the two of them stood there in the window spying on the town, pointing out people and making up stories about what they were up to that holiday afternoon.

When her adventures with Harriett came to an end, Molly joined her aunts in the kitchen and insisted that they let her help with preparations for the holiday meal. The baking was well underway and the sweet aroma of yeast perfumed the room, making Molly's mouth salivate. She was put in charge of rolling out and shaping the crescent rolls for dinner that evening, while Gertrude worked on a fruit-and-nut coffee cake for Christmas morning breakfast and Mildred put the finishing touches on her eggnog pies. While Molly worked the dough for the rolls that had been rising since that morning, her grandmother followed Mildred around the kitchen, drooling over the famous eggnog pies that were laced with brandy, a once-a-year treat.

Around three-thirty that afternoon, when the baking crew was sitting down to a much deserved cup of tea and relishing in the comforting aromas coming out of the oven, the telephone rang. Harriett answered it and exchanged a few quips with Simon before handing the phone over to Molly.

"Where are you?" Molly asked.

"Hi, birthday girl," Simon replied cheerfully, ignoring her question. "How are you? Have you had a good day?"

"I'm missing you. That's how I am," Molly said unashamedly in front of her grandmother and aunts.

"I promise we'll be together soon," Simon said, smiling to himself on the other end of the line. "Are you going to be ready by five o'clock?"

"We've been through this."

"I know . . . just checking."

"Where are we going?"

"Don't ask questions. Just be ready," Simon instructed.

"All right. But . . ."

"I love you, honey. I'll see you in awhile," Simon said excitedly before hanging up.

"Simon?"

Chapter Sixteen

Molly was on the landing at five o'clock when she heard Simon's deep voice coming from the direction of the kitchen. "I'll just go up and check on her," he was saying.

Her heart pounded with excitement as she struck a pose, her arms akimbo, her new coat draped over one of them, and her holiday ensemble presented in the best light. Simon did not notice her until he set one foot upon the bottom step. When he caught sight of her, he froze with his other foot dangling in midair. He ogled her from head to toe. "Wow! You look fantastic!"

Beaming down at him from her place on high, she took Simon completely by surprise and slid down the banister. "Molly!" he cried, catching her before she hit the newel post at the bottom and wrapping her up in his arms. "You're insane!"

"No, I'm not," she protested. "I have all my wits about me, thank you very much. I'm just happy to see you." Then she snaked her arms around his neck and kissed him hungrily, kicking his passion into overdrive.

"Ahem," Harriett said, clearing her throat as she stood not a few feet away in the foyer with her arms folded across her chest, a disapproving look upon her face.

Simon and Molly unlocked their lips and dropped their chins to their chests in feigned shame. Then Simon propped his chin on top of Molly's head and glared at Harriett. "Are you going to spoil my fun every chance you get?"

"Damn straight," Harriett said without any expression on her face whatsoever. "Just keep your hands to yourself," Harriett warned, "and bring my granddaughter back here in plenty of time for supper."

"What about me? Am I still invited to dinner?" Simon teased.

"Don't be such a pain in the ass," Harriett said, wagging a crooked finger at him. "Just behave yourselves."

"We will, Granny," Molly promised, untangling herself from Simon and crossing over to where her grandmother stood. She planted a quick kiss on Harriett's cheek and added, "And I promise we will be home in time for dinner."

"Well, enjoy your special surprise, Molly," she said as she turned away.

Sliding her arms into the new coat, and pulling it closed in front to get the feel of it, Molly replied, "Thank you. I'm sure I will." Then she quickly did up the buttons and caught her grandmother's attention. "What do you think, Granny?" Molly twirled around.

Harriett turned and with a great ping of pleasure noticed the garnet earrings dangling from Molly's lobes. "Actually, that looks quite smart," Harriett replied, referring to the coat. She was somewhat amazed that Gertrude had chosen something so stylish. Then she startled both Simon and Molly by bellowing toward the kitchen, "Gertie get out here and take a look at Molly in her new coat!"

In an instant, the two aunts came scurrying out of the kitchen in excitement, singing the praises of Molly as they examined her new finery. Aware that the little gathering in the foyer was about to turn into a mutual admiration society meeting, Simon intervened and whisked her away.

When they were alone, outside on the porch, Simon let out a sigh of relief and said, "Whew! That was close. I thought I might never get you out of there."

"They just wanted to admire my new coat," Molly said, smoothing down the front of it with a gloved hand. "I really like it. What do you think of it?"

"I think it looks fabulous on you," Simon replied, as he walked her down the porch steps and onto the sidewalk, where delicate ice crystals were glittering as they fell into the soft beams of light radiating from the streetlamps. "But I would rather talk about what you're wearing underneath. You purposely wore that form-fitting, ass-hugging outfit in order to get me all hot and bothered so that I'd be tempted to break our pact, didn't you?"

Molly did not even pretend to deny the fact that what Simon said was true. "Well, it is my birthday . . ." she said coyly.

"Not fair, Moll," Simon moaned. "That's just dirty pool." He reached for her, but she got away.

Molly laughed and ran toward the driveway. She stopped suddenly at the sight of a shiny black SUV standing in front of her. "You got a new truck!" she cried, looking to Simon for confirmation.

Reaching into his pocket, Simon pulled out a key ring and held it out to Molly. "Happy birthday, honey." His eyes danced with light.

She stared at the key ring dangling from Simon's hand, then at the SUV and then back at Simon. "I don't understand."

"It's for you," Simon explained, forcing the keys into the palm of her hand.

"What? Why?" Molly cried, visibly distressed.

Simon was stunned.

"I can't accept it. It's much too expensive." She stuffed the keys back in his hand. "You can't spend that kind of money on me!"

"Honey, I've got more money than I know what to do with, and now I finally have someone to spend it on." Simon grabbed her upper arms. "I don't just get a salary from the business; I get a percentage of the profits at the end of every year. So don't worry about the money, Moll. I'm excited to be able to do this for you."

"What do you mean? Do what?"

"Give you back some of the independence your father stole from you when he took your car away," Simon explained. "Your grand-mother and I thought it was time you had your own car again."

"Who are you to decide?" Molly said angrily, pulling away from him. "I can save my money and buy my own damn car! I don't need you and Granny making such a big decision for me." Molly began to pace back and forth in the snow.

"Whoa. Just calm down."

"No. Don't tell me to calm down," she yelled. "I don't need you to tell me how to behave or what kind of car I should be driving or when I should be allowed to do it!"

"Nobody is trying to tell you what to do," Simon said evenly. "I gave you this car because I love you and because I wanted you to have a safe, reliable vehicle to get you back and forth from the University when you go back to school. And your grandmother is paying for your car insurance because she loves you and wants to show you how proud she is of all that you've accomplished." Simon took several steps toward Molly and glowered at her. "Don't you dare group us with your parents, Moll. We're not trying to tell you how to live your life. It's simply a gift that we put a lot of thought into."

Molly stared at Simon. He returned her steady gaze, trying to mask the hurt and disappointment he was feeling.

"If you don't want the car, I'll keep and drive it," he said quietly. "If you decide you want it, just let me know and it's yours. I honestly never imagined that you would react this way, and maybe that's something I should've thought of before buying it for you."

Molly turned away from him. Her heart burned with shame, and she did not know how to redeem herself without looking like more of a fool.

"I think I should go," Simon said, turning to leave.

"Simon, no!" Molly cried. She launched herself at him and wrapped her arms around his neck. "I'm sorry. Please don't go." She started kissing him, and Simon tried to fend her off so that he could straighten things out with her. But she was determined, and he quickly gave up the fight. It was the easy way out and he knew it.

Simon staggered toward the car with Molly glued to him and he opened the passenger door. Tearing his lips away from hers, he said, "Get in."

Molly crawled up into the seat and he shut the door on her. After taking several deep breaths, Simon walked around to the driver's side of the SUV and climbed in. He turned in his seat to say something to Molly and she silenced him with another powerful kiss. When he finally broke away from her, he breathlessly said, "We need to talk about what just happened."

"I know," Molly said, pulling down the zipper on his leather jacket and kissing his neck. "Take me to your house."

Simon dropped his head back against the seat and groaned in pleasure. "Moll," he whispered. "You have to stop. We need to talk."

"We'll talk after," she said in a husky voice.

"As much as I want to give into this, honey, I can't." Simon grabbed her by the wrists to stop her hands from roaming all over his body. "If our situation were different, I'd be all for getting naked and letting off steam to get over this fight, or whatever the hell it is. But I don't think we should ignore your little meltdown or the way you were feeling. Having sex won't solve the problem you've got with the way you think I'm treating you."

"I said I was sorry. Can't we just forget what a fool I made of myself?" Molly gazed at him with imploring eyes. "This is such an amazing gift, and I'm overwhelmed by your generosity. But you caught me off guard. Do you understand?"

"Yes, I do." Simon nodded. "But you freaked out on me, Moll, and I don't want this to happen again. I don't want to have to worry about my intentions being misunderstood or about what kind of gifts I can give you. I want to give you gifts, honey, and I want you to accept them and appreciate them. It's pretty standard stuff."

Molly turned away from him.

"Don't turn away," Simon said, tugging on her wrists. "I'd rather have you scream at me than give me the silent treatment."

Molly was so ashamed that she could not look at him. Lowering her eyes, she quietly said, "I'm acting like a spoiled child. I'm sorry. I clearly don't deserve your gift."

"Yes, you do." Simon released her wrists and took her face between his hands. "Don't you see? You do deserve it. That's what your grandmother and I are trying to show you."

Molly's eyes glistened with tears. "I'm sorry if I hurt your feelings. I never wanted to hurt you like that."

"Don't worry about it. No permanent damage done." Simon smiled at her. Then he kissed her lightly on the lips and said, "Come on, let's take it for a test drive around town and we can talk some more. If you don't like it, we'll go pick out a different car together."

"I like this one," Molly said looking directly into his eyes. "And I like you."

"I'm glad." Simon gently brushed his thumbs across her cheekbones. Then he pulled her into his arms and kissed her tenderly.

They took Molly's new vehicle for a drive along the river and over into Wisconsin, and then they came back and tested the four-wheel-drive on the unplowed hills in Stillwater. Molly had never cared much about cars, but she had to admit that she really liked the way the SUV handled and she especially liked how safe she felt driving it. When they finished their talk about Molly's initial reaction to the car, they drove back to The Aunt Hill to celebrate the holiday with their families.

When Simon and Molly returned to the house, they found the assembled holiday crowd gathered in the kitchen, all of them trying to help with dinner preparations and some of them getting quite ornery. Standing in the doorway to the kitchen, watching the mayhem with amusement, Simon and Molly started laughing. Then Simon silenced them all with a high-pitched whistle that required the use of two of his fingers in his mouth. When the aunts, Harriett and his parents stopped to look at him, he cried, "What the hell is going on in here?"

"You're back!" Gertrude cried, running toward the young couple. "What was the big surprise?"

Molly jangled a set of keys above her head. "An amazing car!"

"Oh, Simon," Mildred gasped.

"Ooh, let's go have a look," Gertrude said excitedly, grabbing Mildred by the hand and tugging her toward the front door.

"Happy birthday, dear," Lillian said, leaning in to give Molly a kiss on the cheek. She stepped aside and gave Simon a quick hug.

"Well, what do you think of your new ride, birthday girl?" Henry said, pulling Molly into his arms for one of his bear hugs. "That's a pretty fancy SUV . . ."

Harriett grabbed Simon by the elbow and dragged him down the hallway. "I take it things didn't go as smoothly as you hoped."

"How do you know?" Simon grinned at her. "Were you spying on us?"

"Never mind that," Harriett said angrily. "What happened?"

"She was upset at first because she thought you and I were try-ing to make decisions for her, just like her parents," Simon ex-plained. "Then she got a little wild, and I calmed her down and we drove around town and talked it out. She's fine now."

Harriett eyed him with skepticism.

"I swear to God," Simon said, holding up a hand. "Ask her yourself."

"Don't get so defensive," Harriett said, shoving him back to-ward the kitchen. "I believe you."

Laughing, Simon walked back into the kitchen with Harriet directly behind him. He stepped up behind Molly, who was chat-ting happily with his parents, and wrapped his arms around her. Nuzzling her ear, his whispered, "You should thank Granny."

Molly turned in his arms and saw her grandmother standing behind him. Simon released her and she walked toward her grand-mother with open arms. Hugging Harriett tightly, she softly said, "Thank you, Granny, for your generous gift. But most of all, thank you for believing that I deserved Simon's present."

"You're welcome," Harriett said gruffly. Molly quickly re-leased her.

"What a day to be born on," Henry commented in an attempt to lighten the mood. "I'll bet you always got cheated on the presents."

Molly laughed. "I never really thought about it because I always felt bad about being born on Christmas Eve and spoiling the holi-day for my parents."

"What do you mean?" Lillian asked.

"My mother always said that I ruined that Christmas for her," Molly explained. Simon, Lillian and Henry all winced. "It's all right. She always said stupid things like that."

"No, it's not all right," Henry said in his booming voice.

"What do you say we forget about your mother this evening and really enjoy ourselves," Simon suggested, giving Molly's shoulder a gentle squeeze.

"I'd say that's a good idea," she responded.

"Come on, Henry. Let's go have another look at that fancy

SUV," Lillian said, taking her husband by the hand and dragging him out of the kitchen. Harriett followed them.

"Sorry about that," Molly said, dropping her chin to her chest. "I didn't mean to make your parents uncomfortable."

"You didn't," Simon assured her. "Right now they're both just pumped up because they want to give your mother a piece of their mind. Me, too."

"Like you said, let's just forget about her and enjoy this Christmas Eve." Molly turned to face him and reached her arms around his middle. "Thank you for making this a special day and for giving me such an incredible gift. Again, I'm sorry–"

Simon silenced her with a kiss. The crowd came barreling back into the kitchen and they broke apart.

"All right, everybody out of the kitchen!" Mildred commanded, waving a wooden spoon to show that she meant business. Stopping next to Simon and Molly, she said, "Simon that is quite a special gift." She kissed both of them on the cheek and then made a bee-line for the stove. "The food will be on the table in fifteen minutes," she called over her shoulder.

"Go on," Lillian said, shooing everyone out of the room. "You heard the woman." Then she turned to Mildred. "I'll help you get things onto the table, Millie."

Mildred nodded her approval and bent over to check on her roast in the oven. The crowd dissipated, leaving Mildred the space and peace and quiet that she needed. As soon as they were alone, Mildred barked orders at Lillian, who followed them cheerfully and with great precision, pleasing Mildred immensely. She and Lillian made a great team, and, as promised, they were setting dishes of piping hot food on the table within fifteen minutes time, delighting the hungry horde.

Everyone agreed that Mildred's roast was superb and some asked for seconds and thirds. They also stuffed themselves with mashed potatoes, gravy, vegetables and Molly's fresh-baked crescent rolls. The only one who did not eat very much that evening was Harriett, who complained of a sudden headache, no doubt brought on by the chaos in the house and the two glasses of scotch she had consumed before dinner. She was also intent upon saving room for several pieces of the much anticipated liquor-laced, egg-nog pie.

When the dishes were clean and dry, and the roast pan was soaking in soapy water, they all gathered around the Christmas tree in the parlor to open gifts. Molly was so excited about the presents that she had selected and paid for with her own hard-earned money that she insisted on passing hers out first. Simon helped her, and then she sat down in front of the tree to eagerly watch everyone open her gifts.

Lillian quickly tore the wrapping paper from her present to find a delicate Limoge tea cup and saucer carefully swathed in tissue paper. "Molly, this is lovely!" she cried. "Thank you so much, dear."

"I noticed that you had a collection of tea cups in that hutch in the dining room," Molly said happily, glad that Lillian liked her gift, "and I thought this might be a nice addition."

"Oh it is," Lillian cooed. "I just love it. Thank you."

"You're welcome."

Then Henry opened his parcel to find a wide-brimmed straw hat with a leather strap around the crown. He laughed out loud at the sight of it. "So, Molly, you don't like my beat up old hat with the brim ripping away, eh?"

"Well, it's a beauty, but it no longer suits a dapper gentleman like yourself."

"You have a point," Henry said, placing the hat upon his head and settling it securely. "Well, what do you think?"

"I think you look very handsome," Molly replied, smiling warmly at him.

"Oh, Molly, that's a fine hat," Lillian said, admiring her husband's new chapeau. "Ten thousand times better than that soiled disaster he's been wearing. What a perfect gift, dear."

Next, the aunts opened their presents. Gertrude was delighted to find new rose pruning shears, leather gardening gloves and a kit to make mosaic stepping stones for the garden. Molly gave her Aunt Mildred a special reading lamp and several of the current bestsellers in hardcover because her aunt loved to read. In a separate envelope, Mildred found a beautiful leather bookmark and a twenty dollar gift card for Starbucks so that she could treat herself to her favorite mocha coffee drink whenever she liked. Both Gertrude and Mildred gushed with gratitude, making their elder sister want to scream.

Finally, Harriett opened her gift, and she was rendered speechless. Carefully laid out in a large rectangular box were four antique silver frames, each very unique in their design. In the frames were old black and white photographs. One of the photos was of Harriett with her young boys, one a toddler, one an infant. Another was of Harriett and her two sisters on the porch swing of The Aunt Hill, taken when they were teenagers. The third photo was of Harriett and her parents, and the final picture was of Harriett holding Molly when she was just a year old. Harriett kept her head lowered and stared at the framed photographs. Her first thought was why Molly would do such a thing for her, go to such effort on her behalf; and her second thought was that she had never received a better gift. The photographs meant the world to her as they were all memories of some of the happy moments in her life. She wanted to throw her arms around her granddaughter, tell her how much she appreciated the gifts, and show her how much she truly loved her.

Without raising her eyes from the box, Harriett softly said, "Thank you, Molly. What a tremendously thoughtful gift."

"You're welcome, Granny," Molly replied, crawling across the room to where her grandmother sat on the sofa. Leaning against the arm of the sofa, invading her grandmother's space, she said, "I like this one the best." Molly pointed to the picture of the three sisters on the porch swing. "You all look so young and beautiful and happy."

"Yes," Harriett agreed, looking intently at the photograph. "Yes, we were."

"May I have a look?" Simon asked, holding out a hand. "Molly was very secretive about this project and didn't give me a preview."

Harriett offered the box of frames to Simon. "Pass it around," she said in gravelly voice.

Finally, it was Simon's turn to open his present from Molly and he took pure delight in torturing her by pretending to be distracted from opening his gift while she sat on her knees in front of him chewing on a finger nail in anticipation. In due course,

Simon opened the gift box and discovered a cream colored cashmere turtleneck sweater. And when he held it up for inspection, all the ladies "oohed" and "aahed." Bending down to kiss Molly in gratitude, he whispered, "You shouldn't have spent so much money on me."

"I wanted to buy you something nice."

"Well, this certainly is nice," Simon said most sincerely.

"Ooh, Molly," Lillian chimed in, "what a good choice. He'll look so handsome in that."

"Won't he," Molly said enthusiastically, knowing that was exactly why she had purchased it.

"All right, enough of that," Simon protested. "Let's keep it moving or we'll be here all night."

After all the gifts had been passed out and torn into, they circled the room for inspection and comment. From her aunts and grandmother, Molly received more maternity outfits and essentials for which she was immensely grateful, and from Henry and Lillian, she received two pairs of maternity overalls, a basketful of all different types of garden gloves for work, and a boxy, flannel-lined barn jacket to keep her warm in the greenhouses during the bitter cold winter months. And as an extra little trinket, Lillian gave her a silver charm bracelet with gardening charms dangling from the links which made a little tinkling sound when it was shaken.

"Well, that's it!" Molly said cheerfully, looking under the tree as she sat amidst a pile of crumbled up wrapping paper balls and gift boxes.

"Not quite," Simon said evenly. "Why don't you take a look in the tree branches?"

Molly thought she had already received her gift from Simon— the new car was certainly enough to last for several birthdays and Christmases—so she was convinced that he was playing a joke on her. But she pulled down the evergreen's branches and peered into the depths of the tree, looking for hints of Christmas wrap. About three quarters of the way up the trunk, perched a small, shiny silver box tied with a white ribbon. She carefully extracted it from the prickly pine branches. Crossing the room to sit down on the floor in front of Simon, Molly glanced around the room at everyone with sparkling eyes.

"What's this?" she mused.

"Open it and find out," Simon suggested.

She opened the box to find a gold necklace with a solid heart pendant resting upon a bed of white satin. "Simon, it's beautiful." She looked up into his eyes. "But you already gave me a present."

"That was for your birthday. This is your Christmas present."

"Oh, Simon, I love it!" Molly squealed. She sprang off the floor and wrapped her arms around his neck. "Thank you."

"You're welcome." Simon breathed a sigh of relief that he had not touched off another bout of resentment. "Turn around and I'll put it on you." After Simon had secured the clasp at the back of her neck, Molly circled the room to show off her new bauble, pausing to peer into the mirror above the fireplace to admire her gold heart.

Simon sat contentedly in his chair watching her, happy in the knowledge that Molly's twentieth birthday had been special for her—a day she would never forget because of the love and affection that had been showered upon her by her family and his. And when Molly turned from admiring her necklace in the mirror to look at Simon with love-filled eyes, he knew he would remember the look upon her face for the rest of his life.

Chapter Seventeen

After two pieces of eggnog pie each and several games of cards, Molly and Simon freshened up to join Harriett and the aunts for midnight mass at St. Michael's. With many thanks and warm embraces, Lillian and Henry bid everyone adieu and went home to bed. Interested to see what Molly's church and religion was all about, Simon decided to go along with her to the special Christmas mass. He promised his parents that he would join them in the morning for services with their congregation at First Presbyterian.

Arriving back at The Aunt Hill at two o'clock in the morning, tired and chilled, hardly a word was exchanged as everyone headed for their warm, soft beds. As the three sisters started climbing the stairs to their rooms, Simon offered to turn off lights and use Molly's keys to lock up.

"As long as you are out of here in five minutes," Harriett said, yawning.

"Hattie, please," Mildred said angrily. Looking down into the foyer at Molly and Simon she said, "Thank you, Simon. That's so kind of you." Then she blew Molly a kiss. "Sleep well, sweetheart. Merry Christmas."

"Merry Christmas, Aunt Millie," Molly said, returning the kiss. "Goodnight, Granny. Goodnight, Aunt Gertie."

"Sleep well," Gertrude said, reaching the top of the stairs and waving over the railing at Molly and Simon.

"You, too," they said in unison.

Harriett simply dismissed them with a wave and lumbered down the hallway to her bedroom.

Simon turned Molly to face him and he gently brushed the hair back from her face with his hands. Looking into her eyes, he asked, "Did you have a good birthday?"

"The best," she replied, nodding her head. "It was full of surprises, and you were a part of it. Thank you for everything."

"My pleasure." Simon smiled.

"Sorry, I acted like such a jerk." Molly lowered her eyes. "I'm pretty sure it's the hormones."

"Hey, look at me." Simon lifted her chin with his finger. "Let's not talk about it anymore. It's over and done with. All's forgiven and forgotten."

Simon placed his hands on her shoulders and began to massage her tired muscles. Molly closed her eyes and let her chin flop to her chest. "You're exhausted," Simon pointed out. "Why don't you go up to bed and I'll lock up and get out of here."

"I want you to stay with me," Molly said softly.

"I know, honey." Simon sighed, wrapping his arms around her shoulders and resting his chin on top of her head. "I wish more than anything I could, but I don't want to offend your grandmother and get her mad at us. She's just starting to come around."

"How do you figure?" Molly asked, peering at him out of the corner of her eye.

Simon smiled and clasped her face between his hands.

Harriett, who had been lurking in the shadows upstairs, moved a little closer to the railing to see why the young lovers had suddenly gone silent. She was careful not to step on the squeaky floorboards as she peeped down at them. As she suspected, they were locked in a romantic embrace, and she was pleased to see that they were not mauling each other but that Simon was kissing her granddaughter with great tenderness. Slinking back toward the wall, Harriett waited to see what would happen next.

"Goodnight, my love," she heard Simon say softly. "Sleep well. I'll see you in the morning and we'll have another great day."

Molly said, "Goodnight." And then Harriett realized that she was maneuvering toward the stairs. Moving as fast as her limbs could manage, she scurried down the hall and into her room.

Simon moved like a zombie from room to room, switching off lights and double checking to make certain that no candles had been left burning. Then he helped himself to a glass of water in the kitchen and grabbed one of Molly's crescent rolls to keep him awake on his short drive home. Back in the foyer, he stood for a moment and gazed up the stairwell, thinking about Molly getting ready for bed. He stood there for a long time, listening to the muffled sounds of the women moving about in their rooms, and just as Molly opened her door to take her turn in the bathroom, Simon dashed out the front door and locked it securely behind him.

A gentle hush settled over The Aunt Hill early that Christmas morning as a light snow drifted softly down from the sky and frosted the snow-covered town with a fine sheet of glittering crystals. The streets of Stillwater were deserted; not a car, delivery truck or taxi crept along under the dim glow of the street lamps. In the silence, down by the river, one could hear the ice cracking as the water shifted and froze in the cold winter night. And the only creature to hear this wondrous sound was a ravenous raccoon that had crawled up from the sewer drain to rummage through the trash bins behind the Freight House restaurant.

Around five o'clock Christmas morning, just as Jack Frost was finishing a masterpiece on one of Harriett's bedroom windows, she awoke with a start from a nightmare in which she had died. When Harriett realized that she was indeed awake and alive, her first thought was of the leaf she had pressed in the dictionary on Halloween. She had not checked on it for awhile and she needed to know that it was still there. That precious maple leaf had drifted gracefully down from the tree to a peaceful death when it landed on Harriett's shoe and she had envied its beautiful ending, hoping for the same for herself when the time came.

Crawling out of bed with great difficulty, she struggled to move her right arm and leg which seemed to have turned into tree stumps while she had been sleeping. When she finally made it to her feet, she was struck with a dizzy spell that forced her to sit back down on the mattress. As she sat there, alone in the dark light of Christmas morning, her heart seized with panic as she again thought about getting to the maple leaf down in the library. What were the headings of the pages where she had pressed it into the dictionary? Her mind felt quite muddled and she was having trouble organizing her thoughts.

She finally rose from the bed and made another attempt to propel herself out of her room and downstairs. Slightly off balance and dragging her right leg along with her, Harriett's stubbornness and sheer determination helped her make it across the room and out of her door. In the hallway, she became even more confused and her vision seemed to fade in and out like a dimming light bulb. She grappled her way along the wall and doorways en route to the staircase. Suddenly, an agonizing pain pierced the left side of her head. The blow came so swiftly that she did not have time to cry out before she fell to the floor.

Molly sat up in bed and cocked an ear. Something had disturbed her slumber. For a minute or two she sat there holding her breath, listening, but all she heard was the grandfather clock ticking out in the hall. She tried to ignore the nagging in the pit of her stomach telling her that something was wrong. The beat of Molly's heart began to thump in her ears, finally driving her into action. She slid out of bed, grabbed her robe, and tiptoed out into the dark hallway. Molly nearly tripped over her prone grandmother, who was splayed out atop the Oriental runner that had cushioned her fall.

Molly's screams sent terror through the hearts of her great-aunts. They both shot up in bed, clutching at their chests, fearing the absolute worst. Mildred had the sense to grab the baseball bat that she kept tucked away behind her bedside table before she ventured out of her room, but Gertrude was trembling so violently that she could not move.

Bolstered by a sudden surge of adrenalin, Mildred sprang from her door and flicked on the overhead light in the hallway. She was poised with her bat ready to strike when she saw Molly down on her knees, shaking Harriett by the shoulders. "Granny! Granny!" Molly was crying.

"Gertrude," Mildred yelled, "dial nine-one-one!" Then she rushed to her sister's aid. Rolling Harriett onto her back, Mildred lowered an ear to her chest. She heard the faint beating of her sister's heart and felt her chest rising and falling with each inhalation and exhalation of air.

"She's still alive, Molly," Mildred said, taking the girl by the shoulders to get her attention. Molly's tear-stained face stared back at her as if the words had not registered. Pulling her grand-niece into her arms, she again called, "Gertie! Get out here and dial nine-one-one!"

Finally, Gertrude found the courage to come out of her room, but when she saw Harriett collapsed in the hall, she became hysterical. She fell to her knees beside Harriett and sobbed, which frustrated Mildred to the point of anger. Suddenly, Molly regained her wits and dashed for the telephone.

First she dialed the emergency number and begged them to hurry to the house. Then she called Simon who picked up the phone on the first ring. "Simon, help," was all she managed to say.

"I'm on my way," he cried, tossing the phone on the floor. He flew out of bed as if he had been catapulted across the room and dressed himself in a heart beat. In less than forty-five seconds, he was out the door and racing to The Aunt Hill. Simon reached the house before the paramedics and let himself in with Molly's key.

Bursting into the foyer, he yelled, "Molly?"

"We're up here!" she leaned over the stairwell railing to get his attention.

Flying up the stairs, Simon stopped cold when he saw Harriett's prostrate form and Gertrude weeping over her. "What happened?" he asked, pulling Molly into his arms and hugging her fiercely.

"We don't know," Mildred said sadly. "Molly heard a noise and found Hattie here, like this. Her heart is still beating, but she won't wake up."

Simon dropped to his knees and lowered his face near Harriett's. "Granny?" he said loudly. "Come on, Granny, wake up." Just then, they heard the sound of the ambulance siren. "I'll be right back." Simon squeezed Molly's hand. He ran down the stairs and out of the house.

The moment that the ambulance skidded to a stop at the curb in front of The Aunt Hill, the doors flew open and two EMTs jumped out. Quickly grabbing their medical kits, they ran toward Simon and followed him up the stairs. The two men visually assessed the situation and asked everyone to move away from Harriett. Then they got to work.

Simon stood several feet away with his arms around Molly and the aunts. As they watched, he realized that Harriett was not going to wake up. "Ladies, why don't you get dressed so that we can follow them to the hospital."

"Good thinking," Mildred said quickly. She grabbed Gertrude by the arm and pulled her toward her bedroom.

"Honey, get dressed. I'll stay out here with Granny," Simon said, gently pushing Molly toward her room. Molly nodded and moved swiftly into the chamber, emerging a minute later in a pair of sweatpants and a sweatshirt. Hobbling on one foot at a time, she pulled on her socks and then she pulled her hair back into a pony tail and secured it with a band.

It took Mildred and Gertrude a little longer to get ready, but they were dressed and back out in the hallway in time to see the paramedics carrying Harriett down the stairs on a gurney. At the bottom of the stairs, Molly and her aunts stepped into boots and pulled on their coats. Mildred grabbed her handbag and they breezed out the front door. They all piled into Molly's new vehicle, then Simon backed the SUV out of the driveway and sped off after the ambulance.

With their eyes focused upon the road in front of them, not one of them noticed that the lights were on in all of the homes around their little corner of Chestnut Street and that the faces peering from the windows of the houses were wrinkled with genuine concern. Oblivious to all, they rode along in deadly silence. When they finally reached the hospital emergency entrance, Harriett was nowhere to be seen. They were informed that she had been taken to a room to be examined and then she would be sent to a different area of the hospital for tests. They had nothing more to do but find a seat in the waiting room and keep themselves distracted until someone brought them news of Harriett's condition.

Around eight o'clock in the morning, Simon stepped outside

with his mobile phone and called his parents to let them know what had happened and to not plan on them for Christmas dinner. Lillian and Henry told him that they would be at the hospital as soon as they could get there.

By eight-thirty, they were all starting to lose patience. Just as Mildred was about to start raising hell with the emergency room receptionist, a doctor in scrubs and a white lab coat popped through a set of swinging doors and asked one of the emergency room nurses where Harriett O'Connor's family was seated. They waved to get the doctor's attention, and he walked swiftly toward them.

The doctor held out his hand to Mildred and said, "Hello, I'm Doctor Richardson. I am a neurologist." The doctor looked to be in his mid-fifties which instilled confidence in terms of his experience. Dr. Richardson had a thick head of steel gray hair and a neatly trimmed mustache framing his upper lip, both of which gave him an air of distinction.

"Hello," Mildred replied, firmly shaking his hand. "What news do you have about my sister?"

"We believe that she's had stroke," he informed them. "At least that's our best guess right now. I was just about to have a good look at the results of her MRI to see what exactly has gone on in her brain and once I have that information I will know much more."

"How is she doing otherwise?" Simon asked.

"Well, she's in a coma, but once the swelling in her brain subsides, I'm hoping she will come right out of it. Her vital signs are good and we've already started her on clot-busting drugs. She appears to have quite a strong constitution for an eighty-year-old woman." Both Mildred and Simon smiled at his statement.

"When do you think we will be able to see her?" Molly asked.

"They're getting her situated in a bed in ICU, and once she is settled, I'll have someone come down to get you," Doctor Richardson promised. "I will visit with all of you again when I have her test results." The doctor started to turn away. "Oh," he said, stopping midstep, "and when you visit her, go in one at a time, and be sure to touch her and talk to her. I want to get that brain of hers working again as soon as possible." Then the doctor disappeared through the same doors through which he had come.

Later, Henry and Lillian came rushing into the emergency room with a picnic hamper and a tote full of magazines and newspapers, obviously prepared to settle in and wait for news about Harriett. When they were all comfortably seated and thinking positively about what little information the doctor had given them, Simon rose and pulled Mildred aside. He noted that her smooth, delicate features were lost behind a veil of worry, and her hazel-green eyes seemed to be searching for reassurance. Her bobbed silver hair was free of the barrettes she normally wore to keep it back, and she nervously tucked it behind her ears. Simon wanted to pull her small frame into his arms and comfort her.

"Do you think we should call Molly's father and uncle?" he whispered.

"I hadn't even thought," Mildred said absently. Looking over at Molly and then up into Simon's eyes, she said, "Yes, we must. They have a right to know."

"Do you want me to do it?"

"I can't ask that of you," Mildred said, shaking her head. "I'll take care of it."

"Would you like to use my phone?" Simon offered, holding it out to her.

"Thank you." Mildred took the mobile phone and stared at it for a moment.

"You'll get better reception near the outer door," he suggested. "And that way, Molly won't hear you."

"Exactly," Mildred replied, rubbing a hand on Simon's back. She excused herself and walked out the automatic doors.

"Wow! What a Christmas," Simon whispered as he watched her go.

Chapter Eighteen

Late morning, a friendly nurse led them to the ICU. After they got themselves settled in the waiting area, it was decided that Mildred would be the first to visit with Harriett. When she saw her sister for the first time since that morning, Mildred was pleased to see that Harriett's color was better, yet at the same time she was disturbed by the eerie silence hovering over her sister's comatose form. Taking a seat beside Harriett, Mildred gently picked up her hand and stroked the back of it. Softly she said, "Hattie, you don't have to hold on for any of us. You can go if you want to. I know how unhappy you've been in this life and I wish you only peace and joy in the next. Just know that I love you, Hattie, for always." Mildred leaned over and kissed Harriett's forehead and then paused a moment to look for any signs of recognition in her sister's lifeless face. She noticed a slight droop on the right side of her sister's mouth. Then she added, "And Molly loves you so dearly. You know that."

Mildred stayed with her sister for about ten minutes, silently caressing her hand and remembering the happier moments of their childhood. Then she gave up her spot to Gertrude, who cried nonstop and soon returned to the waiting area. Despite the ICU rules, Simon accompanied Molly to her grandmother's bedside. He was awed by Molly's poise and composure as she sat talking cheerfully to Harriett, holding her grandmother's hand and gently rubbing the bruised and paper thin skin on her forearm.

"Come on, Granny, open those eyes," Molly coaxed. "We need you here with us a while longer. I want you to be there when I graduate from college. I want you to be proud of me." Simon gently squeezed her shoulder. "I know we all probably annoy the hell out of you, Granny," Molly added lightly, "but we like being with you. We love you. So, please open your eyes. Please, come back to us."

Lillian and Henry each spent a few moments at Harriett's bedside, and then Lillian tried to talk everyone into eating a little something to keep up their strength while they waited for an update from the neurologist. Molly developed a headache as a result of stress and exhaustion, and Simon took her to the nurses' station to see if there was anything she could take for the pain that was safe for the baby. As they were returning to the waiting area, Dr. Richardson appeared and motioned for all of them to follow him. Then the doctor led them down the hallway to a small conference room where they took a seat around a rectangular oak table.

Seated at the head of the table, the doctor began, "Hello, again. We've done many tests on Harriett and I finally have some results and concrete information for you. What we know is that she has suffered a stroke, specifically an ischemic stroke, which is caused by a blood clot in the brain. The clot produced a blockage in the left hemisphere of her cerebrum that cut off blood flow to her brain cells, destroying quite a few of them." Dr. Richardson looked around the table to make sure they were all still with him.

"Now, the left side of the brain controls the right side of the body as well as speech function, so some of the things we might expect for Harriett include paralysis on her right side and speech difficulties. There are also some other results that can be expected from such a brain injury, but we won't know if they're present until she has awoken from the coma. The good news is," he added quickly, "that in the first few days after a stroke there is a spontaneous recovery period during which some of the damage can be repaired by the body."

Leaning back in his chair, Dr. Richardson glanced around the table, looking each and every one in the eye. "I won't lie to you. She's still in danger, and the damage to her brain could be severe due to the length of time the brain cells were deprived of oxygen. And there's always the risk of another stroke. So, right now, I'm focusing on getting her through this episode, trying to prevent another stroke, and hoping for the best case scenario. She seems to have a strong constitution and that can work in her favor, even for someone of her age."

"When do you think she will wake up?" Molly asked.

"What is your name?" Dr. Richardson asked politely.

"Molly. I'm her granddaughter."

"It's nice to meet you, Molly," Dr. Richardson said smiling. "In all honesty I have no idea when she'll wake up. It could be this evening or two days from now. But, based on the information that I have and the way things look in her brain, along with the course of drug therapy that we have her on, I am confident that she will come out of the coma."

"So, all we can do is wait," Simon said.

"I'm afraid so," Dr. Richardson replied. "At this point, we have to let the stroke run its course and hope for the best outcome under the circumstances."

Everyone looked helplessly around the room at one another and then Mildred said, "Thank you for taking the time to explain all of this, Doctor Richardson."

"And you are?"

"Mildred, Harriett's sister."

Dr. Richardson reached over and covered Mildred's hand with his own, the touch of his warm flesh bringing her comfort. "I promise you that I will do my best for your sister."

"Thank you, Doctor," Mildred replied, patting his hand. "And thank you for being here on Christmas day."

Smiling at her in sympathy, Dr. Richardson said, "People have emergencies every day of the year. We can't pick and choose when these things will happen."

"We certainly can't," she agreed.

The doctor glanced around the room. "Are there any more questions before I leave?"

They all looked at him and then at one another with blank expressions, and Henry said, "I don't think so, Doc."

"All right." Dr. Richardson gently rapped his knuckles on the table top. "Let's all hope for the best." He waved a hand and left the room.

"Well, I am going to the chapel to do my part," Mildred said wearily, pushing herself out of her chair.

"I'll come with you," Gertrude said as she rose from her chair with a helping hand from Henry.

Simon grabbed Molly by the hands and pulled her out of her chair. "Moll, I think I should take you home so you can get some rest."

"No!" Molly cried with panic in her eyes. "I want to be here if she wakes up."

"But, honey," Simon said brushing the hair back from her face with both of his hands, "you look absolutely exhausted. I think you could use some sleep."

"He's right, dear," Mildred said, looking her over.

"I want to stay with Granny," Molly said in a trembling voice.

Sensing that Molly was about to fall to pieces, Simon pulled her into his arms. "All right. Don't get upset. We'll stay for a while longer."

"Why don't you come to the chapel with us," Gertrude suggested, gently taking Molly by the elbow.

"All right," Molly agreed, leaving Simon's side to go along with her great-aunts.

Out in the corridor, Henry stepped up beside Simon and wrapped an arm around his son's shoulders. "How are you doing, kid?"

"It's hard, Dad," he confessed. "It's hard to see someone you care about suspended between life and death, and it's even harder to know that it's breaking the heart of the one you love and there's not a damn thing you can do about it."

"I understand," Henry said, pulling Simon closer. "That's exactly how I felt when Lil's mom died. But everything works out the way it's supposed to and in the end your relationship with Molly will be even stronger because you have shared this experience."

"Thanks, Dad. That's comforting to hear."

Lillian stood in the doorway of the conference room listening to their exchange. Simon's words touched her deeply. He was truly in love with Molly; she did not need any more proof. Marching past them, she hurried to catch up with the group going to the chapel.

As he watched the women moving down the corridor, Simon

suddenly bolted after them and pulled Mildred aside. She waved the rest of them on and promised to catch up.

"Did you get a hold of Molly's father?" Simon asked anxiously. "Is he coming?"

"Yes," she whispered, even though Molly was well out of earshot. "He'll be arriving by plane this evening and catching a cab directly to the hospital. His brother, on the other hand, couldn't care less. He still harbors so much resentment for Hattie."

Simon covered his mouth with a hand and thought for a moment. "I'd better take Molly home for a nap so that she's not overly tired when she sees him. I don't want her to be at a disadvantage."

"Good thinking," Mildred agreed. "Why don't you come with us to the chapel and take her away after a few minutes? Take her back to your house," she suggested. "The memories of last night might still be too fresh and she may not be able to sleep at home."

"I think you're right."

Mildred looped her arm through his and they started walking down the corridor.

"What did her father say?" he asked.

"Not much. He didn't even ask about Molly."

"Bastard," Simon said angrily.

"Yes, he is," she agreed.

"Promise you'll be my ally and not let him take her away from me?"

Mildred stopped and stared up at Simon. Reaching up to take his face between her hands, she said, "My dear Simon that is not going to happen. Molly is not going to leave you. This is her home now. We are her family, and you are the love of her life."

"I know. I'm just being paranoid," he said looking away from her.

"No, you're not," Mildred assured him. "It's perfectly normal for you to be feeling insecure. I guarantee that George is not going to like you and that you are going to have to fight for what's best for Molly. But we're all going to be fighting along with you, including Molly. I don't think she's going to take much of anything from him anymore. So, don't worry yourself." Mildred smiled at Simon and patted his cheek.

"Thank you," he said, embracing her. "I needed that little pep talk."

"I know," she said wisely. "Now, let's go say a prayer for Hattie."

Simon released her from the embrace and wrapped an arm around her shoulder as they walked in the direction of the chapel. Suddenly, Mildred burst our laughing and Simon eyed her with concern.

"Can you imagine what Hattie would say about you taking Molly back to your house?"

Simon thought for a moment and laughed. "She would definitely have *something* to say about it," he agreed. And then they both sobered as they wished she were there to voice her protest.

Simon took Molly back to his bungalow while the aunts and his parents remained at the hospital with Harriett. On the drive back to his house, he wrestled with telling Molly that her father was coming that evening so that she could prepare herself for the confrontation. But, in the end, he decided that it would be better to give her the news after she had slept and regained some of her strength.

When he drove into the driveway at his house, Simon completely forgot his worries as Molly's face lit up with excitement. "I get to sleep here?"

"Yes, you do," Simon said, laughing. "And I swear that it was Aunt Millie's idea."

After helping her out of the truck, Simon glanced toward Mrs. Sullivan's kitchen window as he walked with Molly toward the house. There was the old busybody with her face pressed to glass. He waved at her.

"Who are you waving at?" Molly asked.

"My nosy neighbor," he said grinning. "I can't wait to hear the gossip she drums up about this."

"Oh, God," Molly said wincing, "She'll probably call Granny again and tell her all sorts of lies." Realizing what she had just said, she covered her face with a hand. "I can't believe I just said that."

"Honey, you're tired. Don't worry about it." They tromped up the back stairs. "Besides, Granny will be awake and ready to take Mrs. Sullivan's calls before you know it."

Molly sighed heavily and leaned into his chest. Kissing her on the top of the head, Simon reached into his pocket for his keys and realized that he had forgotten to grab them when he made his mad dash out of the house in the wee hours of the morning. He turned the door knob and they stepped into the kitchen.

Simon helped Molly out of her coat, bolted the door behind them and asked, "Would you like something to eat or drink? Some soup? A cup of tea?"

"No thank you," she replied. Then she stepped into his unsuspecting arms and snuggled into his chest. "Please just take me to bed. I'm exhausted."

Simon gathered her up in his arms and carried her to the bedroom.

Simon and Molly slept soundly for nearly four hours, and they would have continued slumbering peacefully in each other's arms had it not been for the shrill ringing of the telephone around five o'clock. Simon woke with a start and reached for the phone, only to realize that he had tossed it in a panic that morning. Propping himself up on his elbows, he spied it resting underneath his dresser. He willed the voice messaging to pick up so that the racket would cease.

"Too early," Molly groaned, rolling over on the pillow and bumping her nose into his arm. Turning her head, she saw Simon's face. "Hello," she said happily.

"Hello," Simon replied, lying back down beside her and draping an arm around her middle. "How are you?"

"Much better," she assured him. Then she placed her hand upon his cheek and traced her thumb across his brow and asked, "How about you?"

"I'm great. I love sleeping with you in my arms."

Staring into the depths of his dark brown eyes, she softly said, "I love you, Simon . . . so deeply."

"Then marry me and let me be the father of your child." The words were out of his mouth before he could catch them.

Speechless, Molly stared at him with wide eyes. "I'm serious, Moll. I want to spend the rest of my life with you, for better or worse . . . for all of it."

Molly's bright green eyes flooded with tears as she said, "Yes . . . I mean, no . . . I'm not sure about the baby thing." She closed her eyes tightly and stuffed her face into the pillow.

"What about the marriage thing?" Simon asked hopefully.

Molly pulled her face out of the pillow and smiled. "Yes, I want to marry you and spend the rest of my life with you," she answered. "I have no doubts about that." Simon kissed her lips softly. She put a hand against his chest, and added, "But, I don't know about the baby, Simon. I need to think about it."

"I understand."

Looking at him curiously, she said, "Why do you want this baby so much? Why do you care about it?"

"Because it's a part of you, and I don't want to let it go." He reached under the bedcovers to place his hand on her slightly rounded abdomen. "I think that together we would make great parents."

"I don't know about that," she said doubtfully. "Look at my parents. What if I turn out to be like them?"

"Honey, that's not going to happen," Simon assured her. "You're nothing like them. You're patient, tolerant, and forgiving, and you give your love so freely. And those are just a few of the items on the long list of reasons why I love you so much."

Molly laughed. "That was almost a tongue twister," she teased.

"I'm serious. I think you are going to be a terrific mother." He patted her warm belly.

"But not to this baby," she said sadly. "I just don't think I can live with the reminder for the rest of my life."

"I see," Simon said, turning away from her. Perhaps he was wrong about her having a change of heart about the baby. That meant they would have to wait until after the baby was born to get married, and the fact was that he didn't want to wait another day.

Simon's reaction filled Molly's heart with remorse, and she panicked at the sudden thought that he might change his mind about wanting to marry her. Snuggling up against his side, she said, "But someday I want to have lots of babies with you."

Simon wrapped an arm around her and pulled her closer. "But not until you've finished school and started a career. You should to do some things for yourself first."

"I'm glad you think that way."

"I honestly do," he assured her.

The phone rang again and Molly jumped. "That might be about Granny!"

Simon crawled out of bed and went to retrieve the phone from under the dresser. "Hello? Hi, Mom. Is there any news about Harriett?" Molly sat up and looked expectantly at him.

"No change," Simon said, looking sympathetically at her. He walked to the bed and sat back down. Reaching for Molly's hand, he clasped it to his chest. She draped her other arm over his shoulder from behind and rested her chin on his shoulder, listening as he continued the conversation with his mother.

"She's fine. We both got some sleep." Simon tugged on her hand and turned to smile at her. "That sounds great," he said into the phone. "We'll see you around six." Simon put the phone back in its cradle.

"What's up?" Molly asked.

"They're putting together a little Christmas dinner at The Aunt Hill and then everyone plans to go back to the hospital until visiting hours are over."

"No change in Granny, then," Molly said sadly.

"Not yet," Simon said optimistically. "Just give her some time, honey. The doctor said that once the swelling goes down in her brain she should wake up."

"She has to wake up," Molly said firmly. "It's too soon for her to go."

"I know," Simon said. Then he kissed her hard on the lips. "Come on. Let's take a shower and head over there." He moved to get up but she held him down. "What?" he asked, cranking his head back to look at her.

Grinning, Molly said, "You asked me to marry you."

"Yes, I did."

Chapter Nineteen

Molly and Simon arrived at The Aunt Hill a little after six and found the family gathered around the kitchen table speaking in subdued tones. They all looked exhausted which made Molly feel terrible about sneaking away with Simon for the afternoon, leaving them to stand vigil. Yet, she wouldn't have given up their time together now that she knew the outcome. She was engaged to Simon Mulberry. For both of them, it was a dream come true, but they agreed on the drive over to keep their secret until a more appropriate time. Right now, it was imperative that they all focus upon Harriett's recovery.

Mildred noticed that something was different about Simon and Molly, but she could not put her finger on it. Her first thought was that they had been drawn closer by Harriett's tragedy, but then she went a step further and a lovely thought blossomed in her mind. Watching them closely, Mildred smiled to herself.

After a quick supper, they headed back to the hospital. They were disappointed to learn that Harriett's condition had not changed and that she was still lost in a coma. Mildred went in to visit with her first and Gertrude followed. Then it was Molly's turn, and she stayed with her grandmother for a long time. She had found a discarded paperback novel in the waiting area, and after chatting with Harriett for awhile, she began to read the murder mystery aloud. She droned on for several chapters before giving up on the exercise and leaving her grandmother in peace. She strolled back down the corridor lost in deep thought.

Molly heard a familiar voice as she neared the ICU reception desk, and curiously, she looked up to see a man standing there in a long camel hair coat. When she saw the man's face, she froze in her tracks. The man glanced over at her and their eyes locked. As they held each other's gaze in silence, Molly felt as though she were suspended in time while the world continued on around them. He was the first to move, and as he came toward her, Molly unconsciously took a few steps backward. He immediately stopped advancing.

"Hello, Molly."

"Hello, Father."

George O'Connor almost did not recognize his own daughter. Molly had truly changed. She looked more mature, more experienced, definitely transfigured by all that had happened. As they stood there staring at one another across a space of about ten feet, George marveled at the transformation in the girl who had captured his heart as a baby.

Simon was paging through a tattered *Sports Illustrated* magazine when he looked up to see Molly standing rigidly in front of a gentleman with graying temples. Mildred was sitting on the sofa beside him and he grabbed her arm in panic.

"Is that him?" Simon croaked.

"Oh, dear," Mildred cried. "You didn't get a chance to warn her."

"Shit!" Simon hissed, jumping up from the sofa.

"Simon wait!" Mildred called, racing after him. She caught him by the shirt and pulled him back. "Let me handle this, please. I have a little more experience with George than you do."

"All right. But I'm coming with you."

Together they approached the pair, who were poised for a face off. Raising her eyes to the ceiling, Mildred silently begged, "Oh, please. Not here."

Approaching her nephew with an outstretched hand, Mildred said, "George, you made it safely." She shook his hand quickly. "I'm so glad that you came. Your mother will be touched and pleased."

"Hello, Aunt Millie," George said gruffly.

Simon stepped in between Mildred and Molly, and George eyed him suspiciously. "Who are you?" he asked rudely.

"I'm Simon Mulberry, a friend of Molly's." Simon held a hand out to Molly and she grabbed it as if it were a lifeline.

George eyed their clasped hands and fury bubbled up inside of him. "Don't touch my daughter," he said through clenched teeth.

"Why don't you ask Molly if she wants me to touch her?" Simon said defensively.

"Simon, please," Mildred begged.

"How dare you talk to me that way, boy," George said disdainfully.

"Excuse me?" Simon said in disbelief.

The slur against Simon was all Molly needed to find her voice and courage. "Don't talk to my fiancé that way," she ordered.

"Your what?" George cried. "Like hell he is." Mildred eyed them both and then gave Molly a look of warning.

"You have absolutely no say in what goes on in my life any more," Molly informed her father. "I'm no longer your daughter, remember?"

"How dare you talk to me that way!"

"That's enough!" Mildred warned, muffling a shout. "This is a hospital, not an arena." Turning to Molly and Simon, she said, "Simon, take Molly home to our house and wait for us." Without a word, Simon pulled Molly away with him.

"As for you," Mildred said, turning to George. "Don't you ever speak to your daughter or Simon like that again, or I will kick your sorry behind all the way back to Chicago. You always were an insolent little boy and I am ashamed to see that you have not grown out of it." Mildred felt nothing but disgust. "What on earth could you possibly be thinking to come here and pick another fight with your daughter when your mother is lying in a hospital bed fighting for her life?"

"It's Molly who started all of this," he said defensively.

"No, George, a perverted college boy started all of this," Mildred corrected. "What Molly told you was true, you cretin. Think about what was done to her, to your daughter. Where is your love and compassion?"

George lowered his eyes.

"Molly went through something awful, and she survived and is moving on with her life," Mildred continued. "That man who you regarded with such disdain, and for which I am utterly ashamed of you, is the reason she has been able to move on. He's the primary

source of happiness in her life. She loves him deeply, and I promise you that she will choose him over you if you make it a contest."

George felt as if his aunt had slapped him hard across the face.
He colored with humiliation.

"I know you have a heart, George," she said in a softer tone,
"and that your wife has turned it to stone. But you had better find
a way to use it again or you will die a lonely, miserable old man."

When George looked up, she could see the fear in his eyes. "Now,
forget about Molly and Simon for the time being and go make
amends with your mother before she dies and it's too late," Mildred
instructed. "She's unconscious but perhaps she can hear you."

He looked down the corridor in the direction from which Molly
had come. Then he looked back at Mildred. "Where do I go?"

"Follow me," Mildred said in vexation.

Molly paced back and forth in the parking lot, her breath puff-
ing into little clouds in the cold night air. Simon stood by her
new SUV and watched her with his arms folded tightly across his
chest and his jaw set in anger. He wanted to strike out, but not at
her, so he bit his tongue and waited for her to calm down and get
into the car. George had cut him and the wound still stung. Why
hadn't Molly warned him that her father was a bigot? Then again,
he had not warned her about his coming, and she had definitely
been blind-sided. But why did she have to go and announce their
engagement like that? It made him feel like she had only said yes
to his proposal to get back at her parents.

"Damn it, Molly, why did you announce our engagement like
that?" he suddenly shouted.

"Why didn't you warn me that he was coming?" she shouted
back. "You knew. I could see it in your eyes." She stopped pacing
and pointed an accusing finger at him.

"I wanted to tell you earlier, but you were so tired and I was
afraid you would flip out," he cried. "Then I was going to tell you
when you came out of your visit with Granny. I didn't think he
would arrive this soon."

"You should have told me!"

"And you should have told me that the color of my skin was
going to be an issue with him!"

Molly slowly dropped her finger and stared at him. Her eyes suddenly filled with tears and she said, "I hate him for the way he treated you."

Simon opened his arms to her. Molly walked into them and buried her face in his shoulder. "I'm sorry," he whispered. "I screwed up. That all played out badly because I was afraid to tell you he was coming."

"I'm so sorry he treated you that way," Molly said to his chest.

Simon hugged her tightly and said, "Don't validate his actions by apologizing for him. It's not your responsibility."

"But you're not going to want to have to deal with him as a father-in-law." Molly looked up into his eyes to see his reaction to her words.

"Don't even think it. We can't let him split us up, Moll," Simon said firmly.

"I'm an adult now; he has no control over me."

"My head knows that but my heart still has doubts."

"Doubts about me?" she asked fearfully.

"I confess that I wondered if you agreed to marry me just to get back at him," Simon said, looking away.

Molly stared up at his profile, completely at a loss for words. A car drove into the parking lot and pulled into a space not far from them. She could feel Simon start to pull away, and she reached up to turn his face back to look at her. Tears spilled from her eyes and rolled down her cheeks. "Please don't think that. I swear to you that I never once thought about it because I don't see you as different. To me you're just beautiful. You make me feel safe and I trust you like no one else." she explained. "I want to marry you because I love you and want to be with you. I promise. Please don't ever think so badly of me again."

"Oh, honey," Simon whispered, caressing her cheek with his gloved hand. Then he seized the back of her neck and kissed her, and all the anger, frustration and fear poured out of him. Molly felt all of his emotions in the kiss, and she held on for dear life to ride out the storm with him.

On the drive back to The Aunt Hill, Mildred was still fuming, Gertrude was fretting, and George was stewing. George had visited briefly with his mother, becoming extremely upset at the sight of her. It dawned on him that she actually might die, and then she would be gone from his life forever. For years he had believed that such an event would bring him great relief, but now he felt the complete opposite. They had never really gotten along, but he was suddenly able to remember loving her as a child and believing that her warm lap was the best place to be on earth. George felt only confusion as he tried to determine how he had become such an ungrateful son and unloving father. When they drove up to The Aunt Hill and he thought about seeing Molly and Simon again, his hands began to tremble.

Mildred stormed into the house and immediately went in search of Simon and Molly, while Gertrude held the door for George to bring his luggage inside. Mildred's search ended abruptly in the kitchen where the young couple was sitting at the table having a drink. She spied the glass of scotch in front of Simon and then the glass of wine in front of Molly. "Do you think that's wise?" she asked.

"I've just taken a few sips to help me relax," Molly explained. "I don't want to lose control and say stupid things again."

"I see." Mildred shrugged her coat off and draped it over the chair next to Simon. Putting a hand on his shoulder, she stood between the two of them, looking back and forth. "Is it true that you're engaged?"

"Yes," Molly said shyly.

"Yes," Simon concurred.

"Very well," Mildred said, taking Molly by the hand. "Come with me and tell that to your father, and tell him exactly how you feel about everything."

Simon rose from his chair and Mildred held out a hand to his chest. "You stay put," she instructed. "After Molly has had a chance to set her father straight, you'll get to have a few words with George."

Simon held up his hands as a sign of surrender and then stepped in to give Molly a kiss on the forehead. "Good luck," he said softly.

The women walked out of the kitchen, hand in hand. "George," Mildred ordered. "Come into the parlor."

Crossing the foyer, George peered into the parlor and saw

Mildred and Molly standing near the sofa holding hands. Motioning for him to enter the room, Mildred said, "Come, come."

Moving across the parlor and stopping just a few feet from them, George stuffed his trembling hands into his pants pockets. "Hello, again, Molly."

"What else do you have to say to your daughter, George?" Mildred asked impatiently.

Looking into Molly's eyes, he paused, and then said, "I'm sorry for what I said at the hospital. I'm sorry if I offended your friend."

"He's more than my friend," Molly corrected. "And I want you to apologize to him for your despicable behavior."

"Why him, Molly?" George demanded. "Are you just trying to get back at your mother and me?"

"Believe it or not, everything is not about you two," Molly said evenly. "Why not him? You don't know anything about Simon. Does the color of his skin frighten you that much? How does it hurt you? How has he offended you? Simply by being?"

"I didn't say that," George snapped.

"You didn't have to," Molly snapped back.

"Listen," George instructed.

"No, you listen." Molly silenced him with a stare. "Simon is everything to me. You are nothing."

Mildred dropped her head and closed her eyes.

"You never wanted me or loved me so I went and found people who would," Molly continued. "They are my family now and I won't let you and mother take them away from me the way you took my friends away when I was growing up. You said I was no longer your daughter, so why do you care what I do?"

"How dare you throw that back in my face," George hissed.

"How dare you judge me the way you did when you and mother had to get married because she was pregnant."

Mildred looked up at George to see his reaction. His face flushed scarlet. He had no come-back for his daughter. "Well, George," she said. "Do you think an apology is in order? Perhaps you might ask your daughter's forgiveness for your inexcusable behavior."

Molly placed a hand on Mildred's arm. "I can handle this, Aunt Millie."

"I know you can, dear," Mildred replied, patting her hand. Mildred glanced over at George. "Very well, I'll leave you two to get this sorted out." She walked swiftly out of the parlor.

Molly planted her feet, crossed her arms over her chest and glared at her father.

George lowered his eyes to the floor and then looked up at his daughter. For a long time, they stared silently at one another. "I'm sorry, Molly," George said quietly. "I've been incredibly unfair. Please forgive me for the way I've treated you."

"What about Simon?" Molly demanded. "Will you apologize to him?"

George nodded his head, pulled his hands out of his pockets, and gestured in the air. "He's obviously important to you."

"Extremely," Molly said passionately.

"All right. But you'll have to give me some time to get used to the idea of the two of you together."

"Why? Simon's just a man, a very good man," Molly said matter-of-factly. "If you need time to get used to the color of his skin, then I feel sorry for you."

"Well, I'm ashamed to say that I do, Molly. And it's not something that I can change in an instant. So, what do you say, you cut me some slack?" George turned away and thought for a moment. "You've changed so much that I hardly know you."

"I've had to grow up."

"Yes, I know." A big lump lodged itself in George's throat. Swallowing hard, he said, "I'm sorry that I didn't believe you when you told us what happened. I guess I couldn't bear the thought of such a thing being done to you. And now that I've accepted it," he said, choking on his words, "I know that I can't bear it."

George's tears were Molly's undoing. She moved toward him and reached for his hand. Squeezing it tightly, she said, "It's all right, Father. If I can bear it, so can you."

George was awed by her strength and dignity. Where had it all come from? Certainly, his strong-willed mother had played a part in her growth process, but he suspected an influence from a source outside the family, and he knew exactly to whom he should give credit. It was a sharp blow to him to realize that Molly had already chosen Simon to be the male influence in her life and that he had already become irrelevant to her. It had been different when it was him choosing to cut her out of his life, but when the tables were turned it hurt more deeply than he could have imagined. He was beginning to understand what he had done to his daughter.

George gestured toward the sofa and said, "Do you mind if we sit down?"

"Sure." Molly took a seat. And when George sat down next to her, she slid back a bit on the cushions.

George crossed and uncrossed his legs and tried to find something to do with his hands. "You seem very happy here," he commented.

"I am," Molly answered quietly. "Granny, Aunt Millie, and Aunt Gertie have given me a true home, a home full of love and acceptance."

George felt the jab and had to admit that it stung. "I'm glad that you're happy."

"Thank you."

"And your grandmother told me that you have a job . . ."

"Yes, with Simon at his family's nursery." Molly's face lit up. "I love it, and I'm good at working with plants. I'm going back to school in the fall to get a degree in horticulture.

"That sounds great," George said enthusiastically. "Especially if it's something you find interesting."

"I do."

George could not stand the stilted conversation any further. Turning to face her on the sofa, he asked, "Are you still pregnant?"

"Yes, I am."

"What are you going to do with it?"

"You mean with the baby," Molly said, purposely saying the word. George nodded.

"I'm going to have the baby and give it up for adoption."

George gazed at her with eyes full of remorse. "I'm sorry you have to go through all of this."

"What's done is done. I can't change it," Molly said, shrugging.

"Forgive me, Molly. Please. What I did to you was so wrong."

George clasped Molly's hands and looked into her eyes. "Please, forgive me."

Molly searched for the forgiveness in her heart and found it. "I forgive you," she whispered. "But you still have to make amends with Simon. I'm going to marry him. He will be the father of your grandchildren."

Molly's words hit him like a punch in the gut. George took a few deep breaths and said, "I'll try. I promise that I'll try."

Mildred came walking back into the parlor with a tray and smiled at the sight of them sitting together and holding hands. "Now, that's much better," she said happily. Mildred set the tray on the coffee table. "Here you are," she said, handing a glass of scotch to George.

George took the glass from her and quickly swallowed two huge gulps. Mildred frowned at him and then handed Molly a cup of tea.

"Thanks, Aunt Millie," Molly said, smiling sheepishly. She was afraid she had been a bit dismissive when she sent her aunt away. "I'm sorry for the way I treated you."

"You don't have to apologize, dear." Mildred bent over and kissed her on the forehead. "I understand your feelings well enough to know why you did what you did."

Mildred straightened and glanced at both of them. "Well, is it time to bring Simon in here? I don't think I can keep him restrained in the kitchen much longer."

Molly looked to her father.

"Yes, bring him in," George instructed.

Mildred left, and George quickly took two more gulps of scotch. Molly watched him and realized he was nervous, not confident or arrogant.

"Don't worry. Simon won't bite," she assured him. George took another big gulp of his drink. "Remember what you promised," Molly warned him.

Simon and Mildred came strolling into the parlor holding hands, and when Molly saw her fiancé, George noticed that her face lit up like the sun. George quickly stood and smoothed down the front of his blazer.

"George," Mildred said, "I would like to introduce you to Simon Mulberry."

Simon held out his hand and George took it and shook it quickly. "Hello."

Mildred scowled at her nephew.

"Hello, Sir," Simon replied. "It's good to meet you properly."

"Listen," George said, glancing at the floor, "I'm sorry about the incident at the hospital. Please accept my apology."

"Apology accepted," Simon said quickly. "I'm sorry, too. I think we all got a little heated."

"Well, it's a beginning," Mildred said, hopefully.

Molly rose from the sofa and walked over to Simon. When she wrapped her arms around his mid-section, Simon noticed George starting to squirm. "There's a lot more to say but it's been a long day for everyone, and I think we should save it for another time," Simon suggested.

"Yes, of course," George agreed.

"Simon and I have to get up at the crack of dawn for the After Christmas Sale at the garden center tomorrow," Molly informed him.

"It's been a very long and stressful day," Mildred said, yawning. "I think a good night's sleep will do us all a world of good."

George eyed Molly and Simon and wondered where the young man intended to sleep. Mildred noticed her nephew glaring at Simon. "Molly, why don't you lock up after you've said goodbye to Simon, and I'll take your father up to his room." Mildred moved toward the foyer. "Gertrude went up awhile ago so you don't have to worry about her prowling around down here."

"All right," she said, glancing at her father. "Good night, Father."

"Good night, Molly, Simon." George followed Mildred out of the parlor.

"Good night, Sir," Simon said. "We'll see you tomorrow."

"Yes."

When George and Mildred were out of earshot, Simon asked, "So, how did it go? Your father seems to have mellowed out a bit."

"I told him exactly how I feel and how much you mean to me. I also told him that he had to make amends with you."

"He was at least civil to me."

"I want him to be more than civil," Molly said forcefully. "He knows that, and I think he'll try for my sake."

"Good." Simon wrapped her up in his arms. "And I promise that I'll make an effort with him."

"I don't doubt it." Molly rested her head on his chest. "I have complete faith in you."

"Wow. Thank you," Simon said, hugging her tightly. "I hope I don't let you down."

"You won't," Molly said confidently. She snaked her hands up underneath his turtleneck and ran them over his abdomen.

Simon stared down at her in surprise. "Moll, what do you think you're doing?"

"You heard Aunt Millie; everybody's gone upstairs for the night."

"Including your father," Simon said, trapping her hands underneath his shirt. "Who would like nothing more than to catch us in the act so that he can kill me."

Molly laughed.

"Time for bed, you wanton woman." Simon extracted her hands from under his shirt. "Tomorrow is going to be another long day. Between the sale and Granny, we've got a lot on our plate."

"You're no fun," Molly pouted.

"Oh, how wrong you are," Simon whispered near her ear. "I'm lots of fun. And as soon as you marry me, you'll find out just how much fun I can be, day and night."

A shiver ran along Molly's spine. "Oh my," she sighed.

Simon threw his head back and laughed. Draping an arm around Molly's shoulders, he walked her toward the front door.

As he was putting on his coat, Molly playfully said, "You're mean to leave me like this."

He looked up at her and smiled. "No, I'm not, honey. I'm just keeping things interesting." Then he took her in his arms and kissed her goodnight.

Chapter Twenty

The day after Christmas dawned cloudy and cold. Molly was up at the crack of dawn in anticipation of the After Christmas Sale. She ate a quick bowl of cereal and two pieces of toast and then dashed out to the car when Simon pulled up in her birthday present, which she realized she had yet to officially take possession of and drive on her own. The rest of the house was still sleeping when she left for work.

As they were pulling away from The Aunt Hill, Molly said, "I sure hope Granny wakes up today."

Taking her hand and giving it a tight squeeze, Simon said, "She will. I have a feeling this is the day."

"I hope her brain is not too damaged."

"Keep a positive attitude, honey," Simon suggested. "It was not that long from the time she had the stroke until they started treating her with the clot-busting drugs. The damage should be minimal. If she comes out of this partially paralyzed or with some speech difficulties, there's a lot they can do for her with physical and occupational therapy."

Molly looked quizzically at him. "How do you know so much?"

"I read that pamphlet that the nurse gave to everyone yesterday."

"Oh."

Smiling, Simon took his eyes off the road for a second to look over at her. "Don't worry. Granny is a tough old bird. She's going to be just fine."

"I sure hope so. I'm not ready to lose her. We were just getting to really know each other and there's still so much more for us to say to one another."

"She knows that," Simon assured her. He turned on the radio to get a weather report and to distract them both from unpleasant thoughts.

When Molly and Simon entered the garden center, Henry and Lillian were there, and bargain hunters were already lining up outside the doors. Simon had overstaffed the store with fifteen extra employees, on top of the usual six who rotated through the registers. With Molly and his parents there to help, he felt that they were properly staffed to handle the volume they expected to do that morning.

Molly and Lillian took up positions at the check-out counters where their sole duty would be to tissue wrap and bag purchases. Simon and Henry took up posts on the floor where they could answer questions, help take ornaments off trees, and, most importantly, keep an eye on people; t'was the season for shoplifters. With all the Christmas items fifty percent off and some of the other store merchandise at thirty percent off, there was a great deal for everyone to keep track of that day.

When Henry opened the doors at nine o'clock to welcome the shoppers, he was nearly run down by a band of crazed women who headed straight for the artificial tree covered with Radko ornaments, which they frantically plucked off the branches as if it were an apple picking contest. Molly had never seen anything like it. At first she was completely overwhelmed with the quantities of each customer's purchase and was in a panic as she tried to wrap and bag the items. After an hour and several reassuring winks from Lillian, she settled down into a comfortable rhythm which afforded her the luxury of handing each overfilled bag to its owner with a cheery, "Thank you and have a great day!"

While the mayhem was occurring at Mulberry's, George, Mildred and Gertrude were on their way to the hospital in the Comet, which was giving Mildred some trouble in the cold. After chugging their way to Lakeview Memorial, they arrived to the welcome news that Harriett had come out of her coma. The nurse tried to call them the moment it happened, but they were en route to the hospital. Anxious to see her, they moved in the direction of the ward. The nurse stopped their collective advance with her outstretched arms. "Doctor Richardson is in with her now and should be out shortly. After he has had a chance to examine her, I know he'll have more information about her condition to share with you." So it was back to the waiting room. When the doctor appeared, he motioned them all into the same conference room he had addressed them in the previous day.

When they were all seated around the small table, Dr. Richardson and George introduced themselves. Then, leaning his elbows on the table, the doctor said, "Well, the good news, which I assume you have already heard, is that Harriett is awake. She's very alert and she understands what I'm saying to her. The bad news is that the damage to her brain cells was rather extensive. She's paralyzed on her right side and she has lost her power of speech." Dr. Richardson paused a moment to let his words register. "Now, we are in the spontaneous recovery period so we could still see some improvements over the next few days. We will get her started with some physical and occupational therapy right away, which can be very helpful."

At Dr. Richardson's words, Gertrude started to cry, and Mildred wrapped her arm around her for comfort. She asked, "So, what can we expect when we go in there?"

"Well, I don't know if any of you have noticed yet, but the right side of her face is drooping from the paralysis; you especially notice this at the corner of her mouth and her eye," Dr. Richardson said evenly. "You also need to be prepared for the fact that she may be emotional, sudden bursts of crying and anger. She cannot respond to you even though she understands what you're saying and this will be frustrating for her."

"What do you think her quality of life will be like?" George asked sternly.

Dr. Richardson responded, "There's a lot that can be done for her, and she obviously has a family who loves her and will be there to keep her life interesting." Glancing around the table at the faces staring back at him, he added, "You must all keep in mind that there's always the risk of another stroke, which may or may not end her life. But with the drugs we have and with monitoring her diet, we can do our best to try and prevent such an occurrence."

"How long will she have to stay in the hospital?" Mildred asked nervously.

"We're going to move her to a different room this afternoon," Dr. Richardson said, smiling sweetly at Mildred. "And I would like to keep her here for about a week to see how her recovery is going. Then we will discuss what comes next. But, don't worry about that now. Just talk to her, give her support and encouragement, and be happy that she is alive for you to do that."

At his words, Mildred's eyes welled with tears and Dr. Richardson reached a comforting hand across the table toward her. Taking it, Mildred smiled through her tears and said, "Thank you, Doctor, for taking such good care of Hattie."

"You're very welcome," he replied, giving her hand a gentle squeeze. He looked around the table. "Do you have any more questions for me?" There was a collective shaking of heads in response. "Well, if you think of anything or have any concerns, just have the nurses page me." Dr. Richardson rose from his chair and left the room.

There was an awful silence that followed his departure. Nobody moved. Nobody volunteered to be the first to visit Harriett. For some time, they all sat there silently wondering about Harriett's present and future. Mildred finally stood up. "I'm going to visit with Hattie now. I think it's best if we go in one at a time." Looking down at George, she added, "You should come next, George. It will make her happy to know that you came all this way for her." Then Mildred walked out of the room.

Cautiously approaching Harriett's bed, Mildred forced herself to unclench her hands and drop them to her sides so that her sister would not see her anxiety. Harriett's face was turned away from her, and when Mildred gently touched her left arm to get her attention, it took a moment before Harriett turned her face on the pillow and looked back at her sister. Mildred was immediately shocked by the transformation of her sister's face which had not been so noticeable when Harriett was sleeping peacefully in her coma. The right corner of her mouth was down-turned in an exaggerated frown and the lower lid of her right eye sagged down into the outer corner of her eye socket. It was almost too much for Mildred to bear. Her sister had already suffered so much hardship during her life. Harriett did not deserve this current imprisonment. Being trapped in one's own body without any way to express feelings, thoughts or opinions was tantamount to a death sentence as far as Mildred was concerned. What had God been thinking when he decided not to take Harriett from a life she had grown to despise?

While Mildred was pondering her questions, she realized that Harriett was looking at her as if she did not know her, as if she could not see her. Suddenly, Mildred remembered her sister's eyeglasses which they had tucked into the drawer of the console near Harriett's bed. She quickly retrieved them and placed them on her sister's face. Mildred watched with relief as recognition dawned in Harriett's eyes. "Hello, Hattie. Did you have a nice rest?" Harriett did not respond. She simply stared back at her sister as if she were seeing her for the very first time.

"You gave us quite a scare, you know. But Doctor Richardson—he's your neurologist—says that you're going to be just fine. He's going to help you get better. We all are."

Much to Mildred's surprise and horror, Harriett responded to her gentle words with tears that suddenly sprang from her eyes and rolled down the sides of her face. Looking around the room for a box of tissue, Mildred hurried to pull a few sheets from the box sitting atop the bedside table and then began mopping her sister's tear-stained face.

"It's perfectly all right to cry, Hattie," Mildred assured her. "Your life has been turned upside down in a horrible way, but, I'm here and Gertie's here, and Molly, and Simon. We all love you, Hattie, and we are going to help you through this."

Mildred's words brought more tears and she simply continued to mop them up with the tissues. She figured that it was her sister's only way of expressing herself at that moment, and it was certainly better for her to cry in front of Mildred than any other member of the family. Harriett was so proud, and Mildred knew that this had to be the most awful blow she had experienced in her life of misery and disappointment. So, with a heart full of sympathy and love, Mildred sat there wiping away Harriett's tears and cooing to her that everything would be all right. There really was not much more to say, and Mildred knew that it would be torture to ask Harriett questions that she could not answer.

Eventually, Harriett stopped crying and Mildred rose to leave so that George could visit with her next. As she stood up, she felt a fierce grip on her wrist. She looked down at Harriett to see her good eye filled with panic. "Don't worry, I'm not leaving you. But I have a surprise for you, and I would like to go get it." Reluctantly, Harriett released her sister's arm and Mildred walked away.

Like a scared child, George first peaked at his mother from a distance until he found the courage to approach her. When he came into her vision, the look of surprise in Harriett's one eye was undeniable. At first she looked at him in wonder, then with anger, and finally affection, and as George watched all these emotions alter her face, he remembered being six years old and coming home to his mother, having torn his best pair of pants while play-ing stickball with his friends in the street one Sunday after church. Back then, Harriett had first looked at him with surprise, as if she could not believe that he would wear his Sunday pants to play stickball, and then she had scowled at him in anger which made him cry and say that he was sorry, and finally she had smiled at him affectionately and opened her arms to him, wrapping him in a bear hug that made him feel loved and forgiven. George's quick trip down memory lane brought unwanted tears to his eyes that he tried desperately to blink away. He had not cried in front of his mother since he was a child.

"Mom, I'm so sorry about what has happened to you," he said woefully, taking a seat beside her and clasping her hand. "Please forgive me for being such a miserable son and for what I did to Molly. You were right, and I was very wrong." George paused and looked down at the floor beside the bed. He felt a tugging on his hand and glanced back to find Harriett eyeing him sternly. Some-how, he understood her.

"Yes, I had a talk with Molly and I think we understand each other better now. She has forgiven me to a point." Leaning closer to his mother's deformed face, he continued, "I'm still trying to get used to the idea of Simon, but they seem to really love each other."

Harriett nodded and smiled with the left side of her face which twisted her lips into an elongated S-shape, the sight of which made George want to weep. Instead of losing his composure, George tried to be reassuring. "I'm going to get you the best therapists, Mom, even if it means carting you down to the Mayo Clinic in Rochester, where they will get you walking and talking again in no time," George said.

Harriett was unconvinced but thought it was sweet nonetheless. It was something that a little boy would say to his adored mother which is one thing that Harriett never had felt she had been.

Harriett had so many regrets about how she behaved when she was married to Gerald O'Connor, and now that she no longer had the power to do so, there was suddenly so much she wanted to say to her sons. Trapped in her silent world, listening and understanding, but having no idea how to form a word in response, Harriett silently prayed to God that her children would understand and be able to forgive her for being such an angry, unhappy person all of their lives. Deep down inside, Harriett had a feeling that her time on earth might soon be coming to an end. She had so much mending of relationships to work on and so little time to do it.

In desperation, she tugged on George's arm with her good hand and tried to convey to him with her eyes what she was thinking. Smiling tenderly at her, and completely misunderstanding her gesture, George said, "Don't worry, Mom. I'm going to stay around for a while and see that you get the care you need. Then, I'll just commute back and forth from Chicago until you are on your feet again." Rising from the chair beside the bed, he added, "Now, I'm going to get Aunt Gertie. She's most anxious to see you. Molly and Simon had to work the big sale at the nursery this morning, but they'll be here as soon as they can get away. Molly has taken this pretty hard. She's the one who found you, and she's so worried about you."

The knowledge that Molly had come across her after her episode made Harriett's heart sick. The poor girl had enough on her plate without having to worry about her decaying grandmother. But hearing that Molly was so concerned about her was enough to start the tears flowing again. Shocked to see his mother crying and feeling extremely uncomfortable, George grabbed a tissue for her, stuffed it in her left hand and raised her hand to her face so that she could mop up her tears by herself. Then he quickly left the room to get Gertrude.

When Gertrude approached Harriett's bedside, she was already crying. Harriett wished that her sister had not come to visit. Even as a child, Harriett had never been able to stand Gertrude's crying because she did it so often and it grated on Harriett's nerves. The last thing she needed right now was Gertrude blubbering at her bedside. She was frustrated enough being trapped inside of her head without any way to express herself. Gertrude would just add to her frustration.

Predictable as ever, Gertrude took Harriett's hand and whined, "I'm so sorry, Hattie. I can't believe this happened to you. I wish it had happened to me, instead. I don't think it would bother me as much as it will bother you."

Harriett thought she had a point, but that was neither here nor there since she was the one lying in a hospital bed, partially paralyzed and rendered mute. She instantly wished that Gertrude would stop crying and talk about something else. Even a boring tutorial on her rose garden would be more pleasant than watching her sister's contorted face flood with tears.

Sniffing and dabbing at her eyes with a hankie, Gertrude asked, "Is there anything I can get you, Hattie? Do you want some water? Should I make you some special food for dinner? Of course, I don't know if they will let me bring food into you and Doctor Richardson did say that you needed to go on a special diet, but I can ask if you would like." While Gertrude rambled on nervously, Harriett tuned her out and thought about her son. Maybe he did actually care for her after all.

"Hattie?" Gertrude interrupted Harriett's pleasant thoughts and she scowled at her sister in annoyance. "Oh dear," Gertrude whined. "Maybe I should just leave you alone."

Harriett tugged on her sister's arm to get her attention. When

Gertrude looked at her, Harriett nodded and pointed her finger toward the corridor in an attempt to instruct her sister to leave. It took Gertrude a moment to get the meaning of Harriett's gestures. Eventually, she left her sister in peace. Inside, Harriett breathed a sigh of relief and closed her eyes. Then she thought of Molly and Simon and the baby and remembered the file that she had received from the private investigator.

While Harriett lay in her hospital bed thinking about her granddaughter, Molly was at Mulberry's thinking about her grandmother. She watched a woman pushing her baby up to the checkout in a grocery cart containing four small ornaments for purchase. The mother was singing Christmas carols to the child and playing silly games with the pink-cheeked cherub that had her squealing with delight. As she observed this special mother-daughter interaction, something shifted in Molly. She began to wonder what it would be like to have what that fortunate woman had, a smiling baby to love and cuddle and laugh with.

When traffic at the checkout had slowed to a trickle around noon, and the store had been nearly emptied of all the holiday merchandise, Lillian sent Molly to find Simon so that they could leave for the hospital to see Harriett. Molly found him at the information desk, trying to calmly explain to an irate customer that all the Radko ornaments had gone in the first half hour of opening and that he could not order one for her and give it to her at fifty percent off.

Molly tugged on his shirt to get his attention. Simon glanced behind him to see her looking expectantly at him. "Can we go see Granny, now?" she asked hopefully.

Simon smiled and turned back to the overbearing woman he had been unable to appease and said, "I'm sorry. You'll have to excuse me—important family business."

When they were out of the mayhem and into the serenity of the quiet greenhouses, Simon wrapped an arm around Molly. "Thanks for rescuing me from that battleaxe! She wouldn't take no for an answer." Molly laughed and snuggled into his side as they walked along. Looking down at her, Simon asked, "How are you doing? Are you exhausted from the morning?"

"No," Molly replied softly. "I'm just anxious to see Granny."

"Well, hopefully she'll see you today, too."

Molly smiled up at Simon and said, "I sure hope so."

When they reached the office, Simon held the door open for Molly and followed her inside. He grabbed their coats from the back of the desk chair and helped Molly into hers.

"Do you think Granny would rather have died?" Molly asked.

"What?" Simon said, pulling on his jacket. "Why do you ask that?"

"I'm just afraid that I prayed too hard for Granny to survive for my sake, and what if she would rather be dead than live with being paralyzed or not able to speak, or whatever might be wrong with her."

Looking directly into Molly's eyes, Simon said, "Honey, I don't think Granny wants to go anywhere now that she's found your love. You've made her life happy, Moll. You make her feel loved and needed. So, don't feel bad about wanting more time with her. I think she feels the same way about you."

Molly smiled at him and he kissed her quickly. "Let's go see what Granny has to say about all this, shall we?" Simon took her by the hand and led her out of the office.

Simon and Molly arrived at the Intensive Care Unit at Lakeside Memorial and walked cautiously hand in hand toward the waiting area. The smiles on the faces of Harriett's kin told them everything they needed to know. Molly let go of Simon's hand and ran directly into Mildred's outstretched arms and cried, "She's awake?"

Wrapping her arms tightly around Molly and hugging her close, Mildred softly said, "Yes she is, sweetheart, but she's very much altered."

Molly pulled back instantly to look at her great-aunt. "What do you mean? What's wrong with her?"

"She's awake and alert and understands what's being said to her," Mildred explained, "but she can't respond to what you say because her speech has been affected by the stroke. And the right side of her face and body are paralyzed."

"But Doctor Richardson said that it could take her a few days to recover, right? So, she may be talking again and not be paralyzed after all."

"Let's hope for that," Simon said, rubbing Molly's back.

"That's right," George said approaching the group. "And I'm going to get her the best therapists, Molly. They'll get her walking again."

"Don't worry, dear," Gertrude said, wrapping her arms around Molly. "I'm going to take care of Hattie. She's going to be fine."

"But Granny can't live like that!" Molly cried, backing away from Gertrude.

"Honey," Simon said gently, "why don't we go see how she's doing? I'm sure that she's anxious to see you."

Molly turned to look at Simon, first with annoyance and then with understanding. "You're right," she agreed. "We should go see her."

Harriett was sleeping when they approached her bed. Molly and Simon both paused to look for the transformation in her. Asleep, she did not look all that different, especially with her eyeglasses on, but upon closer inspection, Molly noticed the dramatic downward turn of the right side of her mouth which for some reason she had failed to notice the day before. Without thinking, Molly reached over to gently push the skin upward with her index finger. As a result, Harriett's eyes fluttered opened and she turned to look up at Molly and Simon. When her eyes focused upon their bright young faces, she could not help but smile. Forgetting about her recently acquired disabilities, she opened her mouth to tell them how happy she was to see them and a funny little sound escaped her throat. To Harriett's ears, it sounded like a dolphin. To Molly, it sounded like the word, "bee," drawn out for several syllables.

Again Harriett opened her mouth to try and tell them how glad she was that they had come and the same, drawn out, "Beeeeeeeee" sound came out of her mouth. The horror on Molly's face in response to the strange sound was unmistakable. Harriett turned away in embarrassment.

"Aunt Millie tried to tell us that you couldn't talk, but listen to you; you have already made some progress," Simon said, gently pulling Molly down to sit with him beside Harriett on the bed.

Slowly, Harriett turned back to look at them. "We're glad to see that you're recovering. Aren't we, Moll?" Simon prodded Molly with a little poke in the ribs.

"Oh, Granny," Molly said tearfully, "I'm so glad you woke up. I was so scared to lose you and I prayed so hard for you to stay." She paused a moment and then added, "Is that all right?"

Tears sprang into Harriett's eyes and obliterated her vision. With her good arm, she reached up to locate Molly's face, and when she did, she cupped the girl's cheek with her hand and nodded her answer. Molly made her feel truly loved and wanted, which was something Harriett had not felt since her boys were very young. Her life had been a dark, dismal canvass, but since Molly's arrival at The Aunt Hill, Harriett's life had become a rainbow of color, full of just as many emotions.

Molly grabbed a tissue and gently dabbed at her grandmother's cheeks. "I'm so lucky to have you, Granny," she said seriously. "You changed my life by allowing me to stay in your home."

Harriett shook her head.

"It's true, Granny," Molly protested. "You, especially, have helped me to grow up and learn to be independent and to take on the responsibility of a job. And speaking of jobs, you should have seen the madhouse at the garden center today. There were crazy women running all over the place, and we could hardly keep up with all the purchases . . ."

As Molly and Simon rambled on about their hectic morning at work, Harriett gazed at her granddaughter with great pride and thought, *You did it all on your own and overcame tremendous obstacles to achieve so much.* Molly had truly earned her grandmother's respect, and Harriett felt a tiny twinge of remorse for being so hard on her from the start. But, she also knew that her treatment of Molly had helped the girl toughen up, set some goals for herself, and work to achieve them, and Harriett knew that this, along with a good education, is what would pave the way for a bright future for Molly. Of course, Molly really did not need her grandmother prodding her along anymore because she now had the love and support of Simon, who seemed to have all the right answers when it came to finding happiness in life.

Molly stopped talking when she noticed her grandmother's eyes drooping. Simon noticed as well and asked, "Are you all right? Are we tiring you out?"

Harriett shook her head. She loved having them near and listening to them talk so excitedly about their day. They were both so young and full of life and she was drawing from their energy and enthusiasm. It made her feel like anything was possible.

A nurse breezed in. "Well, Mrs. O'Connor, we've got a room all ready for you, and I think you'll be much more comfortable with some privacy and a nice view out your window. I've got two handsome orderlies coming to take you for a ride."

Harriett eyed the nurse suspiciously with her good eye. For some reason, she was afraid of being moved about. She felt safe in that bed and with the familiar nurses tending to her. She did not want to go to a strange place. Harriett's left hand moved over and clutched the edge of the bed.

The nurse took note of Harriett's expression and her grip on the bed. "There's nothing to worry about. You'll be perfectly safe, and your family can escort you all the way to your new room."

Molly and Simon both gave her a peck on the cheek and slid off the bed. "We'll see you down the hall, Granny," Molly said cheerfully.

Harriett was ensconced in a private room on the third floor of the hospital which had a nice view of a small lake. The room was soon filled with baskets and vases of bright flowers, as well as her doting family, making it feel like a celebration. Lillian and Henry arrived in the late afternoon loaded down with flowers and sacks of Subway sandwiches, which added to the festive mood. They were immediately introduced to George, who was perplexed by the color of their skin. Gertrude noted his confusion and promised to explain everything to him later.

At first, Harriett loved having her family near and receiving so much attention. Then all the fussing started to grate on her nerves, and she wanted to scream at them to leave her alone.

Mildred finally realized that they were making Harriett agitated, and she suggested that it was time for everyone to leave

Harriett to rest and recuperate. She gently pushed them all out of Harriett's room after they had said a quick goodbye.

When they had gone, Harriett relaxed back into the mattress and pillows of her hospital bed and glanced around the small room. It was a riot of color with all the flowers that Lillian and Henry had brought and all the bouquets that had been sent by family friends and her friends from church. Yes, word had spread quickly through the town that Harriett O'Connor had suffered a debilitating stroke, and it made her angry just thinking about all the pity swirling around with the cold winter wind. Harriett did not like the idea of people feeling sorry for her or whispering about her newly acquired physical limitations. She was tremendously proud and extremely private, and these qualities had seen her through many an ordeal in her life without anyone ever knowing what she was suffering. Then again, perhaps if she had shared her misfortunes and miseries with someone she would not have suffered so cruelly in the silent world that she had created for herself. Harriett suddenly thought how ironic it was that she was now rendered silent so that there was no way of anyone knowing what she was feeling. She had always maintained that God had a nasty sense of humor. Now she had proof.

With the room to herself, Harriett felt more at peace. Her overtaxed brain began to settle down. She had been fortunate enough to avoid thinking about what had happened to her and just what it meant for the future because her family had been there to distract her. Who knew that they would come to her aid like they had? Harriett was more surprised than anyone that her family actually cared for her, even loved her, as Molly was so free to express. Closing her eyes, she took the thought with her into her dreams.

Supper time arrived and Mildred had a small battle to win in order to convince everyone that Harriett would not want any of them to see her being fed her food, let alone have one of her family members spoon-feeding her. It would be the ultimate humiliation for her and she reasoned that Harriett had already suffered enough. So, the O'Connors, the Haydens and the Mulberrys propelled themselves down to the hospital cafeteria, where they had a surprisingly decent meal and some moments of laughter.

Then it was back upstairs to visit with Harriett before they were kicked out for the night.

Harriett became rather frightened when they all left at the close of visiting hours. Unable to control her emotions, she started to cry. The night nurse slipped into the room and sat beside her on the bed. Gently taking Harriett's hand, the nurse softly rubbed her forearm and cooed, "Shh, you're not alone. I'm here for the night if you need me, and after you fall asleep, it will be no time before your family is back again in the morning."

Harriett could not place the accent she was hearing; she thought maybe it was African. She looked up at the nurse and immediately became distracted by the color of her skin. She had never been so close to a person that dark and she marveled at how the woman's skin shone like polished mahogany. She stared freely at the young woman and she thought of how she had come to accept and admire Simon. It dawned on her that every human being on earth was the same; everyone was equipped with the same sets of feelings, and ruled by his or her own fears and desires. There were more religions on earth than one could possibly need and thousands of different cultures with their own rules and traditions. These were the things that made the world so volatile and interesting. But, in the end, people were just people, Harriett reasoned, and each person should try to live his or her own life to the fullest and try and not to hurt anyone along the way. If everyone did this, what a different world it would be. If she had done this, what a different life she would have led.

Harriett wondered what on earth she was doing with such thoughts in her brain. Yes, they were good ideas, but now that she was speechless no one would ever hear them. Harriett's head began to ache and she feared that all this newfound introspection might short circuit her brain.

The nurse began fluffing the pillows and neatly arranging the bed covers on top of Harriett. "Now, it's time for you to sleep. Tomorrow is a new day that will be full of possibilities, and your family will be back again. Sleep well." The nurse smiled sweetly at her, turned off the lights, and left the room.

Utterly exhausted from her physical ordeal and the frustration of trying to communicate, Harriett closed her eyes and wished for a peaceful night of sleep. But worry crept in, slowly circling until her brain started to spin. Horrifying thoughts began to gnaw at Harriett, sending her into a state of panic. *What if she never walked or talked again? How would she live with such humiliation and frustration? Why did God insist on keeping her on earth in such a half state?*

Harriett opened her eyes to chase away the thoughts that were terrorizing her. She focused on the enormous bouquet of roses that Lillian and Henry had brought her. It was a mere silhouette in the dark, but she could smell their fragrance and it reminded her of Gertrude's rose garden. She closed her eyes to envision all of her sister's rose bushes bursting with brilliant color in the bright sunshine. Then she heard the riverboat whistle down on the lazy river, and she imagined the sound of the water rushing over the paddlewheel as the boat approached the dock. She was sitting on the porch swing at The Aunt Hill on a hot August afternoon, sipping ice tea and watching her sister toil in the garden.

For a brief time, she found peace.

Chapter Twenty-one

Molly had a hard time leaving her grandmother that night. She thought of Harriett lying there all alone in the dark haunted by her thoughts of what her future might be and it terrified her. When she asked the pasty-faced nurse at the desk if she could stay with her grandmother until she fell asleep, she was flatly refused. Visiting hours were strictly observed and there were no exceptions. Irked by the nurse's rudeness and lack of feelings, Molly started to argue with her, which forced Mildred and Simon to drag her out of the hospital with the rest of their group.

When they were out in the parking lot, Molly apologized. "Sorry about the little scene in there. I must be having a hormone surge."

"That's all right, dear," Mildred said, patting her arm. "That nasty old nurse was terribly rude. I think she's been working here too long; she looks as old as I am."

"Oh, you don't look that old," Henry said in his booming voice.

"Don't worry about it, honey," Simon said, wrapping an arm around her shoulders. "It's been another long day, and your nerves are probably wearing thin."

"I think you're right. It's time to go home to bed."

As Simon and Molly walked toward their vehicle, George cleared his throat and said, "Are you too tired to go for a drink, Simon?"

Simon quickly turned to look at him. "Just you and me?"

"Yes, if you're up for it," George said, looking down at the ground.

Molly smiled and nudged Simon in the ribs. "I'd like that," he said. "I know a great little neighborhood joint that serves tasty German beers."

"That sounds perfect," George replied.

"I'll ride home with Aunt Millie and Aunt Gertie and you can take my car," Molly suggested. She quickly kissed Simon on the lips, wished him goodnight and hurried to catch up with her great-aunts and Simon's parents as they walked toward their cars.

After everyone had called goodnight to one another, George and Simon crawled into the SUV and drove the short distance to the bar. They settled into a booth and each ordered a stein of beer. When the waitress left, George glanced nervously around the room. Simon could see that he was uneasy so he took it upon himself to get the conversation rolling.

"Is there anything in particular you wanted to talk about?" he asked.

George shrugged. "Not really. I just thought we could get to know each other a little better for Molly's sake."

"I think that's a good idea. It's important to Moll. She really needs your love and support right now, despite what has occurred between you."

"I understand that," George said flatly. "I also understand that you mean more to her than all of the rest of us combined."

"I'm sorry if that upsets you, but some things you have no control over," Simon said sincerely. "I truly believe we were brought together for a reason."

George slowly nodded. "When do you two intend to get married?"

"That's up to Molly," Simon answered. "I have offered to be the father of her child if she decides to keep it, so I would like to marry her before the baby is born."

George stared at Simon in silence. The waitress set their beers on the table. Simon stared back at George and smiled to himself.

"You're wondering why the hell I would want that baby," Simon said knowingly. "First of all, I was unwanted. My parents saved me and gave me a wonderful childhood; this is my opportunity to do the same. Second of all, that baby is a part of Molly and she may realize that and not want to give it up. I just want to give her an option when the time comes."

"You love her that much?" George said in amazement.

"Oh, much more," Simon assured him. "That's why I want us all to get along. It's very important to her."

"I want that, too," George assured him. "I would like to have an adult relationship with my daughter." He and Molly had shared a special bond when she was a little girl, and he had let it be destroyed by an unstable woman who held all the financial cards in their marriage. He was utterly ashamed to realize just how much of a coward he truly was and just how much time had been lost with his daughter.

"What about your wife? Do you think she'll come around?"

"Realistically, no," George said sadly. "She lives in a different world, and quite frankly, she has been jealous of Molly since she was a little girl."

"What do you mean?" Simon asked in confusion.

"Gillian is a bit complicated. From the time Molly was very little, she has never been able to stand anyone giving Molly attention." George shook his head as he thought about it. "For example, when Molly was in second grade, there was a little boy in her class who absolutely adored her. He followed her everywhere and carried her things for her, and when the teachers mentioned it to us, Gillian sent Molly back down to first grade to get her away from the boy."

"That's just twisted," Simon said in disbelief.

George paused to take a drink of his beer. "You don't know the half of it."

"Wow! Poor Moll," Simon said miserably. "How could anyone treat her that way, especially her own mother? Molly is so loveable and forgiving."

George did not have an answer for him because he had never understood it himself. And he was ashamed to think that he had allowed himself to get caught up in Gillian's mad world, doing the same thing to his daughter. And now, Molly was grown up with a life of her own that had very little to do with him. All he had was a wife he despised, a mansion on the shores of Lake Michigan that belonged to her family, and a son who had always treated him with great disrespect. In the end, he had nothing, except a chance with Molly. Simon was the channel by which he could reach her.

Simon had taken a few swigs of his beer and was staring forlornly into the amber liquid when George stopped his musing and studied him. He ventured a guess as to what Simon was thinking, and decided to change the subject to a much less depressing topic.

"Why don't you tell me about the nursery?" George suggested. "From what I can gather it sounds like quite the operation."

Simon nodded. "Yes, it has grown considerably over the years."

"Well, tell me about it." George leaned back in the booth and focused his attention on Simon. Simon happily described the business that he was so proud of his father for building and that he had put so much of himself into.

While Simon and George were out at the bar, Mildred, Gertrude and Molly were having milk and cookies in the kitchen at The Aunt Hill. Gertrude, who was worrying about Harriett and fretting about Simon and George, soon excused herself and went sadly to bed. She wanted Harriett home, where she could nurse her properly, just as she had done for her parents. She believed that if Harriett were home in her own bed she would feel much better and recover more quickly. Gertrude knew that she could be helpful, but Mildred seemed to be ignoring her and making decisions without consulting her. She was also jealous of the relationship Mildred was forming with Molly and Simon. She felt very left out, as if they were keeping secrets from her.

When Gertrude had gone, Mildred seized upon the opportunity to discuss Molly's surprise announcement and find out just what was going on between her and Simon. More importantly, she did not want the young couple springing the news on Harriett when she was in such a fragile condition.

"Molly, dear," Mildred said as she refilled their glasses, "what are you and Simon thinking with regard to your engagement?"

"I don't understand what you mean," Molly answered. "He asked me to marry him and I said yes."

"I'm asking when you intend to marry," Mildred clarified.

"Oh. I really don't know. We haven't talked about that. But Simon wants to be this baby's father and wants to have his name on the birth certificate, with both of us sharing the same last name."

"And how do you feel about that?"

"Miserable," Molly said plainly. "I've already made the decision to give it away and now I'm worried about hurting him by doing it."

"I don't think Simon means for you to feel that way, dear. I believe he just wants to give you another choice in case you decide you can't give it away."

"But, why would he ever dream that I would want to keep it?" she demanded.

"Because something happens to a woman when she feels her child start to move inside of her," Mildred replied. "You either fall in love with the little creature or grow to resent it taking over your body. In my case, I fell so profoundly in love with my baby that I would still give up all the life that I have lived for just one year with her."

Molly stared at her for a moment and then said, "Please tell me about your marriage and your baby, Aunt Millie. You promised that you would one day."

"I did, didn't I."

"Please, Aunt Millie. I would really like to know."

Mildred could see how eager Molly was to hear her tale, and despite how much she knew it was going to hurt, she took a deep breath and started her sad story. "I was close to your age when I left home to go do a secretarial course in Saint Paul," she began. "You see, I was always interested in business but at that time the only careers available to women were teaching, nursing and secretarial work. Otherwise, you married a man and gave your life and money over to him, while he, in turn, provided for you and your children. It was a very different time, my dear," Mildred informed her. "You don't know how fortunate you are to be starting your life now when women can do or be anything they desire."

Molly nodded her head in understanding but did not say a word for fear of causing her aunt to lose her momentum.

"Anyway," Mildred continued, "I at least got to try my wings and live in the big city which was such a gift to me back then. I had such hopes and dreams and I was determined to realize them. I didn't want to end up like Hattie, with bad, selfish men dictating my life and deciding my fate. So I enrolled in the secretarial school and moved into a house on Cathedral Hill with three of the other girls in the course. We became fast friends and had loads of fun going to parties and dance clubs."

Molly liked the way the story was going, and she leaned her chin on her hands and listened intently.

"There was a girl in our group named Isabella Martini. We called her Bella," Mildred said smiling. "She was this beautiful Italian girl with flawless olive skin and long, black curly hair. Her family owned a restaurant on the east side of the city. One night she took all the roommates there for dinner and to meet her family. That night I met her brother, Angelo, and I fell head over heels in love with him the moment I saw him."

Molly smiled at Mildred, knowing exactly how she felt, having gone through it so recently with Simon. "I understand completely."

"Of course, you do," Mildred said, smiling sweetly at her. "And Angelo was very much like Simon in that he was beautiful, almost too beautiful. He had this dark, thick hair and eyebrows and these sexy charcoal eyes with lashes as long as a paint brush. His skin was so smooth and dark that I wanted to touch him all the time. Blind as a bat, I entered into a wild affair with him."

Molly, who was becoming more intrigued with every word that Mildred spoke, was not at all shocked by her great-aunt's revelations. She had always sensed that they were kindred spirits when it came to love and passion, and Molly was pleased to discover that her intuition was worth trusting. "What happened?"

"Well," Mildred replied, "life was bliss. We seemed so in love with each other, especially each other's bodies, and his family adored me and strongly encouraged our union. Sometime later I learned that his parents actually blackmailed him into marrying me by threatening to take his birthright, the restaurant, away from him."

"What? Why?"

"You'll see," Mildred promised. She paused to take a sip of her milk. "Anyway, to make a long story short, all I wanted was Angelo.

So I married him without question or reservation. The only thing I wanted as much as I wanted Angelo was to have his babies. So, I got pregnant right after we were married—I had been very careful up to that point because of what had happened to Hattie. Anyway, about four months into our marriage and my pregnancy, Angelo started staying out very late at night and disappearing during the day for hours at a time. I was working at the restaurant to help out so I was with him and noticed his odd behavior. I became suspicious and started asking my in-laws and Bella if they knew what was going on. They all dismissed my fears and told me that Angelo would never leave me, which I thought was putting the cart before the horse and was rather compelling evidence that he was up to something. Not to mention the fact that he had stopped sleeping with me in our bed, giving me some excuse about not wanting to risk losing the baby. For two people who had not been able to get enough of each other, even for the first few months of my pregnancy, it was all the damning proof I needed that he had found someone else."

"Oh, Aunt Millie," Molly said sadly.

"Well, I confronted him several times, and each time, his denials became more vehement and his temper more volatile. But I was never afraid of him; I could give as good as I got. Besides, I still loved him and wanted him, and I tried my hardest to win him back. But he simply stayed away more and hardly ever looked at me, let alone laid a hand on me. Finally one night, I really lost my temper. I was nearly seven months pregnant and feeling miserable about Angelo's blatant rejection of me. I confronted him one last time."

Mildred took a deep breath and Molly could see that the story was becoming more painful by the minute. But she could not let her stop without finishing the story; she had to know what happened to the baby.

"We were out in the hallway, outside our bedroom, yelling at one another," Mildred said softly. "I was accusing Angelo of all sorts of things, not the least of which was lying to our families and God when he said his vows at the altar. I told him that he never really loved me and then, without batting an eyelash, he admitted that he never had. He told me that he had been in love with the same woman since he was a child and that their families, who had been feuding for years over a loan or something like that, had kept them apart by sending her away to school. Apparently, they thought it was safe to bring her back when Angelo had married me and he had gotten me pregnant. But now, Angelo said that he did not care what his family thought or did; he was going to marry her because she was pregnant with his child."

Molly gasped and gripped Mildred's hand.

"I was so full of rage and pain that I lunged at him. I beat Angelo's chest with my fists until his anger bubbled over and he shoved me away from him. Then I tripped over my nightgown and tumbled down the stairs."

"Oh no, Aunt Millie," Molly said, covering her mouth with a hand.

"I woke up two days later in the hospital to discover that I had lost my baby and my husband. My baby girl had been born and died moments later, and Angelo had run off to Italy with the woman he loved. When she found out what had happened, your grandmother rushed to the Cities to be with me. She was there to explain everything to me when I woke up. You can imagine how hysterical I was," Mildred said, tears flooding her eyes. "I didn't care about Angelo, but I wanted my baby back. And when Hattie told me that the Martinis had taken her to bury her in their family plot, I went quite literally insane. It took all her power and some sedatives to calm me. Several hours later, she brought my baby to me and placed her in my arms."

Molly was crying openly and wiping her nose on the sleeve of her shirt.

"To this day, I am so grateful to your grandmother," Mildred said with tears streaming down her cheeks. "Hattie fought the Martinis and organized a separate burial for my baby in our family plot at Fairview Cemetery. I named her Rosemary Elizabeth Hayden, and every night of my life I have prayed to someday meet her in heaven. She was so beautiful, so precious to me."

Molly wondered why such a terrible thing happened to someone as dear and sweet as her Aunt Millie; it just didn't seem fair.

And why had her grandmother's life turned out so miserably? And why had she been raped and become pregnant during the first week of her independence from her mother? Suddenly, Molly's heart was filled with rage and she wanted to strike out at someone for what had been done to all of them.

"Why did God do that to you?" Molly cried. "You didn't deserve it. I didn't deserve what happened to me. And neither does Granny!"

Mildred immediately sobered. Clasping Molly's face between her hands, she looked directly into her eyes. "Don't blame God, Molly. He gave us free will, the ability to make our own choices and to live with the consequences whatever they may be. You and I and Hattie, we made our choices. I could have walked away from a man who did not want me and kept my precious baby. Harriett could have asked more questions about Raymond Archer and taken precautions to not get pregnant. And you could have refused that drink. But that does not mean that it's our fault, do you see? It's not our fault, Molly. Someone else has to live with the knowledge that they will perhaps have to answer for it some day. The important thing is that we survived and learned to make better choices."

Releasing Molly from her vice grip, Mildred gently smoothed the long auburn strands of hair away from the girl's face. "We learn from our mistakes, my dear. That's what life is all about. And unfortunately, some of us have to find a way to unburden ourselves from the weight of regret that accompanies the really bad mistakes."

Molly gripped Mildred's hands between her own and said, "I'm so sorry about your baby, Aunt Millie. And I'm so sorry about what Angelo Martini did to you."

"Just as I am sorry about what happened to you, my dear," Mildred replied. "But we cannot change what happened, and we both have to live the life that God gave us and make the best of it."

"How do you mean?" Molly asked.

"Hold that thought," Mildred said, pulling her hands away from Molly and rising from her chair. "Let's get ourselves cleaned up a bit, shall we? Then I'll explain." Mildred walked over to the counter near the telephone and picked up the box of tissues. Then she sat back down, pulled a tissue from the box and handed it to Molly. She pulled one out for herself and went to work, mopping up her tear-stained face and blowing her stuffy nose.

Molly did the same, along with taking several gulps of her milk. Finally, Mildred was her composed self again. "After all of that tragedy, I got an annulment, took my maiden name back, and then went on to open and successfully run my own business." Mildred smiled. "The Martinis felt so terrible about what Angelo had done to me that they gave me a large sum of money so that I could get myself back on my feet and try to live my life. The doctors said I could never have any more children after the accident, and I think they blamed themselves for destroying that part of my life. Little did they understand that my heart was so shattered that no one, except you," Mildred reached across the table and gave Molly's arm a gentle squeeze, "could ever make it whole again."

Molly chewed on her bottom lip, determined not to start crying again and force her great-aunt to delay the telling of her story. This was the good part, and Molly was most anxious to know if her Aunt Mildred had once again found happiness.

"So, I took the money and opened a little market in the Crocus Hill neighborhood of Saint Paul. I had a butcher and a store manager and several stock and delivery boys. We delivered groceries to the customers' homes and put them away in the cupboards— can you imagine that? My little business became a great success, and I managed to afford a wonderful little bungalow of a house on Portland Avenue near the University Club and the Cathedral. I made lots of wonderful friends, grew a beautiful garden and got two golden retrievers for companionship. It was a very good life."

"Weren't you lonely?" Molly asked with concern. "Didn't you want a husband?"

"I did not want to give up my business. It meant too much to me," Mildred explained. "I built a very good business, and I didn't want to marry a man and have him take it all away from me, or worse yet, make me give it up."

"No," Mildred said without an ounce of regret, "I was very content in the life that I created for myself. The only thing missing was Rosemary, and yet, she was always with me. I realize that now.

I haven't lived a day without thinking of her, which means she has never left my side. And now I have you."

"I am so in awe of you, Aunt Millie," Molly whispered. "I'm so grateful to have you in my life."

"Thank you, dear," Mildred said smiling.

"I'm so lucky to have Simon," she said thinking out loud.

"Yes, you are, and now I hope you see that you chose the man that Hattie and I were dreaming of so long ago. God gave you the prize, Molly; you got the genuinely good one. I don't believe that Simon could ever wound you so deeply. So, don't ever let him go, dear. Don't ever think that the grass is greener somewhere else—it will never be so."

"I would never think that," Molly said, taking offense.

"Never say never, my dear," Mildred warned. "People often start looking elsewhere for excitement when the passion begins to fade years down the road. And I'm just saying that if that ever happens, remember this conversation and remember how you love Simon right now and how hard it is to keep your hands off of him, and then you will be fine."

Molly stared at Mildred as she drank in the old woman's wisdom. Yes, she would always listen to whatever her Aunt Millie had to say and would heed her advice. Mildred had lived her life fully and appeared to understand life better than anyone that Molly knew. It would be wise of her to pay attention to her guidance.

"You and Simon have something special," Mildred continued. "We all can feel it and we all love being a part of it. Your grandmother, especially. She doesn't trust a soul in this world and yet she's given him her stamp of approval. I think I can safely say that you have her blessing for your union, but I definitely think we should give her a little more time before you tell her."

"I couldn't agree more, Aunt Millie," Molly replied. "I wouldn't want to upset her and possibly cause another stroke."

"Well, let's give her a couple of weeks to adjust to her new life before you spring it on her," she suggested.

"Okay. I'll talk to Simon about it."

"Good," Mildred said, rising from her chair. "Now, it's time for you and that baby to get some sleep."

Molly glanced up at the clock.

"Don't worry about Simon and your father. I'm sure they're having a good conversation. You don't need to be waiting up like a nervous Nelly to find out what was said. Ask Simon on the way to work in the morning."

"Good thinking," Molly said, pointing her index finger at Mildred. Molly rose from her chair and stretched. "Well, I'm off to bed then."

"Good night, dear," Mildred said, hugging her tightly. "Sleep well."

"Good night, Aunt Millie."

Molly walked toward the kitchen door and then stopped to look back at her great-aunt. "I just know that you and Rosemary will be together again, Aunt Millie."

"Yes, we will," Mildred said nodding. Molly smiled and left the room. Then Mildred cleaned up, allowing herself to dream about seeing her baby again.

Chapter Twenty-two

The next five days were hell on earth for Harriett. Absolutely nothing changed for her; there was no spontaneous recovery of any kind. Her right side remained paralyzed, she had no control over her bladder and bowels, and the only word that would come out of her mouth wasn't even a word at all; it was simply baby babble. More than anything she wanted to rip off a few choice swear words to make herself feel better, but she had to settle for thinking them in her mind, letting them ricochet around and around in her brain.

The therapists arrived to work their magic, and they angered and frustrated Harriett all the more. The occupational therapist was a very large woman in her mid-forties who wore too much make-up and talked to Harriett as if she were a child. The condescension in the woman's voice was like fingernails on a chalkboard to Harriett. She tried her best to tune out the woman's high-pitched squeak and refrain from punching her in the nose with her good hand.

The physical therapist was a young woman with bleached, blond hair, and deeply tanned skin. It annoyed Harriett to no end the way the girl paid absolutely no attention to her because her radar was on for any and all warm-bodied males passing their way. One morning, Harriett, fed up with the girl's inattentiveness and frustrated by her new physical limitations, kicked the girl's backside with her left foot and pretended that she had simply lost control. The satisfaction derived from this simple act of malice did a world of good for Harriett's psyche and made her feel like her old self again, if only for a moment.

The speech therapist was a lovely woman in her late thirties who really seemed to know what she was doing. But despite the woman's efforts, Harriett did not seem to make any strides with regard to her verbal capabilities. She seemed doomed to a life limited to a one-word vocabulary. Harriett actually felt sorry for the therapist because the woman seemed to care so much about helping her regain her speech. She seemed genuinely defeated as Harriett stared helplessly at her after uttering her now familiar "Beee, beee, beee" in response to every exercise.

So, Harriett struck out in all three areas during her first week of recovery. Disappointment became the prevailing sentiment for her family and caregivers. But no one felt this disappointment more keenly than the patient. Harriett began to wonder what the point of her living might be. She begged God to be merciful and free her from the insufferable imprisonment that had been thrust upon her, but he did not seem to be listening. She began to despair.

Despite Harriett's lack of progress and her depressed state, Dr. Richardson told the family not to give up hope. He encouraged them all to get comfortable with her physical limitations and decide how they were going to work with the challenges. He assured them that she would need around-the-clock care which would include lifting her, bathing her and changing soiled undergarment pads. The reality of this led to a tense family discussion about Harriett's future living arrangements. In one camp, Gertrude, George, and Molly wanted to bring her home to The Aunt Hill so that she could be taken care of by family. In the other camp, Mildred and Simon reasoned that this would be the ultimate humiliation for her. Mildred gently explained to Molly that having one of her sisters or her granddaughter changing her Depends or bathing her chubby old body would be too much for Harriett to bear. Simon reasoned that Harriett would be allowed to maintain some semblance of dignity if strangers were paid to do such things for her and she was able to look her family in the face without suffering the embarrassment of having them perform such tasks for her. Their logic eventually swayed Molly's and George's opinion. Gertrude remained alone in her belief that she should be the one to care for Harriett the way she had cared for her parents, until each of them had died in her arms.

While they were hashing out the logistics of Harriett's care, one of the nurses suggested that they call the Stillwater Good Shepherd Care Center and see if they had a bed available. She believed the facility to be well managed and clean and knew the resident care was quite good. When a consensus was finally reached by the family and it was decided that the best option for Harriett was the full-time care provided in a nursing home, George made the call.

It was decided that Mildred would be the one to explain the nursing home move to Harriett. For the first time in days, Harriett did not break out in tears. She simply nodded her head in understanding and agreement. The last thing in the world she wanted was her sisters or her granddaughter wiping her bottom or washing underneath her drooping breasts. The humiliation would be insufferable. Even though the prospect of a nursing home made Harriett sick, it was the only option for her now that she could no longer take care of herself.

On the morning of New Year's Eve, Harriett was loaded into a medical transport and driven to the Good Shepherd Care Center. Her family was there to greet her, which brought a smile to her face. George pushed her wheelchair through the maze of corridors while they all looked around and got a feel for the place. It smelled and felt like a nursing home to Harriett, but an obvious attempt had been made to make the interior bright and cheerful in an effort to buoy the spirits of those who resided within its walls.

When George rolled her into her room, she was pleased to see many of her own things. This immediately brought her comfort and she began to relax a bit. Henry and Lillian arrived soon thereafter and filled her room with vases of bright flowers, which brightened her spirits further. Harriett was actually beginning to like flowers; their bright colors and happy blooms made her smile. Lillian had also brought a pan of fresh baked brownies—one of Harriett's favorite treats—and a bag of oatmeal raisin cookies for the family to munch on as they got Harriett settled. The whole transition went more smoothly than any of them could have imagined.

While they were showing Harriett her bathroom, a young, fresh-faced woman, dressed in pastel scrubs, walked into the room and caught their attention. Harriett looked her over, noting her bright smile, long blond hair and sparkling blue eyes. She decided that the woman did not look too menacing.

"Hi, everyone," the girl said cheerfully. "I'm Katie. I'm a nursing assistant, and I'll be helping Harriett while she's here." She gently shook Harriett's hand and said, "Hello. It's a pleasure to meet you."

Harriett nodded in response, and then waved a hand around the room at her family. Katie greeted and welcomed them all, and then she asked if they had any concerns or questions. George came up with a few and captured her attention for a minute while Harriett followed them around with her eyes and listened to their conversation. Then Katie shooed them all out of the room so that she could give Harriett her medicine and tend to any of her needs.

Out in the hall, they were greeted by the Care Center manager, whom Mildred and George had met and talked with the previous day. He introduced himself to the rest of the family and took them on a tour of the facility, answering their questions and trying to convince them that Harriett would be well cared for. Molly still did not like the idea of leaving her grandmother there but she resigned herself to the fact that it was the best option for Harriett. Gertrude, on the other hand, was still pouting about not winning the argument to bring her sister back home. She could not bear the thought of Harriett living amongst strangers without her sisters there to care for her. It simply was not right.

After the tour, the family went back to visit with Harriett until lunch time. Then they left her to eat her meal in peace and have a nap before they all returned that evening to celebrate New Year's Eve with her. Harriett was glad for the break from all the commotion and she happily waved goodbye. After managing to feed herself lunch without too many spills and dribbles, she had

Katie help her into bed for a nap. She was both physically and emotionally exhausted from the events of that morning, and she fell sound asleep. No dreams found their way out of the attic in her head.

The family returned to the care center at seven o'clock to toast the New Year with Harriett. Simon brought some delicious champagne that she thoroughly enjoyed, and they all were highly amused when she nudged him with her empty glass. George proposed a toast to his mother's recovery and to a new beginning for Molly. And Simon proposed a toast to a "year filled with wonderful surprises."

As Harriett sat enjoying the company of her family and the effects of the wine, she observed that her sisters looked very tired, their weary eyes ravaged by the stress of the past week. This made her feel guilty even though she was fully aware that it was due to circumstances completely beyond her control. Hopefully, now that she was settled in the nursing home with round-the-clock care, Millie and Gertie could catch up on their sleep and breathe a collective sigh of relief. Harriett noted that her son, George, also looked extremely weary and spent most of the evening lost in his own thoughts.

For a more uplifting scene, Harriett turned her attention to Simon and Molly who appeared absolutely smitten with each other. Her whole life long, all Harriett ever wanted was to be adored by a wonderful man, someone who made her laugh and smile and who did not already have a wife and children. She had never found such a thing, but she could see that her granddaughter had, and it made her happy. She did not begrudge Molly her happiness and good fortune, for her granddaughter most certainly deserved it after all that she had been through.

Too soon, a new nursing assistant entered the room and put the kibosh on their little party. Sticking to procedure, she shooed everyone out of the room as it was eight o'clock and the end of visiting hours. Reluctant to leave her alone for the first time in her new home, Mildred, Gertrude and Molly hung back and encircled Harriett's wheelchair. With their hands on Harriett's arms and shoulders, they stayed until the last possible moment—until they were forced by the nursing assistant to say their goodbyes and make their exit.

Outside the nursing home, the group split up. George took Mildred and Gertrude home to play a game of Scrabble, and Simon and Molly went off to a party at the home of one of Simon's friends. He was anxious to introduce Molly to everyone, and she was curious to see what type of people Simon chose to associate with. Hopefully, they would become her friends, as well. Molly had never had many friends growing up because her mother always seemed to have reasons why she could not play with certain girls, and she was certainly never allowed to play with boys. So this was her opportunity to benefit from Simon's introductions.

The Sunday after New Year's was a miserable day for everyone. Clouds hanging low with the threat of snow made the world gray and gloomy. A wet chill in the air crept into the bones and threatened to stay for the duration of the winter. Molly was suffering from the same sickness she had felt at the beginning of her pregnancy, and it was all she could do to keep anything in her stomach, which brought anxiety to Mildred and Gertrude and worried Simon to no end.

Harriett was in a terrible state, knowing that George was going back to Chicago and thinking that she might never see him again. "I promise that I'll get back here as often as I can." George tried to be reassuring as Harriett wept openly. "Don't cry, Mom. You're going to be fine. The aunts and Molly and Simon will take good care of you." George wrapped an arm around Harriett's shoulders as she sat in her wheelchair. When he clasped her good hand, Harriett cried even harder.

"Listen, Mom, I've done a lot of soul searching while I've been here, and I may be back sooner than you think." Harriett stopped crying and looked at her son. "It's time Gillian and I had it out and did something about our sham of a marriage. I want to be near you and Molly; you're my family."

Harriett smiled at him and tugged on his hand. "Beee, beee," she said, nodding her head.

"I'm going to start searching for a position with a law firm in the Twin Cities as soon as I get back to Chicago," George assured her. "But don't tell Molly, yet. Let's wait until things are a little further down the pike."

Harriett nodded. She was happy to keep the secret. Even though Molly still had issues with her father, Harriett hoped they would reconcile their differences. They were family, and they needed each other.

After George said good-bye to Harriett, Simon drove him to the airport to catch his flight. Then he went to the nursery to get some work done. When Simon and George had gone, Molly retired to her bed with a cup of broth and the desire to be left alone. Determined not to get drawn down into everyone's depression, Mildred started putting away the holiday decorations and cleaning the house. Gertrude spent the day fussing over Molly and fretting about Harriett, which suited her perfectly fine.

Chapter Twenty-three

After the hustle and bustle of the holidays and the shock of Harriett's stroke, everyone fell back into their old routines with the exception of carving out sections of their day to visit Harriett at the care center. Mildred and Gertrude spent much of their day there, arriving sometime after Harriett's breakfast, staying until eleven o'clock, and returning again around two o'clock to visit until dinner time. They had come to respect Harriett's need to be left alone at certain points of the day, and when they were with her, they did not push her to try to talk or move her dead limbs. They realized that she was not only badgered enough during her therapy sessions but frustrated with her lack of progress.

Simon had rigged up a little chalk board to hang around Harriett's neck so that she could scribble out words with her left hand in order to communicate, and he worked diligently with her to help her form letters with her untrained hand. Along with letters and words, they worked out symbols for certain things, and Harriett was soon communicating on a level that eased her frustration. In terms of her therapy, Simon seemed to be the only one Harriett would listen to and the only one who seemed to be making any progress with her.

Every Tuesday evening, Harriett and Simon had a special date to play cribbage, just the two of them. Harriett looked forward to his visit with great anticipation each week. Simon had purchased a large cribbage board with big pegs and had manufactured a homemade card holder for Harriett whereby she could see all her cards without having to hold them in her hand and fan them out. Simon did all the scoring for her, but he insisted that she do all her own pegging on the game board, which Harriett did with great pleasure when she was winning. She still had her sharp mind and her reasoning capabilities, but they were trapped inside her head and often expressed with the ridiculous little "bee" sound that escaped her throat when she got excited about something. Yet, despite all of her failings, Simon still came each week to entertain her and help her with her letters. She adored him for making time for her in his busy life.

Molly had taken to visiting with Harriett every evening after supper or in the afternoons on her days off. As the pregnancy progressed, she regained some of her youthful energy and accomplished more each day so she had lots of activities to report on. During her visits with her grandmother, Molly would relay news from the nursery and talk about her dates with Simon, where they had gone to dinner or what movie they had seen. Harriett drank it all in like a soothing tonic and cherished every minute she spent with her granddaughter. On Sundays, after church, Molly brought in a curling iron, hair pins and barrettes to work her grandmother's thick hair into a charming coif. She understood that the tiniest bit of self-esteem was itself a gift for her grandmother. Harriett enjoyed this weekly ritual, especially the scalp massage Molly gave her when she shampooed her hair. And for a few days of the week, she did not feel so frumpy and frightening to look at.

Some of the new developments in Molly's life included regular phone calls from her father that brought a happy new dimension to her world. George's calls were brief but punctuated with love and concern and the ever lingering remorse he felt for his behavior toward her over the years. Slowly, but surely, they were developing a relationship, and Molly was beginning to forget about the way he had treated her. The days when he called somehow seemed brighter.

Another new development in Molly's life, which she only shared with her silent grandmother, was that she had begun to feel the baby moving inside of her. One night toward the end of January, she had been soaking in a warm bath when she suddenly felt something strange in her abdomen. At first, she thought it was gas bubbles in her intestines. It felt like tiny fingers scraping the inside of a balloon, and Molly was so overcome when she realized what it was that she nearly wept. She sobered when she reminded herself not to get attached to something that she intended to give away.

What Molly did not bargain for were the loving feelings that she began to have toward the little creature in her womb. Mildred's words came back to haunt her. She was delighted by the baby's antics, and she began to anticipate its movements and place her hand upon her abdomen. Molly became more and more enchanted by her little companion with each passing day.

One day at the garden center she had watched a mother slap her toddler across the face for crying, and it immediately frightened Molly to think that her baby could end up in the hands of such a horrible person. Little signs of encouragement for her to rescind her decision began to creep up everywhere, as if Simon were plotting a campaign to try and convince her to keep the baby. And Molly's heart and head were both in a muddle over what to do with the little creature that had so drastically altered her life.

Getting back to a routine after the holidays and after Harriett's medical emergency meant Molly returning to her counseling sessions with Helen Faraday. Understandably, the focus of their sessions turned into discussions of Harriett's tragedy and Molly's feelings about what had happened to her grandmother. That is, until one afternoon in late January when Simon appeared at Molly's side and asked Helen if he could partake in their discussions that day. Helen was delighted to have him and very curious about his true feelings with regard to what had happened to Molly at college. She welcomed him into her office after making sure Molly was comfortable with the idea.

They had a great session, resulting in further understanding of each other's feelings about the rape. And Helen helped to facilitate a major breakthrough, when she asked Molly to express her feelings about Simon wanting to keep her baby.

"I love him for it," Molly answered. "But I just don't know if I want this reminder in our life." She turned to look at Simon and explained, "Don't you see that there would be too many opportunities for either of us to get angry and to say terrible things to each other about how this baby came to be, about how it's not really your child?"

"Moll, I don't think like that," Simon said forcefully. "I would never want to hurt you that way. I want you and your baby because I love you both."

"It's going to be hard enough to give this baby away for all the right reasons without having to worry about how I'm hurting you," Molly said sadly.

"Honey," Simon said, his face twisted with remorse, "I never meant to put such pressure on you and add to the difficulty of your decision. I just wanted to give you another option in case you changed your mind."

"Aunt Millie said that was what you were doing, but I just wasn't sure."

"I love children, Moll," he said softly. "And I can't wait to have them with you. But, more importantly, I support any decision that you make with regard to this baby." Simon clasped her hands. "I swear to you that I will love it as my own if you decide to keep it. I will never remind you how it came to be. And if you decide to give it away, I'll help you and accept your decision without question." Looking deeply into her eyes, Simon added, "This is all about your peace of mind, honey. I wanted to give you another option because I don't want you to be torn in pieces when it comes time to make the final decision."

"Then you won't be angry with me?"

"God, no," Simon said, hurt by her suggestion. "I thought I made that clear from the beginning, but obviously I didn't. I'm sorry. Do you understand now?"

Gazing at Simon with clear, green eyes, Molly said, "Yes. I do."

Simon smiled in response. "Now, let's not talk or worry about this again. You decide and let me know what you want me to do. And I promise that I'll be there for you."

"All right," Molly replied, nodding her head.

"Well," Helen said, startling them both. "I'm glad you have a better understanding of one another. Molly has been twisted up inside over this for some time."

"Why didn't you just tell me?" Simon asked in disbelief. "You know you can tell me anything." Then he said more gently, "You've had enough to worry about without my selfish behavior adding stress to your life."

"Sometimes you just need the right environment for things to come spilling out," Helen said wisely. "And for the record, your offer is hardly selfish." Helen looked directly at Simon. Then she shifted in her seat, and continued, "It was good that you came today, Simon. I hope that you'll come every now and again. I think it would be good for both of you."

"I think you're right," Simon agreed wholeheartedly. "I didn't realize how easy it could be to miscalculate one another's feelings. I've just been so certain that Molly and I know each other inside and out."

"You haven't known each other that long," Helen pointed out.

"It feels like forever," Simon challenged.

"I understand. I really do." Helen smiled. "But the exciting bit is that there's so much that you don't know about each other, so much to discover as you move through life together."

"That's the part I'm looking forward to," Simon replied evenly.

Ever focused upon ending their sessions on a positive note, Helen changed the subject of their discussion to Harriett's continued progress and the return of a normal routine at The Aunt Hill. Afterward, Simon treated Molly to her favorite decaffeinated coffee drink at Starbucks where they settled into a pair of easy chairs in front of the fireplace and rehashed their session with Helen.

Molly was glad that Simon had come along because his clear explanation of his feelings toward her baby eased the burden of her decision considerably. She had been too tied up in knots trying to decide what was best for all of them when, in fact, as Simon pointed out, all she had to do was decide what was best for her. Now that she knew who she was making the decision for, Molly felt that she could make the decision without regret. And she hoped that she could find peace afterward.

A few days later, Molly was busy working in one of the greenhouses at the nursery, getting it cleaned and prepared for the first wave of spring seedlings. And as she hosed down the flower benches, she suddenly felt a sharp pain in her lower back. Dropping the hose, she reached around with one hand to her backside and grabbed the flower table for support with the other. She gripped the table and waited for the pain to come again. Was she losing her baby? Terror flowed through her body like a tidal wave. Her knees buckled.

"Oh God, no!" she cried out. "Please, no." Molly froze, convinced that if she did not move the baby would settle down safely in her womb and stay where it belonged. Standing there, paralyzed with fear, Molly realized that she could never give the little person inside of her away. She had grown to love it too much. The mere thought of anything bad happening to her baby made her recognize the fact that she would do anything to save it, even risk her life for it, just as Aunt Millie had told her she might. She knew she was too young to be a mother, but maybe she could manage it. She had Simon, after all. Startled, she realized she needed to talk to Simon right away.

Molly pushed back from the table and slowly straightened her torso, fearfully anticipating another attack of pain. But to her surprise and relief, she felt nothing. Moving a few steps back and forth to test for any hints of discomfort, Molly was further relieved to feel nothing. Resting against the table behind her, Molly gently placed her hands on her swollen belly and waited for some sign of life. She was instantly rewarded with a good swift kick on her right side. She sighed in relief. Then the baby did a tap dance before poking a few fingers into the area near her belly button.

"Are you okay, then, little one?" Molly asked softly. "Please, God, let it be all right. I promise You that I will do my best to take care of this baby and raise it well if You'll just let it be all right." The baby moved again and Molly began to relax.

Glancing around the barren, silent greenhouse, Molly's words echoed softly in her head and trickled down to her heart. What had she just promised? Had she just made her decision?

Molly's heart began to race with excitement at all the wonderful thoughts flooding her brain. She pushed herself off the table and hurried through the greenhouse to search for Simon. She scoured the greenhouses, stopped by the office, and then headed for the store. As she was passing through the last greenhouse near the shop, Henry called down to Molly from the top of a ladder.

"My goodness, you startled me!" Molly gasped. "What on earth are you doing up there?"

"Sorry, sweetheart," Henry apologized as he climbed down. "I was just fixing a leak on one of the watering pipes. Where are you off to in such a hurry?" Henry pulled a rag from the back pocket of his overalls and wiped his hands on the tattered piece of cloth.

"I'm looking for Simon," Molly explained. "I need to talk with him."

"He was in the store entertaining some children the last time I saw him. Let's go find him together, shall we."

"Thank you. I would definitely enjoy your company."

Henry wrapped an arm around her shoulders. "How are you feeling today? You look a little flushed."

"I'm fine," Molly assured him. "I've just been frantically searching for Simon."

"What's wrong?" Henry asked with concern, stopping to take a good look at Molly.

"Nothing, really. I just need to tell him something important."

"There he is, sweetie," Henry said, catching sight of his son over the top of Molly's head.

Molly turned around and saw Simon standing in front of the information desk with a little boy perched on his shoulders and a little girl twirling like a ballerina around his legs. Molly's eyes took in the scene and quickly noted the woman standing in front of Simon. The woman was tall, pretty and clearly flirting with Simon.

"Who is Simon talking to?"

Squinting to adjust the focus of his eyes, Henry worked to put a name with a face and finally said, "Oh, that's Diane Swenson. Simon dated her years ago. Now, she's married with children and lives down in Bayport."

Molly was instantly consumed by jealousy and rage. There Simon stood, laughing and talking with his ex-girlfriend and her children, looking like one big happy family, while Molly, his fiancée, was forgotten and not even noticed. She had been searching for Simon to tell him her exciting news while he was playing with another woman's children, giving them all his attention.

Molly began to wonder why on earth Simon would want an immature, college girl, like her, when he could have his pick of half of the sophisticated women in Stillwater and its surrounding towns. And furthermore, why would he want a girl with someone else's baby in her belly to have to worry about for the rest of his life. What a fool she was! What a fool she had been! How could she ever have believed that they had a future together?

With the pandemonium occurring inside of her, Molly did not notice when Simon caught sight of her and waved her over. Blinded with rage, Molly remained trapped by fear and hysteria. Calling to her once and receiving no response, Simon quickly handed the little urchins over to their mother and started in her direction.

"Molly?" Henry said, nudging her side. "Simon is calling you."

Hearing Henry through the cacophony of frenzied questions in her head, Molly turned to look at Henry and then at Simon.

"Honey," Simon called as he approached her. "I want to introduce you to someone."

Molly turned and fled through the greenhouse from which she had just come. When she heard Simon yell her name, she picked up the pace, running between the benches. She managed to cover a fair amount of ground before he finally caught up to her. He grabbed her from behind.

"Molly, what the hell has gotten into you?" Simon cried, spinning her around to face him. "What was that all about?"

"Let me go! Let go of me!" She managed to break free and start fleeing again.

"Damn it, Molly!" Simon yelled, racing after her, catching her once again from behind and spinning her around. "What's wrong? Stop this nonsense and tell me what's going on." Simon wrapped his arms around her and pinned her so tightly against him that she could not move.

Molly turned her face away from him as her heart burned with fury. "Just go back to your old girlfriend and leave me alone," she mumbled.

"You've got to be kidding me," Simon cried incredulously. Taking Molly firmly by the arm, he dragged her through the greenhouse. "Come with me," he instructed.

"Stop treating me like a child," Molly screamed as she tried to yank her arm from Simon's stronghold.

"Then stop acting like one!" Simon shot back angrily.

"You're hurting me!" Molly cried, still fighting to be free.

Simon continued to escort Molly toward his office. Once they were in the privacy of the small structure, he released her and she immediately backed herself into a corner. Closing the door behind him and locking it, Simon turned to Molly with such fury in his eyes that her defenses immediately rose to the surface.

"Would you mind telling me what the hell just happened back there?" Simon demanded.

"Why don't *you* tell me what was going on back there? Why were you so cozy and chummy with your old girlfriend and her kids?"

Simon dropped his head and shook it back and forth in disappointment. "I can't believe this is coming from you, Moll. You're so far above this."

"Just let me go," she demanded, taking a step out of the corner. "I don't want to talk to you any more."

"Molly, please. Calm down," Simon pleaded holding up his hands. "Do you want to know who that woman was?" Without waiting for a reply or expecting one, Simon continued, "She was an old girlfriend that I dated for a very short period of time many years ago." Molly's stare did not waver so Simon continued, "Did I have sex with her? Yes, twice." Simon was relieved when Molly closed her eyes in reaction to his statement. "And it was honestly the worst sex I've ever had. Diane is the most dispassionate person I've ever known, and I, quite frankly, can't even begin to imagine how her husband got two children out of her."

"Why were you so chummy with her children?" Molly snarled.

"Because I love children," Simon wailed, throwing his hands up into the air. "How many times do I have to tell you that before you understand? It's a part of who I am. I think they're funny and interesting and I enjoy their candor. Those two kids were bored out of their skulls waiting for their mother to finish shopping so I rescued them and entertained them for awhile," he explained. "Why on earth would you think that I was interested in their mother?"

"Because why would you want me when you could have a so-phisticated woman who's not getting fatter and frumpier by the day?" Molly turned away.

"Oh, honey," Simon sighed. "I want *you* because I love you, body and soul. Don't you get that? I simply wanted you to come over and meet Diane so that I could show her how lucky I was to be with you. I wanted to show you off. Don't you see?" Simon asked, his eyes pleading for her understanding. "And you're not getting fatter and frumpier," he added for good measure. "No one can even tell that you're pregnant, for crying out loud." Closing the distance between them, Simon reached out a hand to cup her cheek and added, "You're simply growing more beautiful every day."

Molly turned her face away from Simon's hand and ducked to avoid his lips as he bent to kiss her. "Please don't touch me like that," she said, stepping around him. "I can't think clearly when you do and I have so much more that I want to say."

"All right," Simon replied, turning in time to see her making her way toward the office door. "I promise that I won't touch you, but you have to stay until you've said all that you need to say." Simon stuffed his hands into the pockets of his jeans. "What's on your mind, Moll?"

Molly stopped with her hand on the doorknob. She was pleased to realize that the jealousy had dissipated and that her heart was once again full of love, and not rage, for Simon.

"Tell me what's bothering you, aside from the attack of jeal-ousy," Simon said quietly.

"I just don't know if I can do this," Molly said softly, dropping her eyes to the floor.

"What are you talking about?"

"You love children so much and will be such a great father but I have no idea how to be a good mother," Molly said. "And when I promised God that I would love and take care of this baby the best that I could if He would not let anything bad happen to it, I'd for-gotten that I'm not fit to be its mother."

"I'm not following you." Simon pulled his right hand out of his pocket and rubbed the back of his neck. He crossed the room to where she stood, stopping short when he remembered his promise not to touch her.

"Just before I came to find you," she explained, "I had a sharp pain in my lower back and I was terrified that I was going to lose the baby."

Simon's heart fluttered with concern. "Are you all right, now?"

"I think I'm all right," Molly said softly, turning to face him. "I haven't had any more pains and the baby is moving around like it normally does."

"You can feel the baby moving?"

Closing her eyes, Molly wrapped her arms around her abdomen. "Yes, for some time, now."

"Why didn't you tell me?"

"Because I knew that you would get excited and want to feel it," she explained, "and then you would want it even more."

"You're right, of course," Simon admitted. "I'm sorry that you felt you had to hide it from me."

Molly realized that Simon wanted to love her baby the way she had come to love it, and she felt like she had cheated him cruelly with her omission. This thought was her undoing and it shattered her composure. "I'm so sorry, Simon," she cried. "I never meant to hurt you."

"You don't have to apologize, honey. I understand." Simon stood in front of her dying to reach out and touch her.

"No! No you don't understand!" Molly suddenly cried with her hands fisted at her sides. "I feel this baby moving around inside of me and I think that there's no way in the world I can give it away. I've fallen in love with it. But I don't know how to be a good mother to it, and I would rather die than hurt it the way my mother has hurt me all my life." Tears streamed down Molly's cheeks. "Don't you see that I don't want you to be ashamed of me and want to leave me? I don't want to become like my mother and have you despise me."

"Honey, you're going to be a wonderful mother. I have no doubts whatsoever," Simon assured her. "You're so loving, committed and creative, and you give your heart so freely to those who love you." Simon clasped her face between his hands. "You know how parents can hurt their child by not showing them they are loved, and you'll do everything in your power to avoid causing such pain. I know you will."

"I can't give this baby away, Simon. I can't," Molly wailed. "I can't give it to someone who might hurt it."

"Then don't," Simon said forcefully. "Marry me now. Let's give this baby a loving home and a loving family." Simon quickly kissed her lips, then her cheeks and her forehead. "We can do this, honey. I know we can."

"I just don't know," Molly said, closing her eyes and shaking her head back and forth.

"What don't you know?" Simon asked frantically. "Do you love me?" Molly did not respond. "Look at me," Simon instructed, lifting her chin up with his fingers. "Do you love me?"

"More than anyone in my life."

"And do you want to spend a lifetime with me?"

"Yes," Molly sighed, dropping her head back and closing her weary eyes. "But what if . . ."

"No, 'what ifs,' Moll. That's no way to live a life."

Chapter Twenty-four

Simon convinced Molly that they should keep their wedding plans and impending parenthood a secret for just a while longer because he had a special surprise in mind for her, and he needed time to prepare for it. She agreed, and they both tried to behave as if nothing had changed between them. Molly was dying to tell her grandmother and her aunts and nearly did on several occasions. But she bit her tongue and held onto her treasured secret because she had made a promise to Simon.

On February fourteenth, Simon came to pick her up for their special Valentine's Day date, looking amazing in a dark, double-breasted suit. Molly was simply beaming with happiness when she met him at the door, having resolved her inner conflict and knowing that she would soon be his wife.

After showering Mildred and Gertrude with valentines and chocolates, Simon and Molly drove off in her car and down into town. Molly suspected that they were having dinner at the cozy French restaurant on Main Street, but Simon surprised her by heading in the opposite direction and north out of town. When he pulled into the parking lot in front of the Minnesota Zephyr, she grew excited. She had heard about the romantic dinner train from several people and had wanted to try it out with Simon. And now, here they were, taking the short trip by rail along the St. Croix River Valley on such a romantic evening.

After boarding the train, they located the Stillwater dining car and found their table. An exquisite centerpiece made of red and white roses sat on the starched white cloth. Molly laughed out

loud. Earlier that day, Simon had asked her to make a special centerpiece for a very important customer, and there it was in front
of her. There was also a small stack of red and white envelopes, a
box of Godiva chocolates, a little box sitting atop the white tablecloth, and a split of champagne, chilling in an ice bucket beside
the table.

Simon helped Molly with her chair and then sat down across
from her. They were the only ones seated in the train car, as people
were still arriving and stopping for a drink in the bar car. Molly
took the opportunity to glance around at the decor and the other
tables situated near them. The car was quite long. A waiter's station stood in the middle and she could not see beyond it, but she
assumed the same amount of tables and same type of decor were
at the opposite end. A waiter stepped up with two champagne
glasses and went about uncorking the small bottle for them. He
poured the wine and then left them in peace.

Raising his glass, Simon quietly said, "Here's to an unforget-
table evening and an amazing adventure through life together."

"Here, here," Molly said, clinking her glass against his. They
both took a sip of the bubbling liquid. "Mm, that's good," she
commented.

"Just a few sips for you," Simon warned. "I didn't tell them that
you were underage, and we don't want a brain-damaged baby."

"No we don't," Molly replied. "I'll be good."

"Now, open your cards before people start pouring in here and
looking over your shoulder," Simon suggested.

Molly grabbed her purse and pulled out a pile of cards for
Simon. "There were so many fun cards to choose from that I
couldn't help myself," she said, handing them over.

Simon eyed the stack and laughed. "Well, we'd both better start
reading or we're going to be at this all night."

They each picked up a knife from the place setting in front of
them and began slicing open envelopes. And after they had read
all the loving sentiments, Molly picked up the box of chocolates.
"Can we open this and have one?"

Simon laughed at her. "It's your candy, honey. You don't need
my permission."

As Molly was trying to zero in on a caramel in the box, the other diners began to stroll into the car and take their seats. Simon greeted everyone that passed by their table, and Molly smiled and waved. She thought she recognized some of the people seated around them from the New Year's Eve party she had attended with Simon, but he acted as if he did not know any of them.

The waiter distracted her by placing a glass of sparkling water in front of her that she was certain they had not asked for and by setting a small teaser in front of both of them. It was a little puff pastry filled with what looked like a creamy mushroom concoction. It tasted heavenly. While Molly was expressing her opinion about it, Simon reached over and picked up the little box sitting in front of her.

"We're doing presents now?" Molly said in surprise.

"Now is as good a time as any," Simon ventured.

"Wait," Molly said reaching for her purse. "I want to give you mine first."

Simon's face crinkled; he had forgotten that she might have a gift for him. "All right." He took a small, wrapped parcel from her and quickly tore off the paper. Inside was a shiny gold pocket watch. "Molly!" he gasped.

"It was my grandfather Ferguson's," she explained. "For some reason he left it to me when he died."

"Honey, this is an amazing gift," Simon said softly, as he examined the antique and opened the lid to look at the clock face. He reached for her hand. "I'll treasure it always," he said. "Thank you."

"You're welcome." Molly beamed with delight. She was overjoyed that he liked the gift and happy that she had such a treasure to give him.

"All right, your turn," Simon said, placing the watch carefully back in the box.

Molly pulled the ribbon on her gift and peeled off the paper. Opening the lid, she found a small velvet jewelry case.

"Open it," he whispered.

Molly lifted the velvet lid and stared in awe at the platinum and diamond ring glittering back at her. Transfixed by the sparkling object and its significance, she did not notice Simon move around the table and drop to a knee beside her, nor did she notice that the other diners in the train car were gathered around to watch.

Gently taking the box from her hands, Simon caught her attention, and she turned in her chair to face him. Pulling the ring from the box and taking her left hand, Simon said, "Molly Frances O'Connor, will you marry me?"

Molly's face lit up with an enormous smile. "Yes, I will marry you."

Simon slipped the ring on her finger and then kissed her lovingly. The crowd around them erupted with applause and shouts. Molly quickly pulled back. She glanced at the other diners in astonishment, her face flushed in embarrassment. She suddenly spied Henry and Lillian, who were clapping frantically and smiling broadly at them. Her great-aunts were there, too, and some of her friends from the nursery. Then she started recognizing Simon's friends. Grabbing Simon's face between her hands, she cried, "You set this all up!"

"Yes, I did." Simon grinned. "I thought you deserved a proper proposal. Have you got a problem with that?" he teased.

"None whatsoever," she said. She kissed him again as the waiters passed out flutes of champagne to all the guests.

For the next three and a half hours, Simon and Molly and their guests dined on a delicious five-course meal as they rolled along the rails in the darkness. Their dining car was by far the rowdiest, with toasts being offered by their family and friends. Laughter bounced off the ceiling and windows of the train. Then the Zephyr Cabaret-Singers joined the party and things really got going.

It was, to date, the most incredible event in Molly's life, and she knew she would never forget it. The amazing support group gave her confidence that they were definitely doing the right thing by getting married and keeping her baby. And Molly knew, without a doubt, that she could leave the past behind and move forward toward all the wonderful things that she dreamed of for her future. She was strong and brave. She would never go back to being her mother's puppet. And she would never let a man harm her again.

When they told Harriett the exciting news the next morning and described Simon's proposal on the train, she surprised them all with her reaction. She was absolutely overjoyed and beside herself with excitement. There was so much she wanted to say but she could not scribble the words and symbols fast enough on her chalkboard. Mildred and Simon had to calm her down so that they could understand what she was attempting to tell them. When she placed her hand upon Molly's belly and started crying, they all wondered if she was happy or distressed about Molly and Simon keeping the baby. She managed to write, "So happy baby," on her chalkboard and they all breathed a sigh of relief.

After awhile, Gertrude mentioned that they had a wedding to pull off within a few weeks and that they were to meet Simon's parents for a planning session. Harriett shooed them all out of her room, waving her good hand frantically, practically chasing them down with her wheelchair. Molly and Simon hugged and kissed her goodbye, and they went to meet with Lillian and Henry.

Harriett remained in her room, marveling at the turn of events. For some time she had been hoping that Molly would decide to keep her baby because she wanted to see it. She wanted to hold her great-grandchild in her arms before she died, and she wanted to love it for Molly's sake. She knew that Simon would be the perfect father for the baby and that he was going to be a good husband to Molly. Most importantly, she believed that her granddaughter would have a happy life, a life full of love and adventure, a canvas full of color. Unlike her grandmother, Molly would not die with a mound of regrets weighing her down.

These thoughts brought Harriett's leaf to mind, and she realized that she had to find a way to get back to The Aunt Hill. She needed to get her leaf and the file from the investigator—especially the file—before Simon and Molly got married.

Chapter Twenty-five

By some miracle, Molly and Simon were married on the seventh of March in front of a small group of family and friends on an uncharacteristically spring-like day. The ceremony took place at St. Michael's at two o'clock in the afternoon, followed by a reception at The Aunt Hill. Molly and Simon did not mind that it was not a grand affair for the whole town to witness because they did not want to draw attention to themselves. They just wanted to be married, to be living together, and to be preparing for the arrival of their child. Their families gave them a day full of beautiful memories that promised to see them through difficult times in the future.

Molly's brother surprised her by arriving three days before the wedding. He spent a lot of the time with his grandmother and the rest of it getting to know Simon. But the morning of the wedding he reserved for Molly. He snuck into his sister's room very early and found her staring up at the ceiling.

"Can I join you, kiddo?" he asked, crossing over to the bed.

Molly smiled at him. "Certainly."

Tim sat down on the bed and leaned back against the footboard. Molly propped herself up on her pillows and looked across the bed at him. "What were you thinking when I walked in?" he asked.

"About the day I came here," Molly answered. "I was such a mess."

"I'll bet," Tim said sadly. "I'm sorry I wasn't there for you."

"Don't be. You have your own life to lead."

"But I abandoned you, Molly." Tim gazed at her with eyes full of remorse. "I wanted to get away from Mother and Father as soon as I possibly could, and I left you behind, alone with that crazy woman."

Molly placed her hand on Tim's ankle. "I wasn't your responsibility."

"I always felt like you were. I wanted to protect you from Mother and her bizarre behavior."

"I'll never understand why she dislikes me so much," Molly said, staring down at her hands.

"I had my ideas when I lived there, but I've thought about it a lot since I left," Tim said pensively. "I think all her problems stem from the fact that she was an only child who was spoiled rotten and had everyone's attention. That, and she turned into a religious fanatic."

"I don't understand what that has to do with me."

"You don't remember, but there was a time when you and Father were inseparable. He adored you Molly. We both did." Tim looked at her lovingly. "You were such a sweet, lovable baby. You were also very pretty and drew all sorts of outside attention. Mother couldn't stand it. I remember her throwing tantrums when people would moon over you, and when you got a little older, she started taking her jealousy out on you. That's when Father stopped showing you affection and paying so much attention to you. I realize now that he did it to protect you from her."

Molly stared at her brother.

"He loves you, Molly. He always has. He just got caught up in all the money, and didn't want to lose it. People get comfortable in a lifestyle," Tim said matter-of-factly. "If Father leaves her, he gets nothing. The house, the law firm—it's all hers, thanks to Grandpa Ferguson."

"Poor, Father," Molly said softly.

"Don't feel sorry for him. He made his bed. He married Mother for the money and he's been paying for it ever since."

"It has to be eating her up inside that he's coming to visit me and giving me away at my wedding, especially when she thinks I should be burning in Hell for my sins." Molly twisted the quilt around one of her hands. "It's not fair, Tim. I never did anything to deserve her animosity. I spent my whole childhood trying not to upset her because I wanted her to love me. She was never going to love me."

"No," Tim said bluntly. "But let's face it, she's quite unstable. That's why she's gone so overboard with her religion. Religious fanatics usually are quite nuts."

"Why does Father stay with her? He has to be miserable."

Tim smiled and glanced down at the floor. "I'm not supposed to tell you this, but he's in the process of divorcing her and negotiating a partnership with a law firm in the Twin Cities. He wants to be near you and his grandchild. Finally, I have a little respect for the man."

Molly's heart overflowed with emotion at Tim's revelation, and her eyes filled with tears. "He really wants to be near me?"

Tim nodded. "He loves you, Molly. We all do, especially Simon," he said with exaggeration. "I've never seen a man so head over heels in all my life. The sorry sap thinks the sun rises and sets with you!" Molly giggled. "But that's all right," Tim said more gently. "You deserve to be loved like that."

Molly gazed at her brother, with his rumpled straw-colored hair and unshaven face, and she smiled warmly. His dark brown eyes still looked at her the same way they had when they were children, but they were both adults now. It was time to say goodbye to the past and start focusing on the future. Molly crawled out from under the covers and wrapped her arms around her brother's neck. Hugging him tightly, she said, "I love you, Tim. Thank you for coming."

Tim wrapped his strong arms around her and pulled her close. "I love you, kiddo. I promise I'll be here for you from now on."

"I wish you lived closer."

"As a matter-of-fact . . ."

Molly sat back on top of his outstretched legs and eyed him suspiciously.

"I got into the U of M Med School," Tim said, grinning. "I'll be moving into The Aunt Hill sometime in June."

"What?" Molly yelped. "That's fantastic!" She threw her arms around him and nearly squeezed the life out of him.

When George gave his daughter away at the altar that afternoon, he shocked the bride and groom when he started crying like a baby as he handed Molly over to Simon. Mildred came to his rescue, and Harriett reached into the pew from her wheelchair to hold his hand during the ceremony. And as he quieted and watched his beautiful, poised daughter take her wedding vows, his heart swelled with pride. Her future was bright, of that he was certain, and he so much wanted to be a part of it and to know and love his grandchild. They had a long way to go in mending their relationship, but he was determined to make the journey, no matter how difficult or long.

Mildred stood up for Molly, while Henry stood beside Simon during the ceremony. Lillian and Gertrude both wept into their handkerchiefs on their respective sides of the church while Tim filmed the blessed event on his video camera. The church was overflowing with flowers and heavily perfumed with their fragrance. And many of the wedding guests were having a hard time deciding who looked more beautiful, the bride or the groom.

Molly and Simon exchanged their vows with strong, clear voices, and when the priest asked them if they would accept children lovingly from God, they smiled at one another and answered with an enthusiastic "Yes." Even though Molly's ivory gown hid the bulge in her abdomen, all present in the church that afternoon knew of her condition. Simon had given a version of the truth to those outside their immediate families so that they understood why the wedding had been such a rushed affair. He did not care what anyone thought about their situation, but, again, he felt compelled to protect Molly from gossip and ridicule. It was not that he believed that any of their friends would behave in such a manner, but one never knew.

When George rolled Harriett into The Aunt Hill for the reception, she was overwhelmed by feelings of nostalgia. She had always loved the house and the comfort that it brought to her. And despite the throng of people loitering in its rooms, she was glad to be home. Searching the crowd for her granddaughter, Harriett managed to get Molly's attention, communicating through Simon that she wanted to be alone with her in the library. Rolling her grandmother down the hallway in her wheelchair, Molly wondered why Harriett had excluded Simon from their little gathering. He seemed quite upset and had whispered something in Harriett's ear before Molly took her away.

For once, Harriett was glad to see that there was a fire in the hearth in the library, and she immediately indicated to Molly to wheel her over to the desk. Pulling out the file drawer, she thumbed through the file tabs twice until she found the one she was looking for. Molly watched her grandmother with great interest. She could not imagine what she was up to or what she wanted to show her.

Placing the file on her lap, Harriett pointed toward the fireplace and Molly dutifully rolled her over. She motioned to Molly to take the screen from the hearth and then she held the file folder out to her.

"Do you want me to destroy this, Granny?" Molly asked in confusion. "Or do you want me to look at it?"

Harriett took up her chalkboard and laboriously wrote, "You decide" upon the slate. She held it up to Molly.

Molly looked down at the file in her hand and she felt the hair stand up on the back of her neck. There was obviously something in it that Harriett had been hiding from her. She could not imagine what it held, but the file gave her a very eerie feeling. Looking back and forth between her grandmother and the folder, Molly suddenly tossed it onto the coals and then rubbed her hand on her wedding dress.

Harriett stared into the flames, knowing that their chance to see justice served had just been forfeited by the person that the decision affected the most. Granted, Molly had no clue what was inside the folder, but Harriett had given her the chance to look, which she believed was the proper thing to do. And if Molly ever got curious and demanded to know what had been in the file, Harriett would be able to truthfully point out that it had been Molly's choice to destroy the information.

Gazing up at her granddaughter with great love and pride,

Harriett reached for her hand. Then she pointed to the diction-ary on the shelf. Molly brought the large tome over to her grand-mother and set it gently on her lap. Flipping through the pages, Harriett soon found her precious leaf. It was perfectly pressed and dried, and it had lost its vibrancy. She held it out to Molly.

Carefully taking it from her, Molly said, "This leaf means some-thing special to you, doesn't it?"

Harriett nodded.

Molly held it up near the light and twirled it in her fingers. "The colors really are extraordinary. It's beautiful."

Harriett scribbled the words, "For you," on her chalkboard and held it up for Molly to read.

"My wedding gift?" Molly asked, smiling at her grandmother.

Harriett nodded, and Molly said, "I will treasure it always, Granny. Thank you." Then she kissed her grandmother's cheek before wrapping her up in a hug. "I love you so much."

When Molly released her, Harriett took up her little chalkboard and wrote, "Love you," and Molly's eyes instantly pooled with tears.

Simon was standing in the hallway waiting for them when they came out of the library. His heart sank through the floor when he saw Molly's wet eyes.

When she noticed the expression on his face, Molly said, "Simon what is it? What's wrong?"

He looked down at Harriett, who shook her head at him. He let out a sigh of relief. "Nothing, I was just missing you," he said, step-ping forward to kiss her. "What were you two up to in there?"

"Granny gave me her special leaf!" Molly said, holding it up for Simon's inspection.

"That's beautiful," he commented. He noticed the fire burn-ing in the library and caught sight of the remains of the file. He had no idea if Molly had looked at the contents before burning it. Looking into her eyes, he said, "Is there anything else you want to tell me, honey?"

Molly thought for a moment and then said, "Well, I have to go to the bathroom and I've got to find a safe place for my leaf."

Simon laughed. "Go ahead. I'll take care of Granny."

Molly dashed away, and Simon squatted in front of Harriett's wheelchair. "Thank you," he said softly. "You did the right thing."

Harriett picked up her chalkboard and wrote, "Her choice." Simon closed his eyes and dropped his head. Pulling his chin up, Harriett looked into his tear-filled eyes and nodded.

"I love you," Simon whispered as he wrapped his arms around her. Harriett embraced him with her good arm and gently patted him on the back. Then they went back to join the party and celebrate the happy day.

That evening, Simon whisked Molly away to a five-star resort in the middle of Wisconsin, where they honeymooned for three days. The resort was tucked deep in the woods and situated around a small lake, perfectly isolated from the rest of the world. They had a small cabin all to themselves with two fireplaces, a large Jacuzzi and a combination shower/steam room. There was a kitchenette in the cabin, but the resort provided full room service which they made use of the entire time they were there. They spent most of their honeymoon in the comfortable king-size bed, with its silky sheets and downy duvet, and, as promised, Simon showed Molly just how much fun he could be, day and night. Twice, they ventured out to tromp through the woods in snowshoes, but Molly got cold quickly and they hurried back to the warmth of their cozy cottage.

On their last night, as they were snuggled under the duvet, staring at the flames in the fireplace, Molly said, "Wouldn't it be wonderful if we could stay here forever."

"That would be nice," Simon agreed. "But after awhile it wouldn't be so special anymore."

"I guess you're right."

"So, we'll just have to come back here a few times a year and relive our honeymoon."

Molly smiled. "That sounds good to me."

Simon rolled on top of her and looked down into her eyes. "I take it you're happy being Mrs. Mulberry, then?"

Molly nodded. "I'm over the moon," she whispered. Then she wrapped her arms around his neck and pulled him down to her.

Chapter Twenty-six

One bright Sunday in May, Molly and Harriett were sitting on the patio at the care center, soaking up the sun's warm rays and drinking in the sweet aroma of blooming hyacinth and daffodils. Suddenly, Harriett put her hand on Molly's bulging belly. Placing a hand on top of her grandmother's, Molly smiled, and then laughed, knowing they were thinking the same thing. "Pretty soon, Granny. Pretty soon you shall meet your great-grandchild."

Clearly pleased, Harriett nodded and gently patted her granddaughter's stomach. She was instantly rewarded with a nice big kick and her good eye grew wide with astonishment.

"Simon and I decided last night that if it's a girl we're going to name her after you."

Harriett shook her head violently in response to Molly's words and picked up her chalkboard. As fast as she could scribble, she wrote, "Bad name."

"No it's not, Granny. It's a good strong name," Molly countered. "We're going to call her Rosemary Harriett Mulberry. Don't you think that's a wonderful name?"

Harriett's eyes immediately flooded with tears at the thought of Mildred's little baby. She was surprised that her sister had shared her tragic story, and yet so proud that her granddaughter would honor her sister in such a way. Harriett knew that it would touch Mildred to her very core, bringing something very special back into her life. Harriett prayed that Molly's baby would be a girl.

"Oh, I almost forgot to tell you," Molly said excitedly. "I framed your special leaf, and it's hanging in the baby's room. You'll have to come over and see it soon. Maybe you can come for Sunday dinner."

Harriett wrote, "Like that," on her chalkboard.

The Friday after Memorial Day, Molly was working at the nursery, answering questions at the information desk, when she began to feel nauseated. She grabbed another employee to take her place and went in search of Simon. She found Lillian first and was informed that Simon had gone to oversee a planting at an office building.

"What's wrong?" Lillian asked, taking a closer look at her daughter-in-law. "Aren't you feeling well?"

"No. My stomach doesn't feel well," Molly replied, rubbing her protruding belly.

"Do you think you're having contractions?" Lillian asked anxiously.

"No," Molly said, thinking for a moment. "No, I feel like I'm getting the stomach flu."

"Come on," Lillian said taking her gently by the arm. "I'm taking you home to bed. I'll call Simon on his mobile phone and let him know that you're at home. I'm sure he will be there as soon as he can."

"Thank you, Mom," Molly said gratefully.

"You're welcome, dear." Lillian ushered her out of the nursery, took her home, and tucked her in with a glass of ginger ale.

Simon arrived home soon thereafter and found Molly lounging in bed, sipping her ginger ale and watching Oprah. She seemed just fine and explained that she thought that the Chinese take-out they had eaten the night before had simply not agreed with her. Simon laughed, kissed her sweetly, and then hurried back to work.

That night, when Simon came home late from the nursery, he found Molly still tucked up in bed and feeling no better. "Maybe I should take you to the doctor," he suggested.

"No. It's just something I ate," Molly explained. "I feel like I want to throw up but I haven't at all. I'm sure I'll feel better by morning."

Simon sat down on the bed beside her. "Well then, I'm going to make you some soup, my love. And then we'll pop a romantic comedy into the DVD and snuggle up in bed because I'm beat."

"My poor, sweet husband," Molly sighed as she ran her fingers through Simon's curly hair. "You worked yourself ragged today while I was home lounging about, eating bon-bons."

"And that's the way it should be for awhile," Simon said seriously. "Today was your last day of work. I'm firing you until further notice. So don't even think about getting out of bed tomorrow morning and following me out the door."

"Aren't you a nasty boss," Molly teased. "For your information, I wouldn't do that anyway. I have my session with Helen tomorrow because she's not available for our regular appointment next Wednesday."

"Oh shit! That's right," Simon said, smacking himself on the forehead with his palm. "I wanted to come along. It's been a month since our last session together."

"That's all right. Don't worry about it." Molly wrapped her arms around Simon's neck. "You can come next time. Things should be a lot slower at the nursery by then."

"Honey, we're going to have a baby any minute now. I don't think we'll be visiting Helen in the next few weeks."

"Oh, good point."

Simon kissed her and jumped off the bed. He took a quick shower, and then prepared a light supper before returning to the bedroom. He popped a movie into the DVD player and crawled into bed with his wife.

About three in the morning, Molly awoke feeling strange. There was a weird pressure in her abdomen along with a pain in her lower back. She crawled out of bed for a trip to the bathroom. As she closed the bathroom door, an intense tightening in her abdomen produced a flush of liquid that cascaded down her inner thighs. Flipping on the light switch, she took a step back and looked down at the tile floor. There was a pool of pinkish liquid beneath her. She immediately wrapped her arms around her abdomen and froze in place. "Simon!" Molly cried out in panic. "Simon, help me!"

Violently awakened from a deep sleep, Simon sat bolt upright and felt for Molly beside him. "Molly?" he cried, jumping out of bed and racing for the door. "Honey, where are you?"

"In here!" Molly cried from the bathroom.

Just as Simon flung the door open, a contraction clutched Molly's middle. It took Simon's eyes a moment to adjust to the light, and when they did, the first thing he noticed was the fear in Molly's eyes. He looked down to see her arms clutching her belly and then noticed the pool of liquid on the floor.

"Holy shit!" was all he could think to say.

"I think it's time," Molly said frantically.

Simon stepped over the mess and wrapped Molly in his arms. "Shh. It's all right. Everything's going to be all right," he said in his most soothing voice.

Molly felt instantly better, knowing that Simon was so calm and sure. She clung to him, drawing out some of his tranquility. Then she pulled back and said, "I had a contraction just as you opened the door so I think we'd better start timing them."

"Good idea." Simon put an arm around Molly's back and led her toward the bedroom. "Now, you sit down on the bed and I'll get dressed first. Then I'll get you dressed. We have the bag packed so we're in good shape. There's nothing to panic about."

"Okay," Molly said, taking a deep breath as she sat down on the bed.

Simon paused a moment to kiss her tenderly on the forehead, before dashing across the room to the dresser. As he opened his jeans drawer, Molly cried out in pain. "What? What is it?" Simon cried, turning to look back at her.

Molly clutched her abdomen with one arm and reached out a hand to him.

"Another contraction already!" Simon squawked hurrying over to grab her hand. "Okay, okay. Just breathe. Remember our childbirth classes," Simon instructed. "Look at me, Moll. Look into my eyes and concentrate."

Molly did as she was told and soon the pain passed. After a couple of cleansing breaths she nodded at Simon.

"Are you okay?" Simon asked as he rubbed her back gently.

"I think so."

"All right. I think we need to get you to the hospital quickly. You must have been having contractions while you were sleeping." Simon gave Molly's hand a hard squeeze. "Let's get a move on." Simon released Molly's hand and dashed back to the dresser, where he quickly jumped into jeans and a tee shirt. Then he rushed over to the closet and pulled an oxford shirt from its hanger and a pair of drawstring sweatpants from a shelf.

Hurrying back to Molly, Simon quickly pulled Molly's nightgown over her head and stuffed her arms into the shirt and began buttoning it. Suddenly, Molly grabbed his wrists so tightly that he lost the circulation in his fingers and had to give up on the shirt buttons.

"Okay, honey. Remember your breathing," Simon instructed, unable to do anything but coach her.

Slowly the gripping in Molly's belly eased and she blew out a long slow breath of relief. "I'm starting to get scared," she confessed, looking to Simon to allay her fears.

"There's nothing to worry about," Simon cooed as he quickly finished the buttons and helped Molly step into the sweatpants. "You're doing great. Things seem to be going along quite normally," he lied as he darted back to the dresser and snatched a pair of cotton socks. Pulling them onto Molly's feet, he said, "Okay! Let's go. We'll call the doctor on the way to the hospital."

Then Simon hefted Molly into his arms, stooped to grab her bag next to their bedroom door and hurried through the house to the back door. There he stuffed his bare feet into a pair of flip-flops, snatched a set of car keys off the counter and grabbed his mobile phone before busting out the door.

When they arrived at the hospital, Molly was in terrific pain. Her contractions were coming one on top of the other without any break in between. Simon blew into the Emergency Room with Molly in his arms and called out for help. His panicked request was answered immediately by a nurse and two orderlies, who placed Molly in a wheelchair and rushed her to the maternity ward.

Once they reached the ward, the maternity nurses took over with practiced efficiency and had Molly in a bed with an IV tube stuck into the top of her hand and round tabs on her belly to monitor her contractions and the baby's heart beat. One of the nurses announced that Molly was already six centimeters dilated. It was time to summon the doctor so she ran off to make a call, leaving Molly clinging to Simon and burying her face in his shirt to muffle her cries.

At one point the pain was so intense that Molly simply wanted to crawl right out of her skin. She started to chant, "Get it out. Just get it out," over and over again. Simon flew into a rage and demanded that someone give Molly something to ease her pain. Her body was shaking so violently that he feared she might go into shock.

Mercifully, the nurse gave Molly something to relax her muscles and she calmed a bit which helped Simon settle down and focus on how to help Molly during delivery. Shortly thereafter the doctor arrived. After a quick check, she announced that it was time for Molly to push. At this point, Molly was not listening to a word anyone was saying, except for Simon. It took all of his coaxing to get her to cooperate with her breathing and pushing when the time came to do so. After three attempts at pushing, Molly lost all heart and started crying, "I can't do this. I can't."

In response, Simon took Molly's face between his hands and calmly said, "Listen to me. You can do this. It's almost over, honey. The pain will soon go away, but you're going to have to cooperate and push the baby out." Then Simon crawled behind her on the bed, placing his legs on either side of her. He pulled her torso back against his. "I'm going to help you, honey. Just lean on me, and we'll do this together."

The doctor looked up at Simon and mouthed "thank you." Then she instructed Molly to give one big push on her count and together Molly and Simon breathed and pushed, with Simon propping her up and rubbing his hands on her belly. Suddenly, Molly released a piercing scream as the pain of the baby's head popping out tore through her. Simon pulled her back with him so that she could rest a moment while he caressed her arms and praised her for being so brave. After a few more pushes, the baby was delivered and the doctor announced that they had a beautiful girl with ten fingers and ten toes.

Simon crawled off the bed to look at their baby. When he saw her, he started laughing and crying at the same time. "Oh, God," he said in astonishment. "She really is our baby, Moll."

Mystified by Simon's comment, Molly lifted her head from the bed and tried to see over her draped belly. When the doctor placed the squirming, brown infant on top of Molly's abdomen, she understood Simon's wonderment. Overcome with emotion, Molly's eyes flooded with tears as she reached out to the messy creature and caressed its cheek with the back of her finger. Wiping the tears from his eyes so that he could see properly, Simon did his duty and cut the umbilical cord, and then a nurse took the baby away to clean it up.

Returning to Molly's side, Simon leaned in to kiss her tenderly. "She's ours. She's truly ours," Simon said softly, with tears streaming down his face.

"She looks just like you," Molly cried. "How did this happen?"

"It was meant to be," he suggested.

They were interrupted by the nurse, who handed them a swaddled bundle wearing a little pink cap, and they both held onto her and stared in awe. They marveled at how tiny she was, just six pounds four ounces according to the nurse. They laughed at her wrinkly little face when she closed her eyes against the assault of the bright lights. She was beautiful. She was perfect. She was their little Rosemary Harriett, and she was as brown as a milk chocolate bar, just like her father.

When Molly had been cleaned up and given a fresh bed to lie in, a member of the Leche League came in to help her take a crack at breast feeding. Since it was nothing that he could participate in, Simon took the opportunity to call all their family members and announce the good news. Simon called his parents first, and they were so excited that they hung up on him and bolted out the door. Mildred and Gertrude were just making breakfast when Simon called, and they both broke down into tears of joy. Simon did not tell Mildred what they had named the baby because he wanted Molly to be the one to do the honor. Finally, Simon called George who was so overcome with emotion that he sobbed into the phone. When he regained his composure, he inquired after the health of his daughter and granddaughter and told Simon to give them his love, and he promised to be on the first available flight out of O'Hare to the Twin Cities.

With his duties out of the way, Simon tossed the phone onto a chair in the corner of the room and looked over to see his baby daughter nursing at Molly's breast. He was suddenly hit with a sense of the miraculous. How had everything turned out the way it had? Surely, someone had a hand in all of this. Simon had always leaned toward the idea of fate and destiny and now he could not help but become a believer. Certainly, Molly was sent to him after the unfortunate incident in her life because he was meant to become little Rose's father. And Simon was truly relieved and delighted that with her skin and hair color there would never be any reason to question his paternity. Rose would be his daughter forever.

During his phone calls, Simon had not mentioned anything about Rose's appearance. All he had said was that she was beautiful and perfect. He wanted the rest of their family to be as surprised as he and Molly were when they laid eyes on her for the first time. He could just imagine all of their reactions. And then he thought of Harriett and realized that she already knew. He laughed aloud and grabbed the phone to call the care center to have them relay the good news to her.

Running through the corridors of Lakeview Memorial Hospital like young, spry gals, Mildred and Gertrude rushed to the maternity ward to find Molly's room. Henry and Lillian had beaten them there and the room was already filled with bouquets of flowers, helium balloons and stuffed animals. When Mildred and Gertrude walked in the door, Henry was holding the baby, mooning over the little darling.

When Molly caught sight of her great-aunts, she shouted with joy, "Aunt Millie! Aunt Gertie! You're finally here!"

Quickly the sisters rushed to her bedside and hugged her tightly. After kisses and congratulations, Mildred held out her hands for the baby. "Hand her over, Henry." He dutifully placed the pink bundle in Mildred's arms. When Mildred and Gertrude saw the color of the baby's skin, their eyes nearly popped out of their heads.

"Aunt Millie," Molly said, carefully eyeing her great-aunt, "we're pleased to introduce you to Rosemary Harriett Mulberry, our little Rose." Simon was sitting beside Molly on the bed. He wrapped an arm around her and pulled her close.

When Mildred heard the name, she closed her eyes and raised the baby in her arms so that she could rest her cheek against her forehead. Holding Rosemary brought back so many memories that Mildred could not stop the flood of tears. "Dear, sweet, Rosemary," she whispered. "You are so welcome and so loved."

Gertrude interrupted Mildred's special moment by exclaiming, "Look at her! She looks just like Simon!"

"Yes, she does," Simon said proudly.

"She sure does," Henry chimed in. "Baby Rose is our little miracle. She's the perfect ending to this part of the story. Now begins a whole new chapter with exciting discoveries and adventures for all of us. And just so everyone knows, Lil and I get to baby-sit first."

"That's right," Lillian concurred.

"Oh, no you don't," Mildred said, laughing through her tears. "This little sweetheart is mine the first time Molly and Simon want to go out."

"Oh, yes. We want her first," Gertrude said excitedly.

"All right, that's enough!" Molly said loudly. "Rose is not going anywhere without me and Simon for a long time. So stop bickering. For crying out loud, I've hardly had a chance to hold her since you all arrived."

"Here, dear," Mildred said, handing the baby over to Molly.

"Oh no, Aunt Millie," Molly protested. "I didn't mean for you to give her up already."

"That's perfectly all right, dear. She's your little girl."

"Do you just love her?" Molly asked hopefully.

"I do. Very much," Mildred answered, smiling. "And I am deeply honored and touched that you named her Rosemary."

"That's why we did it," Simon said, reaching out a hand to Mildred. Then he leaned across Molly and gave Mildred a kiss on the cheek.

"Could I please hold her, Molly?" Gertrude asked sheepishly, stepping close to the head of the bed.

"Of course, Aunt Gertie," Molly said, placing the baby in her great-aunt's arms. "You must have your turn, too."

While Molly was distracted by Gertrude, Henry pulled Simon aside and whispered, "You could find him now. With a DNA test and Rose's skin color, it wouldn't be that difficult."

"No," Simon said forcefully. "Rose is mine. Don't you see, now she can truly be mine. That asshole lost out. I get Molly and Rose, and he gets to live with what he did for the rest of his life. I think that's punishment enough. Now, Rose will never have to question whether or not I'm her biological father, and more importantly, she'll never have to know anything about the evil act that brought her into this world. That's enough justice for all of us."

"Just checking," Henry said, slapping him on the back and smiling.

Simon returned to his wife who was happily feeding their infant daughter, while his mother and the aunts were tidying up the hospital room and rearranging the bouquets of flowers. Taking a seat beside Molly on the bed, Simon put an arm around her shoulder and then pressed his lips to her forehead, holding her tightly against him for some time.

"Where have you been?" Molly said softly.

Simon removed his lips from her forehead and looked down at the baby. Gently rubbing the back of his finger against her soft cheek as she nursed, Simon replied, "I was talking with my dad."

Eyeing him curiously, Molly asked, "About what?"

"About you and Rose and about how much I love you both," Simon said, smiling down upon his daughter. "And about how Rose is truly mine now."

Placing her finger tips under his chin, Molly turned Simon's face to look at her and she said, "Thank you for wanting her so much, and thank you for loving me so much. I couldn't have given her away."

"You don't ever have to thank me, Moll. You've given me the greatest gift."

"Oh, Simon," Molly said tearfully. The baby broke away from Molly's breast and started wailing. "Oh, sweetie, it's all right," Molly cooed, bringing the baby close to her face. "Shh, you're fine."

"Why don't you all take a walk to the cafeteria and grab some coffee and pastries so that Molly can finish feeding Rose without any distractions," Simon suggested. "Then come back and you can all hold the baby for awhile."

"That sounds like a good idea," Henry said, trying to keep his booming voice in check so as not to scare Rose. He spread his long arms out and collected the women, moving them toward the door. "We'll see you in bit," he said, winking at Molly and Simon.

When they had gone, Molly switched Rose over to her other breast and relaxed back into the pillows on her bed. Simon leaned back with her and they both closed their eyes for just a moment. The nurse popped into the room several minutes later and found Molly and Simon sound asleep and Rose happily suckling, kneading her mother's breast with her tiny brown fists. Smiling to herself, the nurse gave Rose a few more minutes to nurse and then she pulled the baby away. Molly awoke instantly and the nurse placed a reassuring hand upon her arm and told her to go back to sleep. Then she covered Molly up, swaddled little Rose in her pink blanket and patted her back to get her to burp.

George arrived at the hospital around noon and walked into Molly's crowded room. The new parents and the baby had awoken from their nap an hour earlier and the rest of the family was taking turns holding Rose while they all visited. Molly and Simon both smiled broadly when they saw George's face, and the rest of the family greeted him warmly. Cautiously approaching the bed, George looked proudly at Molly before wrapping her up in a loving embrace.

"Congratulations, my beautiful daughter," he whispered in her ear.

"I'm so glad you're here," Molly said sincerely.

Then George released Molly and held out a hand to his son-in-law. "Congratulations, Simon."

Grabbing his hand firmly, Simon said, "Thanks, George. We're happy that you could get here so quickly."

"Well, where is she?" George asked anxiously as he scanned the crowd. "Where is my granddaughter?"

Mildred, who was holding the baby at that time, rose from the chair she was seated in and walked toward George. Cradling the bundle in her arms, she said, "Say hello to your granddaughter, Miss Rosemary Harriett Mulberry."

When George saw the baby's chocolaty brown skin he was utterly stunned. He turned a suspicious eye on his son-in-law.

"Don't even think it," Simon said, half laughing. "But no one should ever question the fact that she's my daughter."

"All right," George replied with a serious look upon his face. "I understand." Then his countenance changed and he sheepishly asked, "May I please hold her?"

"Yes, of course," Mildred replied, holding the baby out to George.

Carefully and awkwardly settling the baby in his arms, George looked down upon her sleeping form and was overcome with emotion. Hot tears stung at his eyeballs, blurring his vision. "Hello, my beautiful Rose. I'm your grandpa George and we're going to have lots of fun together. I promise."

"That's right," Mildred said softly, wrapping the blanket more tightly around the baby. "Your grandfather will be moving in with us soon, and so will your uncle. You're going to love coming to our house."

Rose squirmed in George's arms and opened her eyes to look up at her grandfather. In that moment, she stole George's heart forever. He marveled at the intensity of his emotions. Finally, George was free to give his heart away to those he loved.

Three days after Rose's birth, Molly and the baby were released from the hospital and Simon drove them directly over to the Good Shepherd Care Center. Harriett gave Simon a smug look when he kissed her hello, having known all along how the baby would look, laughing inside at the thought of what a wonderful surprise she must have been for him. She was reassured by the way Molly treated the baby with such love and tenderness. Things had definitely worked out for the best. Molly had Simon, Rose had two loving parents, and Harriett had them all in her life.

Harriett already loved Rose, but she felt something more when she held her for the first time and looked down at her tiny face. The baby seemed to already know her and to love her back which made Harriett feel rather special. As she was marveling over her great-grandchild, Rose opened her eyes, blinked several times, and squirmed until her arms were free from her blanket. After inspecting her delicate fingers to make certain they were all there, Harriett leaned down to kiss the baby's forehead. *I wouldn't have missed this for the world,* she thought. And in that moment she realized that her life paralleled that of her prized leaf. Since the day the leaf had landed on her shoe, her dark, dismal world had been transformed into all the colors of the rainbow. Harriett now had love, joy and happiness in her heart because of a beloved family that would carry on long after she fell from the branch, going out in a blaze of glory.